Praise for The Words

"The Words that Made Us" takes the epic approach to the Romany story. A thousand years deep, five thousand miles wide, it explains the vast, outstretched tale of the Gypsies from the Punjab to Paris through a variety of characters. Beginning from the perspective of Mala, a street-smart, educated 21st Century Roma girl, it shuttles back and forth through a raft of characters living in 21st Century France; Romania under both the Communists and the feudal Voivodes; Constantinople before its fall; Islamic Khorasan, and lastly India during the 11th century Mughal invasion. The arc of this east-to-west history is colourful, well-realised, riven by armies and cruel lords and silk-covered pasts. I found it all rather enrapturing, so must offer apologies to Edward W. Saïd.

Most people are still completely unaware of the bones of this great ethnic story, and many Romany people (I am one) still don't know how scholars traced the great westward journey of the Gypsies through our language: an Indian backbone, with fine ribs of Persian, Byzantine Greek and Slavonic sprouting out from the spine, telling the tale of our lineage. The extent of Gypsy suffering during the Holocaust is not widely taught. So, a novel like Andrea Busfield's – painstakingly written, rooted in research, linguistically well executed – is a rare event indeed.

We could do with more books like this in school libraries; in libraries in general."

Damian Le Bas, editor of Travellers' Times

"It has been my privilege to have worked with Andrea Busfield, almost from the inception of this book as her guide to Romani history and culture. Unlike the majority of authors of fiction who write about Roma or "Gypsies," and who simply cater to the "Big Fat Gypsy Myth" Ms. Busfield has done her best to present an accurate and sympathetic portrayal of the Romani people. She has also worked in the timeline of Romani history, from our distant origin in India through our current Diaspora throughout Europe and the world beyond. Through a series of five vignettes, she deftly covers the Muslim invasion of India that displaced the ancestors of the Roma, the passage through Byzantium, the centuries of Romani slavery in Wallachia and Moldavia, the Nazi death camps and the current discrimination and persecution in Europe where Roma are living in a state of undeclared Apartheid. As a Romani author, educator and social activist, I highly recommend this novel for its memorable cast of characters and its hard-hitting portrayal of historical reality."

Ronald Lee, LLD, author of The Living Fire and Romani Dictionary: English - Kalderash

The Words That Made Us

a novel by

Andrea Busfield

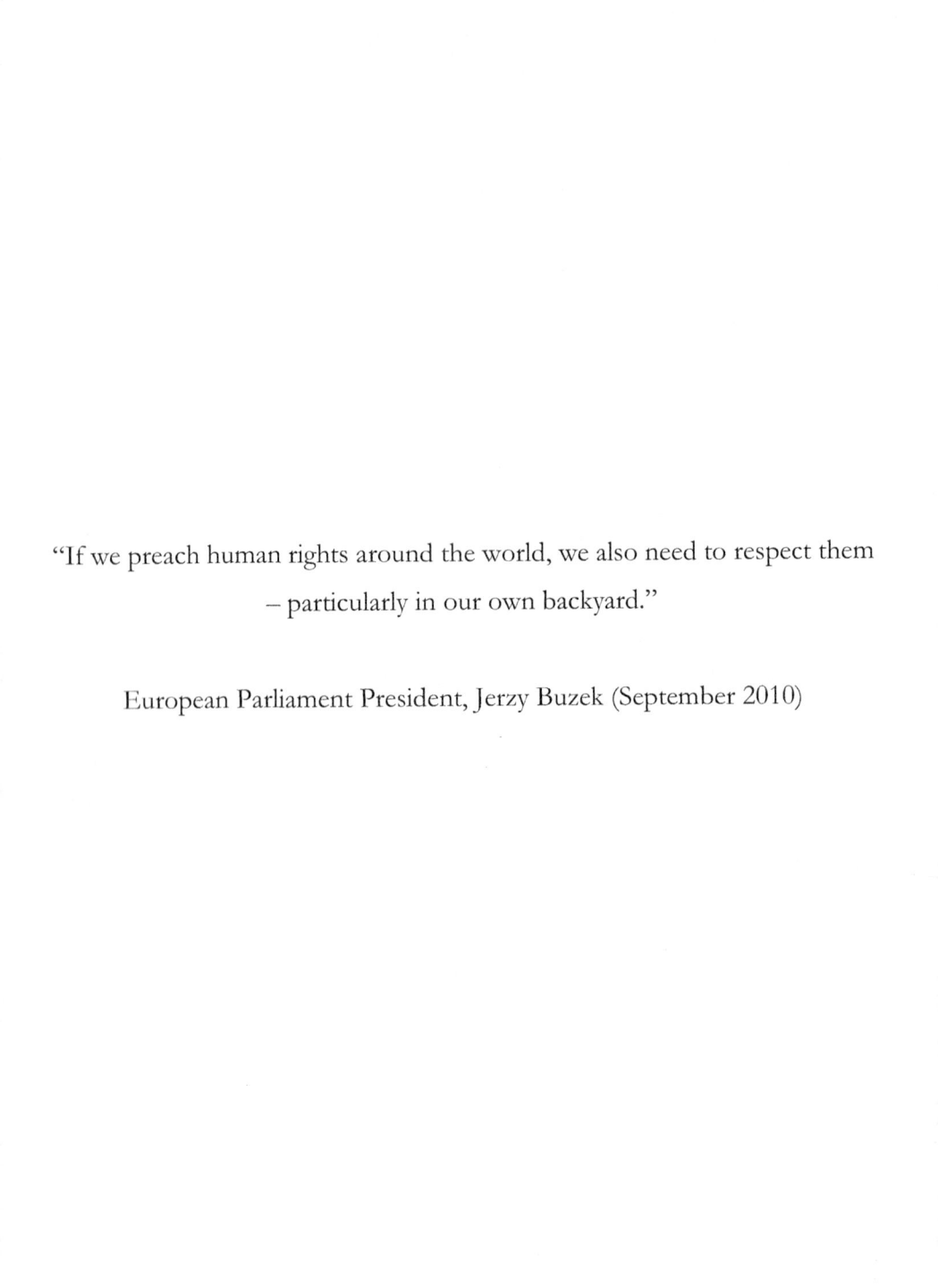

"If we preach human rights around the world, we also need to respect them – particularly in our own backyard."

European Parliament President, Jerzy Buzek (September 2010)

We took a road into night
Unaware of where it might lead
We left behind a great land
And started our journey of sorrow.

The Long Road by Saban Iliaz

Prologue

I have a name though it's unlikely you've heard of it. Instead, you'll recognise and claim to know me through words of your own making such as *gitano*, *ijito*, *gjupci*, *sipsiwn*, and *yiftos*. In England – the birthplace of Shakespeare and Dickens – I'm known as gypsy, my people as gypsies. In other places, at other times, there have been other names, most of them stemming from a medieval belief that we were Egyptian. Sometime later, when this was clipped to 'gypcian, we lost not only the truth, but also entitlement to a capital letter – something the rest of the world's nations appear to enjoy.

However, our journey doesn't stop there.

In the Netherlands we've been *Heiden*, in Sweden *Tattare*, while in Germany we're known as *Zigeuner* – a derivative spawned from a misconception of the Byzantine Greeks who described us as '*atsingani*', meaning 'don't touch'. It referred to our habit of not mixing. Further mutations included *Tsigani*, *Cingano*, *Cikan* and *Cigani*. And though the original meaning became lost, a number of modern interpretations helpfully filled the void – usually casting aspersions on our personal hygiene.

Still, these are only names. And really, what do they matter as long as we have food in our bellies?

Of course, way back in the sands of time, perhaps if someone had stopped to think – and deigned to ask who we were – we might have shaken our heads at the very notion of 'gypcians and '*atsingani*'. We might have revealed that we call ourselves Romani and even divulged some of the less-complex rules that govern our habits and rituals. Of course, way back in the sands of time no one did stop to think – so no one thought it necessary to ask – and before we realised what was happening our worldly identity was forged by those who didn't know us, and who later decided not to like us.

Here in France, things are much the same as they ever were. The people call us *'les gitans'*, *'les bohémien'* or *'les gens du voyage'*. Occasionally I've heard shouts of *"les caraques"* possibly from *"los caracoles"* meaning snails – no doubt implying we carry our homes upon our backs. Still, is it so bad? It's only a name after all; yet another name given to us by those who don't know us and who appear to hate us just as much as the next non-caraque.

But prejudice is a two-way mirror and the truth is we don't like you much either.

Given our apparent inclination to wander aimlessly upon other people's land it might come as little surprise to hear that we remain equally free of geographical boundaries when talking about Germans, Spaniards, Slovaks, Swedes, Romanians, Russians, the English or French. For us, everyone unlucky enough not to be us is called *gadje*.

Loosely interpreted, *gadje* means 'peasants', 'uneducated persons' or 'barbarians.' And though it might seem uncharitable towards the civilised few who hold degrees and ideals, and who regularly march against capitalist aggression while demanding equality in the workplace, I have to ask you – what does it matter? I mean, come on, really? It's only a name. And as the children's rhyme teaches, 'sticks and stones...'

However, in the interests of accuracy – and in the apparent absence of any desire for truth – I should state for the record that I have never been to Egypt. As far as I am aware no member of my family, past or present, has set foot on the Pharaohs' soil either. Furthermore, I endeavour to clean myself as best as I can, even in the direst of circumstances and, once upon a time, I even found myself the subject of cruel gossip due to my habit of mixing with the peasant-like barbarians surrounding us. Of course, that was then, and this is now – and now I'm no longer so sociable.

Less than a year ago, everything changed for my family. Our lives exploded and all the small things began to revolt. The change was immediate and irrevocable, and in the space of one night, all those names did come to matter. They *were* important. So, whether you choose to hear me or not, the fact is I am no Egyptian. Nor am I an untouchable or even a snail.

My name is Mala and with pride beating in my chest I tell you I'm a Romani.

FRANCE
2010

Chapter One

When the Big Man asked if I'd speak to the *gadje* I laughed because it seemed warranted. Then, when I saw he was serious, I refused. And really that should have been the end of the matter, but before I could run, he looked up at me – for he was unusually small for a Big Man – and his eyes demanded more than his lips.

"Think about it, Mala. It's just a little history they want."

"Then you tell it."

"I don't know it."

"Oh, come on, Marko, we all do."

"No, we don't."

As I drew breath, the Big Man rubbed at the broach he wore and I lowered my head. It was a clumsy reminder, but it was a reminder nonetheless, and though the Big Man may have been tiny – standing a scratch under five feet tall – he was still the authority among us, and deservedly so.

"I'm sorry," I said.

"I know," he replied. And we both stood facing each other, trying to pretend it wasn't awkward.

A little over a month ago Miko and I pulled into the Big Man's site, broke and unable to communicate with anyone outside of our own. Having completed the pilgrimage to Saintes Maries de la Mer we needed a place to stay in order to think up our future. During the drive north we spotted the telltale signs of our people; the tired caravans; the lines of washing; the metal hill built from scrap and scavenging; and the nearby dump that declared the land free of interest beyond waste disposal units. After parking in a lay by we went in search of the Big Man. As the site was purposely small, it didn't take long to find him and once he heard our story he found us space. Though it went with the job, the Big Man also supplied a few Euros for our purse while his wife emptied her cupboards to put food on our plates. Their kindness deserved more than the blunt refusal I'd now given Marko, and we both knew that at the very least I could have said that I'd think about the *gadje's* request. So, knowing this, I apologised a second time for my lack of good manners and told the Big Man I'd give the matter serious consideration. When he remained rooted, and clearly expectant, I wound up the charade and said I'd speak to the *gadje* if that's what he truly wanted. With a nod of his head, he confirmed that it was and he walked away smiling. A second later I returned to the caravan to find a spoon with which I could dig out my heart.

"I'm proud of you," Miko insisted later that night as we waited for sleep on a folded blanket. "It's time we spoke up."

"Do you think so?" I asked. "I can't see the sense in it when no one listens."

"Then make them listen, Mala. Prick the *gadje's* conscience, if they have one. And maybe, once you've managed that you could sting them for a little cash and some roofing work."

I turned to catch Miko's smile and found him watching me, his hazel eyes warmed to chocolate in the candlelight. Above his head, standing upon a Bible, the flame began to sputter, ready to breathe its last. I reached for my husband's hand and ran my fingers along the bumps and burns caused by a lifetime of welding and digging.

"You should moisturise," I muttered, and Miko promised that he would – just as soon as he'd plucked his eyebrows and waxed his legs.

Under the sheet we shared, I smiled a little.

"Nice to see," he whispered.

And I smiled a little more.

It was hard to believe that more than twelve years had passed since I first laid eyes on Miko. The occasion had been a wedding, our own in fact. I was 15, he was 24 and, as was the custom, our marriage was by arrangement, a contract between families. The ceremony was traditional – involving bread and salt – and I shook with nerves as I watched Miko raise a glass to seal our fate. To my young mind he appeared huge, a little rough and distressingly worldly. He was also drunk. But once he sobered, and we fell into our pattern, I found a keen mind sadly thwarted by life, and a heart that was as substantial as the moustache he wore. In truth, I'd be hard pressed to pinpoint the moment it arrived, but love came to bless our marriage – and overtime it grew into a bond that could bend trees.

"I'm nervous about this *gadje* nonsense," I confessed. "I don't know what to tell them."

"Just tell them the truth."

"Whose truth?"

"Oh, Mala." Miko rubbed at his eyes. Beneath the short-sleeves of his t-shirt I saw his arms were thinner than they used to be. "Don't let the past eat you. Simply tell the *gadje* how it is, or how it was seeing as they're asking for a history lesson. Tell them your grandmother's stories. God knows she'd have loved that."

"You needn't speak ill of the dead, Miko."

"You think I'd dare?"

"You never liked *Mami*."

"*Mami* didn't like me."

"You called her a witch."

"She broke my arm!"

"You were drunk when you fell off that roof!"

"That is a fact that I cannot deny, however your grandmother was the one who supplied the whisky that almost killed me."

I flashed a warning from my eyes only to watch it nimbly deflected by the challenge in my husband's raised eyebrows.

"My grandmother didn't try to kill you," I insisted.

"Perhaps not, but she certainly wanted to."

"Well, yes. That's true enough."

And under the sheet we shared, I couldn't help but laugh a little.

Like me, Miko was a Kalderash Romani, something that had persuaded my parents of the match if not my grandmother who became an enthusiastic and vocal opponent of our marriage as soon as she discovered the groom-to-be was barely literate. Her upset was further fuelled by a mystical belief that I was somehow special and destined for greatness – whereas Miko was not.

"Perhaps you're right," I conceded. "Maybe I could share *Mami's* tales, if the *gadje* are willing to listen."

"Of course they'll listen. You'll amaze and delight them. And when you're finished with this lot, we'll put you on a train to Paris – so you can educate that Monsieur Sarkozy."

Miko chuckled at his joke only to be abruptly silenced by two small feet crashing into his thigh. Between us, Mirela stretched her tiny neck taut, straining to escape a pain we couldn't see, and I released Miko's hand to attend to our daughter. As gently as I could, I cradled her head and told her I was there, whispering our prayers into her hair, just as I'd done every night since she returned to us – seven years old and already lost in a way that we'd never recover and no longer able to sleep in her own bed.

"Two eyes, two hands, two legs, pain in the eyes go away into the legs. Go away from the legs into the earth. Go away from the earth into death. Two eyes, two hands, two legs, pain in the eyes go away into the legs. Go away from the legs into the earth. Go away from the earth into death."

"Go away from the earth into death," Miko echoed. Then, unable to bear the sight of our daughter's struggle a moment longer, he kissed her lightly upon the forehead and nipped the last of the candle between his fingers.

In the dark, once the fit had passed and Mirela had drifted into a gentler sleep, I could tell from his breathing that Miko remained awake.

"Speak to the *gadje*," he eventually whispered. "Tell them who we are and what we have suffered. After that, we leave it to God."

Swallowing the bitterness in my throat, I promised him I would.

The following morning as I dragged Miko's shirts over a soapy washboard Donka emerged from her caravan. She yawned shamelessly and I looked to the sun. It was nearing ten thirty.

"Mala," she greeted.

"Donka," I replied.

"Washing your husband's shirts?"

"Looks like it."

"And your skirts?"

"A little later."

Though I was on my knees with my back to her, I could sense Donka smirking. Not that it mattered. She was what she was, and I'd never eat from her plates.

"Is there anything you need?" I asked, feeling the cold of her shadow hovering over me.

Glancing backwards I saw a piece of paper clutched between her ring-laden fingers. It looked typed and possibly official. It was also quickly gone, buried within the folds of her skirt. Donka stepped closer, so I could better talk to her feet.

"I don't know why you bother," she stated, waving a glittering hand over my washing.

"You know why."

I rose to fetch another basin and Donka snorted as I placed my skirts in it. Again, I tried to ignore the inference that I was somehow archaic; a relic of a quaint yet preposterous time now usurped by electrical white goods. More than that, I tried not to blame her. Donka wasn't our kind of Romani, nothing more. Besides, a loss of tradition wasn't always the fault of the individual. Sometimes the world simply ran out of patience for it.

"A washing machine gets your clothes done in half of the time with none of the effort," she noted.

"Yes," I agreed, and I went back to scrubbing Miko's shirts.

"As you like," Donka laughed. Then, without a care for who might see, she slung her own bundle of laundry over a shoulder. As she walked away, heading for town and the nearest launderette, her long skirt swayed with the gentle rocking of her ample hips. Taking a moment to watch her go I wondered whether her husband knew she washed their clothes in the same load. Perhaps he didn't even care. They were young after all, and more than ever before our customs were dying with the old.

As Donka sashayed to the gate, she passed the Big Man who happened to be sandwiched between a middle-aged woman wearing skinny jeans and a scowl, and a middle-aged man wearing straight jeans and a grin. The man's good mood appeared to be partly, if not wholly, due to the passing charms of Donka's full figure. As my husband once bravely remarked, the woman had a body that could start wars.

I dropped my head and carried on scrubbing even though I knew the group was heading my way. I knew this because I recognised the couple in much the same way they might recognise me. The *gadje* had come.

Although we usually spoke Romani on site, when the Big Man approached, he made his introductions in Romanian. It was a language that suited at least three of us present. "Mala let me introduce you to Monsieur Jacques Coran and his translator Francoise."

The Big Man propelled his male guest forward by the elbow and though I got to my feet I raised my soapy hands to stop him venturing closer. A second later, the woman stepped forward offering a smile and a greeting. Though her name was French, her accent revealed the rest of her came from somewhere near Bucharest.

"It's a pleasure to meet you, Mala. My name is Francoise and I am here to assist Monsieur Caron and help you with any questions you might have."

On hearing his name, the Frenchman flashed a toothy smile. It was clearly practised but not unpleasant. "Jack," he confirmed, "spelt the English way."

After the Romanian woman with the French name duly translated that the Frenchman took an English spelling, I paused to grapple with the complexities of this first meeting. If the conversation made little sense to me then it made even less when I translated it into Romani for the benefit of our neighbours that evening.

"And they say we've got identity issues," cracked Donka's husband Tanko, and his wife's face glowed with cheap wine and sweet pride as everyone laughed in response.

"So how can I help you?" I asked Jacques-spelt-Jack via Francoise who looked more like an Anca.

"I'm told you're a teacher and I'm here to learn," Jack revealed. He leant back in a chair that had been provided by the Big Man and smiled magnanimously; as though he'd gifted me the Holy Grail or the wherewithal to split the atom.

"Learn what?" I asked.

"Learn what?" repeated Francoise, and the mask of composure momentarily slipped from the Frenchman's face. A second later he repositioned his eyebrows to affect a look of deep sincerity.

"I want to know your history, Mala. Actually, I want to understand it, to understand it in a way that I can give reasoned argument to all the prejudice that you face here in my country. With all that is currently happening, I want to learn of the long road that brought you to France."

Jack kept his eyes trained on me as Francoise duly translated, and though my initial reaction was to reveal 'I came down the E60', I resisted. There was something sad hovering about the man, and the more he hung onto my eyes, the weaker I became. I didn't like him, or rather I didn't like what he represented, but now, with him sat opposite, staring intently into my face, my anger felt close to childish and certainly misplaced. The man's government was threatening to evict us, but here he was, looking to understand. Furthermore, I could smell the need sweating from his pores and, to my surprise, it aroused a small hope in me that I thought had long ago died. I wanted people to know. No, more than that; I wanted *the gadje* to know, and after that, I wanted them to leave us alone.

"Okay, I'll help you," I agreed after the Big Man completed the formalities. "We can start tomorrow, but come in the afternoon because I'm busy before lunch, and only come if the sun shines."

As this was translated, Jack nodded earnestly before flashing his straight, white teeth.

"Coming with the sun – a gypsy superstition?"

"No, not at all," I corrected. "We need the good weather if we're to speak outside. I don't want you in my home."

As the sun set, streaking purple and gold across the sky, everyone took their places around the small communal fire, sitting on whatever they could find; plastic chairs, boxes, tin cans and tree stumps. One by one the men regaled each other with exaggerations of their day while the women worked their chores and the children dodged flying backhanders in between their own fights. A little quieter than the rest, I watched Mirela playing with a puppy. She looked almost happy.

Once the food had been served, the talk made way for compliments as everyone commented on the meat my new 'job' had bought. Then, after the plates were cleared, the men reached for their beers whilst the women sipped at sweet wine, and everyone chewed over the possibilities of the *gadje's* real intentions. Looking around the group, sat in a circle of sorts, emitting clouds of smoke from a dozen pipes and cigarettes, the scene could have come straight from the pages of a dozen or more 'gypsy novellas' – though the wagons had evolved into battered caravans and the violins had been silenced by Eminem.

"I don't trust it," Rami grumbled as he opened a bottle with his teeth. White-haired and bow-legged, the old man was more unwavering than he looked. "One day they shoot us, the next day they're asking to be friends?"

"It was the police that shot that boy, not this curious *gadjo*," Miko replied.

"It's much the same and I still don't like it," the older man insisted before nodding his head at the chief. "What's the fellow's story, Marko? You said he was an actor?"

The Big Man pulled the pipe from his lips.

"He's a singer, or at least he was in the day. Got to be pretty big by all accounts; records, magazine covers – they called him the French David Essex."

"The French David Essex..." the small crowd cooed, sounding impressed though it was clear from their faces that they had no idea who the original Mr Essex might be.

"If I'm honest..."

"That'll be the day!" teased Tanko.

"If I'm honest," repeated the Big Man, calmly ignoring the jibe, "I'm not sure what the *gadjo's* motives are, beyond that of being interested, but right now we could do with a few friends. The government wants us gone, pure and simple."

Around the fire a number of the men nodded while others clicked their tongues. Sat in their own group the women cast their eyes to the floor or sought out their children, revealing the truth of the Big Man's statement in their own, less vocal, responses.

Some weeks earlier, a surge of anti-Roma sentiment had coursed through the country following an attack on a police station in Saint Aignan. During the rampage trees were felled, cars were burned, and the media reported that 50 French Roma were to blame having taken matters into their own hands after a boy had been shot at a checkpoint. News of the attack spread like wildfire among the Roma, with initial interest quickly mutating into worry after President Sarkozy felt it necessary to highlight "a certain kind of behaviour" within the Romani and Traveller communities. After lighting the touch paper, the President announced a meeting at the Palais de l'Élysée to find a way to deal with the problem that was us.

"The government wants the Roma gone, yet this singer wants to sit with us. I tell you, I don't trust it, not one bit," grumbled Rami, and though he was repetitive, and tight with his money, most of the gathering agreed. Recently widowed, the old man had six strapping sons. They had been on the receiving end of unwarranted attention more than most and the last time they were stung for an arbitrary fine it had taken Rami and four of his sons to hold back the eldest boy, Bo.

"Look, I'm as wary as the next Rom," the Big Man assured us, "but let's give these *gadje* the benefit of the doubt."

He then reminded everyone that the Frenchman's interest had paid for their meal that night, not to mention the extra fuel for the generators. Nothing if not practical, the families agreed to watch the passage of the wind. Even so, I felt the weight of their fears pile upon my shoulders, and before Rami retired for the night, he addressed me directly.

"Don't give away too many of our secrets," he warned. "They'll only use them against us."

Chapter Two

I looked at the floor. I glanced at my hands. I thought about Rami's warning, and I wondered how long the milk would keep without a fridge to keep it chilled. In short, I thought about anything but what to write on the piece of paper laid in front of me. In truth, it was a kind of torture; the more I tried to concentrate the more paralysed my mind became. I simply had no idea how to start. It wasn't the stories that were the problem. They had become such a part of me they could be summoned at will. No, it was the beginning that dragged at my brain; how to speak to the *gadje* in a way they might hear. The fact was, they weren't like us; they didn't behave like us and neither did they think like us. They were a different breed, and to reach them I'd have to walk in their shoes for a while so as to find the right path. Metaphorical or not, it made me feel dirty.

"Don't over-complicate things" Miko advised. He dug his knife into an apple and presented a slice of it on the blade to Mirela. She barely managed a bite before deciding to speak.

"I don't think I want to be here when the *gadje* come," she said quietly.

Though Miko's knife continued to carve, I saw the breath still in his chest.

"Don't worry, I won't let them inside our home," I assured our daughter, but Mirela shook her head.

"That's not what I mean, *Mamo*. I mean, I don't want to be *here*."

Mirela waved a tiny hand above her head before turning her attention to Miko, the plea evident in her eyes.

"You don't have to be," he told her emphatically. "I'll take you away for the day. We'll go for a walk or a drive somewhere in the car."

"You promise?"

"I promise."

"Well, that's alright then," our daughter agreed. "It's not that I'm afraid or anything."

"Nobody thinks you're afraid, Mirela, though I'd say you'd have every right to be."

Miko glanced at me, looking for support, but the casual truth of his statement caught me by surprise. I turned to Mirela, unwilling to let the weight of my husband's words hang unchecked so close to bedtime

"Every one of us ought to be cautious," I admitted. "But these *gadje* seem honest, Mirela. They say they want to help us. And maybe we should let them. Saying that, I'd actually prefer you to spend the day with your father rather than sit around here, watching me go through the motions."

I clasped our daughter's hand and she gave a brief nod of satisfaction before turning on her stool to slip from the table. After untwisting her pyjama bottoms, she went to lie on the blanket I'd placed on the floor. Before settling under the sheet we all shared, she threw me a last, careful look.

"Whatever you do, *Mamo*, don't sit too close to the *gadje*. They're *marime*, you know."

"I'll do my best not to," I promised.

I looked over to Miko who attempted a smile. We had taught our daughter well – although it was clear we had also failed her – and for a moment the two of us sat in silence. Then, flashing a cigarette by way of explanation, Miko took his leave.

As the door closed behind him, I looked again at Mirela. Her thick hair was draped away from her neck and her eyes were closed. It was doubtful she had found sleep so quickly – she was her mother's daughter after all – and I sensed rather than saw the pictures playing in her head; ones she couldn't yet bring herself to discuss. Still, she had been correct in what she said; even if the *gadje* did come with their fists unclenched, their presence would be polluting. It was their nature. They possessed little sense of justice or indeed decency, they didn't respect age, their talk was shameless, their women immodest, and it was said that they liked to sleep with pets on their beds. The *gadje's* ways were as strange to us as the fish is to the fox, which is why I struggled to understand why the Big Man had invited them into our lives and all but forced me to deal with them. What on earth was he thinking of? Granted, the Frenchman had spoken prettily about wanting to understand, but I'd rarely seen a concern that hadn't been planted by seeds of self-interest. For all we knew, the *gadje* might be agents of the police or government spies. God forbid, they might even be reporters. No, something wasn't right. The truth had yet to be spoken. And though it had stung at the time, Rami's warning had been warranted. Our secrets were our strength. They were the armour we wore to defend ourselves against the world. And yet I had to tell the *gadje* something. But how much was too much?

Felled by the mathematics of an impossible equation, I continued to glance around the caravan, looking for something to occupy my mind until the door opened to offer fresh distraction. Returning from his bedtime smoke, Miko took a handkerchief from his pocket and wiped at his face before grumbling about it being another close night. I felt the truth of his words in the air that failed to follow him into the room.

"Still struggling?" he asked, coming to sit by my side. He picked up the paper before me. The lines remained blank.

"I'm trying to make sense of something," I explained, "but I swear I can smell the *gadje's* pollution already."

"What, even above their pretty perfumes and sprays?"

I smiled in response and Miko returned the sheet of paper to the table. With the light fading at the open window, he reached for a candle. As the flame flickered into life, casting shadows across his strong nose, it was a comfort to have him close.

"I've been giving your predicament some thought," he whispered, tilting my face upwards as he spoke, "and I'm minded of the advice a Rom fisherman once gave me. He said that if you ever find yourself in the sea with a shark the last thing you do is swim for it – you'll be caught and eaten. He said the only way to manage a shark is to face it head on and then punch it hard in the nose."

I looked at Miko and raised my left eyebrow; partly to reveal doubt and partly out of habit. It was a trick that used to hold great sway over my husband.

"Are you suggesting, my love, that I start the *gadje's* lessons by thumping them in the face?"

Miko shrugged. "Well, it might get their attention."

"Do you think?"

"I'm pretty sure," he insisted.

"Well then," I sighed, "if you're sure…"

Chapter Three

"In the beginning God created the earth. When He was done making the mountains and the seas, the plants and the trees He created Adam out of mud and the first gypsy out of shit."

I paused to give Francoise time to translate. Beyond a twitch of her pencil-thin eyebrows she betrayed no emotion as she spoke. In contrast, Jack grimaced, ran his fingers through the quiff of his unnaturally dark hair and inhaled deeply, no doubt ready to fight the Romani corner. I continued before he could start.

"A variation of the theme has God making both out of mud before breathing life into Adam and breaking wind into the gypsy. In other accounts, Eve gave birth to the first gypsy after mating with Adam once he was dead."

As Francoise translated, Jack's face grew increasingly pained; not like a stunned shark, but more like a middle-aged man battling indigestion.

"This is awful," he finally mumbled.

"Yes, it is," I agreed. "And it's hurtful. Needless to say, these aren't the stories we tell our own children. In the version handed down to us by our grandparents, God made the sun and then He made the moon. After that He took a handful of clay and moulded a statue of a man. Placing it in an oven, He went for a stroll. By the time He returned the clay man was burnt. Still, God loved His creation and He breathed life into the figure. This became the first ancestor of the Black People. The following day God tried again. He moulded a clay statue, put it in the oven and waited. Pretty soon He became bored and He removed the statue too early. It emerged from the oven as white as it went in. Even so, God loved the man and He breathed life into the statue which became the ancestor of the White People. God then tried again, but this time – after kneading the clay and placing it in the oven – He became neither distracted nor impatient and, just at the right time, He opened the oven door to pull out the most beautiful, brown-coloured man. God was so pleased with His work that He blew not only the breath of life into the figure, but also His wealth of experience and emotion. His work done, God made the brown-coloured man the ancestor of the Romani People."

I reached for my tea and waited for Jack's response. When it came, it was fairly predictable; a patient smile, an earnest nod of the head followed by a carefully worded 'But...'

"It's a charming story," he said, "really it is, although I'm more Darwinist in my beliefs." Jack released a self-conscious laugh that wasn't repeated in Francoise's more stoical delivery. I watched him carefully and then I watched her, and I had to wonder how the two of them had ever found each other. "What I'm trying to say is, Mala, that I'm more interested in the history of the Roma. It's the *real* story of your people I want."

"Oh, the *real* story," I responded. "In that case, you won't want to hear of how we emerged from the lost city of Atlantis, or how our descendants roamed the earth as prehistoric horsemen, or how we were supposedly Egyptians or depraved Europeans hiding our white faces under layers of walnut oil?"

"Walnut oil?" inquired Francoise.

"Yes, walnut oil," I repeated.

I waited patiently for Jack's face to settle into confusion before continuing. "I'll assume then that you want to hear about the place of our birth, our first birth – the place you call India."

"Your first birth?" Jack interrupted.

"India was the seed, Monsieur Caron, she wasn't the flower."

"Interesting," he replied. He then nodded his head, three times in fact, before lifting his pen, allowing it to hover over a moleskin notebook even though the cogs of a tape recorder turned on the table between us. I risked a glance into his eyes, but I still couldn't fathom his interest.

"Once again there are differing accounts of our beginning," I revealed. "Some say we left India as 12,000 musicians gifted by a Raja to the Shah of Persia in the 5th century. Others say we were members of a wandering, criminal tribe; a clan of robbers, murderers, hangmen and baby-stealers."

Jack's pen hung in the air: his sword of truth momentarily blunted. "Well, which is it?" he asked, and I prickled at the irritation I heard.

"None of the above."

"But you did come from India?"

"No, my ancestors came from India. I was born in a village near Sibiu."

Jack threw me a look that needed no interpreting, and I saw a hint of amusement brighten the face of his translator. It was to be my first clue that Francoise wasn't so much a member of the team as the hired help. She also needed more sunshine. A glance at her hands further revealed she needed a husband, and despite the disdain that hardened her eyes it was perfectly possible she'd like that husband to be Jack. Unluckily for Francoise, Jack appeared to be a man clearly confident in his powers of attraction, and like all men who have never had to work for the attention of others, he took interest as a given rather than a compliment.

"Mala?"

Francoise stared at me, and feeling my cheeks warm I apologised. "Sorry, I got distracted while you were translating."

"It happens," she admitted, and smiled a little, which made a world of difference to her face. She was pretty in a way – blue eyes, high cheek bones, strong hair – yet it appeared she was as blind to this fact as Jack was.

"So yes, India: my ancestors came from India," I confirmed. "But not as a band of roguish outcastes as some would have it written. In my family's case, we can trace our line back to Angha Paramichi, the daughter of a warrior once hired to keep the barbarous Moslems at bay. Her father failed in this task, as it turned out, and it heralded the start of our journey. Therefore, what I tell you now is Angha's story; preserved by my ancestors so that it might keep us strong – and one day fill the pages of your notebook, Monsieur Caron."

Jack tilted his head, flashed his teeth, and lifted his notes in a gesture of solidarity.

I closed my eyes. He really was something else.

INDIA
1011

Chapter Four

Angha was three days old when her mother died and, for the first year of her life, her father stayed away from the world as he sought to rid himself of the impurity that followed such an inauspicious passing. Instead of being a time of celebration, Angha's arrival drove Bir Paramichi into the holy waters of the Ganges so that he might cleanse himself through ritual and ceremony. Throughout it all, Angha lived at her grandparents' house, which was also the place of her birth. Her father stayed with her, in self-imposed isolation; shunning his friends and keeping all contact to the absolute minimum. By the time Bir took his daughter home, she was walking.

Due to Angha's young age, coupled with her father's distractions and paternal uncertainty, her grandparents accompanied her to the vast confines of the Paramichi compound; a sprawling estate of sword smiths, pyrotechnicians, soldiers, and families who had built their lives around war. A son of the nomadic Bhairaqis, Bir descended from a tribe of warriors who earned their finery as hired mercenaries. For much of his career he had prospered handsomely under the patronage of Rajapala, the King of Kanauj.

Three years after Angha's birth her grandfather died, followed by his wife four hours later when she set herself on fire so that her husband might be freed from his earthly sins to enjoy the afterlife. Though Bir was required once again to bathe in the Ganges, the deaths were less inauspicious and his isolation lasted only six days. This was the world Angha was born into; one of superstition, ritual and death. This was India, albeit the one that came second – after the great flood which washed away the first.

Originally named after a hundred hunchbacked maidens, the city of Kanauj was a coveted prize among India's ever-squabbling elite. Standing on the hip of the Ganges, below and east of the five rivers, her walls rose from a great cliff with seven huge forts to defend her. Over the years a succession of Rajas had died trying to take her, and the kingdom had passed through the fingers of all manner of despots, father-killers, beheaders – and at least one dwarf descended to earth – until it came to rest with Rajapala, a man claiming royal descent from the Lords Rama and Krishna. Given the dichotomy of his religious heritage, Rajapala proved to be a magnanimous ruler, allowing each to their own in matters of worship and encouraging a society that was less formal than most. Unfortunately for him, he ascended the throne when Kanauj faced not only threats from Hindu aspirations in the south and the east, but also from the Moslems sweeping in from the west. Therefore, when Angha was born, in the year 1011, Kanauj was feeling distinctly vulnerable – which was good for business, as far as her father was concerned.

Unlike the rest of Kanauj which hummed to a gentle tune of learning and devotion, the Paramichi compound was a clatter of metal on metal as warriors practised their art in sandy circles, and blacksmiths toiled in the seemingly endless pursuit of shoeing cavalry horses. Occasionally, over the hammering of men, the compound's war elephants trumpeted for food. Louder still were the women – berating their husbands and children for the many wrongs that made their lives hell – and at least once a week an expert in explosives would set fire to his workshop. When the men rallied to douse the flames, they would bark orders in a language that was part Hindi, part Persian.

"We fight where we're paid to," Angha's father once explained. "And if the Persian-speaking Shahi orders you to charge and you have no idea what he's saying you'll find a sword leaving your belly with your guts decorating the tip."

Angha looked carefully at her father, who was evidently a man unused to the sensitivity of little girls. According to his friend, Patag, the Punjabi Shahi ruled the land northwest of Kanauj. His territory stood between the Moslems and the rest of India and, for the past 15 years, his armies had taken a regular spanking from the scimitars of Islam. Although Bir Paramichi had yet to test himself against the curved swords of the Ghaznavids, many of the compound's older men had, and they all agreed it was an experience they wouldn't wish to repeat. Among their number was Patag, who regularly blamed the Battle of Peshawar for turning his hair white and making him reliant on a form of alcohol he called "medicine". It was a dependency shared by his war elephant, Sabal.

Surrounded by men whose talk centred round war and a sword's point of balance, it was only ever going to be a matter of time before Angha heard the name 'Mahmud of Ghazna', the man who would play such a pivotal role in her life. When that moment came, she was four years old. She would always remember the occasion because it occurred on the very same day that she met the boy who would become the man she would love for eternity.

Having woken with the first rays of the sun, Angha had sought out her father only to find he had left for his office. He hadn't always spent so much time at the palace, but Patag said the king was nervous and therefore Angha accepted her father's absence because, when she was afraid, she also liked to have him close by. Padding barefoot to the dining hall, she heard the maid Lungri rattling among her pans behind a closed door. Angha looked about her and felt the full force of her loneliness bouncing off the whitewashed walls and high ceilings. So out of habit, and indeed preference, she did as she usually did in times of paternal absence and left for Patag's home with its one room painted red and its warm floor made from purified cow dung.

Although her father worshipped Vishnu, Patag was a follower of the Sun God, as well as an occasional Buddhist. The Hindu part of his devotion sometimes required him to coat his body in saffron paste and kneel to the east holding a jar of lotus flowers.

"Red is the colour of protection," Patag informed her and, naturally, Angha believed him because the only alternative was to think him insane.

Turning right at the blacksmith's forge, Angha was greeted by Sabal. She saw the door to Patag's home was shut and she braced herself for the inevitable punch to the stomach as the elephant looked to her for food. Taking a handful of peanuts from a leather purse strapped about her neck, Angha passed them to Sabal who took them with a grunt before letting her pass. Once inside Patag's hut, Angha grimaced at the smell of old men and bad medicine. On a leafy mattress Patag snored loudly with one hand twitching on the hilt of his sword whilst the other cradled a jug of wine to his bare chest. Angha worked the vessel free and took it outside to Sabal because she knew that sometimes old war elephants needed medicine too.

Using the jug to coax Sabal to the wall, Angha clicked her tongue, imitating Patag's instructions, and the elephant duly offered his trunk so she might use it as a ladder. After rewarding Sabal with what was left of Patag's wine, she scurried across the wall to a nearby tree branch and made good her escape knowing that, should she return before lunch, her father would be none the wiser and Lungri would imagine she was with Patag. Patag, should he awake, would assume she had stayed home. Life wasn't that complicated in the compound.

Out on the street, the city moved at a faster pace than her father's world and Angha marvelled at the people already going about their business. Through narrow passages separating family homes, barracks and stables, she made her way to the heart of Kanauj where hundreds of Buddhist monasteries and many more temples stretched glittering fingers to the sky. At regular intervals, small gardens appeared – spraying colour and perfume into the air – and in tanks of clear water strange creatures from other lands swam for the amusement of the city's residents. Among the shouts of vendors and labourers, she heard holy men chanting for the pleasure of whichever god they served, whilst pockets of scholars congregated in the sunshine to steal ideas from one another. Her father once said that if you wanted the impossible you asked for Kanauj. The city was rich beyond imagination – and the eye of the storm circled around the huge wealth of the king's palace. Though Angha had never set foot inside the high walls, her father spoke of vast halls shining with panels of gold; a place where fist-size jewels, abundant as pebbles, hid inside vaults the size of small cities. To Angha's mind such opulence was staggering, but at that stage she was still too young to understand that a man's worth was usually measured by the amount of gold he carried.

Ahead of her, a little to the right, the palace gates swung open bringing a flurry of excitement from the city folk walking nearby. Hearing the sound of hooves Angha slipped into the shadows of an alleyway, concerned that her father might be leading the charge. Although Bir Paramichi wasn't an angry man, Angha assumed he would kill her if he caught her out of the compound, which is why, with her heart pounding in her chest she nearly choked on her own spit when a voice came to challenge her.

"What are you doing? Why are you hiding?"

Angha span on her heels to find a boy scratching at his armpit. He stood a head taller than she did and he was dirtier than she was used to.

"I'm not hiding, I'm being careful," she hissed.

"And why would that be?"

"Because..." Angha paused and slumped against the wall as she contemplated the best answer to give. After a while she simply said, "Just because, that's all."

The boy sucked in his thin cheeks, looking far from convinced. "Come with me," he ordered.

"Why?"

"Because..."

Angha tutted and the boy laughed. "Come on, I've got something to show you," he urged her, and unable to find a reason not to, Angha got to her feet.

As the boy broke into a run, she followed suit and together they jumped over water channels, dodging people, goats and a succession of carts loaded with Kusha grass, until they emerged on the outskirts of the spice bazaar where huge hessian bags displayed India's flavours in the colours of autumn.

Amid the chaos of the market, street performers worked for whatever they could get as a crazy man with matted hair darted in between the crowds, completely naked save for the mud that coated his stringy limbs.

"Here!" the boy shouted over the cacophony of noise and Angha followed him as he disappeared behind one of the spice stalls. There, among the rubbish and rotten fruit, a rusty drum lid was propped against a wall. The boy pulled it away with a triumphant smile to reveal a two-headed snake that was very much dead. Angha wasn't sure how to respond. For close to two minutes, she stared at the creature before taking it in her hands and raising both heads to the sun. That done, she burst into tears.

The boy was stunned. He was also a little sorry.

"I thought you'd like it," he said.

"I do, it's a beautiful snake," Angha sobbed. "But it's dead!"

The boy stopped to consider the reality of her statement. His features were fine, almost delicate, and they pointed to a sensitivity his life probably didn't indulge. He was touched by the girl's sadness. Bending towards Angha, now in tears on the ground, he took the snake from her hands and examined it more closely. Slowly, he turned both heads towards her.

"I think he died happy," he assured her. "See how the heads smile in their sleep?"

At his gentle insistence, Angha looked again, and because she wanted to believe him, she smiled too. For a while longer she sat in the dirt, cradling the snake until her sobs and her interest gradually subsided.

"What's your name?" she eventually asked.

"Sohan."

"My name is Angha."

"I know. I dreamt you here," replied the boy. Angha giggled, but his face remained serious.

"I'm hungry," she announced, taking the boy by the hand. "And now it's your turn to come with me."

Sohan shrugged and perhaps because he'd made the little girl cry, and he had nothing better to do, he told her to lead the way.

As they walked, Angha chattered, speaking a little about the place where she lived and a lot about Sabal – thinking sword-fighting and elephants might please the boy. Occasionally, Sohan managed to get a word in edgeways, and when he did, he mostly spoke about food because he was really quite hungry.

"Not long now," Angha encouraged, even as she quietly wondered how they might get into the compound to feed her friend's stomach. She needn't have worried. By the time they reached the main gate, the warriors were awake and typically fractious, and as the guards threw themselves into an altercation with a cart driver, the two children crept by unchallenged. Once inside, no one paid them a blind bit of notice.

In front of Patag's hut, they found Sabal crunching through a small hill of grass. With food to distract him, the old elephant accepted the company of the children, but because they were young, they soon lost interest in the view of his leathery backside and Angha pulled her new friend away.

"My house is here," she said pointing to the huge building before them. Feeling Sohan's reticence in her hand she added, "I thought you were hungry."

"I am, but I'm not sure this is a good idea," he replied. "Won't your father be angry?"

"Why should he be?"

"Men usually are," he said, and Angha laughed because she had never known it to be true.

After dragging Sohan into the main hall, Angha finally released her grip. On the floor, sat cross legged on a cushion, Patag greeted them with a nod. With no wife to cook for him the old man practically lived at the house, and Angha decided he looked especially bad that morning. Patag's eyes were red, his moustache was askew, and his hair looked particularly shocking. Only the gold draped about his neck and the bangles clasped to his upper arms gave any indication of his status.

"Don't shout," he ordered gruffly before Angha had chance to utter a word.

"You need new medicine," she chided, and the old man nodded in agreement before blaming the Great War.

"It scarred my soul and it scarred my elephant," he muttered.

Angha raised her eyes to the heavens and sat herself on the floor, gesturing to Sohan to do the same. As they settled themselves, Lungri appeared with a jug of clean water which she poured over the children's hands and into a bowl. The maid had worked for Bir Paramichi ever since Angha's grandparents died. She had no family of her own because fate had been less than kind to her. With a leg turned inwards and a face misshapen by a nose knocked sideways, Lungri had the look of a woman sliding slowly to the right.

"Did you say a war scarred your elephant?" Sohan asked Patag as he inspected the dried bread Lungri placed in front of him. The old man looked up in surprise, as if noticing the child for the first time.

"I've not seen you before," he mumbled in the hybrid language of the compound. "Who's your father?"

Noticing her friend's confusion, Angha told Patag to speak in Hindi. "He's not from here. He doesn't know any Persian"

Patag sniffed, but he dropped the Persian from his speech.

"Who's your father?" he repeated.

"Sumed. He's at the palace."

Patag raised his eyebrows, impressed in spite of his personal doubts on the necessity of royalty.

"Well, Son of Sumed, I was talking about the Battle of Peshawar. It took place long before you were born – when I was still considered handsome – and they said it would be the war to end all wars. Until we lost it, that is. Now it's just another war to add to all the rest. Honestly, have you not heard of it?"

"No," Sohan replied honestly, and Patag shook his head in dismay. He grabbed a chicken leg, pausing to chew slowly because he had fewer teeth than in the day, and tried to keep his voice neutral as he dealt with the ignorance at his table.

"Well, the bastard Moslems started it," he grumbled. "For years they'd been raiding the Punjab and finally the Shahi decided enough was enough. He sent his ambassadors to all of India's kings telling them that it was no longer a matter of honour, but a sacred duty to rid the land of these mongrels who call themselves Ghaznavids. The Rajas agreed and three years ago they united under one banner led by Anandpal, the Shahi himself. Six kingdoms rallied to the cause, including the King of Kanauj who sent men, horses and elephants. It was the greatest army the world had ever seen. Our men marched to the beat of a thousand drums and the gold and silver of our armour blinded the birds in the sky. With the swords of Kanauj, Ujjain, Gwalior, Kalanjara, Delhi and Ajmer at his side, Anandpal could have finished the enemy in one day. Unfortunately, when we arrived at Peshawar, our sea of men stood ready for battle whilst the great Shahi sat back and dithered. Across the vast plain, the Moslems faced us like a black cloud hugging the horizon whilst Anandpal remained in his tent conversing with ministers and starry-eyed astrologers. As the days dragged on, we warriors became restless. Then, on the fortieth day, as the talk grew mutinous, the Shahi finally appeared. By the time he had mounted his elephant, the wild tribes from the lower hills of Kashmir had gathered in formation, all 30,000 of them."

"The Khokars?"

Patag smiled at the boy's wide eyes. "The very ones – a breed of men who know no fear, and know no sandals."

Patag paused to laugh at his own joke before continuing. "The barefooted Khokars hurled themselves at both sides of the black cloud. Like ants they swarmed over dugouts and threw themselves upon the Moslems, gouging guts from black cloth and cleaving heads with their stone axes. Smothered under an unexpected fury, the Ghaznavid horses reared in panic, bolting to escape. But there was no escape and the Khokars inflicted immediate and heavy losses. Sensing victory, Anandpal sounded the charge and his war elephants – roused by atmosphere and alcohol – surged forward smashing into the Moslem fighters to scatter them like skittles. As our swords cut and scythed through the great mass of black, explosives were fired into the rearguard of the Ghaznavid army. Within an hour, the ground was a carpet of broken, bloodied bodies and with every step I heard the bones of men crunching under Sabal's feet."

"That's disgusting," Angha muttered as she mopped up her eggs with a pinch of warm bread.

"No one said war was pretty, my pretty," Patag replied. "Anyway, with the Ghaznavids in disarray, the battle was all but won until, in the dying breaths of the fight, Anandpal's elephant bolted for home. We had no idea, no clue, what was going on. And given his previous record, we naturally thought the Shahi had fled. So, with no king to fight behind, the Rajput army sputtered to a stop, collectively losing its will and reason. Sensing our confusion, the Moslems acted swiftly. Their leader, Mahmud, rallied his men and counterattacked, scything us down like a farmer harvesting hay. Anandpal's great army fled and though it went against every bone in our bodies, the warriors of Kanauj got out of there too. And here lies the nature of the Ghaznavids; instead of taking their victory like men, they gave chase and embarked on a massacre. Less than a third of the greatest army the world had ever seen survived."

"But you escaped?"

"I'm here, aren't I?" Patag glanced towards the door, roughly towards the place he imagined his elephant might be. "Where Sabal got the strength from, I still don't know, but that elephant saved my life that day. Chunks of his legs were hacked away and his trunk was torn where the armour couldn't protect him. But the old boy did well – and I swore I'd never drag him into that hell again. The Ksatriya code of honour calls for death in battle. Cowardice is a sin, as is begging for mercy and fleeing the enemy. But on that day, we were willing to fight for the man who paid us. It was our job and our duty. But when a king loses heart, there's no shame in retreat. We kept our side of the bargain – and when we returned to Kanauj, me and the old boy retired. There was no dishonour in it."

"No dishonour at all," Bir repeated as he walked through the door to catch the end of Patag's tale. He bent to ruffle Angha's hair before loosening the straps of the leather jerkin he wore and came to sit cross-legged at the mat. Lungri instantly shuffled to his side, carrying a jug of water which she emptied over his hands. After thanking her, he picked over what was left of the chicken.

"Mahmud of Ghazna is a new breed of warrior," Bir said, seamlessly continuing the line of conversation Patag had begun. "His army is light, it's mobile and it's fanatical. In contrast we've grown fat, complacent and cumbersome – no disrespect."

Patag inclined his head to show no offence had been taken.

"Our kings are slow to respond and hunger only for a quiet life," Bir finished.

"So why not fight like the Moslems?" asked Sohan.

Bir looked at the boy, as though seeing him for the first time. He wasn't especially tolerant of children, but he appreciated the child's interest.

"It's not for us to change the way of things," he explained. "We can guide, but in the end, we fight as we are instructed whether it be for the King of Kanauj or the Punjab's Shahi. Besides, Mahmud's stolen so many of our elephants his army resembles more of a Rajput force with each passing year."

"Which means we can beat him," stated Sohan, and both Bir and Patag chuckled at the boy's confidence.

"Perhaps you might, one day, but I'm getting old," Bir replied. "Tell me, who is your father?"

"Sumed," Sohan told him.

"He's over at the palace," Patag revealed, jerking his head backwards towards a place where he thought the palace might be.

"Really?" replied Bir. "What office does he hold?"

Sohan shifted uncomfortably on his heels. "It's not a position as such," he admitted. "He's the rubbish collector."

To the right of Angha, Patag's mouth suddenly exploded, showering chicken and bread into her hair. About to protest, she was silenced by the two fingers the old man subsequently shoved down his throat, releasing the full contents of his stomach into a nearby dish. Angha looked to her father in confusion, but though Bir's response was less grotesque it was equally as baffling. He stopped chewing and took the food from his mouth, throwing it back on his plate. Angha was astounded. Sohan was quiet.

"The kid's an outcaste," spluttered Patag, wiping at his chin.

Bir nodded and rang the bell at his feet, bringing Lungri limping back into the room.

"My robes," he ordered before asking her to find someone who might return the boy to his own part of the city.

Before she could respond, Sohan rose to his feet. "I can find my way," he said quietly, and Angha screamed in furious shame as he walked away.

Ignoring Angha's protests, Bir Paramichi then dragged his daughter to the Ganges where he did his best to cleanse them both of the contamination she had brought into their house.

The next time Angha saw Sohan she was five years old. Needless to say, she had been schooled on India's caste system by then, as well as its horrible implications for manners and humanity. According to the rules, those with jobs considered ritually impure, such as rubbish collectors, were known as outcastes. This meant they weren't allowed to worship with the other castes, nor were they permitted to draw water from the same source, and though Kanauj was more tolerant than other cities – meaning the outcastes weren't required to warn of their approach – it remained highly inappropriate to dine with them. Should such an anomaly occur, the higher caste member had to bathe thoroughly in order to purge himself of the impurity to which he had laid himself open. This was India. This was the world Angha was born into. This was the thinking of the civilised.

"It is what it is," her father half-apologised.

"It's a pile of elephant crap," Angha responded and Bir clipped her about the ear before visiting Patag and asking him to temper his language in front of the child.

From the moment Angha learned how the world worked, she felt scarred from the inside. Worse than that, she despised her own weakness because despite her heart telling her to find Sohan and apologise, her legs lacked the courage to defy her father's orders. She had to admit it; she was no friend at all. Even so, on a day when she found something interesting – be it a curiously-shaped mango or a set of teeth lodged in a rotting chunk of wood – she always left it in a box covered by an old drum lid a little to the right of the compound gate. By the next morning, the oddity would be gone and a rainbow-coloured flower would stand in its place. Though Angha hoped with every beat of her heart that it was Sohan accepting her gifts, she could never be certain – not until the day her father took her to the banks of the Ganges to honour the goddess Kali, the many-armed protector of Kanauj.

To Angha's eyes the entire city appeared to have left their homes that day. People poured from every alleyway, spilling onto the road like a great flood. Every face carried a smile, and every man, woman and child shone in their finest clothes, including Angha who had been dressed by Lungri and wore a white silk tunic with beads of gold dangling from her ears and around her neck. Before they left for the holy river, Patag swore he had never seen her look more beautiful. It was the first compliment Angha ever remembered receiving.

To save her from falling under a thousand or more feet, Bir hoisted his daughter onto his shoulders and she giggled as he cantered upon the cobbled pathway that slipped down to the Ganges until, finally, the wall of flesh became too deep to pass.

"Ksatriyas!" bellowed Patag. "Clear a path for the warrior class!"

The old man was clearly joking, but old habits die hard and the people around them parted to give Angha a first-class view of a procession of men carrying statues of Kali to the water. Every year after the great rains, mud was gathered from the sacred river and a likeness of the goddess was moulded, fired and painted a thousand times over. On the last day of the celebration, her statues were carried from their shrines and released into the Ganges. As they floated away, they gradually melted, allowing the goddess to return to heaven.

Caught up in the happiness of the moment Angha could hardly still her eyes. They darted from river to bank, from Brahman to warrior, from woman to child, from Kali to Kali, from ground to wall, until they found what they hardly knew they were searching for. Sitting among a group of men crowding a high wall, one leg dangling over the edge, she saw Sohan. His hair looked coarser than she remembered and his body longer, but his dark eyes remained the same and she saw they were watching her. Giddy and strangely nervous, Angha smiled – happier than she could ever remember being. In response, Sohan lifted a flower to his nose. It was the colour of dawn. He twirled it in front of his face and then leapt from the wall to be swallowed by the crowd.

Later that afternoon, after all the Kalis in the whole of Kanauj had been released, Angha ran to the box that she kept by the wall of the compound. Removing the drum lid, she found the orange and red petals that Sohan had played with earlier that day. She was so pleased, she went home and cried.

As the months went by, Angha continued to leave presents for Sohan – a blue feather here, a lizard's tail there, and a scrap of burnt bread bearing the face of Lord Shiva. In turn, Sohan left his flowers and kept to the shadows where his own caste resided. Meanwhile at home, surrounded by men bred for war, the talk grew ever more serious.

Bir was worried about the Moslem's Mahmud. Following the disaster in Peshawar, the Ghaznavids had been riding in and out of India at will, filling their coffers with the riches of the Rajas and flooding slave markets with so many captives that the price of bread was now dearer than a man. By spring, many believed the Moslems would next target Kanauj and every night scouts galloped back and forth through the gates of the fortress city, charting the Ghaznavids' advance, while the Ksatriyas discussed battle plans until their candles grew short. The sense of foreboding was such that Patag no longer took his medicine.

"We can't hope to match the Islamists," the old man growled.

"I hate to say it, but you might have a point," accepted Danvish, one of Bir's most trusted commanders whose bravery was carved in the scars on his arms. "The Ghaznavids will fight until the earth is stained red. More than that, they have a mighty God on their side. Mahmud seems unstoppable."

"They say his men have caught frostbite in the time it takes them to count the spoils," said Rahul a red-haired man who was another of Bir's favoured few.

"A wolf attacking sheep," grunted Patag.

"And yet they rarely change tactics," Bir interrupted, trying to halt the growing despondency surrounding him. "They lure the fight into the open, dividing their horses into packs which then circle and swoop in succession. It's an efficient method, but one that requires space."

"So, what do you suggest?" Danvish asked. "Bring the fight to the city?" He looked around him, barely willing to contemplate the thought, but the other men muttered in agreement.

Behind the door where she listened, Angha's heart thumped at the thought of the barbarous Moslems charging through the city's clean streets. Surely, there had to be another way.

"It's the only way," her father concluded inside the war room, and though he didn't sound especially pleased, she recognised a tremor of excitement breaking his voice. When a week later Mahmud's army turned left – away from Kanauj, heading for Kashmir – Angha couldn't be sure her father wasn't disappointed.

As Angha entered her seventh year, the Moslems finally pointed their scimitars towards Kanauj. With war an ever-nearing reality, Bir arranged for the compound's women and children to leave the city; taken to a place where they would be guarded by those either too old or too young for battle. It took the best part of a fortnight to dismantle the vast number of lives in his care and, as the evacuees loaded up their carts, they moved to the rhythm of hammers hitting anvils as the blacksmiths and sword smiths worked without end.

Although her father assured her that all would be well, Angha instinctively knew she would never return to Kanauj, so with everyone busy she managed to creep away to say goodbye to the city she had always called home. By now, the bustle of privileged life had been swept away leaving the empty streets echoing to the march of soldiers' feet, the shouts of engineers, and the desperate implorations of priests and Buddhists. Above them all, the clouds hung still in the blue sky, as if soaking up the end of an era.

As she gravitated towards the palace, Angha was stopped in her tracks by the sight of a beautiful horse roaming untethered. A proud grey stallion, he was as fine an animal as any her father had ever bartered from the Arabs in Gujarat. He also happened to be trailed by a hundred young men dressed in the robes of royalty. Behind the nobles walked an even larger crowd whose chatter barely lifted above a whisper. Curious, Angha followed them.

As the stallion neared the outer wall, a fanfare of trumpets sounded and Angha was further amazed to see the king had left his palace. Seated in an ornate litter, Rajapala was accompanied by a multitude of servants who wafted perfumed flowers under his nose to disguise the sweat of the crowd. The king was slighter than Angha had imagined, like a man whose finery was trying to swallow him. Dressed in a blue and gold tunic, a silver belt gripped his waist bearing a large ruby clasp. His feet were covered by slippers that curled upwards and his fingers shone with emeralds. Upon his knee sat a great sword, sheathed in embroidered leather. Despite him looking as terrifying as a painted doll, Angha cheered.

Moving towards the Ganges, the king, his followers, and the beautiful horse came to a stop at the river's edge. Immediately, a group of men stepped forward and with great care they harnessed the stallion to a golden chariot. With so many wrestling to watch the spectacle, Angha lost sight of the ceremony and fell back. Looking about her, she saw steps leading to the wall of a nearby monastery and raced to climb them. By the time she was seated the horse and the chariot were both in the water, and along the bank she noticed a dozen or more animals tied to wooden stakes including a wild ox and a hornless goat. After bathing the stallion, the Brahman priests led him back to dry land where, to murmurs of appreciation, three women – remarkable for their beauty – unharnessed the animal. They then anointed him with oils before decorating him with gold. Angha could almost sense the horse's pride as he calmly took their offerings. Once the women were done, six men then approached holding a heavy-looking cloak, but instead of placing it upon the stallion's back, as Angha expected, they threw it over his head causing the horse to rear in panic. Immediately, the men used their weight to pull at the bridle, wrestling the animal to the ground, and in the mud of the Ganges, the stallion's legs lashed out, kicking furiously as he fought to regain his feet. More men came running to help, and Angha realised, all too late, that they were in fact suffocating the animal. Horrified, she screamed and span away – crashing blindly into a pair of waiting arms.

"Make them stop," she begged.

"I can't. It's too late," the boy replied, and Sohan dragged her away because there was nothing that he could do. On the eve of war, the gods demanded sacrifice and the king had obliged.

"When we grow up, we must never, ever treat a horse like that. Not ever," Angha sobbed. Sohan pulled her deep into his chest and promised that they wouldn't. He then waited for Angha to calm herself. As he held her in his arms, he realised she was getting tall for a girl.

Once she blew the last of her tears into the hem of her robe, Angha dried her eyes to look at her friend. Her shock was immediate and nothing she could disguise. Sohan's skin was dark as charcoal and his delicate features had settled into creases of stern acceptance. His hair was thick and roughly cut and for some reason he wore only one earring.

"I took out the other when my mother died," he explained when he saw her looking.

"That's sad," Angha sympathised.

"That's death," he replied.

A little more shyly than they once did before, they walked back to the city and Angha belatedly apologised for the spectacle of vomiting that had marred his last and only visit to her home. Sohan shrugged and said that he should have known better. Angha insisted that he should have known no such thing, and Sohan dismissed the retort for making no sense at all. Accepting he might be right, Angha moved onto safer ground by echoing the concerns of the Paramichi compound.

"The Moslems are coming."

"I know," he said.

"Are you scared?"

"A little."

"You should be more. Patag says that Mahmud is the worst bastard devil who's ever walked the earth and that he'll feast on our livers before our dead bodies hit the ground."

"The old man could be right."

"Do you think?" Angha's eyes widened.

"No, I don't think he'll feast on our livers," Sohan laughed easily, "but I'm sure he'll try and kill us."

"Oh."

Looking to the sun, Angha noted the time and knew she couldn't delay much longer. Trying to sound matter-of-fact, she revealed she would be leaving the city the following day.

"If you can, watch where we go," she urged, and Sohan replied that he would.

The boy then walked away, knowing sleep would be short.

That night, Kanauj remained restless, but ready. Giant stockades covered trenches hiding iron spikes, and all the tar available waited to be boiled in mammoth black pots. Meanwhile, in the privacy of their homes, residents veered between bravado and unchecked tears. Although Angha was sent to bed early, for much of the night she remained in the great hall, going largely unnoticed, as the warriors discussed tactics for the coming battle. A three-day ride away, Mahmud headed an army of 100,000 horses and 10,000 foot soldiers as well as 20,000 mercenaries hired from the wilds of Turkistan, Transoxiana and Khorasan.

"The Turkmen are savages," Patag declared, and nobody at the war council seemed inclined to disagree.

"That's enough now," Lungri whispered as she emerged from the kitchen to find Angha listening, pale-faced and slightly tearful. Thankful for the intervention, the girl traipsed wearily to bed.

At dawn, Angha was summoned from a sleep she hardly remembered having to be brought before her father. Bir was dressed in his best armour and his broad chest was covered by a silver plate emblazoned with the sun.

"Be brave and be patient because we will win and then I will come for you," he said. "In the meantime, Lungri, Patag and Sabal will take care of you."

Bir bent to kiss his daughter, but the metal he wore restricted all movement and so he sank to his knees to take hold of her.

"You are my proudest moment," he whispered. He then nodded to Patag and the old man stepped forward to take the child from her father, kicking and screaming.

It was a grim trail of two thousand or more miserable faces that left the city that morning, winding its way alongside the Ganges before turning right to lose itself in the rich swell of trees that India wore like a mantle. Eight hours from Kanauj, the evacuees rolled to a stop in a clearing their warriors had found a week or so earlier. It lay by a freshwater stream and a number of trees had already been felled to help speed the construction of the camp. With few words, the group got to work; cutting branches and plaiting leaves to make homes they had no idea how long they might need. Sabal was the only elephant among them and he helped where he could – pushing down trees and rolling great logs. All the while, the cooks stoked their fires, ready to feed anyone who had regained an appetite.

After the horses were penned, everyone converged on the centre of the camp to take food and elect Patag as the head of the group. The old man took their trust with thanks. He then organised a troop of boys to act as scouts. Each of them was given a horse and they were to share the responsibility of bringing news from Kanauj.

"In the meantime, we get on with living," Patag concluded, and the camp returned to building corrals and erecting shelters whilst the young mothers among them attempted to discourage their children from crying.

With Patag busy, Angha retreated into Sabal's shadow. As if sensing her need the elephant was gentler than usual, and whenever she could Lungri also did her best to supply the human contact a little girl might need. Though she'd never said it, Lungri loved Angha as completely as if she were her own. Deep in her heart, she knew she would never bear children – her body's betrayals had made her unmarketable, and her father had lacked the dowry to change that – so Lungri had put all of her care into the child that was there. She couldn't claim to be happy, but she felt secure, and that was a condition she owed to Bir Paramichi. He was a stern man, but he had always been good to her. Therefore, when she saw the little boy who had caused such a frenzy of vomiting in her master's home, she was torn. On the one hand, he was an outcaste. On the other, he was a child. Further complicating the matter was the knowledge that he had become a friend to Angha; their closeness being all too apparent when Lungri fell upon the pair talking behind the bulk of Patag's elephant.

"Don't make him go," Angha pleaded when she realised that they had been caught.

Lungri looked at the boy, seeing little more than the injustice that had blighted both their lives. "Keep out of Patag's way," she stiffly advised before limping back to whatever chores she could find in order to ignore the possible repercussions of turning a blind eye.

"That lady seems nice," Sohan commented once they were alone.

"Her name is Lungri," Angha replied. "She loves my father, but she's too lopsided for him."

"Too bad."

"Yes, it is. She's a good cook."

On the third night of their flight, as the evacuees struggled to find sleep, a scout thundered into the camp, ending all hope of rest. With the flanks of his horse frothing with exertion, the boy came to a halt outside Patag's shack. After relaying his news in short desperate gasps, Patag's head sank to his chest. King Rajapala had fled Kanauj, taking his family and bodyguards with him. Apparently, his cowardice only came to light when Mahmud arrived at the gates of the city to find no ruler to bargain with. The camp's shock was immediate.

"Our men?" demanded one of the women.

"My father?" shouted Angha. "What about my father?"

Hearing her distress, Sohan approached, coming to stand at Angha's shoulder. Patag's eyes flickered in recognition, but he had more pressing matters to deal with.

"Your father fights," Patag told Angha before turning to the waiting crowd. "Kanauj now rests or falls on the swords of the Ksatriyas!"

Patag's war cry was met with a stony silence. The king had fled, the fight was pointless. "They have no choice," Patag insisted, albeit more quietly. "It's their fate," he added, and everyone knew it could be no other way.

"What will become of us?" one of the wives sobbed, and Lungri ushered Angha away because the child needed hope, not the despair of others who ought to know better. As she clasped the child's shoulders she told her, "Be brave; your father will win." She then willed herself to believe it too.

As Lungri guided Angha back to her bed she nodded towards Sohan, suggesting the boy might follow. Quickly glancing at Patag, Lungri registered the frown on the old man's face, but they both knew that rules were less rigid during times of war. It was a small relief, and it was one that was quickly swallowed by the morning when Lungri awoke to find Angha already up and sitting cross-legged. At first the maid thought nothing of it – the girl was peculiar in her habits – but then she saw the child was alone.

"Where's the boy?" she asked.

Angha's face was pale but resolute. "I asked him to save my father."

"Oh Angha, you didn't."

Lungri ran from the hut as fast as her gammy leg would allow her. At the gate of the clearing she saw Patag. "I'm looking for the boy!"

"So am I," he grumbled, pausing to swat a fly from his face. "The little bastard has stolen my sword."

Despite Patag's efforts, Sohan avoided detection simply by keeping off the trodden path. He had never considered himself bright, but Patag's scouts couldn't have been more obvious if they'd conducted their search on the back of fifty rutting elephants strutting to the beat of a thousand drummers. Occasionally, he cursed the sword in his hands as it grew heavier with each passing hour, but mostly he struggled with the weight of Angha's request, and the fear he might disappoint her.

By the time Sohan came within hearing distance of Kanauj the sun was in full retreat and Patag's sword dragged behind him, picking up nicks and scratches that couldn't be avoided. As the screams of men became ever more distinct his legs began to falter, and for a moment, but no more, Sohan thought of his own father. They had never been close and he had only ever known the touch of his backhand. Still, he'd never wished him any harm. He'd only ever wished him gone.

Beneath his tunic Sohan felt his heart pounding. He pulled from his pocket the last piece of meat Angha had given him before quenching his thirst in a nearby stream. The water was cool – the sounds of death close – and after splashing his face he raised Patag's sword with renewed purpose. His resolve lasted until he met the road to Kanauj where he saw, from the safety of the trees, that the battle was over – and the Moslems had won.

At the mouth of the city, the Ghaznavids were busy; dragging out their dead and hauling the spoils of their victory onto wagons that now glittered with jewels and jagged plates of gold that had been stripped from the temples' many idols. The ground was a mess of torn cloth, globs of flesh and puddles of blood. In a pen at the left of the gate, stood a number of men, women and children – survivors of the battle, destined to become slaves. Sohan scoured the group. Beneath the grime and the blood that covered them, he recognised the terror he saw, but none of the faces. Then, in the distance, he heard the clash of metal upon metal. The war had been won, but some fights were clearly not over.

Skirting the edge of the forest, Sohan passed a slum of empty shacks that had once housed the city's flotsam and jetsam – the pariahs of a society now lost. Every dwelling stood abandoned, all had fled, save for a few stray dogs fighting over a dismembered hand. Sohan slung Patag's sword about his neck and finding the point where the battle was loudest, he scaled the wall using whatever nooks and crannies his feet could fit into. As he pulled himself upwards his arms trembled with effort. Twice he lost his footing and a scrape on his chin began to pulse blood. With one last heave, Sohan hurled himself onto the wall-walk. Ignoring the pain in his chest, he looked into the courtyard below to see 600 or more Rajput warriors backed into a corner by a larger force of Ghaznavids. At their feet many lay dead or dying, and it was clear that the Islamists were steadily hacking their way to victory.

Among the surviving warriors, his helmet gone and a large gash running along the length of his face, was Bir Paramichi. The strain showed in the fixed snarl he wore and beneath his chest plate his tunic dripped red. To the right of him, a man fell as a sword twisted in his throat. Bir repositioned himself and found a stomach to gouge before spinning to block another blade. Even as he swung, he was conscious of the support dwindling around him. His men had fought bravely. He was proud of them. "Kanauj!" he roared, and the men around him took up the cry. With an increasing sense of desperation, Bir's sword sliced through the neck of the man in front of him. As he fell, he kicked the body away, but the Moslems were like ants and another filled the gap before Bir barely had time to pull back his weapon. Over his shoulder a head flew past, slamming into the chest of an approaching Ghaznavid. It had once belonged to the body of Rahul, and Bir's shock was such that he felt no pain when a scimitar carved into him. Only when his right arm failed to respond did Bir notice the flesh ripped open, oozing blood. He swapped the weapon to his left hand, but it felt unnatural, almost too slow to be of any use and within seconds another blade scythed through the air, hitting his thigh. The wound was shallow, but it added to the blood already lost and Bir felt his body waver.

"No!"

From behind him, a young boy ran screaming, holding aloft a sword that was almost as tall as he was. He struck the Moslem who should have ended Bir's life squarely upon the head. The weapon bounced on the Ghaznavid's skull and he reeled backwards, stunned but otherwise uninjured. Again, the boy lifted his sword and Bir became aware of having seen him before. He grabbed the youngster and threw him aside as a sword flashed through the dusk to take him. The child leapt back to his feet, and Bir moved to protect him just as a horn sounded, breaking through the grunts and screams of battle. Its effect was instant.

"Enough!" barked a command in Persian, and like a pack of dogs denied a bone, the Moslems retreated with their teeth still bared.

Bir was stunned, unsure what to make of the sudden impasse. Around him, his men struggled for breath and a quick glance at their sword arms revealed they remained tense. At his side he noticed the boy who had come to save him, trembling under the weight of his weapon. Bir took hold of the sword, thinking as he did so that it looked an awful lot like Patag's.

"It's OK," he whispered as the child resisted. Only then did the boy relax his grip. As his black eyes looked up, the penny dropped, and Bir felt deeply ashamed.

From out of the shadows, a black horse moved towards the Ksatriyas, directed by the man who had effectively ended the fight. He stopped in front of Bir. His eyes were dark, the horse danced beneath him, and he looked as weary as them all, if less butchered.

"You've a brave boy there," he remarked.

In the strange silence, Bir didn't correct the man's mistake. He turned to Sohan, "The Moslem says you have great courage."

The rider watched the exchange, his black eyes glinting beneath heavy brows. Though he was dressed in the same drab cloth of the other Ghaznavids when he spoke it was with the authority of a king. "These men are now prisoners," he told his men. "Treat them with honour. They fought you well."

At the command, the Moslems lowered their scimitars. The Rajput warriors looked to Bir and he answered them by dropping his own sword to the ground. There was no further honour to be had in dying. Following suit, the men released their weapons. Bir laid a hand on Sohan's shoulder, and together they left the place that had almost cost them their lives, herded by an enemy as grateful for an end to the fight as those they had vanquished.

"Angha asked me to save you," Sohan revealed as they walked through a city destroyed, and Bir swallowed hard. The boy couldn't have been more than a couple of years older than his daughter.

As Bir led his men towards an unknown fate, a day's walk away Patag was grappling with his own uncertainty. At his feet a scout sat shaking with the revelation that Kanauj had fallen.

"It was a massacre," the boy sobbed, unable to deny his tender years.

Patag gazed into the sea of eyes looking to him, pleading for some kind of hope, but for the life of him he had nothing to tell them. As far as he knew, the situation was, in fact, hopeless. The women had become widows, their children fatherless. What could he offer but survival? The Moslems were savages and, more than that, they were unstoppable. Even with the fall of Kanauj, Patag couldn't be sure that their thirst for blood had waned. They might continue their campaign, and in doing so find them hiding. Rubbing his temples, he ordered everyone to leave him. He needed time to think. Yet before he could do that, he knew he should speak with Angha. In the dark, his eyes searched for the girl but found only Lungri.

"She's with Sabal," the maid revealed, and Patag walked to the edge of the camp where his oldest companion stood watching over the child who lay sleeping on a bed of hay. Patag offered Sabal a handful of peanuts, and knowing he'd do Angha no favours by waking her, he let the girl be. Trudging back to the centre of the camp – an open space that had been office and home to him since the day they arrived – he heard hooves approaching from the black of the forest. Patag's blood froze as he braced himself for the worst.

"They live!" screamed the scout, dismounting at a gallop before scrambling to his feet. There wasn't a soul who hadn't heard him and everyone came running from their shelters.

"Who lives?" Patag asked, handing the boy a jug of water. The rider downed the drink in one, wiping the waste from his chin with the back of his hand.

"Bir, I saw Bir and Danvish for sure, and many more. Dhara," he called out, addressing a woman standing close to him, "I saw Ekel!"

At the news the young woman dropped to her knees, holding her head.

"Thank you, thank you," she wept as she rocked.

"I also saw Kuvam and Manit," the young boy revealed spinning wildly in search of the men's wives. From the back of the crowd, a shriek of gratitude escaped into the night whilst the other wives pressed forward, urging the teenager to speak their own husband's names. However, the boy could do no more. "I'm sorry, it was dark. There was no time."

"You did well," Patag assured him, feeling the blood tingling in his fingers. "Get the boy some food," he ordered, "and the rest of you, return to your shelters and try to find sleep – in the morning we leave!"

Four weeks into his captivity, Bir Paramichi was thinner than he used to be and grudgingly impressed. Far from being the crazed sword of Islam, the Ghaznavids were a well-disciplined force. There was no triumphalism in their dealings with the prisoners, no arbitrary acts of brutality, they simply carried out their orders and kept the beast moving. The sheer size of the operation was staggering; tens of thousands of black-turbaned riders, foot soldiers and war elephants, with a few thousand more being tended to in the hospital that travelled with them. Adding to their weight were 50,000 Indians taken during the length of their campaign. Unlike the Rajputs who took hostages for ransom, it was clear the captives were a different kind of commodity – and the wounded were patched up and fed so they could be sold at market along with the cattle. Those beyond help were discarded en route, left to die where they bled. The rolling camp was as big as a city and Bir knew that in the midst of it all there was one man oiling the cogs that kept it all moving; Mahmud of Ghazna.

Having glimpsed the Sultan during the month-long walk, Bir's suspicions had been confirmed – the man who had stayed his execution was indeed the Ghaznavid leader. What he remained uncertain of was why. As Bir pondered the possible reasons, he watched their numbers swell as the Ghaznavids continued to collect trophies on their long journey home. During a siege of Manaich the Moslems made little attempt to scale the fortress, preferring instead to let their reputation do the fighting. On the fifteenth day of waiting, the Hindus complied by running out of the gate and onto the swords of their enemy. "Once terror is attained there's not much left to achieve," Danvish commented dryly, and Bir agreed that fear was as good a weapon as any.

After the carnage of Manaich, other governors fled to a safer distance before suing for peace, and by the time Mahmud cleared India he had collected riches beyond imagination, as well as another 380 war elephants, 85 of which had belonged to Rajapala. Bir spat in the dirt at the very thought of their king. Occasionally he even amused himself with thoughts of slitting the regal throat. But mostly throughout the long walk west, he focussed on surviving so that he might one day find his daughter. Instinctively, Bir turned towards Sohan, asleep on the ground with his head resting against Danvish's thigh. He was a boy of few words and many scowls, and Bir felt strangely awkward around him.

To the left of them, a Ghaznavid guard approached. Picking his way through the human debris of multiple victories, he stopped in front of Bir and ordered him to his feet. At the command Sohan stirred.

"If they'd wanted to kill me, they'd have done it by now," Bir reassured him.

Sohan didn't reply. Neither did he return to sleep. Instead, he sat upright and waited.

Taking care to protect his bandaged arm, Bir followed the guard out of the prisoners' field and into the main camp. Despite the early hour, most of the soldiers slept – a habit amongst men who never know when the next rest might come. Occasionally, a noise of protest met a scheduled shift change, but by and large the camp was quiet, almost peaceful.

Stopping at a large tent, a nod indicated Bir should enter the opening. At the entrance, stood two soldiers of immense proportions and Bir felt his heart quicken as he passed between them. Inside, a wood burner gave light from one corner. Three guards filled the others. Animal skins covered the floor and long cushions were arranged around a mat displaying plates of brown rice, stewed meat and bowls of fruit. Sitting cross-legged on the ground, using scraps of bread to scoop up his meal, was Mahmud. There was nothing regal about his appearance, save for a ruby ring adorning the small finger of his left hand. He gestured to Bir, inviting him to sit.

"Hungry? Thirsty?"

Mahmud pushed forward a jug of wine. Then, noticing the warrior's dilemma, he smiled and nodded to a guard standing to his left. The man unsheathed his dagger and, walking behind Bir's back, he sliced through the ropes binding him. After rubbing his wrists, Bir took the food on offer as well as the drink.

As the two men ate in silence, Bir watched Mahmud with more care than was reciprocated. The Moslem was dressed in practical dark clothes with a turban covering his hair. His beard was thick and unruly and Bir noticed a deep cut slashing the back of one hand. His eyes were black, and keen as a hawk's.

"Do you like what you see?" Mahmud suddenly asked. "The way you're devouring me I feel like a virgin on the point of ravishment."

Unsure whether he was joking, Bir stayed quiet.

"You do speak Persian, don't you?"

"Not so good, but enough to get by," Bir admitted.

"You're too modest. Though, really, I'd no idea our influence stretched this far east."

"Trade," Bir responded, "and war, of course."

"Of course," Mahmud accepted, "unfortunate business, really."

Again, Bir was thrown by the man's choice of words.

"Anyway, as pleasant as this conversation is, you're probably wondering why I've asked you here."

Bir tilted his head to confirm that was exactly what he was wondering.

"Well, something quite curious is occurring and for some reason my eyes are drawn to you." Mahmud paused to take a bite of meat before running the back of his thumb along the edge of his moustache. "For three weeks we've been aware of being followed. Naturally, my first thought was that one of your kings had grown a spine, but I was soon assured this was not the case. So, I went to see for myself – and do you know what I saw?"

Bir waited to be told.

"I saw 2,000 women and children – and a few old men – walking in the shadow of the most decrepit elephant I've ever laid eyes on."

Bir couldn't hide his surprise and Mahmud smiled at his reaction.

"So, they belong to you?"

"I can't say for certain, but yes, it sounds like my people," Bir admitted, trying to blank the whys and wherefores until he had a moment to think.

"And what would be your power over them – Raja or priest?"

Bir shook his head, "Neither. We are Bhairaqis; nomadic warriors. We follow the man who pays us."

"You mean mercenaries?"

"That's another word for it, yes."

Mahmud nodded slowly, taking a moment to evaluate the prisoner at his table. "A man who knows loyalty is worth knowing. How's your arm?"

"It's healing."

"Good."

Mahmud rose to his feet. Bir attempted to follow.

"No, no stay where you are," the Moslem insisted. "Eat. Drink. When you're finished, my guard will take you back to wherever he found you."

Mahmud grabbed a scarf to wipe at his face before leaving the tent. Bir didn't thank the Moslem and neither did he continue eating – after being told his daughter was close his stomach was no longer in the market for food. Instead, he rose to his feet and waited for the guard to shackle him. When he returned to his men, he watched their relief turn to surprise when he repeated the conversation that had taken place.

"They should have stayed put," muttered Danvish.

"Would you have stayed?" Bir inquired with a smile, and his friend released a humourless laugh.

"No, probably not."

A little away from them, Sohan got to his feet and gazed into the distance.

Leaving India's lush valleys, the Ghaznavids squeezed their train of captives, elephants, horses and cattle through narrow gorges shielded by sky-high mountains until they spilled out onto the dusty plains leading the Moslems home. On their journey the weak and injured continued to die and scavenging birds circled their every move. Some way behind the procession, Patag gazed upon the hard, brown landscape with growing despair whilst endeavouring to avoid the carpet of dung that stretched before him, seemingly without end. As if sensing his dismay, Sabal grabbed a passing bush to chew on, recognising it might be his last meal for a while.

Although Patag's plan had been to follow the victors discreetly, by the time they reached the flat expanse of Ghaznavid territory there was little point in pretending; the Moslems had spotted them many moons ago, when the valleys were still green. He glanced behind him, seeing the grim determination of people who believed in him. It was gratifying at his late stage in life, and emotion combined with the dust to choke him.

"Are we there yet?"

Patag looked down to see Angha by his side. She was teasing him, which he thought was admirable given the circumstances. She may look like her mother, but the child was the product of her father. Noting the strip of cloth she had tied around Sabal's left leg he also saw he had played some part in her development.

"Red protects," Angha had explained, in an echo of one of his own statements. She had also tied a scrap about her own wrist and ordered Patag and Lungri to do the same. Naturally, the other children had followed suit until their mothers ran out of dresses or patience. Patag wasn't sure which had come first.

Looking back to the horizon, Patag saw that the Moslems had stopped some several leagues ahead of them. He then noticed the hazy outline of a city, rising from rock.

"Ghazna," he guessed aloud.

Built by the side of a river, the Ghaznavid stronghold lay behind a wall with only the spikes of two immense towers visible to hint at what lay inside. As the war party neared, the gates swung open and Mahmud and a contingent of his men broke away to gallop through. The bulk of his army remained where it stood, and it quickly became apparent that the dusty plain would be home to Bir and his men until the human spoils of war had been bartered over by the gathering slave buyers.

Clearly following orders, the Ghaznavids herded the captives into a collection of groups. Bir and his men were kept together, along with the boy

Sohan, and they all watched in shame as the fair and the dark, the rich and the poor, all suffered the indignity of auction.

For more than a week the bazaar attracted a succession of buyers, arriving on horses or camels from the far reaches of the Ghaznavid Empire to buy slaves by the hundred, destined to be sold again for a better price further afield.

"I'll be no slave," Danvish snarled as he watched the recently sold being led away in shackles, sometimes quiet with terror sometimes screaming.

"Something's not right," Bir replied, and Danvish turned to him, waiting for an explanation.

"See how we're kept apart?" Bir whispered. "No sticks have prodded our thighs. And our families have been left alone. That's telling. For the life of me, I don't know what the Moslem's plan is, but I'd say he has one."

Danvish looked towards their followers, still too distant to view clearly. Every inch of him ached to see the faces of his wife and children, but all he could make out was the dark smudge of Patag's cantankerous elephant. Around his feet, the dust began to fly, stirred up by the warm winds that plagued the flatlands around them. Danvish dropped his head and covered his mouth.

As the sand began to swirl, Angha hid behind Sabal's huge belly, using it as a windbreaker. Seemingly resigned to his role, the elephant also accepted Lungri when she hobbled towards him, which is why, when the Ghaznavids finally approached their group, Angha and Lungri were among the last to realise it.

"Stand firm," Patag instructed as everyone rose to their feet.

Instinctively the smaller children moved closer to their mothers as a hundred or more Moslems surrounded them, all on horseback, all carrying swords.

"Now we will see," Patag whispered to no one, and he clicked at Sabal, urging him to his feet, as the soldiers began herding them towards Ghazna.

As they walked, nobody spoke – their heads were too busy with prayers, their throats too restricted by wishes – but closing in on the men they had followed, pockets of relief gradually escaped in gasps and cries as faces were recognised. Within throwing distance of each other tears began to fall upon the cheeks of both groups, and they barely even noticed when the gates of Ghazna pulled open and twenty men on horseback rode out. The group was led by Mahmud, now dressed like the Sultan he was. Wearing the finest silk, complimented by a tapered gold crown upon his head, his beard had been trimmed and his moustache waxed upwards. The tack on his horse shone with silver buckles and his finery served to heighten the shabby state of those he had vanquished.

The flat plain that had seen tens of thousands come and be sold was now a wasteland offering only litter, discarded rags, heaps of animal dung and a few stragglers from the merchant classes. Mahmud's horse trotted to the front of the Ksatriya warriors. He wore no sword and his eyes sparkled with energy. Bir stepped forward, his joints stiff, but his wounds almost healed. As he did so Sohan came to stand at his side and Bir placed a restraining hand on the child's shoulder. At the same moment, Angha felt two hands land on her own and she looked up to see both Patag and Lungri guarding her. Their faces were tense and Angha followed their gaze.

"As you can see the bazaar is done," Mahmud said loudly, waving a hand across the empty expanse. "So now I come to speak to you, soldier to soldier, with a business deal. You may not like me, you may not even respect me, but if you serve me, you will gain your life and that of your families."

Bir felt the breath of everyone he knew stop in disbelief. Although it hardly needed discussing he turned to read the eyes of his men. Nodding, he returned his attention to Mahmud admitting, "It's a good deal."

But the Moslem hadn't finished.

"The warriors among you will fit into my army and, as you have seen, the rewards are great if you fight for them. Furthermore, you have permission to build homes in my city and to keep with you your parents, wives and daughters. However, I must insist that you hand over your sons."

As the crowd balked, Mahmud lifted a hand.

"They are to live," he said, "but as Ghaznavids, not Rajput warriors. They will board within our barracks. They will be trained and they will be treated well."

Mahmud waited for his words to sink in before delivering the next hammer blow.

"As far as the people who followed you are concerned, I commend their spirit. Loyalty is a trait to be admired. However, any wife who finds herself without a husband will be sold. And so that you're not tempted to claim a few sisters you never had, these too will be traded. These are my terms. You get your parents, your wives and your daughters, no more. I'll give you until the sun stands above your heads to make up your minds."

As Mahmud cantered away, the Moslem guards allowed the two groups to spread out, so they could see what was, or was not, at stake. Within minutes, the line behind Patag began to crumble as one by one the elderly and the widows dropped to the floor, realising it was not to be their day. Those with fatherless daughters pushed their young towards women whose men were still standing. Without a word the wives adopted them even as they shed tears for the sons they would lose. By the time the sun beat directly above them their grief was palpable, and when Mahmud returned the dreadful business of farewell began as Bir grimly accepted the Moslem's terms.

"You're to go to a special kind of school," Bir explained to Sohan as the other boys stepped forward to be taken away. "You will learn how to fight and you will be treated well. When I can, I will find you."

Setting his jaw, Sohan moved to join a hundred or more boys who had gathered near Mahmud. Before disappearing into the throng, he stopped and turned. Finding Angha, he lifted a clenched fist into the air. In response the young girl broke free of Lungri's grasp and stepped forward, her own arm raised high in reply until one of the guards pushed Sohan forward. With swords half-raised the Moslems led the boys up the hill to be swallowed by the great gateway of Ghazna.

On the back of his black horse, Mahmud slapped at the dust settling on his clothes before indicating to Bir that his men should begin retrieving their families. One by one the warriors stepped forward; to claim whomever they could in a ghastly game of choice. As their leader, Bir went last and the sight almost broke him – the boys were gone, wives and daughters had been saved, and only old men and widows remained. People he had known all his life were about to be cast to the wind, and there was not a thing he could do to stop it.

Bir opened his arms and Angha came running. Watching the reunion, Patag smiled and patted Sabal's trunk.

"Father!" Bir shouted. "There's nothing more you can do. Please, come!"

Somewhat confused, Patag saw his friend beckoning him, and though the warriors around him betrayed no surprise, the old man could already hear their laughter. Patag shrugged and clicked his tongue to lead Sabal to Bir's side. At the sight of the moving elephant Mahmud half raised his hand before relenting and allowing the beast to pass.

"You too, Lungri," Bir ordered.

Dipping her head to hide her tears, Lungri shuffled forwards only to find her path quickly blocked.

"I told you, no..." Mahmud stopped, searching for the right word, unsure who the woman might be to the warrior.

"My wife," Bir stated calmly.

"Is that so?"

"Yes, it is. I claim my wife, my father and my daughter – as you permitted."

Mahmud lifted an eyebrow. Bir kept his gaze steady.

"Interesting," the Moslem finally managed. "Well, now you're reunited I look forward to welcoming many more of your children into our lives."

Behind him the Ghaznavids sniggered, but the Ksatriyas remained quiet – and Angha couldn't have been prouder of her father if he'd actually saved Kanauj.

In the face of almost universal scepticism, Mahmud of Ghazna kept his word; he incorporated the warriors into the rank and file of the Ghaznavid army; he allowed families to build homes and prosper at will; and he trained and cared for the boys he had stolen.

Occasionally, missing sons were permitted to visit their parents, but the occurrences were rare and when the boys returned home each appearance revealed less of the Indians they once were. Isolation and training moulded them into mamluks – an elite force of mounted archers – and though they continued to be slaves their position was one of privilege.

"This mighty empire was built by slaves!" Abdul Aziz informed his bright young things during the many hours of training that went into the making of a mamluk.

Sohan listened to the old man whilst oiling a bridle. In a matter of months, he had grasped the words that riddled the speech of Angha's people and as a result he had grown interested in what Abdul had to say – a man who acted as trainer and father to the boys in his care.

"Fifty-eight years ago, the Turkic slave Alptigin broke away from his Persian masters to cross the killer peaks of the Hindu Kush and take this city we proudly call Ghazna."

Abdul flicked his wrist, slapping an inattentive recruit across the head with the stiff handle of his whip. His reach was long and his temper sometimes short.

"Some fourteen years later another ex-slave, Sabuktigin, usurped Alptigin's line and took the sultanate through sheer – and yes, bloody – determination. He then dallied a little with the effeminate forces of the Punjabi and Kabuli

Shahis. However, it wasn't until his son Mahmud ascended the throne that the Ghaznavid Empire was truly born. Today this land, that we call home, stretches from Khorasan in the west to Kashmir in the east. And therein lies the lesson; never think of yourselves as slaves, consider yourselves future kings! Although you'd be wise to keep those thoughts to yourselves – incumbent sultans get touchy about such things."

Along the stable wall, the mamluks greeted the brief lecture with appreciative laughter. Their unlined faces were the living story of Mahmud's conquests; Indian, Turkish, Berber, Armenian and Deylamite – all recruited from the fringes of the great empire.

Close to Sohan's feet, a buckle rattled to the floor. He bent to pick it up and returned it to the boy sat next to him. Naturally, Kerim cracked a joke about polishing his boots while he was down there to which Sohan responded by threatening to sever his friend's knackers, revealing that having mastered the Persian language his speech possessed a distinctly earthy flavour.

Abdul Aziz listened to the exchange, feeling somewhat pleased with himself. Not so long ago the boys had despised each other, which wouldn't have been a problem under normal circumstances, but in a mamluk unit teamwork was everything. For that reason, and that reason only, Abdul Aziz had set about punishing the pair with marathon days and arduous endeavours. When this failed to bring a thaw in relations he tied them together, forcing them to execute their chores as one. He later found them on the stable floor, slipping in and out of consciousness having punched each other senseless. In the end Abdul lost patience and called in the assassins. One afternoon, heading into town, he was confronted – on time –

by a black-robed figure of the guild. With enviable dexterity the assassin juggled his knives as Abdul Aziz groped for a weapon he couldn't find. Sohan and Kerim duly leapt to their tutor's defence, combining their skills in the face of a more agile, fleet-footed and capable foe. Feigning defeat, the assassin left as quickly as he had come, but not before leaving a kiss from his knife upon Abdul's right cheek, something which hadn't actually been part of the contract. Still, the plan had worked; the boys had bonded through necessity and fear, and it was the start of a slow-burning friendship that required few words. Abdul was satisfied, and surprisingly, so was his wife. She found the scar roguish, she said, and with a grin that was more of a grimace given the constraints of his stitches, Abdul threatened to show her just how much of a rogue he could be. Unfortunately, at that point the Indian arrived.

Dressed in the uniform of the palace, the man had introduced himself as Bir Paramichi. He said he was looking for Sohan.

"Are you his father?" Abdul inquired, and the man shook his head before fumbling over the word 'guardian'. The trainer narrowed his eyes. He wasn't sure what the story was, but it stank of unnecessary complication. Therefore, over a cup of green tea, he suggested the warrior might want to leave the child in peace.

"It's more difficult to build a future when you're reminded of the past," he explained.

"Well, perhaps you're right," the Indian agreed wearily. He then left without another word, or even finishing his drink.

Outside the garrison, Bir felt no small measure of guilt at abandoning Sohan, but hearing the mamluk trainer speak of the boy's future had convinced him that he was looking for Sohan for all the wrong reasons. He couldn't offer the boy better, and though it gave him no pleasure, he later told Angha that her friend had been transferred to another city within the Ghaznavid Empire. Naturally, Angha took her father at his word, but ultimately it made little difference to her world – she was in love with Sohan, and distance was merely a journey to be made, not the end of it. So, displaying an acceptance that was woefully misinterpreted by her father, Angha simply got on with the business of living.

Somewhat smaller than Kanauj, Ghazna was very much a work in progress. Streets were part-paved and slave labour toiled from dawn to dusk constructing new schools, museums and minarets. It was a city racing to match the scope of its leader's ambition, and pride of place had been given to a magnificent mosque known as the Celestial Bride in honour of the God who guided him. However, it was in the eclectic mix of races that coloured the city's suburbs that Ghazna revealed the full extent of the Empire's success.

Despite their numbers, Bir and his people had quickly settled into the Indian quarter, a cramped but colourful centre that smelt something like home. The suburb teemed with traders, engineers, labourers and warriors – both hired and enslaved – and the residents, though resigned to their futures, worked to protect the past in the cloak of their language, albeit a more standardised version of the dialects they had left behind. With little room to expand, houses were built, one floor upon another, and though Bir had been gifted a small plot of land it had been commandeered by Patag's elephant.

Along with one hundred of his men, Bir worked at the palace where he acted as bodyguard and watchman over Mahmud's twin sons; Muhamad and Masud. Though the siblings were young men, their privileged lives had left them petulant as teenagers and often too drunk to be cognisant. It was clear that any aspirations they may have once harboured had gradually stagnated in the shade of a man who threatened to outlive them all.

"Muhamad is the better of the two," Bir confided in Patag and Danvish. "The boy's quick and warm-hearted whilst his brother is hard as stone. When the time comes, Masud will be the one to watch not to watch over."

Having been witness to palace intrigues in the past, problematic princes were nothing new to Bir or his men. Neither were the daily jostles for favour amongst ministers, imams, generals and women. From the sidelines, Bir watched as Mahmud sought the advice of many whilst heeding the words of a few. Among those he appeared to trust was the Indian general Tilak, a Turkman called Ariyaruq and the slave Ayaz who, as the Sultan's favourite companion, was duly rewarded for his services with the kingdom of Lahore.

"Keep the big man happy and we might yet see Kanauj," Patag quipped.

"I doubt Bir's pretty enough to warrant such rewards," Danvish responded with a snort, and the men around the table laughed – as did Angha, even though the joke went sailing over her head. Having been in the process of filling their tumblers, Lungri flashed the men a warning and the old warriors coughed with embarrassment before returning to more familiar themes of war and politics. Satisfied, Lungri went back to her work – ensuring the men were fed and watered – just as she had always done.

Once the warriors retired for the night Lungri cleaned and prepared for the morning. Before the sun was up, she would rise to fix Bir's breakfast, and once he had left for the palace, she would wake Angha and Patag. For Lungri, life was the same routine only in a different place, and with few surprises. But then, one hot summer morning, she went to wake Angha only to find the child missing half of her hair.

"I was hot," Angha explained, handing Lungri the knife she had taken from her father's arsenal of weapons.

"Your father will go insane," Lungri warned.

"He won't even notice," Angha replied, and Lungri was stung by the child's loneliness.

"Your father loves you very much."

"I know he does, Lungri. But he doesn't care about hair."

"Of course he does." The maid pulled Angha towards her in order to tidy the mess she had created.

"Really, I wouldn't worry about it," Angha responded. "My father wants me to be happy, that's all."

"Well, that's true enough. That's all any of us want."

"And I tell you I will be – just as soon as I marry Sohan."

At the child's words, Lungri stopped cutting. It was the first time Angha had spoken romantically of the boy her father had hoped she had forgotten, and she could only assume the girl was hurtling towards puberty. For a moment, Lungri considered saying something, but it wasn't in her nature to spoil another's dreams. Sad as it was, Angha would learn soon enough. India might be a world away, but her people remained tied to the old traditions; widows set themselves alight; potatoes were forbidden in times of mourning; and the castes remained separate and married to their own kind. Even now, after everything that had happened, their neighbours continued to treat Lungri as a maid, and though it hurt her pride she knew it was only right. 'Lungri the Wife' lived only in the privacy of Lungri's mind. But that was bearable because sometimes dreams were enough.

A year after Kanauj fell, the Ghaznavids returned to India to avenge the murder of King Rajapala at the hands of some neighbouring Rajas who had failed to agree with his cowardly submission the previous winter. Mahmud interpreted the murder as a direct challenge to his authority whereas Bir believed the traitor deserved no less than a violent death under a storm of Rajput arrows.

"The world has gone mad!" he bellowed in anger, to which Patag could only agree.

"Ghaznavids avenging the death of an Indian – whatever next?"

As expected, Mahmud dealt with the troublesome Rajas by killing tens of thousands of their men and stealing 580 elephants. Three years after that reprimand, the Sultan marched again – returning with another 300 elephants. It was as this particular procession thundered into town that Patag happened to be bathing Sabal in the river. Sadly, the spectacle proved too much for the old grey warrior and he sank to his knees. With a last breath, that Patag swore was a sigh, Sabal passed away. Naturally, the old man was distraught, and because two thousand people had spent much of their lives dodging Sabal's drunken feet, they shared Patag's loss.

As grief hovered over the Indian quarter for an elephant that couldn't have cared less, Bir called for a celebration to lift the cloud, and bring his people back to their senses. With space being sparse, the event was staged in the marketplace and everyone brought cushions and carpets to sit upon. Throughout the day, food was shared, wine was fought over, and stories of Sabal's heroism – both true and embellished – were told amid tuneful laments for the homeland. As the feast was devoured, Lungri did her best to clear away the debris and keep the ewers full, but the day was long and she was no longer the girl she used to be. As the hours dragged by, Lungri's foot, with its stubborn determination to slip inwards, sapped at her strength and her face began to show the strain as the evening arrived to bring many more guests demanding solace in wine. As oil lamps were lit, Lungri found herself momentarily distracted by Bir's laughter coming from the other end of the courtyard. Before she realised her mistake, the red wine she was pouring cascaded onto the dress of the woman before her and a hand rose to slap her sharply across the face. Naturally, Lungri apologised and ordinarily that would have been the end of the matter. But Bir had witnessed the exchange.

"Lungri!" he barked, and the crowd immediately stilled. Flushing wildly, Lungri turned, unable to meet Bir's eyes.

"It wasn't her fault," Angha whispered, tugging at her father's sleeve, but he removed her hand with barely a glance.

"Lungri, come here," he ordered, and she shuffled towards him, feeling herself shrink with each dragging step. As she reached Bir, he cast his angry eyes over the remnants of the meal everyone had enjoyed and reached for a clay tumbler. He then grabbed a husk of bread and after sprinkling it with salt he ripped it in two. Lifting Lungri's hand he forced her to take a piece.

"Eat," he commanded and Lungri ate, though her mouth was dry with humiliation. As she swallowed, Bir took a bite from the other half of the bread before washing it down with wine. He then brought the tumbler to Lungri's lips.

"Drink," he urged, and she did so. When a trickle slipped from her slack lips, Bir reached forward and cleaned it away with the flat of his thumb. After draining his own cup, he threw it against the wall where it shattered. Once satisfied he had everyone's attention Bir proclaimed, "Let every man, woman and child among us see that together this woman and I are as bread and salt!"

The crowd sat in bemused silence, glances were exchanged and confusion hung heavy in the air until, to the right of Bir, Danvish began to slowly applaud and, taking his lead, the rest of the people followed. Only once they had quietened did Bir address the woman still standing in front of him.

"I took you as my wife, Lungri, and I'm sorry I haven't honoured you by making this clear. Now I have corrected this error may you be treated accordingly; please, take your seat at the table and let someone else fetch the wine."

Bir looked towards the woman who had slapped 'Lungri the Maid', and understanding she now needed to correct the dishonour to 'Lungri the Wife', she stepped forward and filled a fresh tumbler to pass to the woman she had so recently assaulted. Lungri's eyes welled as she took hold of the cup.

"Thank you," she said quietly, and though the woman accepted Lungri's gratitude everyone knew she spoke to the man at her side.

From her seat at the table, Angha watched the development with a mixture of pride and dismay; not out of any disrespect for Lungri, she loved the woman like the mother she never knew, but Angha was of an age that could only be embarrassed by such displays of geriatric affection. She quietly retreated from the feast before her father could cause her anymore shame. Squeezing passed Patag, who lay face down on a table – felled by drink and sorrow – she wandered off towards the far reaches of the Indian quarter where she climbed the steps of the outer wall to escape the trapped air of the city. The sun had almost disappeared and the view that met her was one of grey dust.

"Sabal was a fine elephant," a voice sympathised behind her and Angha smiled before turning.

"Yes, he was," she replied calmly, pausing to pick at a scab on her knee because it seemed easier than meeting the boy's gaze.

"I've thought of you often."

"Then you should have visited."

"It's been difficult, but I've been watching when I can."

Angha finally looked up, finding Sohan the same and yet different. The boy remained slim, but much taller and cleaner than she remembered. The brown arms under his linen tunic were lean and faintly muscular and a pale scar ran through one eyebrow.

"What happened there?" she asked, pointing towards the wound.

"I cut it. What happened to your hair?"

"I cut it," she echoed with a giggle.

"Well, I'd rather you didn't."

"Okay."

Sohan came to sit by Angha's side. As he did so a Moslem guard patrolling the wall gave the two of them a quizzical look before covering his heart in greeting as he recognised the mamluk insignia on the soft leather tunic the boy wore.

"How is the training going? Is it hard?" Angha asked, and Sohan's mouth dipped. Every day seemed worse than the last, but what could he tell her? That every inch of him ached from firing arrows, hour after hour, for days without end? That there were nights when he rolled into bed nursing legs that felt snapped from his hips? That his hands were calloused and scarred from the constant pull of reins? That three of his fingers had broken during misfires? That his shoulder had been dislocated so often he feared he'd never lift an arm again let alone a weapon? That he was so lonely he could feel it eating his insides?

"Oh, it's not so bad," he replied.

"That's good. I'm pleased for you. So, you like your new life?"

"Sometimes."

"Like when?"

And without intending to Sohan recalled all the things that he did in fact like. He told Angha about Abdul Aziz and how the man had become the father he had always wanted. He spoke with wonder about Turkmen archers who seemed to have eyes at the front and the back of their heads. He also described his friend Kerim and the two-day journey they had recently made to Kabul so that he might learn to sleep in the saddle.

"I fell off twice before getting the hang of it."

"It sounds like a lot of fun," Angha remarked, trying not to show the disappointment she felt at hearing him enjoy life without her. Sohan shrugged.

"I wouldn't call it fun, but it's useful," he admitted. "Riches are waiting, Angha. And when I get them, I shall bring my wealth to your father and he'll see that I'm no longer an outcaste, but a warrior like him – and when that day comes, we shall be married."

Shocked by the sudden affirmation of the dreams she had harboured, Angha felt her ears burn with embarrassment.

"I'll wait for that day," she managed to reply, and because they were still little more than children the two of them shook hands on the deal, blushing furiously as they did so.

With the light gone and everything said that needed to be said, Sohan jumped from the wall. Angha watched him go before doing the same and with happy feet she raced back to Sabal's wake to find many of the revellers were starting to leave. As she half-expected, Patag remained face down on the table and Bir raised his eyebrows in irritation when Angha suggested they might help the old man to bed. Calling Danvish to aid him, Bir hooked himself under Patag's arms only to jump away, as though bitten. His grief was immediate and before he could stop her, Angha approached their old friend. Turning Patag's face towards the light of an oil lamp she noted the smile playing on his lips. It reminded her of the two-headed snake Sohan had once shown her. Surprising herself, she felt no sadness. It was how it should be, she thought, and she suspected that somewhere close by Sabal had been waiting – urging his master to finish his drink so they might make their final journey together.

It took six years for Sohan's mamluk unit to be considered old enough and hardened enough for battle, and during that time they had been pushed, punished, occasionally praised and frequently broken in order to be reset for war. But with the Ghaznavid ranks flush with hired mercenaries there had been few opportunities for his unit to vent their frustrations, either professional or hormonal.

"I tell you, I'm sick of this," Kerim griped as they continued with the endless task of preparing for a fight that never came. "Let's get out of here."

"And go where?"

"Anywhere."

Sohan shrugged. Grabbing a halter, he followed Kerim to the stables and after ensuring that no one of any great importance was watching, the two friends mounted their horses and trotted away, as capable bareback as they were in the saddle.

As it was Friday the city was quiet with most of the residents busy only with the business of prayer. Even so, the two mamluks attracted a number of admiring glances as they ambled through the streets, albeit mostly from servants beating carpets against the walls of their masters' homes. Breaking into a canter as they passed the outer gates, Sohan and Kerim followed the river with no greater plan in mind than that of feeling the wind in their hair until, an hour into their ride, in the shadow of a small hill, they noticed a dozen or more tents surrounded by a hundred or so goats grazing on the grass that clung to the riverbank.

"If God wills it," Kerim remarked with a wink, and before Sohan could ask what he meant the young man trotted towards the settlement.

At the sight of the two mamluks, a handful of men rose to their feet, allowing flashes of metal to be seen in the process. Kerim raised an arm and kicked his horse forward, shouting a greeting Sohan could barely understand. In response, the men released their leather gilets and covered their weapons. Kerim then dismounted. As he hit the ground a man stepped forward, presumably the chief, and for a few minutes Kerim engaged him in lively conversation. After a firm shake of hands Kerim returned to Sohan's side.

"That's sorted then," he said with a winning smile. "As soon as I have the money, I'll have myself a bride."

Sohan raised his eyebrows and glanced back at the tribesmen. They were Ghuzz Turks given leave to graze their herds within Ghaznavid territory. They also happened to be Kerim's people, and as his 'people' had also been responsible for the murder of his father during one of the many squabbles that broke out between the clans, Sohan was somewhat surprised by the sudden turn of events.

"She must be a beauty," Sohan finally responded.

"Who?"

"Your bride."

"The devil if I know. I've not seen her."

"Then why…"

"A man needs a wife, Sohan. I am a man. I want a wife, and the great beauty of our women is that they expect little from their men and complain even less."

Sohan shook his head, and then – possibly because he was also being troubled by raging hormones – he shared his own marriage plans.

"She's called Angha and she's a Hindu, like me. We'll be married as soon as I find a war to line my pockets."

"Then I hope she doesn't mind waiting," Kerim replied, and Sohan was disheartened to see his friend was serious.

In her room Angha stirred from sleep, convinced she had missed something important. She shook her head, groggy from a nap she'd never intended to take, and moaned at the realisation her tutor would be at the house in a matter of hours. She was woefully unprepared. He'd be annoyed. She'd be ashamed, and her father would grumble about the expense.

Although education had never been high on Bir's list of priorities when it came to his daughter, since his confinement in Ghazna – part slave, part freeman – he had become a fervent advocate of keeping the past alive. "Our language is our strength," he insisted, and so an Indian scholar had been employed to school Angha twice a week in all the things that made her a Hindu. With little else to keep her mind occupied, she had proved a willing student with a passion for writing, and in the words of her birth she tried to recover everything their community had lost in stories that she saved on the parchment Lungri bought from the Arabs' bazaar.

"I'd love it if you could read this to me once you're finished," Lungri once stated, running her chapped fingers over words she couldn't hope to make sense of.

"Over my dead body," Angha had replied before laughing loudly at Lungri's appalled face. "I'm writing about us; about our history and our lives. So really, I'll never be finished, not until the day I die. But yes, I can read it to you as I write."

Lungri beamed broadly, but it was a gift that all too quickly turned sour because once Angha fulfilled her promise, Lungri came to understand the true extent of the girl's feelings for a boy they had once known. It was almost too much for Lungri to bear because she knew how Angha's heart would break once her father announced her engagement to Danvish's eldest boy, Haroon.

As with all the warriors' sons, Haroon had been secreted inside the labyrinth of barracks that housed the Ghaznavid mamluks, and for many years it had been a life he had enjoyed until a riding accident crushed his leg and he was told he would never again ride with any great ability. Haroon was subsequently released from service with little ceremony and returned to his family. Since then, Danvish had worked hard to bring his son back to a level of fitness that would allow him to take a position in the less arduous surroundings of the palace. The Indian general Tilak had also flexed his power in support of their cause, and as Haroon settled into his new routine his father and Bir drew up plans to unite their families in marriage.

"She's too young," Lungri told Bir as she tried, once again, to dissuade him from the match.

Sitting in the room that served as kitchen and meeting hall, Bir took a break from sharpening his sword to look at Lungri as she cooked pastries for the arrival of Angha's tutor – illiterate or not, Lungri knew full well that hospitality was the key to civilisation.

"Too young?" asked Bir with a laugh. "Whatever do you mean, woman? Angha's thirteen years old!"

Unable to argue the point without revealing more, Lungri sighed. Her heart bled for the girl and she knew that at some point in the near future she'd have to explain some of life's realities to the child. Until then, she could only pray that fate would step in and save them from heartache. Little did she know, however, that with the walls being so thin fate had arrived early.

Above their heads, Angha slumped to the floor, appalled by what she had heard. Her fingers trembled as she gagged into her hands. The blood pounded in her skull. She was sure she would die. By the time her tutor arrived, it was clear Angha was in no condition for a lesson, and Lungri sent the man away with an apology. Unnerved by the girl's sudden sickness, Lungri offered to stay with her, but Angha insisted she needed peace. She then stayed in her room, refusing all food, and finding no sleep as she waited for the sun to come up. At that point she was gone.

It took all of the day and three calls to prayer before Angha found Sohan's barracks. By the time she knocked at the wooden door with its iron loop knocker it was dusk, she was tired, her throat hurt and she was distraught. Although her father had led her to believe that Sohan had been posted to another city, and she had forgotten to ask which one in the excitement of their last meeting, she knew Sohan had spent time in Ghazna and that someone, somewhere, in at least one of the many barracks must know where he is.

When Angha finally turned up on Abdul Aziz's doorstep, he listened to her desperate implorations feeling touched but resolute. The old man wasn't made of stone, and neither was he a stranger to love, but ultimately his responsibility lay with the boys in his care, and that morning he had received orders to send them into battle. The call had been a long time in coming and, given the circumstances, he had no option but to say what he did; complications of the heart were dangerous during times of war. So, for that reason and nothing more personal, he told the girl that Sohan was no longer in his company.

"He was here, but he left for the north six months ago, taking a bride with him," Abdul Aziz lied.

At the revelation, Angha's eyes welled and the old man felt his determination falter as tears as large as raindrops caught on her eyelashes. Thankfully before he could react, the girl walked away.

"She'll get over it," his wife later insisted, but Abdul wasn't so sure, and when he retired to bed that night, he couldn't shake the feeling that he had slaughtered a lonely foal.

Because he was a man – and blessed with a short attention span – Abdul's regret was short-lived and he awoke the next day with the excitement of his coming announcement electrifying the roots of what was left of his hair. It was the news his mamluks had been waiting for; they would be serving Mahmud on his next expedition to India.

Barely had the details passed Abdul's lips when his voice became lost in the roar of fame-hungry boys eager to prove themselves as men. In an attempt to regain control, he took out his whip and cracked a few heads, but he might as well have been beating the threads of a carpet. Abdul Aziz left the room to sip tea with his wife, and allow the boys to settle at their own pace.

Two days later, Sohan marched out of the city as part of the great Ghaznavid war machine, expecting to return with honour and the means to acquire a bride. Little did he suspect that even before he reached the vast expanse of the Thar Desert his dream would be turning to ashes; Angha was informed she would be getting engaged and she accepted the arrangement without a word of protest. Only Lungri seemed concerned by the girl's meek compliance.

"I'm of the right age, it's a good match" Angha told her stepmother. However, in the sanctuary of her room, she put away her writing books and cried like she had never cried before.

After clearing the misery of the desert, the Ghaznavids marched south, finding little resistance as they headed towards their goal. Though men were lost on the way their deaths made little impact on the huge army and most sensible Rajas finding themselves in the path of the beast fled it rather than face it. Once Mahmud penetrated the damp heat of India's Gujarat kingdom, he commanded 30,000 men, all of whom were thirsty for reward. Kerim and Sohan remained with them, although the Turkic mamluk was somewhat lighter than he had been the year before.

"You were born in hell," Kerim grumbled as he struggled with the headache of lung-clogging humidity.

"I was born in paradise," Sohan corrected. "It's people who make the world hell."

Though Sohan meant it as a joke, it was a truth that reminded him of every blow he had ever received from his father's fists and of every indignity he had suffered at the hands of those who had thought they were better than him, and by the time he arrived at the gates of Somnath, Sohan knew without a shadow of doubt, that he was no longer an Indian, but a Ghaznavid.

As Sohan stood before the temple city, Angha found herself draped in silk and gold. Her hair shone in the sunlight, her lips were rouged and Lungri thought the girl looked almost perfect – save for the kohl-black tears streaking her cheeks.

"Come on you'll be late for your own party," Lungri urged, dabbing at her own eyes as she dragged the girl to the courtyard.

Sohan squinted into the sun, surveying the challenge that was Somnath. Legend said the city was built by the Moon God, and it went someway to explain the residents' almost mystical belief in their powers of defence. Instead of fleeing, they congregated along the wall to hurl insults at the Ghaznavids below them. From the back of a grey stallion, Mahmud took their jeers in silence, partly because he had no idea what they were saying and partly because he regarded them as little more than perfumed deviants. Once he grew bored of the game, he moved aside to let his archers do the talking. Within a minute, a thousand black arrows cut through the sky, and a hundred surprised Brahmans fell to their deaths. Realising survival might require something more than blind faith, the rest of the priests quickly retreated, and Mahmud indicated that his engineers should get busy. Locking and loading the catapults they carried, his men blasted great rocks into walls that were never designed to withstand the realities of modern warfare. Stone and timber fractured under the onslaught while Mahmud's archers dealt with the occasional flurry of defence. By the second day, whole sections of the wall lay in rubble and the Ghaznavid army stormed the city to lay waste to anything possessing a heartbeat.

Angha tried to admire the ring on her finger; an intricate gold band sparkling with emeralds, but though it was beautiful it meant nothing to her. Neither did the gifts that lined her father's home. In India such generosity would have been saved for the wedding, but times had changed and Bir's bread and salt ceremony had become the fashion. As a result, engagements had taken up the strain of occasion and, at one point, Angha thought she might faint under the suffocating attention of their guests. But then, as she wavered on the brink of collapse, an arm arrived at her back and she looked to her side to see Haroon smiling. His face was gentle, in many respects handsome, and she understood from his eyes that he too was only following the wishes of others. The support was unexpected and its appearance made her feel marginally better. Not that it stopped her wishing for death.

Sohan followed Mahmud into the gloom of the temple, having to blink twice to adjust his eyes to the sudden loss of light. He then had to blink again, in order to comprehend all that he saw. Attached to fifty polished pillars, oil lamps flickered and burned, bringing light to play on giant bells that hung from golden chains as thick as a man's wrist. Clinging to the edges of the great hall, cowering in the shadows, were hundreds of old men and semi-naked women. The incense clogging the air added to the sense of depravity, and in the centre of it all stood a huge phallus-shaped monument glittering with emeralds and rubies, plated with silver and gold. Stunned beyond words, Mahmud faltered before the idol, hardly knowing where to start. Closing his eyes, he raised his head and Sohan saw a prayer pass over his lips. The Moslem then unleashed his fury. Taking the mallet from his belt, he smashed it into the side of the Hindu lingam, again and again. Without pausing for breath, he pounded the monument like a man possessed until it began to crack and spew its treasure onto the floor. As the idol fell, Mahmud dropped his weapon as if scalded.

"Waste them all," he snarled, and the Ghaznavids obliged – embarking on a massacre so great it required a further three days to strip the bodies of their riches.

Angha allowed Lungri to bathe her. The woman was so gentle it made her want to scream. But she didn't. She remained quiet. As she listened to how lucky she was and what a good husband Haroon would make, Angha felt like telling Lungri she could add blindness to her list of disabilities. But she didn't. She merely nodded. Angha then looked at her body, wet and gleaming in the lamplight, finding it young and still forming its shape. Even so, deep down, past the skin – amongst the blood and the bone – she had never felt so old.

Loaded with immeasurable wealth, Mahmud's army retraced its steps across the Thar Desert. The going was brutal, with soldiers dogged by sickness, exhaustion and the unwanted attentions of Jat tribes who buzzed and harried them under an unforgiving sun. Though Sohan's mamluks tried to deal with the nuisance they might as well have been chasing down flies and they felt nothing but relief once they cleared the desert and the Jats simply disappeared. In contrast, Mahmud remained irritated beyond reason.

Angha paused to look one last time at the house she was leaving. It had been a home of sorts, but now she would live with her husband's parents. There were worse fates, she guessed. Not that she could think of any. And blissfully unaware of his daughter's unhappiness, Bir emitted a sigh of satisfaction as the door closed behind her. Perhaps if he had thought less like a soldier and more like a father, he might have recognised Angha's anxiety for the sadness it clearly was. Instead, he honestly believed he had served the girl well; Haroon was a fine boy and he came from good stock. As Bir also happened to be more of a soldier than a husband, he was equally as blind to the dread that crept over Lungri. Their house, small as it was, felt empty without Angha, and in the unaccustomed quiet Lungri was more aware than ever of the sound of her leg dragging along the floor.

Almost two years after they left, Mahmud and his men finally returned to Ghazna where they were showered with flowers as a train of camels revealed the extent of their victory. Even the Caliph of Baghdad was impressed, and he duly bestowed the title of 'Guardian of the State and Islam' upon Mahmud as a reward for laying waste to the fabled centre of Hinduism. In turn, Sohan and his mamluks were paid handsomely for their endeavours and after handing a percentage of his gold to Abdul Aziz, Sohan headed for the home of Bir Paramichi – to ask for his daughter's hand in marriage.

Dressed in his best tunic, with his armour polished to perfection, Sohan rode with hard-earned confidence into the Indian quarter, graciously accepting the courtesies of men who might once have ignored him. He couldn't deny it; their respect gave him great pleasure. In Ghazna the world had spun on its head with outcastes finding social status and the upper classes demoted to servants of shopkeepers. He felt as much pity for them now as they had once shown for him. Furthermore, he couldn't remember a more perfect day; the sun was bright, a gentle wind played in his hair and inside his purse he heard the rest of his life jangling its music.

Resisting the urge to gallop, Sohan fought to steady his nerves as he sighted the walls of Angha's home. The place looked smaller than he remembered, but he was older now and the last few years had shown him bigger things. Dismounting, he threw a coin at a waiting child who happily took the reins of his horse. Slicking back his hair, he knocked and breathed deeply. Impatient as he was, when he received no reply, he stopped short of hammering again. Eventually, the uneven footfalls that could only belong to Lungri approached and he smiled at the thought of her, and of imagining her surprise at seeing the man he had become.

Lungri opened the gate and though many years had passed she immediately recognised the young soldier before her. Sohan had grown handsome and strong, and his uniform spoke of success. She was pleased for him, really, she was, and that only made what she had to say all the more difficult when he expressed a desire to talk to Bir and then to Angha.

"Bir is at the palace and Angha is married."

Sohan was stunned. "I don't believe you. You're lying..." he managed to mutter before shaking his head to regain his composure. "I must speak to her, Lungri. We had... we had an agreement."

"I'm sorry, Sohan." And Lungri meant the apology more than he could know. "Angha is married. She has a good husband and, more than that, she is with child."

The revelation hit Sohan with such force he slammed a fist into the wall, drawing blood. Around him, the breeze seemed to die, the world stopped moving, and if his chest hadn't been protected by the armour he wore, he might have felt his heart breaking. Struggling for breath, he reached for his purse and dropped it at Lungri's feet.

"These coins were for Angha," he said, "but you might as well have them. They're as useless to me now as the trinkets you wear to hide your ugliness."

Without a word more, Sohan returned to his horse, digging nails into the palm of his hand as he took hold of the reins. In the space of seconds, he had proved he was less of a man than he had imagined he was, and he knew that the image of Lungri's shocked face would haunt him for the rest of his days. In turn, Lungri had suffered worse insults in her life and she simply returned to the house wondering what the Ghaznavids had done to the boy.

"Who was it?" Angha asked as Lungri set a pan of water on the stove.

"Just someone looking for your father," she half-lied.

Ten months after Angha was married, she gave birth to her first child, a daughter named Rashmi. Angha was 15 years old.

As tradition demanded, Angha had returned to her father's home the moment she started to show. In turn, Haroon kept his distance until three days after the birth, giving the female spirits plenty of time to determine the child's destiny.

"She's a beauty, just like her mother," Haroon declared when he held his daughter for the first time, and Angha smiled because she saw he was a good man who promised to be a good father. Though she felt no love for Haroon, he had given her life purpose, and finding something close to happiness, she began writing again.

From the day of her birth, Rashmi was as sweet as the morning she entered the world. Her smile was quick and easy to come by, and everyone adored her. Yet it was Lungri she shone brightest for, and the woman could barely disguise her gratitude. As Bir watched his wife play with their grandchild, he found himself regretting that he couldn't give Lungri the one thing she so desperately desired. But even if her womb remained capable it wasn't in his power to bestow such a gift, and he was truly sorry for that.

Getting to his feet Bir released a moan of protest as age scraped along his joints. When Lungri rushed forward to fuss he waved her away, irritated that she had noticed a weakness he wasn't yet ready to accept. His mood wasn't lifted any when an hour later he arrived at the palace to find Mahmud preparing for yet another invasion of India – taking with him a platoon of soldiers who were the elite that Bir had once been.

Mahmud had always been a man of febrile temper, and the recent accolades heaped upon him by the Caliph of Baghdad had merely increased his sense of outrage. His desire for revenge against the Jat tribes who had plagued him that spring had become wholly disproportionate to the effect of their attacks, but as Bir listened to the Sultan's justifications for war, he had to assume it was this kind of unreasoned thinking that made kings out of men. It would later prove to be a move that would cost Mahmud dearly.

As the summer cooled into winter, the Sultan left Ghazna accompanied by a small, highly mobile war party whose mission was not to plunder, but to kill – which they did, almost to a man. But though Mahmud returned victorious, he also returned sick. With dim lighting and careful planning, the Sultan continued to hold court twice a day – dealing as fairly as self-interest would allow – but his stamina often failed him and the sessions were kept short. It was increasingly clear among those in the palace that Mahmud was dying. And he knew it.

One autumn afternoon, as Bir watched the Sultan's sons practise their sword skills, Mahmud approached. His smile was weary and though the two men were not friends, the Sultan spoke as though they were.

"How is your son?" he asked.

For a moment Bir assumed the Ghaznavid chief was suffering an episode, but then he recalled the first time they met – and how a young boy had risked his life to save him. Ten years on, it seemed pointless to continue the charade.

"He was never my son," Bir admitted. "The child was a friend of my daughter's. I have a daughter."

Mahmud's eyes widened – the whites an alarming shade of yellow – but then he shrugged.

"No sons at all?"

"No sons," Bir confirmed, and Mahmud nodded thoughtfully. Beads of sweat had formed on his strong nose and he was unusually pale with cheeks sinking into sallow pits beneath his jaundiced eyes. Ahead of them, Muhamad screamed in fury as Masud's blade connected with his thigh.

Muhamad dropped his weapon and charged at his brother, bowling him to the floor. Bir quickly gestured to the guards and one of them stepped in to separate the brawling twins. Mahmud sighed.

"Perhaps it's just as well," he mumbled. "What will become of them, do you think?"

Mahmud jerked his head towards his sons, both frothing at the mouth and shouting profanities despite the presence of their father. Bir gave no answer, knowing it wasn't his place to pass comment on princes.

"Masud is proud," Mahmud admitted, seemingly oblivious to the indiscretion. "He thinks there's no one better than himself. Whereas Muhamad he is different – stout of heart, generous and fearless. But if Masud indulges in pleasures such as wine and the like, Muhamad easily outdoes him. He has no control over himself and, in the end, Masud will devour him. It amazes me that Muhamad cannot see it."

The Sultan wiped at his eyes whilst Bir focussed on the princes. His armpits itched with discomfort. It was rarely a blessing to have a ruler's confidence.

"You know," Mahmud continued, "I love both my boys, as only a father can, but Masud is greedy. I fear he may destroy everything in order to possess it."

The Sultan pulled at the blanket hanging about his shoulders. "Thanks for listening," he said. He then allowed a small smile to escape from his parched lips, a reminder of the man Bir had once met in a tent during the long walk from Kanauj. As Mahmud shuffled back to his palace, Bir was faintly comforted by the thought that he wasn't alone in suffering the effects of age.

Time was coming to take them all. The new generation was almost upon them.

Faced with a Friday holiday and little to do, Sohan agreed to accompany Kerim as he went in search of the bride he now had the money to pay for. Possessing no knowledge of the realities of marriage his friend was childishly upbeat.

"And what will you do when I get my woman?" Kerim teased.

"Come and live with you, of course."

Sohan kicked his horse into a gallop and though Kerim caught him quickly, he couldn't steal the lead. As the pair raced to the summit of a hill, Sohan turned in his saddle to point over his friend's shoulder. "Turkmen!" he shouted and Kerim span his horse with the skill of his training only to be met by a featureless wasteland. Spitting his annoyance into the earth, he turned again to see Sohan fifty metres ahead of him, at the top of the hill. Sohan reined in his horse, with a triumphant smile.

"Very sly," Kerim applauded after catching him up.

"I can't believe you fell for it," Sohan admitted.

"Well, I've had a lot on my mind."

"Such as the bride we can't find?"

"Partly."

Kerim breathed heavily, as if expelling a great weight from his chest, and Sohan assured his friend he could be trusted.

Kerim nodded. "I'd trust you with my life, Sohan, and whatever happens, I'll always have your back, no matter what."

Sohan frowned at the unfamiliar sentimentality, and Kerim wiped a hand over his face, before shrugging his shoulders. "Don't worry," he sighed. "There's no drama. I'm simply growing tired of this hell, that's all. Every day it's the same: we sleep; we wake; train; fight; eat. If I'm honest, I can't see myself ending my days serving the great Ghaznavid Empire."

"But what else is there to do? Where would you go?"

"Who knows, back to my people, perhaps?"

"I thought 'your people' were wandering nomads."

"Indeed, they are," admitted Kerim, breaking into a broad grin, "which means they're not that easy to find!"

With a swift kick to his horse, Kerim charged ahead. After regaining his wits Sohan chased after him. It was a race with no clear winner and after twenty minutes the two friends paused for breath after spotting a huddle of tents belonging to a crazy Yemeni they both knew. They had met Tariq a handful of times during their rides into the country to blow off steam, and the two mamluks were sure there would be a bowl of hot stew waiting for them if they happened to pass by. So, with a look of inquiry and a nod of agreement, Sohan and Kerim urged their horses forward so they might fill their stomachs.

One of the great Arabic nomads, Tariq made his living selling sheep and antiquities. He also collected wives like other men collected swords.

"I'm my own worst enemy," he admitted as the two mamluks settled themselves in his tent. One of his wives tended the fire and she nodded her head in agreement. Though females were usually forbidden to sit with male visitors, Tariq's first wife was considered too old to garner any interest. His other wives were presumably younger. They were also former slaves, and Tariq admitted that being weak of will and strong in libido he had fathered their children, giving them automatic wife status. As long as his first wife clung on to life the mullah said he could take no more.

"The day I die I'm taking you with me!" his first wife hissed, and though she laughed heartily there wasn't a soul in the tent who believed she was joking.

Moving towards the fire, Tariq winked at his wife, revealing a bond that clearly transcended good looks. "Do you know, I've travelled the length and breadth of the Islamic world," he said. "I've walked through Baghdad's marble corridors where the women are so virtuous they show only one eye, and I've traipsed through the Steppes where girls wrestle oxen to the ground, but I'm telling you now, that the women of the true Arabic nomads outclass them all."

Despite evidence to the contrary, Kerim winked good-naturedly at the wizened face of Tariq's first wife.

"Oh, she may look sweet," the Yemeni warned him, "but she's fiercer than a tiger. During the time of the Prophet, Peace Be upon Him, her ancestors cut the noses from their enemies and wore them on chains around their ankles.

"Well, I like a woman with spirit," Kerim joked.

"Especially if they also attract flies," added Sohan, and Kerim begged Tariq to excuse his friend as he was a heathen from India.

"Actually, the Indians have a civilisation as old as our own," Tariq replied, waving away the apology. "And I have to say, I've never seen a better class of sword than the ones forged by their smiths."

From under the fringe of his hair, that had grown long in the absence of care, Sohan threw Kerim a look. It more or less said 'I told you so'.

Back in the city, Bir finished polishing his armour. It wasn't brilliant, but it would do, and he felt a pang of loss for the heavy breastplate of his Rajput years and the great sword he had once wielded that had been as much a part of him as his right arm. Today, the only reminder of his once-glorious past was the etching of the sun he had commissioned on the hilt of his current blade. Beckoning Rashmi towards him, he measured the child's height. She didn't protest because she was too busy tugging at the red string her mother had tied about her wrist.

"Stop that, it's to keep you safe," Bir ordered the girl, scarcely believing he had spoken the words as they jumped from his mouth. He sighed to himself. Away from the Ganges and its powers of purification, the Indian quarter had become bedevilled with fanciful superstition. He lifted Rashmi's chin to make her stand upright.

"Big?" she asked.

"Huge," he agreed, although his granddaughter barely reached halfway to the pommel.

"Star," she said, pointing to the emblem engraved on the cross guard.

"Sun," he corrected, before noticing the child's use of Persian. He pinched at his nose, feeling yet another loss of the people they once were. In time it could only get worse. Though the Indian quarter had retained its distinctive flavour, minor changes were occurring everyday be it a different cut of cloth, the end of a custom, or the casual slip from Hindi to Persian.

"Come here, you!" Angha ordered, picking up her daughter before bending to kiss the grey crown of her father's still lustrous hair. She noticed his eyes were creased with fatigue. "You should rest more," she advised, and he smiled because it was a nice idea.

"Someone needs to feed Lungri. That woman eats like a horse," he grumbled.

"Father!"

"I'm only joking, although she does have an interesting appetite for someone so scrawny."

"And you? You've lost weight."

"Yes, I believe I have," Bir admitted. He fell quiet for a moment. Then he stood up to face his daughter. "Angha, I hope I've not disappointed you in life."

"What a thing to say! Why would you even think it?"

"Well, maybe because sometimes I catch your face and what I see in it worries me."

Angha bent her head. "Father, I'm fine. I have a good husband, a beautiful daughter, I am safe and I am cared for. You have done your job well."

"I hope so," Bir replied smiling, though it quickly lost heart on the way to his eyes. No matter what his daughter said he could tell she was unhappy, and he worried occasionally that he might have infected his child with his own form of grief. All of his life he had tried to shield his daughter from the pain he had known, but there wasn't a day that passed in which he didn't think of her mother. He had loved that woman in a way that defied reason, even now, more than seventeen years after her death, because once a seed has grown it cannot be undone.

In the spring of 1029, Abdul Aziz bid farewell to his young charges. They had all become men and it was time to let go. More than that, the Sultan had asked for their company. Having grown tired of the Turkmen abusing his generosity, Mahmud had decided to act. For years he had allowed the Ghuzz Turks to graze on his land and yet they rarely paid taxes whilst their cousins across the Oxus seemed hell-bent on harrying his subjects who felt rightly aggrieved. Worse than that, there were reports of the clans uniting. Mahmud knew he had to show his face and bolster his garrisons on the western frontier. So, after seeking his generals' advice, it was agreed that the Hindu ghulams would supply the manpower – having no allegiance to the area or its religion – with a smaller contingent of Moslems in overall command of the area they called Khorasan. Several mamluk units would also be shared between the cities of Balkh, Merv, Nishapur and Herat.
"Where are you going?"
Sohan was saddling his horse and Kerim was wondering why he hadn't been invited.
"I need to see someone."
"Who?"
"Someone."
"It's that girl, isn't it? The one you wanted to marry."

When Sohan made no reply, Kerim readied his horse.

"Mind if I tag along?"

"It's kind of personal."

"Excellent."

Before Sohan could protest, Kerim mounted his ride. He then asked the one question, Sohan was hoping he wouldn't.

"So, what are you going to say to her?"

In all honesty, Sohan had no idea. Therefore, he gave no answer. A part of him fantasised Angha might have been widowed; the rest of him only hoped he wouldn't be unkind, as he had once been to Lungri.

With shame gnawing at his bones, he pushed his horse on.

The city was lively that morning and it took them nearly thirty minutes to reach the Indian quarter. As they skirted the spice bazaar, Kerim grimaced and placed a scarf over his nose. In response Sohan laughed and dismounted. After bartering good-naturedly with one of the vendors he bought several wraps of the spices his friend found so nauseous.

"Everyone needs a little taste of home," the seller remarked, waving a leathery hand at the crowds, many of whom would also be moving west to join the Hindu ghulams charged with taming the Turkmen tribes.

Sohan surveyed the marketplace, imagining it empty of the families he saw there. For a heartbeat he felt something close to affection for his own people until his eyes were taken by a rare beauty emerging from one of the dark alleys that led to the square, and Sohan shrank back into the boy he had once been. Angha was stunning; her hair was blacker than a moonless night and her brown eyes shone with flecks of gold. In every way she was the woman he had imagined she would one day become, and heartbreakingly more – because she was also clearly pregnant.

By her side walked a man dressed in the uniform of the palace. Sohan noted not only the faint limp, but also the child he carried. As the two of them weaved through the mayhem, the man turned to speak and Angha smiled in reply before placing a hand upon her stomach. Unable to bear the sight a second longer, Sohan swung himself into the saddle and headed back the way he had come. Behind him, Kerim dropped his chin to his chest. With one last look at the woman who had caught Sohan's eye, he turned to follow. He made no jokes as they rode away, he passed no comment – he simply accompanied his friend back to the barracks.

The following morning, as Sohan's unit rode out of town, Angha woke up crying. There was no reason for her tears and she sensibly laid them at the door of her growing stomach. Even so, she struggled with a strange grief for the rest of the day. Even Rashmi with her impish games could do little to raise her mother's spirits. Then, when Angha discovered her daughter's red bracelet had gone, it increased her sense of foreboding. She desperately wished Lungri were with her, but only the first pregnancy required a move to the family home. And unable to stop them, or understand why, the tears continued to fall.

Once known as the Land Where the Sun Rises, Khorasan was quite clearly the place where the sun set following its integration into the Ghaznavid Empire – proving that perspective is everything in life. However, perspective was something Sohan was sorely lacking when he arrived in Khorasan and a cruelty seeped into his actions that went well beyond the call of duty. On the open plains, with the roar of survival drumming in his ears, the mamluk quickly carved out a fearsome reputation in the arms, legs, and heads of men he carried no feeling for.

"You need a woman," Kerim declared after another bloody skirmish. But Sohan knew he needed only time and he bided it by giving chase; rising from the saddle as his horse galloped at full stretch to fire arrows at the bare necks of another man's enemy. Given his devotion to the job, it came as little surprise to the rest of the mamluks when he was summoned by Mahmud.

"You fight with great passion," the Sultan commented when Sohan was brought to his chambers. Inside the room, the air was thick with incense, though it did little to disguise the stench of sickness, and even in the candlelight Sohan could see their leader was desperately unwell.

Sitting in a high-backed chair, Mahmud drummed his fingers as he waited for the young mamluk to respond. Eventually he had to ask, "Do any of you Indians ever speak?"

"What do you want me to say?" Sohan inquired, genuinely perplexed.

Mahmud laughed in response, something he hadn't done for some time, and the effort of it jarred his lungs until it developed into a wet, catarrhal cough. A servant handed the Sultan a goblet of wine which he greedily drained. After wiping his beard with the back of a thumb he felt well enough to continue.

"I noticed you, boy, because you seem strangely keen on your work," he stated. "Then I noticed you again because I thought I recognised your face –

from an evening in Kanauj when you could barely lift the sword you then held."

Sohan was surprised, and though he wasn't going to mention it he thought he might as well.

"I'm surprised you remember."

"I remember a lot of things," Mahmud replied drily, "more and more these days, and not all of them pleasant. I guess that's partly why I asked you here. Tell me, boy – and be honest because I need to know the truth – have I visited a great wrong on you?"

Sohan paused, first with shock and then to properly consider the matter. No matter which way he turned, all thoughts ended at Angha.

"You have made my life complicated," was the best answer he could give, and Mahmud raised his eyebrows.

"Considering what you might have said I'll take that as a positive," he replied. "You have performed well for me ..."

"Sohan."

"Sohan. When we reach Merv you'll be promoted to commander. You'll lead a Hindu battalion stationed at Karakhs. I 'm sure you'll find the weather agreeable there."

Sohan stammered his thanks. Mahmud nodded and then coughed into his sleeve, no longer looking as he waved the mamluk away.

Bir made a final circuit of the palace, checking the preparations for the Sultan's return. A fierce wind whistled through the walkways, and he wrapped his furs tighter. The winter promised to be tough and he could feel his bones crumbling under the threat of it. Not that he was the only one suffering. Catching everyone by surprise, Mahmud had sent word that Ghazna should expect him earlier than planned. Most took it as a sign that the campaign had gone well – although Bir had his doubts – and not everyone in the palace welcomed the news. In a small den at the back of the public hall, Bir found Muhamad. The young prince was sat before a dwindling fire, already half drunk. His brother Masud had been dispatched to Hamadan, in the far west of the Empire, and for a time Muhamad had seemed all the better for the distance, demonstrating a greater appreciation of his responsibilities. Now, well, it was as though nothing had changed.

"Pir!" Muhamad roared, spilling his wine with the generosity of his welcome.

"Your Highness," Bir replied, ignoring the Persian word for 'old'.

"Has my father arrived?"

"Not yet, but within days."

"Excellent. So, I've plenty of time to finish my preparations." Muhamad laughed, but there was no joy in the sound and he waved his goblet in explanation. Bir saluted and left the young man to find his courage in whatever way suited him best.

Three days later, Mahmud entered Ghazna with little fanfare – and Bir was shocked by the changes he saw. The fat had fallen from every inch of the man, leaving skin clinging to bone. What was left of his teeth appeared too large for his mouth and his hair had thinned. Mahmud looking shocking and, unable to resist the orders of his doctors, he immediately took to his bed.

Six days later, as Bir prowled the palace, he was puzzled to see servants carrying pails of jewels from the vaults. Tilak emerged from the royal chambers. The general's face was drained of its usual colour and he greeted Bir wearily. Though it wasn't his place, Bir found himself asking about the activity of the servants.

"Mahmud sent for his wealth – every last ruby, emerald and sapphire. It's now piled on the floor of his room and he's crying over it. I ask you, has a man's greed ever been so great that his dying thoughts are consumed with all he must leave behind?"

"It might be remorse," Bir ventured, thinking of the tens of thousands who had died on the man's sword for a room full of baubles.

"Perhaps," said Tilak, "but I doubt it."

Bir saluted as the Indian general continued walking. A few hours later, the mosques informed the city that their Sultan had passed away.

Mahmud's death brought typically mixed reactions; a general sense of grief within the city, a state of alert amongst the generals, trepidation within ministerial chambers, and a quiet jubilation inside the hearts of Indians who had watched the Ghaznavid chief desecrate their temples, kill their kinfolk and steal their freedom.

According to Mahmud's last wishes, his kingdom was to be divided between his two sons; bestowing Ghazna, Khorasan and India on Muhamad and Raiy, Djibal and Isfahan on Masud. Of course, the last wishes of a dying man are only ever respected for as long as he breathes, and with Mahmud's body still warm, his brother-in-law declared Muhamad the new Amir of the empire. Arriving home, Bir hadn't even untied the leather bonds of his armour when he heard the news, and he immediately reached for his sword.

"What are you doing?" asked Lungri as he waved away the dinner she had prepared.

"Expecting trouble," he mumbled before heading out of the door.

Lungri gazed at the food left untouched on the table. Knowing she would be unable to bear the quiet for much longer she then grabbed a woollen scarf and went to visit Angha and her new baby, a little girl she had named Chandra. It was a name Lungri had once known herself; a long time ago, before people saw only her disability and decided 'The Lame' suited her better.

In the short time it took Bir to arrive at the palace, preparations to mark Muhamad's succession were already underway. Servants crawled over the banquet halls, cleaning and polishing, and cronies lined the corridors hoping for an audience with the Empire's new power. Outside in the butchers' yards, sheep were being slaughtered by the hundred and, on the lawns, musicians tuned their instruments. The air was thick with whispers.

"You aren't on duty tonight," Tilak observed as Bir took his spot at the palace door.

"I thought I might be needed."

Tilak paused to consider the older man. He seemed about to speak, but then thought better of it. In turn, Bir was puzzled, but nothing more – not until the next morning when he heard the Indian general had ridden out of Ghazna to meet with Masud.

The days that followed Mahmud's passing were largely filled with prayers until enough time had passed to celebrate the new era. Alms were given and Muhamad marked his ascendency with typical generosity, sealing the goodwill of his subjects in pouches of coins. On the surface, everything appeared calm, but Bir was anxious and his concern was mirrored in the set jaw of one of his oldest friends. Sitting in the sunshine, Danvish casually remarked that they must look like a couple of old war horses put out to pasture. When Haroon emerged from the house, gleaming with youth and a freshly polished breast plate, the two friends exchanged a glance before chuckling as they recognised each other's envy. Angha followed her husband, trailed by their two girls who wanted to wave their father off to work. She took a seat in the small courtyard.

"It's all been too smooth," Bir commented as they returned to the subject of Muhamad's succession.

"Have you heard anything?" Danvish asked.

"Nothing I could pass on with certainty."

"Masud has been quiet."

"Yes, too quiet."

Listening to their concerns, Angha shivered. In the past year, the Indian quarter had shrunk in size with the bulk of their warriors relocated to Khorasan, taking with them their families and followers. It had left the remaining Hindus feeling exposed. Now there were two brothers coveting the same throne and, Moslem or not, the city's residents would need to back the right horse. And seven weeks later, Ghazna made her choice.

Under the cover of night, a huge number of soldiers deserted the palace with more than half of the royal guard disappearing, only to reappear under the banner of Masud. When Muhamad discovered their treachery, he was bewildered and then furious. Bir understood his anger. To the young man's credit, he had worked hard to fill his father's shoes: he had taken daily counsel; given regular audience to his subjects; and been a constant presence among those tasked with protecting him. Yet it hadn't been enough to convince and, in the end, it was mainly the Indians who stayed to be counted. Given their diminished numbers, Bir and Danvish found themselves among the commanders summoned to Muhamad's war chamber to hammer out a response to the betrayal. When volunteers were asked for, both men stepped forward.

"Bir I'd have you stay with me," the young Sultan said. "Danvish, I thank you for your trust and commitment. Please, find these traitors, slay them and hurry back. Your bravery and that of your men will be rewarded, I guarantee it."

The two old warriors stepped away and bowed before turning to leave the room.

"One minute, Bir."

Danvish paused next to his friend. "May we meet again," he said.

"In this life or the next," Bir replied, and Danvish continued.

"Please, close the door," Muhamad instructed.

Bir did as he was bid and then waited. The young man standing before him was a world away from the one he had known. Worry had gouged deep grooves into his forehead and his eyes were already glazed with the wistful acceptance of defeat.

"I'm leaving tonight, when it's dark," Muhamad revealed. "I'll head for Herat where I can still count on good men. Masud will come for Ghazna. I'm certain of it."

"I'll prepare right away," Bir replied, but a raised hand stopped him from leaving.

"I want you here, Bir. You were loyal to my father and you have been loyal to me, as far as I can tell, but as you have seen, I'm no judge of character. Keep the palace safe, we are not in a state of anarchy, merely upheaval. If Allah wills it, I'll see you again when this is all over. Who knows, I may even allow you to retire."

Muhamad tried to laugh, but the sound was quickly strangled and Bir saw how close he was to tears. The young Sultan had taken the best of his father. He had the look of Mahmud and the dry humour was familiar, but it was Masud who had inherited the ruthless determination. Bir feared for Muhamad.

"You will need protection on the road to Herat."

"I will take my bodyguards as well as the ministers and generals I can rely on. You know, I'm sad Tilak never returned. I always admired him."

Unable to do more, Bir assured Muhamad that the palace would remain ready for whoever came to claim it. As he left the room, he thought of offering a few words of kindness to the young man, if not the Sultan, but it wasn't his place and besides, this was the nature of politics; only the strong survived. It was nothing personal, only business. And within a week of Muhamad's departure, the business was resolved.

After arriving in Herat, the ministers Muhamad believed he could rely on, proved him wrong. They imprisoned him in a tower and sent word to Masud. When his brother arrived, he thanked the men for their help – and immediately executed them. He then met with Muhamad and though he didn't kill him, he gouged out his eyes and relocated him to Balkh, where they both stayed for a time. There was no more dissent, the matter was sorted, and the Indian cavalry that had galloped to avenge Muhamad was never heard of again.

When it was clear that their warriors had been lost, the screams of a hundred wives echoed around the empty alleys of the Indian quarter. The next day, at the bank of the river, they turned their grief into flames.

In front of a dying fire, Angha stroked her husband's hair as he wept. Their children watched them, astonished and confused, but there was nothing she could tell them that would make any sense. Their grandfather had died avenging the son of a man who had enslaved them, and their grandmother had committed suicide as was the custom in a world they didn't know. Angha gazed at her children and realised they were lost; belonging neither to the past nor to the present. Their only hope was the future, and the unknown dangers it held. Many of their neighbours had gone, some were dead, others were dying and she saw only a time when they might be swallowed completely, like rats in the mouth of a snake.

It took almost a year for Masud to surface in Ghazna and among the first things he did was to demand the return of all the largesse Muhamad had bestowed upon his subjects on his proclamation as Amir.

"He's a fool," Bir told Lungri.

"A rich fool," his wife corrected, carefully counting the coins they needed to return.

Any affection Ghazna might have felt for the new Sultan vanished on his arrival, and like the disease that ultimately claimed his father this antipathy spread until it clung to every rib of the great body of the Ghaznavid Empire. Of course, a few profited from the change of power, one of them being Tilak, the Indian general who had possessed the foresight to support Masud early on in his claim to the throne. In his fourth year as Sultan, Masud appointed him governor of the Punjab and as Tilak gathered his army together, he asked whether Bir might like to join him.

"It's nearer to home," he said.

"Home is not land, family is," Bir replied, "But if you need my sword, that's a different matter."

As Bir finished, his body shuddered with a cough that stole his breath and pained his lungs. After the fit passed, and embarrassed by his frailty, Bir apologised. Tilak noticed the blood flecking the old man's beard and he waved away his concerns.

"You are right, commander. Stay at home, with your family. I wish you well."

The following day, Tilak was gone. But he left an unexpected gift for his fellow Hindu. Summoned to the finance minister's chambers Bir was told that his service had been appreciated – and he was no longer to consider himself a slave. Along with his freedom he was handed a pension, and though the old warrior felt aggrieved at the assumption he was too old to perform his duties, his overriding emotion was one of relief. He took the purse home and handed it to Lungri who stored it away with another purse she had received some eight years earlier from a young mamluk who had unleashed his grief by insulting her looks.

To the surprise of few, six months after he retired Bir passed away. The sickness that had been eating his insides at last won the battle. It was a quiet end to a vibrant, sometimes cruel, life but he had few regrets and, after asking Lungri to take care of his daughter and grandchildren, he issued one last order.

"You may feel the need to perform sati, Lungri, but I forbid it. You have been a loyal companion and you can do no more for me by setting yourself on fire. Though you may not realise it, you have brought me strength and great pride. My daughter loves you. I ask you to look out for her, and to forgive me."

Before Lungri could summon the courage to respond, the man she had loved the length of her adult life was gone. Blind with tears she ran to fetch Angha. When the young woman saw the shell of her father, she collapsed. She was 24 years old.

Sohan listened to the messenger, being sure to keep his face unreadable. Once he had gone, he cursed under his breath. Leaning against the heavy wooden table, littered with badly drawn maps, he fought to steady his fists though they itched to lash out. Despite evidence to the contrary, he couldn't believe the Sultan could be so blind.

When Mahmud had promoted him, Sohan had risen to the challenge, but under Masud the appointment had become a poisoned chalice. With his hands tied by the Moslems generals in Nishapur he was the head of a battalion without the power to lead. His every movement required their permission, his warnings fell on deaf ears and his request for supplies were virtually ignored. The region had been hit by excessive tax demands causing untold grief to the Ghaznavids charged with administering them, and following Masud's decision to rescind permission to the Ghuzz Turks to graze on his land, the tribes had simply crossed over the Oxus and moved in. Worse than that, the Turkmen had united under the House of Seljuq. There had never been a greater threat to the Empire yet even now, in the face of the coming storm, Masud refused to go on the offensive. Though the Sultan promised reinforcements none ever arrived and just as it seemed Masud was ready to climb on his war elephant it appeared he was heading not for the beleaguered states of Khorasan, but for India. Sohan was outraged. And it was an anger that echoed throughout the breadth of the empire.

"With any luck they'll kill the bastard," Haroon muttered to his wife after the Sultan marched from the city with all the pomp and ceremony of the old Rajas.

Though she understood her husband's resentment, Angha stayed silent. It was true that Masud was partly responsible for the deaths of his parents. However, the Ksatriyas were paid to fight and it seemed futile to rail against an obvious ending. Furthermore, and though she never said it, the practice of sati that took Haroon's mother was an act of superstition they could have easily let go, like many of the other rituals that had fallen into obscurity. Instead, their people had hung on to the strangest habits, which is why, when Lungri continued to live following her own husband's death, she had been talked of and shunned. Angha glanced at Rashmi – eleven years old and but a few years from marriage herself – and she knew without a shadow of doubt that she would never allow her to be tied to a Ksatriya. Though the honour was great the price was heavy, and as a mother she could not allow the possibility that at some point in her daughter's future the girl would be expected to aid the passage of her husband's soul through her own torturous death. Her daughters were too precious for such mindless superstition and she would do everything in her power to furnish them with the means to defy it. Which is why, despite her husband's protests, Angha had insisted their daughters be educated.

Although Rashmi believed she was too beautiful to need letters, Chandra accepted the necessity of her studies, and though she struggled in a way that Rashmi never had, the seven-year-old was determined and conscientious. Lungri often said Chandra carried an old head upon her shoulders, and Angha was glad of it because her eldest daughter seemed bereft of commonsense. Rashmi was very much like her father; vain and foolish.

Although Haroon took care of their needs, Angha had smelt the perfume of other women on his underclothes. She never mentioned it because jealousy needed love to fire it. However, his actions displayed either amazing insensitivity or a complete lack of awareness – and witnessing more of her husband turn up in their eldest daughter she assumed he suffered from the latter. Occasionally, when she lay alone, listening to her girls squabbling in their room, Angha wondered what her children may have been like had they been fathered by Sohan. Naturally, she wouldn't have swapped her daughters for all the riches in Somnath, but she recognised a yearning for more – and it wasn't a desire that extended to her husband.

As the winter took hold of Khorasan, Sohan found himself warmed by the sight of Kerim cantering into the courtyard. Naturally, the first action of his friend was to cover his face with a scarf.

"It stinks of little India," he stated with a grimace.

Sohan embraced him. "Good to see you, old friend."

"You too. How's your wife?"

Sohan laughed even though the joke was getting tired. Since they had left Ghazna, some eight years earlier, Kerim had acquired two wives to Sohan's none. Given his rank, many of the Indian families had tried to push their daughters his way, but he had managed to avoid each proposal without causing offence, until most of the town simply assumed he was homosexual.

"Come, I have a surprise for you," said Kerim, "twenty minutes north from this Godforsaken place."

"What is it?"

"You'll see."

After leaving orders with his second-in-command, Sohan followed Kerim out of the barracks. Heading northwards there was no attempt at conversation because the sleet kept them muffled in fur. Even so, Sohan was grateful for the chance to clear his head of the ills of paralysed leadership.

Although the winter had slowed the Ghuzz Turks' offensives, the weather had brought the onset of other problems – a shortage of food being one of them. The garrison town was close to starving and Sohan had to beg his superiors for every meagre cartload of provisions. It was humiliating. Worse than that, he suspected it was meant to be.

Squinting into the wind, an unexpected smile cracked his lips as a small settlement started to take shape consisting of a handful of camel-hair tents rising out of the bleak landscape. Nearby, a number of animals stood with their backs to the storm and though only two guards were visible, Sohan guessed a dozen more sat close to their swords at the mouths of their homes.

Arriving at the camp, the men shouted their arrival to avoid any mishaps that might require a burial, and from a tent in the centre of the settlement an old man appeared. Sohan had to blink twice; even from a distance Tariq looked ancient. Once inside his home, it was immediately apparent his first wife was also clinging to life, now so old she was practically fossilised.

"Well met," Tariq declared, passing two glasses of warm, sweetened goat's milk to the men. Before Sohan had time to taste the drink, a woman he hadn't noticed rose to her feet from the shadows.

"I'm not interested," she spat, and promptly marched out of the tent. As she disappeared, a gust of snow added to the chill she left behind.

Tariq shook his head, muttering something about sparing the belt and wasting the girl.

"I said he'd be too dark for her," his first wife grumbled. And the penny dropped.

"I'm sorry," Tariq told Sohan who, after recovering from his shock, began to laugh. From the little he had seen of the woman she was no beauty to speak of. She was tall, with a strong face and thick legs.

"I like her," Sohan declared. "Tell me more."

Swiftly swallowing his surprise, Tariq began talking before Sohan could change his mind. He revealed the woman was his daughter, Adiva.

"The name means pleasant and gentle, but as you can see, she is neither," Tariq admitted. Beside him his first wife cackled in agreement.

According to Tariq, the troublesome Adiva had developed an aversion to marriage, and being the favourite daughter of his favourite slave, her father had failed to beat her into submission.

"If we don't find a husband soon, we'll never be rid of her," the first wife muttered, although it was clear from her watery eyes she was joking.

"I'll take her," Sohan informed them, surprising everyone, including himself. It was at that point he realised how tired he had become of living alone. It was time he took a wife.

"It's not going to be easy," Tariq warned. "And there's the small matter of your conversion."

Once again Sohan surprised himself by agreeing to do whatever it took.

"And I want this to be sorted by spring," he told Tariq. "You prepare your daughter. I'll prepare our quarters."

At the home she once shared with Bir, Lungri felt herself slipping away in his absence. She allowed the rooms to gather dust and she rarely ventured into the kitchen. Most days she survived on water and bread, some days she could stomach nothing at all. Her clothes began to hang from her bones like washing on a line, and Angha was deeply concerned.

"I want us to live with Lungri," she told her husband one evening.

Haroon glanced at the mud walls of their house, and feeling no sense of attachment to the place, he agreed. He knew there was little he could do to make his wife happy – he had realised it from the moment of their engagement. However, this he could do. Besides, the neighbourhood they lived in had steadily depleted and Haroon recognised a certain safety in numbers, even among the old and the crippled. Although Masud had taken no umbrage with the Indians who had stayed during his brother's brief rule, everyone felt vulnerable. The Sultan was irrational, and his temper had killed many a man simply for being in the wrong place at the wrong time. A recent embrace of sobriety following his campaign in India had made little difference to his mood and he remained as volatile out of drink as he was in it. Though Ghazna had seemed little more than a prison to the Indians trapped inside her walls, she had always felt safe. Now, the city was shrouded in suspicion and uncertainty – and no one knew what the next day might bring.

Almost tenderly, Tariq removed the silk wrapping protecting the Quran. He held it deferentially in his hands as he concentrated on the devotional element of Sohan's twice-weekly visits to woo the less-than-gentle Adiva.

"As Moslems there are certain rules one must follow," Tariq explained.

"You do surprise me," Sohan replied, before apologising and allowing the old man to catalogue a list that seemed insufferably long.

In short, in order to marry Adiva Sohan would be expected to pray five times a day and forego pork as well as many more pleasures in life. In return he would get a wife and passage to Paradise, a heavenly sanctuary blessed with lush gardens watered by clear, running streams.

"To be fair it sounds a little like Yemen," Tariq admitted.

"Do you miss your home?" Sohan asked, grasping at any diversion on offer.

"Occasionally," the old man replied. "But a country is only soil, son. Land doesn't recognise you – and it will feed anyone if treated right – whereas your family, they are your strength. In their arms is where you'll find home."

And because Sohan was tired of having empty arms, and he really did want to find that home, the next day he returned to Tariq's settlement bringing with him a very fine horse, one that would have been the envy of any man let alone a strong-boned woman who thought him too dark to marry.

"This is a gift," he told Adiva as she collected firewood and attempted to ignore him. "I have some business to attend to so I'll be gone for a while, but when I return, I expect an end to this charade. You either accept my proposal or else I'll wish you luck in your continuing search for a suitable husband. However, before I leave, let me say this to you; I will never mistreat you, I will never abandon you and I will never think of you with anything other than respect. My skin maybe dark, but my mind is enlightened."

With that, and feeling somewhat pleased with himself, Sohan walked away.

Once she was sure she wasn't being watched, Adiva dropped the firewood she held to inspect the horse he had left behind. In truth, it was a fine animal, a beautiful dappled grey with a mane the colour of night. No man had ever been so generous before. In fact, no man had been generous at all. She knew she was not a prized beauty among the clan, although everyone appreciated that she was a capable worker.

"Do you think she'll agree?" Kerim asked as they trotted away. Sohan shrugged. He had no idea, and that kind of excited him.

Before going their separate ways, Sohan swallowed his pride and asked his friend for a favour. "Please, Kerim, I'd ask you to speak to your general on our behalf. For months we've received no flour, my men are hungry and they are dejected. Soon they'll be too weak to fight should they be called on to do so."

Kerim shifted uncomfortably in his saddle, and Sohan immediately apologised.

"It's not that," his friend insisted. "It's true that the Moslems think the Hindus have too much influence, but the fact is we've all been forgotten here. The glory days of the Ghaznavid Empire are gone, Sohan. And I'm sorely tempted to go with them."

"What do you mean?"

"I mean that all of us have choices, slaves or not."

For a second, Sohan wrestled with the weight of the statement, but if Kerim was thinking of elaborating he lost his chance when a messenger came galloping into the courtyard to interrupt their farewell. He carried news from the generals. The Seljuqs had taken the city of Rayy.

"I better return to my garrison," Kerim muttered, and the two friends shook hands, noting the concern in each other's eyes. If the Ghuzz Turks had taken Rayy they were finally playing their hand as a rival for power. It was a realisation that brought a rare rush of mortality surging through

Sohan's veins, and he decided that if he was going to die, he wanted to do so knowing at least some of the pleasure of having been a man. A week later he was married.

Despite converting to Islam, Sohan showed little adherence to the rules of his newly acquired faith and few in the town that the Moslems had dubbed Little Hindustan were any the wiser. Close to the marketplace, he had built a house for his bride and in the first months of their marriage he encouraged Adiva to make friends with their neighbours.

"I have no idea what they are saying," she finally admitted when he returned home one evening to find her sitting alone, as usual.

"Why not?"

"They refuse to speak Persian."

"What? All of them?"

"Pretty much, yes."

At the revelation, a shudder of anger crawled up Sohan's spine, understanding that his wife was being treated as an outcaste simply for the crime of being different. "I'll speak to them."

"Don't be absurd."

"Then what would you have me do?"

"Allow me to find my way."

Sohan paused to contemplate whether Adiva's way might be a road back to her father's tent, but she didn't look like a woman about to flit. If anything, she looked like a woman about to give birth.

"It will get easier," he assured her.

"Only if I learn this language."

"And can you?"

"I can if I want to buy bread."

Adiva laughed and Sohan moved closer, placing a hand on her stomach. Feeling their child kick he thought of Kerim, his friend who had slyly engineered his marriage, and made his current joy possible. He then recalled Kerim's parting shot before he was posted back to Ghazna. All of them had choices, he had said, whether they were slaves or not. Sadly, it might have been a statement made once too often because with his former tribesmen challenging the empire, Kerim had been recalled to the capital to avoid "conflicts of interest". War was looming, the taste of coming battle was hot in the air, and even the horses were getting skittish. But since his marriage to Adiva, Sohan's priorities had changed. He no longer wanted to be a hero, respected for his valour and ability to kill. He wanted to live. He wanted to grow old with his wife. He wanted to welcome the children of his children into the world. And he wanted to be free. He was sick of fighting another man's wars. The Seljuqs were growing in strength – in men and in confidence – and the past year had seen them instigate and win a number of skirmishes within the Khorasan region. The taking of Rayy was merely a taste of what was to come – and it was only when the Seljuq leader, Tugrul Beg, sat himself on the throne of Nishapur that Masud finally acted.

Angha was lying next to her husband, listening to him breathe and wondering why he couldn't wash before coming to their bed, when the sound of a dozen horns shattered the quiet.

"What is it?" she asked as Haroon leapt to his feet.

"An alarm," he answered, hardly believing it himself. Within minutes he was dressed and running for the door, the leather thongs of his armour still waiting to be tied.

Rashmi and Chandra emerged from their rooms, looking sleepy and confused.

"Is it a practise?" Chandra asked as they joined their mother at the window. Though flames lit the sky, Angha told her daughter she expected it was.

As Haroon rushed to answer the emergency, the screams of horses revealed the stables were on fire whilst the shouts of men revealed Ghazna was under attack. The Sultan had only been gone two days, but clearly it was a move that had been anticipated by the Seljuqs who were now stealing his horses and bringing their challenge to the heart of the Ghaznavid Empire.

Nearing the stables Haroon saw the silhouettes of long-haired warriors, black against the orange night. Their swords flashed in the firelight and their ponytails whipped in the breeze like angry snakes on the chase. The palace guard, and what was left of the city's ghulam soldiers, threw themselves into the chaos, scything men from their rides and dying under hooves. Choked by the thick smoke and deafened by the crack of burning wood, the men scrambled to defend the city, but they were woefully unprepared and the battle was wild and messy. By sunrise the horses were lost and though the mamluks gave chase, many of them were Turkic slaves and sluggish in their pursuit.

To the sound of cheers echoing in the distance, the battered Ghaznavids picked up their dead – and Haroon was stretchered back to the city with his stomach open and bleeding. Before he lost consciousness, he asked the man carrying him to send for his wife. It was a request the mamluk could easily have ignored, but the guard was clearly dying and he had done little to repel the Seljuqs responsible. He agreed, acutely conscious of the irony of being posted to a region to avoid conflicts of interest and having them follow him there.

When Angha answered the door, Kerim recognised her instantly. The sight was so unexpected, he found himself lost for words. Naturally, Angha had prepared for the worst and she simply assumed the man at her door was suffering from shock. She invited him in and asked Lungri to make a pot of sweet tea.

Sohan was eating the meat stew Adiva had made when he heard a horseman clatter to a halt outside their door. His first thought was that it was another summons from the Sultan. Masud had arrived some days earlier in a typical rage after being dogged from Ghazna by Seljuq raiders employing hit and run tactics that left his patience short and his army smaller than when he set out.

"Stay here," Sohan ordered his wife, and she instinctively took Abbas from his crib. The baby was as dark as his father, but his face bore the look of his mother – slightly chubby and largely obstinate. She took him to the window where she pointed the boy towards Sohan who was now speaking to a soldier. Noticing her, the man waved in greeting and Adiva smiled in recognition. Kerim had returned. She was glad of it, her husband had missed him, but then she saw the surprise on Sohan's face slip into shock, and the blood in her veins chilled. He glanced up at the window and for a moment their eyes locked before he pulled them away. Two minutes later, Sohan returned to the house to reveal he was leaving. Adiva listened to his explanation, feeling the ground tremble beneath her feet with every word uttered.

"If I don't go and he dies she'll kill herself. I can't allow that to happen," he said, and Adiva understood there was nothing she could say that would make him change his mind. Before he left, Sohan kissed his son and attempted to kiss his wife too, but she felt so betrayed she couldn't raise her lips.

"What is she to you?" Adiva demanded.

"A part of me," he answered, not even trying to cushion the blow, and he ran from the room to save a woman who had once begged him to save her father.

To Sohan's unspoken gratitude, Kerim accompanied him part of the way to Ghazna until half a day into their journey he reined in his horse, and headed west.

"We all have choices," he said, echoing a thought from the past. "I am no more a Ghaznavid than you are, Sohan. Go with God, my friend."

"Stay with God," Sohan replied, and he continued pushing his horse forwards in a desperate race against time that barely gave him space to consider his best friend's desertion.

Lungri was in the yard when Sohan arrived. As he banged on the door he was vaguely distracted by the smell of an elephant.

"Where is she?" he asked, ignoring the woman's shock.

"At the river," she replied. "Her husband died in the night."

From behind her, two girls approached the door, clamping themselves onto Lungri's arm. Both were tearful, but Sohan had no time to care, and seeing his horse was done, he ran.

With every gasp that ripped through his lungs Sohan prayed to Allah and begged for mercy from all the old gods he knew. He jumped over discarded barrels and through debris-littered compounds, clipping walls and an occasional resident as he went. The old city was crumbling, its streets were practically empty, and Sohan felt the breaths of a thousand tortured souls hot upon his neck. Clearing the outer wall he sprinted towards the river. Along the bank he spotted smoke coming from the charred remains of a dozen or more pyres, with only one of them still burning.

"No!" Sohan screamed, feeling the word tear at his throat.

As his heart convulsed, his legs kept up their momentum as though they were somehow detached from his mind and acting on impulse. Over and over Sohan shouted Angha's name as he clawed at the tears falling to blind him. Mere feet from the pyre, he slumped to the floor and let every emotion he had ever buried rise up and take him.

At the sight of him, Angha stopped. Around her lay the clothes and memories of her husband.

"I thought..." Sohan gasped, and Angha moved away from the flames.

"You thought I would kill myself to honour a man I never loved? You thought I'd leave my girls to fend for themselves?"

Sohan nodded as she came to kneel with him in the dirt.

"I will not do it, Sohan. That world no longer belongs to me. I have freed my husband's soul by destroying the earthly bonds that hold him. I can do no more than that, and no woman should ever be required to do so."

For the first time that day, Angha allowed her tears to fall; for a husband she had never loved; for a father she had worshipped; for an old man and an elephant; and for her dreams of a boy who had once shown her a dead mutant snake.

"I'm really so very glad to see you," she eventually revealed.

"Me too," he replied. "I guess we shouldn't leave it so long next time."

Despite her grief, Angha laughed and as she did so Sohan reached for her hand, helping her to her feet. After throwing the last of Haroon's belongings onto the fire, the pair walked back to Ghazna, ignoring the curious stares of any who thought to look at them.

That evening, after Lungri had taken Angha's girls to another room, the two friends who should have been lovers, untangled the past that had worked so hard to betray them.

"I came for you, but you were married," Angha revealed.

"I married only recently," Sohan replied.

"But the old man at the barracks said..."

Sohan groaned, inwardly cursing Abdul Aziz, and not for the first time.

"I also came for you," he admitted later. "But I saw you with your husband, he carried your daughter. You were also pregnant and I assumed, well, I'm not sure what I assumed. We were practically strangers, why would you have left him?"

"We were never strangers, Sohan. To me you were... everything."

"To me you are more than that."

With trembling fingers, Sohan reached for Angha's face and he kissed her for the first time. The next morning, he called for a mullah. Though they had to admit their timing was dreadful, Sohan made Angha his wife, albeit the second one. She was 28 years old.

As Sohan and Angha packed a cart for their journey, Lungri did her best to comfort Rashmi and Chandra; two fatherless girls who had spent much of the morning watching their mother in stunned silence. Angha had tried to explain, but no matter how she put it, the truth sounded awful. Perhaps later, when they had chance to catch breath, she might think of a way to help her girls understand her transformation from widow to wife in the space of one night. Until then, Angha concentrated on loading their cart with everything they might need – as well as a baffling number of handwritten books.

As Sohan expected, the journey north was torturously slow thanks to the inclement weather, two fractious children, a lame, elderly woman and the fear of attack the nearer they travelled to Khorasan. On the fifth day, as they crept past Herat, Sohan spied a line of Seljuq warriors galloping along the horizon. When the danger passed without incident, Sohan relaxed and did his best to make friends with his wife's children. Enjoying some success with fanciful tales of a wondrous city called Kanauj, both Rashmi and Chandra slumped into an exhausted acceptance of the stranger who had somehow married their mother. Of course, once they reached their new home, they were terrified all over again thanks to the tough-looking woman they were now expected to live with.

Ushering his new family into a backroom, Sohan prepared a fire and led Lungri to the kitchen so she might feed them all. He then asked Adiva to join him in the privacy of their sleeping quarters.

"You brought her to my home?" his wife shouted, and it took all of the night and most of his patience before Sohan could get her to accept the change in their lives.

The following morning, after Sohan had left for his office, Adiva prepared a breakfast of warm milk and salted cheese which she took to the woman she was now required to call 'sister'. Angha accepted the plate before promptly offering it back.

"You are first in all things," Angha told her in Persian.

Despite her anger, Adiva was touched by the gesture. When, a few hours later, Angha offered to teach Adiva how to order bread in Hindi, the ice in her veins thawed a little more.

Later that night, after Sohan retired to the bed of his first wife, Angha watched her children's faces in the warmth of the fire. Despite everything they had suffered they slept peacefully. Even Lungri appeared content. With her eyes closed and her face half-shielded by a pillow, she looked like any other woman her age and Angha felt the sting of unexpected tears arrive. Swallowing them away, she reached for her books and began writing. There was so much she hadn't known and it was necessary to be true to it all.

Within a week of Angha's arrival, Sohan was ordered to help the beleaguered city of Nishapur as Masud finally set out to avenge the Empire, cocooned by 80,000 fully-armed soldiers on foot, horseback and elephant.

The sheer size of the army was enough to send the Seljuqs scurrying and the hard-pressed Khorasan generals, who had known only humiliation in recent times, enjoyed once again the agreeable strength of their power. It was a mighty show of force and everyone applauded a job well done – everyone, that is, apart from the Sultan. Against the advice of almost everyone, Masud insisted on pursuing the fleeing Seljuqs; an impossibility for an army of such size. However, the Sultan was beyond reason – and drunk on the power of one victory. With barely a pause, he ordered his men back to the field, and the Seljuqs could scarcely believe their luck. With ruthless efficiency, they wreaked havoc; severing supply lines and poisoning every well they encountered. Yet still Masud thundered on, trailing the Turkmen over land left barren by famine and abandoned by raids. Throughout the journey, the Seljuq archers picked away at the Sultan's soldiers, but this was nothing compared to a new enemy that started to emerge from within. With nothing to be clawed from the land, provisions dried up, along with the water, and horses began to fall. On the periphery of the rolling army, men stumbled with exhaustion and hunger, occasionally pulling knives on each other for scraps of dried meat. All the while, at the heart of the beast, atop of a great elephant cosseted by a hundred or more guards, Masud feasted like the king he was. Therefore, it was little surprise to Sohan when each morning he awoke to find a dozen or more defections among the ranks.

 By the time they reached the flat expanse of Dandanqan, Masud's army had lost 30,000 soldiers – and the Turks had stopped running. The Ghaznavids remained twice as large as the 20,000 Seljuqs who squared up to do battle, but Tughril Beg's army was lightly armoured, mobile and fresh. They had also tasted power and were hungry for more. Luring the Sultan into the open, the Seljuq cavalry acted quickly – circling the beleaguered flanks of Masud's great army before swooping. Their aim was exact and men fell quickly from arrows that skewered necks and split eyes. From deep within the Ghaznavid swell, Sohan saw they had been outmanoeuvred, and every attempt to break free of the trap brought a swift and speedy death. With a professional savagery that had once been the hallmark of the Ghaznavids, the Seljuqs pounded Masud's lines until they were forced to climb walls of corpses to finish off the dying and still fighting. Under the relentless onslaught, amid a carnage that showed no sign of abating – men began to drop their weapons and run. Some were permitted to escape while others were hunted for sport.

As Sohan struggled under a wave of metal that seemed to flow like a river, his back was pushed closer to the core of Masud's inner circle. Only adrenalin kept his arms pumping as he hacked through flesh and bone without feeling the sting of his own wounds, of which there were many. After repelling another charge, Sohan slipped to his knees in the sludge of mud and blood. As he grappled to get to his feet, a huge blow sent him crashing back to the ground. Winded, he swung to his side to haul himself upwards, only to retreat into a ball as a hundred or more hooves thundered over and around him. No longer able to feel the grip of his sword he plunged his hands into the soft ground with increasing desperation until he eventually found the hilt. Pulling it to him he saw the blade had been bent by the foot of an elephant. Sohan glanced behind him to find the Ghaznavids at his back had broken cover. It was their horses that had charged over his head. After everything they had suffered, Masud had abandoned the Hindus to their fate.

As panic gripped Sohan's chest, a horse came thundering towards him only to stop a breath from his face. The legs and flank were splattered with blood and the remnants of men clung to its coat. Sohan readied himself for death.

"Lose your armour, Sohan! Get behind me!"

Kerim fought to keep his horse steady as it danced and shied on the bones of the slain. Immediately ripping the armour from his chest, Sohan reached for his friend's hand and swung himself up and into the saddle. Kerim kicked, but by then there was nowhere to run. Seeing they were trapped, Sohan bent for a sword standing upright in the ground. As he grabbed the hilt a horn broke through the chaos, and to a man, the Seljuqs shuddered to a stop.

In the sudden stillness, the harsh wind carried the death screams of thousands. The battlefield spread before them like a carpet dragged from the caverns of Hell, and the less hardened around them began to vomit in shock. Gradually small cheers began to rise, starting from the right and gathering in ferocity as it followed the path of Tughril Beg. As the Seljuq leader approached, Kerim stood his ground, and Sohan realised the two men were known to each other. It appeared his friend had made his choice.

Holding up a gloved hand Tughril gestured for calm. He cast a slow eye over the remains of the great Ghaznavid army and saw that, under the mask of blood and mud they wore, the faces were those of slaves.

"You have until tomorrow sundown to collect your families and be gone," the man growled. He then turned his horse and cantered away, serenaded by the triumphant shouts of his men. When the cheers died down the Seljuqs got to work, scavenging among the bodies of the dead and injured.

"Where shall we go?" Sohan asked as he slid from Kerim's horse.

His friend shook his head, knowing the options were bleak. The Seljuq warriors were efficient, brutal and looking to build an empire. What they had witnessed today was only the start. A new storm was coming and it would blow the Ghaznavids into oblivion.

"Go west," Kerim advised. "This isn't your war and it's not worth dying for."

"But it's your war?"

Kerim sighed. "They are my people. I know no other way."

"So west it is," Sohan agreed. And the two men parted with an embrace.

Chapter Five

Finally finished, I drank the cup of tea one of the women had brought me shortly before sundown. I hadn't meant to talk so much, but somehow the words had taken on a life of their own. It had been much the same when I had recounted the same tale during the long nights at the hospital – although there, I'd chosen my language more carefully, given the age of the audience.

Turning to stretch the tension from my back, I was surprised and not a little gratified to see that most of our neighbours had gathered. The Big Man sat in a quilted seat while the rest made do with jackets laid on the grass. From the steps of her caravan, Donka watched me, smoking a cigarette.

Jack clicked his tape recorder to a stop and Francoise took the opportunity to drink deeply from a glass of water.

"You've given me a lot to think about," the Frenchman admitted as he got to his feet.

One by one, our neighbours did the same and I told Francoise that with so much to think about perhaps the Frenchman might like to leave it a couple of days before returning.

"Of course," she replied. She then hesitated, and I noticed colour making its first visit to her cheeks. "Bir Paramichi?"

"What about him?"

"Isn't 'paramichi' Romani for folktale?"

I had to admit I was impressed.

"In some dialects there's a certain similarity. But how would you know this?"

Francoise pulled at her ring-less fingers. "I worked with Roma communities in Bucharest, helping them with legal matters and the suchlike. I picked up a few words during that time – nothing to brag about."

"Francoise?" Jack nudged his translator's elbow, evidently tired from the unexpected length of the lesson and the unnecessary chatter of women not thinking to include him. She raised her thin eyebrows a fraction, only enough for me to see, and we shared a smile because I was feeling more amenable than when they arrived.

After the visitors had gone, I took the cups they had drunk from and set them aside from our own. On the steps of her home, Donka jerked her head towards me in a way that looked like a challenge.

"Is it true, what you told the *gadje*?"

I stared at the woman whose face was still fat with youth and possibility, and chose not to bite.

"There's added meat," I admitted. "But the bones are in place."

"I had no idea..." she half-whispered before stubbing out her cigarette.

The next morning, as I washed the previous day's clothes, Donka emerged from her caravan much earlier than usual. In her hands she carried two buckets. Without a word she placed her husband's jeans in one of the pails and her skirts in the other. She then started scrubbing.

Chapter Six

Drina sat in front of me, chewing her bottom lip as if to punish it for the sin of repetition.

"Can you believe such lies?" she demanded.

And what could I tell her? The damage was done, and a million truths would never undo it.

That morning, the French President had ordered 300 traveller sites to be dismantled within the next three months to "combat crime and urban violence". Although the announcement wasn't wholly unexpected, the words he employed were, and he wielded them with such authority that they instantly became 'truth'.

I looked out of the window, surveying the open field with its cropped stubs of wheat and the billowing hedges that had become the frontline in Sarkozy's war on 'urban' violence. A little to the right, within the undrawn perimeter of our 'illegal' settlement, three children rolled a smaller child in the tube of a tyre. I couldn't see Mirela, but she may have been with her father.

I turned my attention back to the cramped confines of our one-berth caravan and back to Drina who had come to me in tears to reveal that the place we called home had been casually damned by the President as a source of illegal trafficking, of profoundly shocking living standards, of prostitution and crime, where children were exploited for begging.

It hardly seemed just.

"I'll never wash his filth from my skin," cried the Big Man's wife in despair. She took a handkerchief from her pocket to at least clean her face.

"We've heard worse," I replied, but it was little comfort and the old woman wasn't in the mood to be reminded.

Drina got to her feet, looking angry yet defeated. Before she left, presumably for her own den of iniquity, she turned to me, barely able to meet my eyes.

"There are bad apples in every cart," she admitted, "but no one sets fire to the cart, not unless it belongs to a Romani."

And what could I say, given our circumstances?

I thanked Drina for keeping me informed, stroking the back of her rounded shoulders as she departed. As the door closed behind her, I took a deep breath, swallowing air that was slowly solidifying under the humiliation that remained. I couldn't say for certain, but I'd wager my health that the old woman had known only one man in her life – the man she had always called 'husband'. In the 45 years they had been married, Marko and Drina had raised three children and buried two more. Although their existence had always relied on the tolerance of another, Drina had known happiness and it had come in the form of her grandchildren and the pride of having a man of status at her side. However, if words can change the course of history, they can do far worse in the present. And now, whenever Drina walked into town – to buy a loaf of bread, a leg of ham or a slab of cheese – people wouldn't see her as the grandmother she was or a person who had earned a community's respect. Instead, they would see the scarf covering her hair, the length of her skirt and the colour of her skin and they would recognise her as something different; something criminal and unsavoury. This was the legacy of the word, as spoken by the most powerful man in one of the wealthiest countries of the world.

With a familiar fury beating at my chest, I reached for a bag of dried rosemary and placed a pinch of it within the lid of an old tin. Before I could set a match to the herbs a thunderous knock arrived at the door. Unlike Drina's gentler announcement, I instantly knew who was behind it.

"Donka," I greeted.

"Mala," she replied, "You weren't at the meeting."

"I'm sick."

The young woman took a step backwards. She clutched at her stomach, but revealed nothing more.

"The Monthly Flower," I explained, and Donka visibly relaxed.

"I call it the Visit of the Moon," she admitted. "Do you need me to cook for Miko and Mirela?"

Taken by surprise – and predictably sensitive given the time of the month – her unexpected kindness made me visibly emotional.

"Christ, I'm not offering to upgrade your caravan," Donka huffed.

"I know, it's just, well, you know..."

Donka rolled her eyes. However, she did know and so she waited for me to gather myself after which I managed to thank her whilst revealing Drina had earlier volunteered to cook for the coming five days.

"Well, the offer stands if you need it. I tell you; my life would be paradise if the Visit of the Moon took up permanent residence. Tanko eats like a horse."

"In that case it would be cheaper too," I replied, and we both laughed a little, feeling the sly warmth of possible friendship enter our veins. After we had calmed ourselves, and settled into the more familiar territory of inconsequential chit chat, Donka revealed the main purpose for her visit.

"I want to know when the *gadje* are coming back."

"I'm not sure," I replied, "perhaps in a day or two."

"And you'll speak to them despite your – you know – flowering."

"There's no polluting the *gadje*, Donka."

"No, I guess not. OK, I'll keep an eye out for them. I'd like to hear more about our past before we run out of time."

Later that afternoon, as I scrubbed the linoleum square that served as a patio in front of our home, Miko returned from a tour of the region's dumping grounds. It wouldn't have been everyone's idea of a fun day out, but he looked uncommonly cheerful.

"Six transistor radios, three computers, a Toshiba laptop and a whisk," he declared.

"I'd have preferred chocolates," I joked, and Miko replied with one of his own, equally lame, about being sweet enough. I groaned in reply, but it was good to see the spark return to my husband's eyes. It wasn't easy for a man of Miko's temperament to have to rely on charity, which is why when Bo revealed he had a man in Amiens who sold reconditioned electrical goods to the Africans, he saw a way he could work for his keep.

"Where's Mirela?" I asked.

"She's helping Bo. I think she's sweet on him."

"And Bo doesn't mind her hanging around?"

"He doesn't seem to."

Miko reached under the sink — a sink that had known no water — and he collected his bar of soap. He then headed for the water pump to prepare for dinner. Understanding that Miko's "doesn't seem to" could possibly mean my husband had "no idea" I left a second after him to go in search of our love-struck seven-year-old. Towards the back of Rami's place, I found Mirela sat among a collection of tools, wires, computers and cables. At her side, Bo was hunched over a dead-looking laptop. Without looking up, he held out his hand.

"Screwdriver."

Mirela immediately supplied the tool, employing all the care of a surgical assistant deeply in love with her doctor.

"Good choice," Bo commented, and I couldn't help but smile when I saw my daughter's face light up. I had to admit, she also showed good taste. Though Rami's eldest was thickset with a rough mop of hair that was forever falling into his eyes, he was unquestionably handsome. As he leaned forward, the back of his shirt gaped open, showing how far the summer sun had darkened his skin, and when he smiled the result was dazzling.

Mirela looked my way, and I jerked my head to show she should follow. Without a word of protest, she rose to her feet and told Bo she would return later if needed.

"Right you are," he replied, which was about as passionate a response as one could expect from a Romani male. As our women are a different breed altogether Mirela's face beamed with unchecked delight.

Running to join me, she grabbed hold of my hand to kiss the back of my fingers. The warmth of her affection stole the breath from my lungs and I welcomed it with a hug. We may have been poor as sparrows but, in many ways, we were rich as kings.

"Has Bo been taking care of you?"

"I'm not a baby, *Mamo*. I'm helping him mend stuff to send to the Africans."

"And do you know where Africa is?"

Mirela frowned and tilted her head to the left.

"Not really," she admitted. "But it must be far from the shops if they need computers from here."

I bent to kiss the top of Mirela's head before supplying the correct answer. Her hair burned against my lips like hot silk. Taking her hand, I led her to the Big Man's caravan where Drina would have a meal waiting.

"Are you learning much from Bo?"

"I guess," Mirela answered, squinting into the sun as she spoke. "I mean, it looks complicated and all that, but it's not that hard once you know what a screwdriver is."

"Is that so?"

"Yes, it is. And Bo says I might even get to fix stuff when I'm older because he'll show me how."

I inwardly winced at Mirela's enthusiasm given my recent understanding of Sarkozy's plans. Bo and his brothers should be safe enough; they were born in France and they would be simply moved on. The Big Man too, although he originally came from Romania. But the others. Us.

"Bo's a good boy," I said, shaking the worry from my mind to keep the smile on my child's face.

"Yes, he is," Mirela agreed. "Bo's nice and I like him a lot."

"Well, I'm sure he likes you too, *shukariyo*. However, he's also much older than you so make sure you find time to play with the other children now and again."

At the advice, Mirela stopped walking and the pull of her hand forced me to follow suit. Her large eyes were serious, almost stern, and I frowned in puzzlement.

"What is it?"

"Well, it's not always easy, that's all," she admitted quietly.

Feeling the full weight of my child's confidence come to land on my chest, I crouched in front of her, taking her tiny hands into my own. "I do understand, Mirela. It takes time to make new friends."

Mirela shook her head furiously, her eyebrows knotting as she rejected the suggestion.

"It's got nothing to do with time, *Mamo*. It's a new face I need. Not everyone wants to play with the ugly kid, you know?"

And before I could stop her, she shrugged her shoulders and continued walking – another 'gypsy' simply accepting that sometimes the world didn't play fair.

Although it played on my mind, I never mentioned Mirela's hurt to Miko. One reason being I loved him too much to keep adding to his pain, another being that I couldn't bear to repeat the words. Letting them loose would only increase their power, and the truth was I wasn't strong enough to face it yet.

There was still too much to recover from. So, the next morning I woke from a sleep that was slow in coming and tried to get on with the life we had.

When Miko surfaced an hour later, he disappeared without a word – to cleanse himself of the pollution haunting the space between sleep and consciousness. When he returned, he greeted me in the manner he used to, a lifetime ago, before everything changed.

"A new day, a new dawn, Mala."

"Pray it will be so," I replied. And I clutched the cross at my neck, to give our wish strength.

Once Miko left for the day – to scavenge among the waste of the wasteful – I sat Mirela at the Formica table we had been gifted by Marko and Drina. I laid out the exercises I had prepared and Mirela got to work. Once we had exhausted our tolerance of maths, we moved on to the mutually more agreeable territory of reading and writing. Although I'd offered to teach the other school-less children on site, few were willing to take up the offer, and I found that a shame. It was a sense of loss shared by my husband who was – for all his own failings in this area – a fierce advocate of education. Once upon a time, in the home we used to own, he even expressed a desire to see Mirela go to university.

"When people have exhausted every path the only road remaining open is that of education," he stated, and I was struck once again by the remarkable man I had had the good fortune to be married to.

Around noon – with everyone I loved currently eating with the Big Man and his wife – I sat alone, struggling to finish a husk of dry bread – partly because the bread needed some kind of spread, but mainly because I wasn't hungry. With no one to cook for my appetite predictably disappeared. It happened every month, and during my more macabre moments I even wondered what I would do if everyone around me suddenly dropped dead. Would I begin to eat again or simply fade away? How strong was the urge to survive if there was no one to live for? And how long would it even take to die? Buddha fasted for 49 days and he not only lived but ended up enlightened.

I swallowed the last of my lunch, crossing myself to balance the ill luck of my thoughts, and did what I always did in times of boredom; sought refuge in scrubbing.

Settling myself in front of a washboard, I was quietly pleased when a few minutes later Donka emerged from her caravan carrying laundry of her own. Naturally, as she got to work, she complained often and stopped frequently, but at least she was trying. The previous evening, before Sarkozy stole the wind from her sails, Drina had further revealed that Donka had sought clarification on a number of our other customs, presumably the ones rendered hazy by time and non-compliance. Though I'm sure she was wholly unaware of the fact, Donka's awakening had had a palpable effect on the women around her because, above all else, Romanies knew they ought to face the same way, which we were – quite literally – when the *gadje* wandered into view.

At the sight of them, I got to my feet and disappeared behind the caravan to retrieve the cups I'd placed there. One of them, a white mug with a tractor on the front, had a snail in its belly. I tipped the creature onto the grass, with an apology, after which I returned to the front of our home to put a pan of water on the gas burner. After a minor detour to the Big Man's quarters, the *gadje* approached carrying their chairs.

"*Sastipe*, Mala!" Jack shouted cheerily.

"*Sastipe, Kako* Jack," I replied with less enthusiasm, wondering where he had picked up the Romani before noticing Francoise standing radiant with the smile of the proud teacher. To my surprise, the Frenchman winked at her. More extraordinarily the Romanian blushed. It was clear there had been something of a thaw since their last visit.

After pouring tea for the *gadje*, but none for the Big Man – due to my sickness – Jack held up the mug with the tractor on it and said something that sounded particularly self-satisfied. I looked to Francoise who smiled patiently. Her lips were painted.

"Jack says you must like him because you've given him his own mug. It's the same one he had last time," she translated.

I kept my face careful, and Francoise leaned closer. I smelt perfume on her skin.

"Actually, I haven't the heart to tell him that our cups will now be reserved for us," she revealed. "Or that once you've seen the last of us, you'll probably smash them into pieces."

Not for the first time I found myself impressed by the woman, not least because she didn't seem the slightest bit offended.

Jack placed his tape recorder on the table and with a crack of his neck – which struck me as a bizarre call to business – he invited me to start where I had previously left off. From the corner of my eye, I saw Donka settle on the steps of her caravan, cigarettes in hand, and I cleared my throat to begin.

However, the ground had shifted around me and it nagged at my attention. I watched Francoise tuck a lock of hair behind her ear and saw she'd had a manicure.

Coughing with the force of the terminal consumptive, I attempted to still my mind so that I might pick up the rhythm of a story that was in constant motion in my mind.

"So, from India to Khorasan," I began, "the first fathers – and mothers – of the Romani people continued south of the Caspian Sea, across the foothills of the Caucasus Mountains into, what is now, modern-day Turkey. At the time of our arrival the Byzantine Greeks were hanging onto the threads of a once-mighty Empire and it was in this place, during a time of urgent upheaval, that the Indians we were grew into the Romanies we are – a race of people unlike any other, with our own language, our own customs and a religion moulded from many parts."

"The Roma are Catholics, are they not?" Jack interrupted. He scribbled in his notepad, underscoring a word he had written there with a confidence that belied his lack of knowledge. My eyes snapped shut as I tried to contain my irritation.

"Yes, the Roma are Catholics," I agreed through clenched teeth, "apart from the ones who happen to be Muslim, Protestant, Greek Orthodox or Jewish, of course."

As Francoise repeated, a swift appeal softened her eyes, and feeling oddly conscious of playing a part in her happiness, I took a breath.

"Joking aside Jack, our faith is as complex as any other," I explained, my voice sounding cheesy with forced affability. "Naturally, because people don't understand it, they tend to belittle it. Some say we have no religion. Others claim we lost it after writing God's instructions on a cabbage leaf that was promptly eaten by a donkey. In Romania they say we built a stone church only to swap it for the locals' church which they had built using ham and bacon. It naturally follows that we ate it."

"I've heard that story," Francoise admitted, taking the opportunity to thank me with her eyes.

"Childish jokes," Jack declared with a dismissive wave of his hand, revealing that he had yet to grasp the insidious nature of such tales.

"Yes, they are," I agreed. "But there's also the story about the gypsy who forged the nails for Christ's crucifixion. It's nonsense of course, and anyone who understands anything about our history will know we didn't leave India until long after Jesus was crucified. Even so, over the centuries, the Church has used this myth to justify our persecution. Like the Jews, 'gypsies' have become Christianity's fall guys."

"Actually, I've heard the nails story," Jack admitted, a little more carefully. "To be honest, and as bad as it sounds, I'd assumed there was some truth in it, like the rest of the Bible."

"Well, if you say something long enough and loud enough it eventually becomes fact," I replied. "Unfortunately, like our history our own Bible is unwritten. It doesn't follow therefore that we have no religion – and as I said earlier, it's complex. We left India with our gods and goddesses; we were sheltered through the ages by the spirit of our ancestors; and we adapted to every new environment. Our religion shadows the story of our survival."

"Then we best get on with the story," Jack interjected jovially, winking as he spoke. It was a tic he repeated again once Francoise had translated. Resisting the urge to ask the woman 'what do you see in this fool?', I breathed in deep to dull my temper and focus my mind on Constantinople, the city where – after much begetting down the ages – one of the descendants of Angha Paramichi found himself at the crossroads of the world; between east and west, the past and the future.

His name was Thomas, and he was quite possibly a giant.

CONSTANTINOPLE

1347

Chapter Seven

Accompanied by their families, followers – and a few terrified others – the Indians of the warrior class, and all who served under them, headed west to discover new countries whose names would one day be confined to the pages of history. As the earth froze, and thawed, beneath their feet, they moved as refugees – fleeing the Seljuq storm that harried their heels along the path of two great seas and the peaks of mountains where the snow never lost its grip.

Reaching Armenia, the Indians paused for breath. Their wagons were lighter, their clothes less fine and they were already drifting from the people they once were. The old had died, the new had been born and their numbers pulsed with the ebb and flow of life. Throughout it all, the spirit of those who began the journey continued to ride with them, and they guided their children through terrain and upheaval that could have spelt the end of their story. With each milestone passed, the living never forgot the dead and they endeavoured to please them with gifts and good behaviour.

With so many lost on the plains of Dandanqan, widows sought new protection – sometimes from the rolling dust of their own, sometimes from the lands that they passed through. And as swords grew blunt with the passage of time and no means to maintain them, other skills were shared among those who had previously known only the power of death in their hands. Warriors became craftsmen, armed with anvils, portable and placed on the ground; mamluks used their expertise to tame horses for trade; the musicians adapted their sound to suit the ears of strangers; the women nurtured their own gifts; and within the forests that shrouded them, bear cubs were trapped so they might bring their own rewards. All the while, the Turkmen pushed them on, ever westwards.

By the time the Indians abandoned Armenia they had gathered new husbands, new skills and a number of new words. Like rain falling on seeds, time, place and necessity combined to nourish the language of their past. Having taken the 'stars' of the Persians and the 'breadcrumbs' of the Arabs their language was cooked in the 'ovens' of the Armenians who also softened the sound, adding a breath of fresh air to old words. Speech became a symphony in progress, and one that reached its crescendo within the boundaries of the once-mighty Byzantine Empire.

Having pierced the drum of Asia Minor, the refugees attracted others displaced by battles that were fought without end. Though the majority fell away, a few opted to stay bringing new words and new blood until, eventually, the lines between what was Indian, Persian, Armenian and Greek became irrevocably blurred. It was here that a new flower was born – that of the Romani people.

As the refugees strayed further from the reach of those who harassed them, they observed the symbol of a new religion, attached to stone and planted in fields of the dead. Those that remembered, recognised Shiva's trident in the Cross of the Christians, and they took it as a sign they were on the right road.

As the years rolled by, in tens and then scores, the refugees' survival necessitated dispersal as the nation they had become required greater yields than a land exhausted by raiding parties and poverty could supply. Larger families broke away to find their own destinies, others simply stopped moving – choosing to settle and sell their skills to Armenian kings and

Turkmen beyliks. The rest walked on, playing to the tune of whoever had means to pay them and stopping whenever they found a place to sustain them. But wherever they went – or wherever they didn't – they remembered who they were, and they carried this knowledge on their backs, in their carts, and in their hearts.

Among those who journeyed westwards were the descendants of Angha and Sohan. At their own pace, they moved deeper into territory that belonged to a king whom the people called 'Emperor'. They arrived at the moment a new storm swept in, led by tall men dressed in metal who wore the sign of the cross on their chests. The Latins, as they were called, appeared in their thousands, rampaging towards a "Holy Land" lying at the centre of the world. It was an endeavour requiring such valour and devotion it permitted the pilgrims to lay waste to everything in their path. Following men addressed as 'Count' or 'Duke', the Latins committed murder on an astonishing scale. From the sidelines of the carnage, the Romanies looked on – appalled and intrigued – until the knights catapulted severed heads into the forts of their enemies, at which point they moved on.

Following the taste of salt on the breeze, the Romanies arrived at Constantinople. It was here, outside the city's vast double walls, built as thick as five men standing, that Thomas was born; a man who would one day be remembered for his innate sense of fairness, his unconscious acts of violence, and his colossal stature.

Initially, there was nothing overtly unusual about Thomas. It was true his skin was a lighter shade than his siblings, but his eyes were dark, his hair was black, he wiggled the preferred number of fingers and toes, and he cried whenever he was hungry. In fact, it was only when his mother rejoined her family that she began to notice that something wasn't so much amiss with her sixth child as amassing.

Her alarm was first triggered by the red twine tied about Thomas's ankle that ate into his flesh a full year earlier than it ought to have done. By the age of six months, his head was the size of a sheep's bladder, and before he could walk, he snapped the neck of a wild rabbit. Although the creature was destined for the pot, its untimely demise signalled the start of a sad and somewhat disastrous relationship with animals that only ended when Thomas was five – and old enough to understand that life was sometimes too fragile to hold on to.

Perhaps unsurprisingly, given his strength and inability to control it, Thomas spent much of his infant years in quiet seclusion. His isolation was further exacerbated by a mother who insisted on rubbing pig fat over his body – out of fear her son's rapid growth might split his skin, like an overripe plum. It was a kindness that left Thomas gleaming and faintly malodorous. Completing the ternion of injustices was the boy's difficulty with speech. Although Thomas created sounds, they were rarely decipherable as words.

"His tongue is too fat, just like the rest of him," his grandmother concluded, oblivious to the anxiety this stirred in her daughter.

"Then what should I do?"

"Starve him."

"But he's a child!"

"Child, maybe, but I'm telling you now, he's the fattest child I've ever laid eyes on – and he's got a fat tongue to match."

"For the love of *Del*, there's nothing wrong with the boy's tongue!" Mihai barked from his corner of the tent.

Rattled, and not a little shamed by the outburst, the two women fell silent. Thomas' father pulled the blanket over his head and returned to sleep. At the far end of the tent, hidden beneath his own covers, Thomas' ears burned. He reached inside his mouth – suddenly aware of a part of his body he'd never given much thought to. It took him only a second to arrive at the same conclusion as his grandmother, and a few hours later he woke them all screaming, having dreamt he was being suffocated by a tongue growing out of control.

"May the gods save us, there's nothing wrong with you," Thomas' father tried to reassure him the next day as they sat by the river waiting to scoop a fish into their nets. "No man has a double. We are all born different."

Thomas gazed across the bank, at the sprawling families of their *kumpania*, and he struggled to believe him. He observed his father's thin arms, the sharp nose and keen eyes, and he saw his image reflected not only in the form of his brothers, but also in their wider community. When Thomas sat among his family he felt like a duck in a nest of sparrows.

"Thomas, you're more like me than you'll ever know," Mihai insisted several months later – once his son had found the wherewithal to articulate his fears. "Watch and learn, boy, and I promise, you will see."

With little else to do in their lives, apart from work, eat, and sleep, Thomas agreed to watch and learn, in the hope that he might one day see what he was currently blind to. Naturally, it took patience and will, but eventually he stopped panicking over the width of his tongue and concentrated instead on the stories his parents shared; of dreamy days in faraway lands where kings went to war on the backs of elephants and where goddesses possessed more arms than were strictly necessary. Unlike his brothers who grew suspicious at the variations that coloured every retelling, Thomas accepted them all, until the past became as real to him as the present he struggled with.

One morning, as he hunted for hedgehogs in the bushes of the plain, Thomas told his father that he would have liked to have met Angha and Sohan. Mihai dragged himself up from the scrub to pinch his son's cheek.

"Well, in some ways you have, Thomas. Their blood is in yours and when you need their help they'll fly to your side. All they ask in return is that you respect their good name and stay true to the life they have given you."

"By sticking to the rules and stuff?"

"By sticking to the rules and stuff, but also by taking care of those around you."

Thomas paused to consider his father's words, but he couldn't marry the sentiment with his limited experience.

"Not everyone takes care, Dad."

"Mostly they do."

"Grandma didn't; she wanted to starve me."

Mihai scratched at his scalp, itchy from the heat and the weight of his hair. A father's instinct told him to lie to his son, but he dismissed the deceit because to lie would be for his own benefit, no one else's.

"The biggest problem I had with your grandmother was that she spoke without thinking, a failing not uncommon amongst women. Had she taken the time to appreciate what she said, she'd have known that starvation would have left you sick and quite possibly dead. It's unlikely she'd have wanted that to happen, and even if she did, I'd have never allowed it."

Thomas's eyes widened at having his death discussed in such a matter-of-fact fashion, and under his breath he quickly blessed his father's legs for bringing him to the rescue. He then followed the blessing with silent prayers to the goddess and the Virgin, thanking them for making his father the one authority in their tent – as well as the wider community.

Following the death of the previous chief, Mihai had become the head of the sixty or so families that made up their *kumpania*. He wasn't the boss, or the ruler of a kingdom, he was simply a voice of reason elected by the majority to keep his head when those about him couldn't. When squabbles erupted, he was called in to adjudicate. If warranted, he administered justice the traditional way through curses, fines and – in the most heinous of cases – banishment. When arguments involved other groups, Mihai was one of several chiefs who met to discuss the roots of the discord and find a solution.

"We don't have much apart from each other and, if we don't look after our own, we stand to lose everything," his father instructed. "Let the foreigners scrap amongst themselves. The Romani survive because we all walk together. And long may it be so."

By the age of twelve Thomas stood as tall as his father and as lean as his brothers. After investigating his hands, his mother saw there was still more to come and accepting there was little she could do about it, she prayed to the Goddess Kali – as well as the Virgin Mary and the sacred soul of St Anne – to build him a woman to match the man he was threatening to become. In contrast, Thomas's father couldn't have cared less. He sensed the boy's power and it lay not in his arms, but in his mind. His son was thoughtful, considerate and eager to learn – soaking up the world's moments like a dry cloth in a river.

"It doesn't look especially grand these days, but Constantinople was once the richest place on earth," Mihai revealed as they turned off Middle Street to trade in the city's most densely populated and squalid suburb. Thomas gazed about him, trying to find proof of a better time beneath the layers of grime and grim reality. It wasn't easy. Away from the main thoroughfare, the streets lost their space and clean edges. Caked in mud and soiled straw, they twisted around towering tenements that blocked the best of the sunshine leaving the area looking sad and dejected. The residents were coarse and quite often angry, and amongst the piles of rotting litter stray dogs scratched for scraps close to where gaudily-painted women shouting for custom. Thomas's father scowled as he passed by. He wasn't a man who cared for prostitutes.

"They're as dirty as the dogs they hang with," he muttered. "Both meddling in areas they shouldn't."

Thomas looked at a dog sniffing around its tail. He then looked to the women, and tried not to blush.

Having negotiated the mesh of channels carrying slop and waste to an undisclosed place, Mihai stopped in front of a black wooden dwelling that appeared to be falling in on itself. He entered and walked up the creaking stairs, calling for business. A couple of doors opened and pots and promises were exchanged with little fuss. He descended the stairs and moved on to the next block, repeating the exercise along the length of the street until they came to a finish at the House of Pigs – a top floor room in the last tenement on their patch in which a farmer lived with two sows and an occasional parcel of piglets.

With their sacks satisfyingly heavy, Mihai and Thomas trudged home. They would return five days later to swap the mended items for money. It was pretty much the same routine, every week – wars and weather permitting. Meanwhile, his mother would peddle the family's wares in the squares of Constantinople. The takings were meagre, but they were enough to survive, and though it was tempting to search for fresh business when times grew lean, every square mile of the Great City had been carved up by previous generations and any attempt to thwart the unwritten agreement would not go unnoticed or unpunished. Besides, in a city rife with superstition, the women were capable of taking up the slack with their gift of divination and posies of blessings, and when times were particularly hard the orchards hugging the walls provided enough for a meal. Survival was attainable for the Romani because it had become second nature.

Back at their village, Thomas's brothers spent much of their days working. Being the youngest, and inherently clumsy, Thomas helped where he could, passing tools or water, or squeezing a leather bag half-buried in the ground that worked to keep a small fire alive as everyone hammered at copper squares ready to fix onto plates, vases and urns. It was a means to an end, but even in those days the craft was nothing Thomas aspired to. Copper left a smell on his hands he could taste and he promised himself that should he ever get the chance he'd seek work in the chaos of Constantinople's harbour; a glittering well that linked the past with the present and where the sweat of men mingled freely with the salt of the sea. It was a thrill Thomas experienced once a week when his father visited the Golden Horn to barter for spices and herbs. In front of creaking ships fastened to the land, Mihai would haggle, trade, and occasionally take, all that they needed, both gastronomically and spiritually.

During these weekly trips, as they ambled along the River Lykos towards the Gate of Adrianople, Mihai would school his son on how the world worked, and why the Romanies did things better. Once inside the city, he would point to the buildings they saw, that defied gravity and belief, opening their chained doors with knowledge gained from those who had trod the road before him. Among the first wonders on their route was the five-domed splendour of the Holy Apostles; once the final resting place of all of Byzantium's emperors, until it ran out of space in 1028.

"So many emperors have come and gone," Mihai remarked. "I tell you; the Great City rejects her rulers more often than a snake sheds its skin. Every few years a new challenger steps forward or a new claimant to the throne and the old emperor inevitably winds up in jail with his eyes gouged out."

As Mihai pretended to skewer his eyes with his fingers, a couple of nobles rode by. Dressed in all their finery, and sitting upon horses that shone with good health, their large noses pointed upwards, towards the heavens. Thomas gazed at the men, imagining their pale cheeks lined with hot blood pouring from sockets burned black and left empty.

"Have you ever seen one of the Emperors?"

"No, not me," Mihai admitted. "I prefer to keep my distance given their habit of dying. But the great-grandfather of your great-grandfather once saw one, shortly before his subjects killed him. They called him Andronicus the Terrible due to his murderous habits and heavy taxation. When his time came, the people severed his right hand and threw him into prison. Several days later he was blinded in one eye and paraded before the masses on a close-to-dead camel. The rabble beat him, stoned him, pelted him with filth. Finally, they poured boiling water over his head before hanging him by his feet until he died. The great-grandfather of your great-grandfather was astonished. He said he'd rarely seen such brutality since the last Emperor died."

Moving eastwards, along Middle Street and past the huge aqueduct that brought water from the rivers of Thrace, several columns speared the skies, appearing behind the roofs of mansions that lined the road which was now terraced on either side. Many of the monuments bore the names of dead emperors – making them a work in progress – and most of them had lost their statues thanks to regular earthquakes and wars.

When Middle Street met the Triumphal Way, Thomas and his father turned left into a vast square known as the Forum of Theodosius, the location of yet another column that stood as tall as seven men. At the bottom, a doorway led to a spiral staircase. Despite Thomas's pleas, his father refused to climb it, insisting that small spaces in high places were an invitation to murder. His mother later dismissed the notion, claiming her husband's reticence had more to do with the price of the entrance fee. Also commanding attention in the square was another huge statue dedicated to another dead Emperor. This one sat astride a horse whose giant hooves hung in their air, threatening to crush a man on the ground. The Emperor was Theodosius, but time had erased the identity of the pitiful figure at his feet.

"He could have been anyone," Mihai admitted, "one of the Latins, or the Venetians, or the mercenary Spaniards. He might even have been an unfortunate tax dodger. I tell you boy..."

"There's nothing more dangerous than the taxman!" Thomas finished and Mihai laughed because his boy learned fast.

In the last of the great squares, which was home to yet another statue of yet another emperor – which had lost some of his gravitas thanks to a family of herons currently nesting on the regal head – Mihai pointed towards the vast expanse of St Sophia, "the greatest church in the whole of Christendom".

"Or at least it was," he added, "before the Latins stole the gold from its altar. I swear those foreigners would steal anything that wasn't nailed down – even Christ Himself."

"But Christ *was* nailed to the Cross," Thomas remarked. His father sighed in reply.

"I was trying to be funny, son."

Contemplating his father's exasperated face, Thomas tried to rectify his mistake by laughing with implausible gusto. By his side, his mother stopped walking, dragging him into her stare. Her gaze wasn't so much perplexed as wary.

"I'm not touched by God," Thomas assured her.

"I never said you were," she replied. However, they both knew it had crossed her mind. Retardation was not unknown in her line.

On the Sundays that Thomas's mother accompanied them into the city it was at St Sophia that she would take her leave, so she might beg for alms from the faithful. If pickings were slim, she would venture inside to watch the spectacle of men and women writhing against the church's marble pillars, believing they possessed the power to heal. She would then head home, chuckling to herself. Meanwhile, Thomas and his father followed the scent of the sea and the cry of the gulls that led them to the glittering blue well of the Golden Horn.

With every inch of his mammoth being, Thomas loved the harbour. The breeze soothed his limbs, alleviating an ache caused by the constant strain of growing, and when he faced the water, he breathed in freedom. The harbour transported him to a place where another time played on the wind. It was the landing dock of all the colours of the world and, as his father talked him through the tastes and smells of their heritage – just as his own father had done and his father before that – it was the place Thomas felt most connected to the ghosts of his ancestors.

"You should never dwell on the past, but you should never forget it either," his father once advised and Thomas promised he never would.

On the way home, with their arms loaded with bags of ginger, cardamom, nutmeg and garlic, it became something of a tradition to stop a while at the Hippodrome where they would buy two tankards of wine and a couple of peaches for a copper coin. It was there that they met with Romanies from other clans who brought their bears to dance for the crowds. Every encounter brought news; some of it funny, some of it sad, and some of it worrying. In the eclectic mix of their language, weddings, births and deaths were revealed in the same breath as a Sultan's manoeuvres and the machinations of the Christian elite. Mihai instructed Thomas to heed it all, insisting that a lack of knowledge was the biggest obstacle in making a wise decision.

"A good wife is as hard to find as a good life, and you'll discover neither if you don't keep your ears open."

Taking the knife from his pocket, Mihai cut up a peach and handed it to his son before continuing his quest for knowledge via a passing spoon-maker. Thomas looked about him, his eyes settling on the space that had once housed the Calydonian Boar. The bronze figure had long ago been melted into coins, but Thomas could still picture the beast. According to his father, one of the emperors had believed the statue to be his alter ego, and when the old ruler's body began to fail, he ordered his craftsmen to sculpt a new set of testicles for the Boar – believing it would restore the same parts on him. Even to a twelve-year-old boy the notion seemed ludicrous, but as his eyes fell on the darting shadow of a cutpurse weaving through the crowd, he saw how easily a fool and his money could be parted.

By the time Thomas turned fourteen he was a good head taller than any man in his village. He possessed a handsome beard and he was deemed ready to take a wife. Two years later – after an agonising search and some brutal bartering – his parents found him one in the robust figure of a daughter of one of the Romani musicians camped outside Adrianople. Her name was

Talaitha, but Thomas called her Tally and for a while he wasn't sure what to do with her. As fate would have it, Tally had been prepared for such an eventuality and a year later she gave birth to a baby so beautiful they called her Callista. Taken by surprise, for his innocence far extended his height, Thomas wept when Tally revealed their daughter – unable to comprehend how something so small could wield such fear and immense power.

"Thank you," he whispered, unable to tear his eyes from the child.

Being of sterner stuff, Tally took the baby and walked away – to hide her own happiness in the palms of the foreigners who occasionally queued along the river to be told their good fortune.

Shortly after Callista arrived, Constantinople was engulfed in a new wave of violence bringing a civil war that pitted the elite against nobles-with-a-gripe and peasants who had grown sick of the rampant corruption and burdensome taxes. Belonging to neither one nor the other, most of the Romanies waited for a winner to emerge before venturing back into the city. However, as the Venetians and the Genoese had also embarked on another of their sporadic sea wars, food started to become a luxury no one could find. In other times, Thomas' *kumpania* might have simply moved on, but after fleeing the Turks in the east and witnessing the God-sanctioned cruelty of the Latins in the west they decided to stay put.

"Better the devil you know," Thomas's mother muttered, and the majority of the Romanies appeared to agree.

Having spent much of his childhood watching how the world worked, Thomas didn't spend the war idly. Without a word to anyone – out of fear his plan might fail – he took a spade and diverted the life of the River Lykos towards patches of green in which he'd sown rows of beans and potatoes. The *kumpania* nodded at his endeavours and waited. Thomas next organised his brothers and a number of other young men into raiding parties, and under the cover of night they crept into the Great City to pick through the spoils of chaos. One way or another, the Romanies got by.

"I'm proud of you all," Mihai told his sons some months into the war as they reaped a meagre harvest of beans and potatoes which they duly shared among the other families.

"You have to look after your own," Thomas replied with a smile.

Mihai raised an eyebrow; surprised and proud that he had somehow brought up a son deserving of the stature fate had given him. Though nothing was said, Thomas read the sentiment in his father's eyes. Sadly, it was to be the last time in a long time that he would feel such satisfaction in his achievements because once Thomas stopped growing the world reacted by collapsing around him.

In his 28th year, shortly after the Greeks had settled on Emperor Andronicus III and two days after his mother passed away, Thomas suffered his first fit. It arrived in the night as he slept. Oblivious to the commotion he had caused, he woke ready to face a new day only to be confronted by the bruised cheek of his wife. When he lifted the youngest of his three daughters she struggled in his arms and cried to be released. Thomas was aghast.

"It wasn't you. It was something that took you," Tally assured him, whilst pressing a tea-soaked rag to her face. Thomas shook his head, unable to speak for shame.

Later that morning he turned to his father, who raised his eyebrows, scratched his head, and promptly fetched one of the older men to purify his son's home. On the patriarch's instructions, Thomas also organised a feast he could barely afford in honour of St Anne, in the hope that the Virgin's mother might intercede with the Almighty on his behalf. Unfortunately, six months later, when Thomas rubbed the sleep from his eyes to find his wife missing a tooth, he realised it would take something stronger than the power of prayer to remove the stench of his disgrace.

Ignoring Tally's protests and the concerns of his family, Thomas banished himself from the *kumpania*, fearing the pollution possessing him would only spread if left unpunished. Naturally, he asked his father to take care of his wife and daughters and after unlinking a crying child from his leg, he bid Tally farewell. Though his wife was distraught, she refused to reveal her fury in front of the others; insisting loudly that her husband acted for the good of them all.

"We'll wait for you," she promised in a whisper, and Thomas drank in his wife's strong face. He wished he could kiss her, but as they were stood in full view of the community he turned away, deciding he was battling enough sin as it was. As he walked away, he shut his eyes, hoping to trap the image of his wife in his head. She was no slip of a girl, that was for sure, and her wild hair was forever locked in battle with the scarf she wore, but he could honestly say he had never noticed a lovelier woman. Thomas felt blessed and yet cursed. And though he'd never told Tally, because it simply wasn't done, he loved his wife dearly.

Parking his troubles further along the River Lykos, out of sight of all he had known, Thomas picked over his life and where it had gone wrong. As the sun set, he was no closer to an answer. The cause of his downfall was as mysterious to him as the stars hanging in the black sky, and he felt paralysed by ignorance. All of his life he had followed his father's example and behaved according to the Romani code. He had controlled his temper, he had prayed and bathed, and he had worked hard and honestly from the moment he could carry a sack. He had even believed himself to be a good husband until he smacked his wife in the mouth.

Thomas surveyed the items he had brought with him, dumped onto the dry grass at his feet. It wasn't much – a blanket, two shirts, a pair of trousers and a jerkin. Even so, the more he stared, the more he smelt his own pollution. Unable to deny his senses, he took a flint from his pocket, sparked up a fire and burnt the lot. By the time he found sleep he didn't feel any cleaner, only colder.

The next day, with nothing to call his own and no instruments to work with, Thomas walked to the Great City to find work in the one place he had known peace – along the docks of the Golden Horn. Having matured into a giant among men, employment came quickly and for a handful of coins he lifted, loaded and carried whatever he was told to. Thomas proved to be tireless, and quite often speechless, traits that appealed to the ships' factors. And though the sun was merciless, he never wilted in the heat and he never cheated his employers. Of course, when a sack of spices fell his way, he accepted his good fortune and took enough to flavour his meat before selling the rest to the apothecaries lining the city's squares.

In the evenings, once Thomas left the harbour for his spot by the river, a distance of five or more miles, he would continue to work on a shelter he had no interest in. Once the sun set, he routinely prayed for his wife and children, and tried to find a reason for their separation. Increasingly his thoughts turned to his ancestors – and how he might appease them.

For two months Thomas laboured at the docks, sweating his penance upon the cobbles of the harbour that rang with the barks of a thousand men in a dozen or more languages. Every colour and creed traded along the Golden Horn: Italians sailed in bearing gold and wool; Russians offered swords, amber and fur; the Bulgarians dealt in linen and honey; and the Arabs and Jews peddled spices, perfumes, porcelain and carpets. In the mix and the heat, fights frequently broke out, and if Thomas was in reach, he would wade in to stop the brawl before knives were pulled and blood was spilt. With greater wars being waged in the empire, such skirmishes were relatively harmless, and usually the product of drink and stale resentments. Besides, there was a common enemy among them, despised by every man at the harbour, and one day it revealed its face to Thomas when the writhing mass of labourers around him suddenly dispersed. The first time this happened, Thomas failed to take notice, intent as he was on getting the job done and returning home to reflect. Before he realised his error, he was looking down a sharp nose protruding from panes of smoky quartz. The man identified himself as Crallus, one of the Emperor's tax collectors, and Thomas swore he heard his father's moan of despair riding the breeze.

"Where do you lodge?" the taxman demanded.

"Out of the city."

"One of the Egyptians, are you? The curious Atsingani?"

"If you like."

Crallus snorted. Using a thumbnail, he picked roughly at a nostril.

"Have you paid your hearth tax?" he demanded.

Though the inspector's men rarely ventured into Romani territory on account of the ferocious curses the women rained upon their heads, Thomas nodded.

"Well, aren't you the model citizen?" Crallus sneered. "Hand over your permit."

At this point, Thomas had to admit he didn't have one.

"Well, if you work in the city you must pay for the privilege. When did you start?"

"This morning."

"Can anyone vouch for that?"

"The man who hired me before his boat sailed."

"How convenient."

The taxman's lips pulled back, revealing teeth that were as black as his fingernails. With his thin lips and sharp face, Thomas was reminded of a rat, albeit one armed with a quill, which Crallus subsequently took from his satchel. "What's your name?"

"Andronicus."

Crallus peered above his spectacles. "Are you being funny?"

"Is honouring your Emperor a joke?"

The taxman held Thomas's stare until the effort of looking up became too much.

"Andronicus," he wrote. "Two copper coins."

"I haven't been paid yet."

"Then I'll come back tomorrow, which would be a personal inconvenience requiring an extra coin."

Thomas briefly considered the merits of further debate, but as he had grown tired of the man he dug into his pockets. Crallus took the coins, licking at the spittle that had formed on his lips as he did so.

"I'll see you in a month," he crowed.

"Not if I see you first," Thomas assured him, and because he was a man of his word, the next occasion the crowd suddenly thinned, he made sure to go with it.

Three months into his exile, Thomas was surprised, and then anxious, to observe his father pushing his way through the squall of sailors and traders to reach him.

"What's happened?" he demanded, his concern overriding good manners. He wiped the sweat from his brow onto a bare arm. "Is Tally sick, or one of the girls?"

"Everyone's fine," his father informed him. The day was as hot as the devil's breath and he leant against the wagon Thomas was loading. "I've come to see you, son, that's all. It's time you came home."

Thomas relaxed his shoulders before deftly steering his father out of the path of a cart moving haphazardly along the cobbles. Mihai muttered a curse under his breath.

"It's madness here, and hot as hell. How do you stand it?"

Thomas shrugged and looked for a slither of shade between the bakeries and sausage sellers. Perhaps it was the harsh glare of the sun, but his father seemed to have aged in the few months he had been gone. He looked smaller and greyer than Thomas remembered, and it seemed as though the confidence had been knocked from his eyes. Flagging down a passing vendor Thomas bought a couple of peaches, which he peeled with a knife.

"That used to be my job," Mihai murmured as his son passed over the fruit.

"Can I not buy my own father a peach?"

"I'd prefer to have your company at home," Mihai replied before shaking his head at the chaos around them. "It looks like hard work you've found here."

"It is, but the money is good, which reminds me..." Thomas delved into his pocket and passed over a purse. "I've been wondering how to get this to Tally."

Mihai weighed up the bag in his hand. "That's a lot of coin."

"I've had little cause to spend it. I also make extra selling spices. The apothecaries here are better stocked than the grocers."

"A Greek and his money..." Thomas's father cast his hooded eyes around the harbour, reassessing it in the face of the fortune he now held. "You seem content here."

"I couldn't say I'm content, but the harbour's been good to me."

"But it's not your home, son, and you've been away long enough."

Thomas slid down the wall, coming to rest on his haunches. He wiped the sweat from his face with a handkerchief.

"I can't come back yet," he insisted softly, "and by rights you shouldn't come here asking me. Banishment doesn't work if you simply choose a different place to meet."

"True, but you haven't been banished, Thomas. There was no court, there was no order. You took it upon yourself to leave."

"I beat up my wife."

"It was the sleep that damaged her, not the man."

"Perhaps so, but I need to find a reason for it – and a solution. Nothing has changed, Dad."

Mihai gazed at his son, his sharp eyes clouding with confusion. Again, Thomas shrugged.

"There are mornings I wake up to find I've pulled the roof on top of me," he explained.

Mihai dipped his head, now understanding why his son kept his distance. After a moment's pause, he finished the peach and moved to wash his hands in a nearby drum.

"I did wonder," he admitted, "which is why I've also been giving your problem some thought. It appears to me that your troubles arrived shortly after your bones stopped growing."

"Meaning what?"

"I'm not rightly sure, but what if the meat inside of you – say, in your head – hasn't stopped growing? Maybe that's why you struggle in the night. Maybe it's bursting to come out."

Thomas raised one of his thick eyebrows in consideration, feeling a vague sense of revulsion.

"And if you're right what's the solution?" he asked.

"We could drill a hole in your skull."

As Thomas paused to weigh up the option, his father knocked his head with the back of his hand to reveal he was joking. For the first time in many months, Thomas felt a smile stretch his face.

"I'll figure this out, Dad, I promise. I know there's an answer to be had. In the meantime, I'll tread carefully. Perhaps – if you think it won't cause too much trouble – I'll return to the village with every new moon, to bring what I've earned. Then, if one day I've fixed this problem, I'll stay."

Despite the shake of his head, Mihai's lips accepted his son's wishes and after telling Thomas to walk with God, he returned home – to give Tally the money she was due, and to deliver the hope she had asked for.

That evening, as Thomas cooked a bony fish over an open fire he chewed over his father's words until he eventually found a plan in the flames that he watched. It was one that he hoped would appeal to the vanity of his ancestors, and relieve some of the pressure possibly building inside his head. Thomas would become a man of letters, and once he had learned them, he would write them all down.

Within the Great City schools were as prevalent as the opium dens their students frequented. However, with seats of learning requiring money, and the kind of information Thomas wasn't willing to part with, he decided against them. For a second, hardly more, he contemplated the docks as a potential place of study, having witnessed men scratching chalk lines onto boards, but he'd seen little more to warrant any inquiry. Therefore, he turned to the only other area he was vaguely acquainted with – the streets selling potions to the sick.

Finding himself not only ignorant but in need of a cure himself, the more Thomas thought about this idea the more it appealed to him. But who should he go to? The physicians were at the pinnacle of their profession and out of the price range of most. Below them came the surgeons, somewhat cheaper but still nothing Thomas could afford. And though their cousins, the barber surgeons, charged less for their services and also gave haircuts, Thomas was offended by the sight of their bloody rags which they hung out to dry in front of their stores. In the end, he looked to the apothecaries, some of whom he knew, and that's where he found Michael.

Slightly built with a frown etched into his face by years of privation, Michael was struggling to pay for a handful of herbs that were barely enough to season a stew when Thomas stepped in line behind him, carrying a sack of Spanish garlic.

"This is an offence to the sick," Michael muttered as he released a copper coin from his reluctant fingers. Pocketing the money with a grin, the apothecary was clearly unmoved.

"We all have to make a living, Doctor."

"And I'll be sure to tell my patients that when I no longer have the means to help them," Michael replied. He spoke with an accent Thomas couldn't place.

Scratching roughly at the crown of his dirty-blond hair, the doctor turned to leave and Thomas was momentarily startled by the soft grey of his eyes.

"Pardon me," Michael apologised as he collided with another man in his haste to vacate the premises. It was a courtesy Thomas appreciated in a city famed for its rudeness and greed. With a shake of his head to the waiting apothecary, he left the premises, still clutching the sack of garlic he had come to sell, and followed the good doctor.

Weaving through the mayhem of the Forum of Theodosius, Thomas looked for an opportune moment to deliver his proposition. To his surprise, the man walked swiftly and within the space of two blocks Thomas was losing the thread of his practised speech as he concentrated solely on keeping up. After turning into Middle Street, the doctor made a right at the Holy Apostles before disappearing into a tired-looking building that clung to the edge of the last stretch of paving before it dissolved into mud. Above a wooden door was a faded painting of a urine flask. Thomas knocked brusquely and entered. Inside, he squinted into the gloom that greeted him.

"I'm closed!"

Thomas looked for the man behind the voice, but found only his back as he rummaged in a closet. Waiting for the doctor to emerge, Thomas inspected the room that was quite obviously some sort of surgery. Taking up most of the space was a desk piled high with papers and Thomas bent to look, finding words he wanted to read and diagrams he couldn't hope to understand. Beneath his feet, the floor felt sticky. Above his head, flies lay motionless in blankets of cobwebs. The place was a mess.

Consumed by second thoughts, Thomas was about to leave when the doctor finally emerged from his cupboard. One look at Thomas and the colour drained from his face. He backed away before stumbling into a chair that wobbled on uneven legs. He then slumped into the seat, defeated.

"Is this how you collect your taxes now?" he asked wearily.

Thomas looked behind him, though it was clear they were alone.

"I told you I needed more time," the doctor continued. "But go on; take what you like. I've got nothing to hide or even worth pawning."

"I'm not a tax collector," Thomas replied, wiping at his hands as he spoke, as if to clean the dirt of association from them.

"Only the muscle, eh?"

"Not even that," Thomas said. He shifted awkwardly on his feet. "I'm looking for help," he finally admitted.

The doctor looked up, his grey eyes narrowing, his mind working through the possibilities.

"You don't look sick."

"Is illness that apparent?"

In spite of his fear, the man laughed. It was a gentle sound and quickly over.

"So, you *are* sick?"

"Not exactly," Thomas admitted. He gestured to an empty chair and the doctor invited him to sit. Somewhat hesitantly, because he hadn't prepared for this particular conversation in his mind, Thomas tried to explain the purpose of his visit. As he spoke the medic shifted between doubtful and intrigued.

"So, you want to write Greek?"

"Not exactly," Thomas replied. "I want to write in the language of my people."

"And that would be Egyptian?"

"Well, no. Not..."

"Exactly?" the doctor finished, and they both smiled at the repetition.

Thomas took a deep breath and delivered his proposal in a manner they might both understand. When he finished, the doctor raised his eyebrows indicating the task might be challenging, but not impossible. Instructing Thomas to speak a few words in his own language, he scratched a quill across the scrap of paper closest at hand. He then repeated the phrase in the softer tune of his accent. Thomas was impressed and Michael, as he then introduced himself, was also rather pleased with his effort.

"I've never spoken Egyptian before."

"Hard to believe," encouraged Thomas.

Reaching under his desk, the doctor produced two clay goblets and a flask. The flask looked suspiciously like the one painted above the door. Pouring two generous measures of wine, Michael revealed he was French born, unmarried and broke.

"I came from Paris twenty years ago to learn from the greatest minds in medicine, little realising that the greatest minds in medicine cost the greatest amount of money. I was penniless within a year."

Thomas commiserated and cast an eye about the room. On the wall, circular charts displayed a series of balls connected by lines. There was a naked but nonspecific drawing of a human divided into parts, and a number of knives were sat on a shelf. Along the windowsill stood a collection of medicine bottles in every size, shape, and colour.

"I can help you with those," Thomas mentioned. Michael followed his gaze.

"With the windows?"

Thomas found himself laughing again. "If you like, but I was thinking more of the spices. I get them for a third of what you pay in the city."

"Really? And how do you manage that?"

"I have contacts."

The revelation brought a flicker of apprehension to Michael's steely gaze as he contemplated the wisdom of doing business with a stranger possessing 'contacts' who happened to be more mountain than man. A minute later his jaw relaxed as he decided his situation could hardly get any worse.

"Shall we start tomorrow?"

Thomas nodded in agreement and handed over his garlic.

Following a pattern of trial and error, mixed with moments of hilarity and utter confusion, Thomas and Michael settled on a largely Latin alphabet with a smattering of Greek to form words in a language only one of them understood. Having been informed of the cause that had driven Thomas to seek help, the doctor also endeavoured to find a medical reason for the nocturnal violence that had left his student isolated. In the end he concluded that the problem was psychological rather than physical. The man appeared to be in enviable health, if unusually large. With this in mind, Michael investigated Thomas's lifestyle, his customs and beliefs – trying to pin a reason on his subconscious sufferings. During the course of their conversations, the Frenchman grew increasingly of the opinion that the *Atsingani* were not only aloof, but impossibly reckless. Whilst modern thinking extolled the virtue of washing one's hands and feet, regular bathing was considered to be highly dangerous because it opened the skin's pores and left the body vulnerable to attack. But if Thomas was to be believed, his people bathed at the drop of a hat, the conclusion of an argument, or the turn of the clock.

"It's complicated," Thomas replied when Michael asked why. However, the greater truth was that much of the logic had been lost in transition.

Paradoxically, where Michael saw only differences, Thomas perceived similarities between his customs and the methods of the foreigners. His people's rituals might appear elaborate or bizarre to the outsider – such as separate washing bowls for different clothes or the danger of handling anything below the waistline – but Thomas noted the amount of time Michael spent examining the stools and cloudy urine of his patients, and for Thomas, this was proof that the most dangerous part of the body was at the bottom end. Furthermore, the Monthly Flower that Michael called 'menstruation' apparently released 'bad humours' – something his ancestors must have known when they ordered their women out of the house until the job was done.

"There are four humours in the human body," Michael explained as Thomas sat at his desk writing lines of clumsy-looking letters. "The humours are yellow bile, black bile, blood and phlegm. According to Hippocrates, the master of all things medical, menstruation is the body's way of ridding itself of bad humours which, if left unchecked, can stagnate in the extremities. Obviously, men are different therefore we have to cut them to release the built up 'pollution', as you call it."

Thomas released the cramp in his fingers and accepted the sense of the doctor's knowledge. Unlike women, who could purge themselves of pollution, men had no natural way of cleaning their bodies. In hindsight, his father's joke about drilling a hole in his head might not have been as laughable as they had thought. When Thomas mentioned this to Michael, the doctor's eyes widened in appalled disbelief. No, he insisted, quite firmly. There was more to releasing bad humours than simply creating a vent. Bloodletting required the examination of various charts to help ascertain the correct vein to slice. Other factors that had to be taken into account included the season, weather, and age of the patient. There were also strict rules governing the amount of blood to be shed. As he listened, Thomas shuddered at the amount of calculation involved. Sometime later, having been invited to witness the practise of bloodletting, he concluded that the doctor's surgery wasn't so much a place of healing as a curiously precise butcher's block. Medicine was a mystery to him, and the more he discovered the more mysterious it became.

"Some physicians consult the planets to help them prepare for coming epidemics," Michael explained when Thomas asked about the chart displayed on the wall showing a series of balls connected by lines. "Any conjunction involving Saturn, Jupiter and Mars tends to be bad. You see, Jupiter is dominated by earth and water. Mars is hot and dry. The two inevitably enflame one another."

"And Saturn?"

"Well, nobody's quite sure what Saturn does, but most of the experts agree that its combination with anything can only be terrible."

Thomas inspected the ringed-entity of Saturn a little more carefully, wondering aloud whether the planets were lining up for any new bedevilment.

"Not that I know of," Michael answered, "but as they all move in circles it can only be a matter of time."

At the return of the full moon, Thomas headed home to give Tally his wages. For close to two seasons, he had been starved of his family and it had taken a lion's strength to stay strong. But Thomas wasn't really a lion – he was a man – and he very nearly ran away again when he arrived at his home to find not only his wife and children waiting for him, but also the head of every family in their *kumpania*.

"We've missed you," Tally whispered as she leant over his shoulder to pass the meat she had been saving since the moon started to reveal her shape.

"I've missed you too," Thomas admitted, and the men who had gathered around the fire pretended not to hear.

After eating, Thomas spoke a while with the men of the group, listening to their complaints and their successes and any news that had drifted in from their brothers further afield. Once the formalities were over, he visited the tent that housed his wife and children. In front of a pile of burning twigs that kept the flies at bay and the good luck in, Tally ran her fingers through the mass of her hair and arched her back to reveal her form. Thomas reacted with predictable longing, but he somehow kept his head – even as he watched his wife's bravery crumble before his eyes. In his heart, he was more upset than he could possibly admit and so he offered what comfort he could by explaining how he was working to resolve their situation.

"I think it might work," he concluded. "I've now got the letters in my head and I'm slowly learning how to use them."

"Perhaps when you're done you could teach the girls," Tally replied, determined to stay positive. And Thomas smiled because he had been thinking much the same thing.

"And how are the nights?" his wife asked, carefully approaching the reason that kept them apart.

"Some nights are better than others," he admitted, "but lately, I don't know, maybe..."

And because Thomas didn't know, and his wife knew only that she loved him, when he left in the early hours of the morning, she tasked one of their girls to follow him. When the child returned three hours later with a smile on her face, Tally packed their meagre belongings into two blankets.

The following day, as Thomas sat by the river bank writing in his journal, he saw Tally and their three girls approaching. He was at once pleased, livid, and thankful. For the briefest of moments, he considered cowing their courage in a rant of disapproval, but Tally's face was set and the truth was he needed her.

"Fine," he accepted as they sat themselves at his fire. "Let it be so. But if you're staying, there are rules to be followed."

That night, after their daughters found sleep, Tally tied her husband's arms with the rope he had bought some weeks previously – in the hope that his family might appear to fight his illness together.

Away from their community, Thomas and Tally entered a new phase of their lives, one that not only involved ropes. With no one but their daughters to steal their time, they spoke more in two weeks than they'd managed in the previous thirteen years. Thomas was not only surprised, but charmed all over again. Tally was resourceful, brilliant, and completely opinionated. While he had been hauling crates from passing ships, she had been bewitching the gullible with staggering success. Of course, it was no surprise to him that his wife had the gift, but far from being steeped in feminine magic, she said the skill had come from a lifetime of looking in, and noticing what others no longer had the ability to see.

"The foreigners are bloated with self-importance," she explained. "Civilisation has blunted their instinct and made them fearful. They believe themselves so worldly, yet they need to be told how they feel in order to make it real, and really, that's not such a mystery. It's not so hard to read sadness in a pair of eyes nor is it difficult to recognise happiness. Similarly, a person's nature is as obvious to me as the clothes that they wear or the perfume hiding their smell. Some people attract bad luck, others know nothing but fortune; it is in their look, in their carriage, in everything they say and do. But this society, I see it drowning in today. People no longer prepare for tomorrow. Worse than that, they only want to know of their own part in this world and what's coming to affect them. The foreigners are selfish and self-obsessed. You can tell them pretty much anything."

"Not all of them are bad," Thomas argued.

"No, not all of them are bad," Tally agreed, knowing her husband was thinking of his French friend because the thoughts that passed over his eyes were no stranger to her either. "But they are not like us, Thomas, and their difference infects them all to some extent."

"And what about their blood that runs in our veins?"

"We haven't so much of it that it's tainted our own. When our numbers grew, our women stopped looking for it."

Thomas considered his wife's face. It was both beautiful and fierce, framing a stare that could pierce eyeballs. It was no wonder people accepted what she told them. Still, she had a point; people had lost the ability to see past the day. One only had to look at Constantinople, once one of the world's most luxurious cities until her children devoured her, leaving only the bones for her enemies to gnaw on. After centuries as the envy of the Christian world, successive emperors had emptied her vaults, decimated her armies, sunk her navy and allowed the Latins to ravage her. If history repeated herself, there would be nothing left to fight over.

"And when that day comes, we'll move on," Tally stated firmly, somewhat startling Thomas. For all of the Empire's faults he considered Constantinople to be home.

A year after Thomas was reunited with his wife and children, his father died. There had been no sickness, no period of suffering, he simply went to bed and failed to wake up. Naturally, the community wept for their loss and honoured Mihai's life by burning his body and all that he owned. Within a week of his passing, they all packed their belongings and moved closer to his youngest son.

With little fuss, Thomas was duly elected the new head of the *kumpania,* in recognition of the strength of his convictions and his unshakeable manner. Though he was grief-stricken, he was humbled by the faith that had been placed in him and he carried the group's concerns on his wide shoulders and worked hard to keep harmony in their lives. Once he had settled into his new role, he further directed his wife and daughters to teach the letters they had learnt to anyone who came asking. Before the second summer was out, the word had spread via visits and marriage to many more tents within their scattered nation.

For many years, Thomas's *kumpania* thrived on the outskirts of Constantinople in much the same way as it had always done, albeit further downstream. The men fired copper plates while the women sold baskets and blessings, and the children grew up and into their own families and alliances. Under his leathery skin, Thomas's bones creaked. Time had faded his black beard into grey. He had found good men to pay for the hands of his daughters and they had rewarded him, frequently, with healthy, normal-sized, grandchildren. It was a period of relative peace during which Thomas not only waved goodbye to his youth, but also to the dreams that had plagued him. He had no idea whether his writing was the trick that kept the devil at bay or whether it was due to old age, but whenever Tally surrendered another tooth, he was simply glad to have played no role in it. Naturally, life was not without its troubles, but by and large Thomas had grown content and he was quietly looking forward to his twilight years – until the Emperor died and the world once again tipped into confusion.

Because Andronicus III had been somewhat frivolous with the finer details of his succession, the country descended into civil war on his death, with the nobles backing the late emperor's best friend and the rest of the Empire supporting his nine-year-old son.

"It's the Church that sits behind this chaos," Michael stated as Thomas helped him replace one of the perpetually loose shelves along the wall of his surgery.

Although the two men no longer shared a student-teacher relationship, Thomas still brought spices and herbs to the doctor in exchange for parchment and ink.

"The boy prince doesn't know his own birthday let alone his birthright," Michael continued. "Will you write the truth of that in your history one day?"

Thomas knocked a final nail into the wall and smiled. If the city's changes affected his life and those of his people, he promised to write of them.

"Every event has repercussions. No one is immune from them," Michael warned. "Food is dearer than gold these days; there are Turks on the loose; and the peasants follow a traitor who keeps a fully-manned ship in the harbour."

"Apocaucus?"

"Who else? He and the Patriarch have dripped poison into the ear of the Empress and she's turned on the one man who could have secured a clean succession with none of this upset, John Cantacuzenus."

Thomas held no interest in politics outside of his own *kumpania*, but even he had heard of Cantacuzenus. It was said the noble was the engine behind the wheel of the Byzantine machine.

"It'll settle soon enough," he declared, but Michael shook his head.

"I'm not so sure. The world is restless and the Empire is weak. I fear Constantinople is nearing her end."

Michael coughed his anxiety into a handkerchief. Stood next to Thomas he looked frail to the point of broken. Perhaps if he had taken a wife, he might have benefitted from her care. Instead, he was married to a city in which he had somehow become stuck.

"Constantinople's not finished yet," Thomas assured the man who had become his friend over the space of two decades. "Keep your head down and wait for her to find her feet."

Michael remained dubious because it was in his nature to be sceptical, but Thomas was eventually proved correct, though it took several years for Constantinople to find her feet and recover her balance. With the war wrecking the economy, the poor quickly forgot about their loyalty to the young prince, and the traitor Apocaucus was unceremoniously butchered by the nobles he had imprisoned. When the eastern part of St Sophia – the greatest church in the whole of Christendom – collapsed without warning, the locals took it as a seriously bad omen. Before the dust had time to settle, the superstitious were praying for the return of Cantacuzenus, and he duly obliged them by arriving under the cover of night accompanied by 1,000 of his soldiers. Within the walls of the Great Palace, peace treaties were drawn up, and hurriedly signed, and it was agreed that the late emperor's best friend would share the throne with the late emperor's son. The populace sighed with relief and all was again peaceful – until everyone inexplicably began dying.

Given their relative isolation, it took a while for the Romanies to realise that all was not well within Constantinople's walls, but when it became apparent that a curious illness was sweeping parts of the capital, Thomas responded by prohibiting all contact with the foreigners until further notice. Naturally, with the coins of the *Atsingani* staying away from the city, it was only a matter of time before the city came looking for them.

On a fresh spring morning, Thomas looked up from his breakfast to see the Emperors' colours approaching, along with ten or more horses. Leading the advance was a man Thomas instantly recognised despite the roll call of years since their last meeting, and as Crallus neared it became increasingly obvious that time had not been kind to the man. He had lost not only his hair, but also one arm.

Pulling his horse to a stop, the taxman briefly surveyed the waiting crowd before settling on Thomas. His eyes flickered as his brain tried to place him. He then released a thin grin.

"The giant from the boatyard," Crallus greeted. "It's been a long time."

"And yet it seems like only yesterday," Thomas replied.

"And yet it's not."

Crallus bent his head towards his one arm, to wipe away the sweat dripping from his nose. Thomas got to his feet. The man was clearly unwell and it made him uneasy.

"What do you want here?" he demanded.

"I'm the taxman, what do you think that I want?" Crallus sneered. "You can run from the city, but you can't hide from the treasury."

"And it appears you can no longer clap hands."

Though Thomas couldn't see Crallus's eyes beneath his dark glasses, he felt them boring into his skull.

"That quip is going to cost you extra," he warned, and the women who had gathered around Thomas reacted quickly to the threat.

Surging forward, with Tally taking the lead, they rained a barrage of colourful curses upon Crallus and his bodyguards. In their hands, they pummelled small bowls of dough, spitting their fury into the mixture before hurling it at the emperors' men. To everyone's surprise – not least the women's – Crallus responded by falling off his horse. One of the soldiers dismounted to help the taxman to his feet only to retreat in horror, quickly crossing his chest.

"He's dead!" he shouted to his men.

Without a word more, Crallus's bodyguards span their horses around and galloped back to the city.

For a while none of the Romanies moved as they tried to make sense of the moment. Perhaps nagged by a sense of responsibility, Thomas was the first to step up to the corpse. In the fall, Crallus's glasses had slipped from his nose, revealing opaque eyes. His mouth lay open, his remaining teeth were rotten to the root, and his throat was blackening with a rash. The marks were nothing Thomas had ever seen before and he ordered everyone to return to their homes.

"Purify them!" he shouted.

With no sense of shame, he then grabbed a plank of wood and shoved the taxman's body some distance from the village before setting it alight.

That afternoon, once the possible pollution that had ridden up to their homes had been neutralised in every possible way, the community gathered around the communal fire. Throwing handfuls of herbs into the flames, they discussed the taxman's strange passing. Some declared it a blessing from God, or a gift from their ancestors, even a sign of the Romanies good favour. Though Thomas nodded, he wasn't convinced, and when he looked to the horizon, he saw a snaking dust of galloping horses pulling carts from the city.

The next day, Thomas watched more traffic leaving Constantinople. Unnerved by the sight, he asked his brothers to accompany him to the highway. As they approached, every horse swerved from their path. If they got too close, men drew their swords, and a terror, like none they had ever witnessed, screamed from the faces that passed by. Eventually, Thomas was forced to shout for news, which a teenage girl supplied from the back of a fleeing wagon.

"The pestilence has come!" she screamed. Before Thomas could ask for more she was gone.

Armed with this small knowledge, the six brothers returned to the *kumpania*. As custom demanded, Thomas gathered the rest of the men to discuss their next move, but it was clear there was only one option worth taking; they had to move west. Unsurprisingly, after witnessing the taxman drop dead at their feet, there wasn't one dissenting voice, and within an hour everyone had dismantled their tents, gathered their children, along with their chickens and sheep, and loaded their lives onto wagons and horses. With everyone ready, Thomas embraced his wife and thrust the journal of his life into her arms. Tally was furious.

"It's the Frenchman, isn't it?" she shouted. "You're not coming with us. You're going in to get him out!"

Around Thomas' shoulders his brothers appeared, and he was reminded once again of being a duck in a nest of sparrows.

"Tally is right," he admitted, allowing them a moment's protest before raising his hand for silence. "Every good man deserves a chance at life. The doctor is my friend. He has been good to me, which means he has been good to us. Let me find him and bring him out. When a week has passed and I'm sure we carry no infection, we'll follow you. Leave signs on your path. I'll know where you are."

Unwilling to say more, Thomas walked briskly away, thankful for the gentle May rain that stopped his wife from reading the fear in his eyes.

Entering the Gate of Adrianople, as he'd done a thousand times before, Thomas was dumbstruck by the changes he found. The orchards lining the wall were littered with fallen fruit, decaying from neglect. The guardhouse was unmanned. Middle Street was deserted, save for cats and dogs staggering listlessly. Others lay in the road, their lifeless bodies humming with flies. In the mansions he passed, all the shutters were drawn. And the only sound was that of cartwheels rattling upon the cobbles, carrying corpses picked up from the steps of locked houses where they had been discarded as though they were rubbish. Not even the salt on the breeze could mask the stench of fear and death. Constantinople was a carcass, rotting from the inside, and Thomas was amazed at the speed of her demise.

Turning left at the Holy Apostles he stopped at the black door that was as familiar to him as his own home. One push confirmed it was bolted and Thomas hammered his fists upon the wooden frame until Michael eventually appeared. The doctor was pale, his eyes feverish, and he looked scared and old.

"You cannot stay," he warned.

"I know, and neither can you."

Michael smiled at his friend's words, a second later he started to weep. He hadn't expected such kindness and he found it overwhelming. Thomas allowed the man a moment to collect himself.

"Is there anything you wish to take with you?" he asked, but Michael was too stunned to answer. Seeing him shiver, Thomas grabbed a worn blanket from the back of a chair and after wrapping it around his friend's shoulders he lifted him into his arms, as though carrying a baby.

"This thing, this pestilence, it respects no man," Michael explained as the two of them sat among the debris and charred circles that had once been a Romani village. Thomas stoked the fire between them and urged the doctor to drink. Michael duly took a sip of wine before continuing. "For three days, I watched it eat its way from the harbour to the suburbs. They say it came in from the sea, from as far away as China, but I don't know. All I can say with any certainty is that it's merciless and it's swift – and there was nothing, absolutely nothing, I could do."

"You did your best," Thomas told him.

"I could have done more. I could have saved you."

Michael lifted his shirt, proving his point in the huge swellings bubbling beneath his arms. The thin skin that clung to the bones of his chest was mottled, almost purple, and sores seeped their disease along the length of his torso.

"I would never have left you there," Thomas replied easily, pulling down the doctor's shirt and tightening the blanket around his shoulders.

"If I'm lucky I'll last another three days," Michael muttered, "other men have fallen in one. I tell you this thing, this vile thing sent by man or the devil, it will kill us all – and that includes you, my good friend. Oh, my very good friend. I am so sorry Thomas, so indescribably sorry."

And having apologised, Michael lay down and never got up again.

Over the next couple of days, the doctor struggled with nightmares, but he never regained consciousness. Thomas continued to tip water into Michael's mouth, but eventually only the shallowest movement of his chest revealed he still lived. All too soon that also stopped. When it did, Thomas shed a tear and buried his friend the Christian way. Thomas was in his 47th year, Michael was perhaps a decade older, and he looked at the mound of earth that spelt the end of his life and he wished with all of his heart that Michael had known the happiness of a good marriage.

"Walk with God, my friend."

During the following days, that passed as slowly as weeks, Thomas comforted himself with thoughts of his family. After deciding on a week of quarantine, he idled away the hours by trying to guess which signs the *kumpania* would have left for him to follow. It was a nice game, and it served to chase the cold from his bones. But every day it grew harder to think straight, and no matter how high he built the fire, he could no longer get warm. The wet cough that seized his chest made him nauseous and unable to eat, and the skin under his breeches was slowly turning blue. Finally, when he coughed up blood, he decided he was done with pretending and he lay down. On the ground that stabbed as sharp as cut glass into his back, he prayed for his family and the souls of all the friends he had known. As he drifted between sleep and pain, he even imagined he saw Tally again. He protested, of course, but his arms had lost their power and she told him to hush.

"You think I'd allow you to leave me again?" she whispered.

Feeling his wife at his side, Thomas wept for her, because he needed her and he was frightened of dying alone.

"Oh, my beautiful man," Tally sang into his ear, "my beautiful Big Man."

Chapter Eight

The gathered Roma got to their feet, offering Marko a pat on the back as they went, expressing their sympathy through one Big Man down to another, locked in a different time. As the small crowd dispersed, Jack shook his head. His eyebrows twitched, perhaps in sympathy or the onset of headache. It was hard to tell which.

"Wow, the Black Death," had been his initial, and succinct, response to a tragedy that had obliterated millions. "You guys, you saw it all."

"Not only us," I replied. "A third of Europe died from the plague."

"Yes, of course, but, even so, it couldn't have been easy."

"Dying?"

"Dying, living, surviving... I once had dysentery. It was pretty bad, but the plague, well, it's a different ball game, isn't it?"

Jack reached for his bag and started packing away his paraphernalia, indicating the end of his interest. I watched – half-amused, half-perplexed – trying to discover what it was that Francoise saw in him. Despite the occasional urge to speak of things better left unsaid, the Frenchman was not unattractive; he was tall and broader than average with a whisper of grey brushing the roots of his thick, dark hair. However, middle age – coupled with easy living – had softened the once-strong chin, and the confidence he projected wasn't matched in his eyes. When I looked at him, I saw only effort and, in all honesty, it made my palms itch.

I got to my feet and Jack followed suit. After a quick tap of his jeans – to find his wallet in the place he had left it – he helped the Big Man clear away the chairs as Francoise reached into her handbag. She passed me several sheets of paper. Her open face was sincere.

"I thought these might be of interest. Originally French, but I translated them."

"What are they?"

"A few reports – nothing much – just to show that some people are trying to help."

As she stopped short of fully explaining, I took the papers from Francoise's manicured hands and acknowledged the kindness.

"It's nothing," she insisted, and I was struck once again by how her gaze flickered between coolness and the vulnerability of a thousand disappointments.

"One day you'll have to tell me what Monsieur Caron plans to do with my stories," I said, just as the Frenchman approached to give me the mug he had emptied.

"Until the next time," Francoise translated for him. As he turned away, she added more quietly, "Jack's an honest man, Mala. Please, don't worry yourself."

"Easy said," I replied, and she told me she knew.

With promises to return in a couple of days – sunshine permitting – Jack and Francoise waved goodbye to the few of us remaining and walked to their car, physically closer than they'd been the visit before. With a nod in their direction, the Big Man came to my side.

"There's something cooking between them two."

"What do you mean?"

"I mean romance."

I laughed at his observation, though it backed up my own.

"Have you developed the sight, Marko?"

"I don't need it," he replied. "I saw him pinch her bum on the way in here."

Over a lonely dinner of peppery beans, I read the papers Francoise had handed me. The first was from an organisation called the European Roma Rights Centre. They had written to the French President demanding an end to his policy of eviction and expulsion, insisting the plans would only reinforce discrimination and enflame public opinion against the Roma and Travellers.

"Nice to see someone gets it," I muttered to no one but myself. Grabbing a pen, I underlined the ERRC acronym provided in brackets.

On another sheet of paper, the organisation was again in attendance; lambasting the European Union for turning a blind eye to the plight of the continent's 16 million Romanies as well as the poverty and prejudice that made their lives unbearable in their countries of origin.

"Hear! Hear!" I applauded, tapping the spoon against my bowl before turning to the final page which simply revealed how unbearable our lives had actually become. As I read, I slid from mumbling defiance into silent depression.

In recent years, Copenhagen had requested government help to deport up to 400 Roma; Swedish police had expelled fifty for the non-criminal activity of begging; a caravan of 700 were chased out of Flanders; Italy was expelling thousands every year; Germany was expatriating children despite many being born there; and the Czech Republic, Hungary, Bulgaria, Slovakia, and the land of my birth, were all charged with widespread discrimination as well as physical attacks.

Needless to say, by the time Miko and Mirela returned home – tired and full-bellied – I felt as though I'd been buried alive, not under sand or stone, but under an accumulative hate.

Over the following days, my dark mood was tempered by the end of my 'flowering' and my family's return to the dinner table – or rather the linoleum covering the dirt outside our home. Traditionally, when the weather was good, we ate in the open air, flavouring our food with the smoke of a fire and the talk of our neighbours. In France, we dined al fresco because it was preferable to being poached alive inside a caravan that doubled as a microwave in the summer heat. Parked in the bowels of a small valley, the days were all-sun and no-breeze, and it was hotter than fire. As a consequence, and though I rarely covered my head, I tied my hair, up and away from my neck, using a thin cotton scarf.

"My God woman, you look like the girl I married," Miko declared, and because a compliment in the right place is as welcome as a longed-for wind, I kissed him.

"Lucky me," he said with a smile. "And if I'd said you looked like the girl I wanted to marry?"

Well, he quickly found out.

As Miko rubbed his ear, Bo walked briskly towards us, chased by Mirela.

"Bo's got something! Bo's got something!" giggled our daughter, clearly excited by whatever Bo had.

"I hope it's not syphilis," Miko quipped, and I clipped him again for wishing a *gadje* disease on one of our own.

Hiding something behind his back, Bo came to a halt in front of us. A broad grin stretched his handsome face and his eyes glinted with triumph and mischief.

"You'll love this," he stated before stepping forward to reveal his big surprise.

Miko and I looked at each other, suspecting we were missing something because on first glance he appeared to be holding a well-thumbed record cover.

"Have you gone into the antiques business?" Miko asked. "I thought you kids listened to CDs these days?"

Reaching for the album, Miko released a warm chuckle before handing it to me. "Oh my, Mala... Look who it is."

I took the record and looked at the face on it. The eyes were dark and somewhat dreamy, the left ear glinted with gold, and the neck was adorned with a bandana tied at a jaunty angle. Under a trilby hat, the hair was stylishly messy, and of a length that no doubt suited the fashion of the time.

"It's Jack."

"It sure is," confirmed Bo. "I found our famous visitor in a house clearance. Have a guess at the name of his record."

"Jacques spelt Jack?"

Bo grinned, but shook his head. Playing to the drama both Miko and Mirela begged him for an answer. Eventually, Rami's eldest ran a thick finger along the letters etched beneath Jack's face. "The record is called... '*My Gypsy Heart Beats On*'."

"Oh, good grief," I groaned, and Mirela giggled like the child she was.

"Is he a Traveller?" asked Miko, turning the album over to find a photo of Jack and his gypsy heart lolling on the steps of a painted wagon. "He's not Romani, surely? He doesn't understand a word we say."

"Hard to be sure," Bo admitted. "He might be one or the other – or just another singer peddling a gimmick."

"Can we listen?" Mirela interrupted, grabbing hold of the record, and Bo stroked her hair with the casual confidence of the admired.

"Of course we can, *shukariyo*, once Stevo finds us a record player."

Miko clapped his hands in approval. "If your brother manages that I'll buy him a beer!"

"Forget the beer, my friend; you might have to post bail. I told him to steal one."

It actually took Stevo two days to find a record player, a feat that cost him three hours at a car boot sale on the wrong side of Lyon and the "scandalous" sum of 10 Euros.

"A duck in a nest of sparrows," Bo sighed, and I smiled at the reference, appreciating the joke and glad to hear my stories finding a new home.

Despite popular opinion, Romanies weren't habitual thieves. Of course, thieves were not unknown in the community – as with every other nation in the world – though it seemed that petty crime was an offence of greater significance once it was tagged with the adjective 'gypsy'. As the saying went, 'The Romani steals a chicken. The non-Romani steals the farm.'

"Are we going to play this thing or look at it all night," Donka moaned as she came to sit by my side. In front of us Bo was tantalising the gathering crowd with the cover of Jack's musical masterpiece.

"The boy's a showman," I replied.

"The boy's a show off."

"And that."

Around us, our neighbours settled themselves on chairs, upturned buckets and worn-out tyres, their bodies aching from another day of scrap collecting and fruit-picking. In front of them an old Dansette record player sat on a table. It was attached to a cable leading from Marko's motor-home, and it held everyone's attention in a way that was mildly disconcerting.

"Now we'll see what the *gadjo* is made of," Rami grumbled as he took a seat in front of us. "You can always trust my boys to get to the heart of the matter."

"That'll be the *Gypsy Heart* of the matter," the Big Man corrected and everyone applauded the joke, despite the puns having worn thin over the past couple of days.

With theatrical loitering, Bo twiddled a few knobs and checked the cable before sliding the record from its sleeve. He blew hard on the vinyl, rubbed it with a handkerchief, and when the heckling got to a respectable level of irritation, he placed the record onto the platter and lowered the needle. The initial reaction was one of wary concentration.

Although the speakers were shot to pieces and the record scratched and jumped in places, the music was pleasant enough. A violin soared over steady beats and a number of tunes were catchy if simplistic. Obviously, the bursts of hilarity from those who understood the lyrics were somewhat distracting and, after the first play, Bo felt obliged to enlighten the non-French speakers among them. It appeared that Jack considered himself to be quite the gypsy lover – glibly breaking hearts wherever he parked his wagon. Over the sound of the ever soaring violin, the Frenchman recounted conquests from "Savannah to Havana, Santa Fe to Mandalay and Arizona to Daytona". Occasionally he drifted from this path to sing of the good old days – fishing in a river, whittling dolly pegs and saddling a piebald pony – but by and large he was touring the world, looking for love, and apparently finding it. Hardly able to contain his laughter, Bo ended the evening by translating the sleeve notes.

"Jack Caron is descended from Hungarian gypsies," he grandly informed his audience. "Furthermore – and I quote directly from the lines written here – Jack 'was born under the stars and raised by the sun, and though his wagon is gone, his Gypsy Heart Beats On'..."

Naturally, the crowd hooted and hollered their disbelief.

"He was raised by the sun? Most people I know were raised by their mothers!" shouted Tanko over his beer.

"Oh please!" retorted Bo. "I met your mother and she told me she never raised no son-of-a-bitch!"

At the challenge, Tanko dropped his tankard and leapt from his seat. The crowd immediately roared its approval.

"Beat him well!" Donka encouraged her husband as he deftly wrestled Rami's boy to the ground.

"Beat me well?" Bo shouted back. "He couldn't beat a tambourine."

Bo bucked and kicked his legs under Tanko's vast chest, sending the bigger man hurling onto his back. As the dogs barked in excitement, he threw a punch that was easily deflected and the men of the camp dipped hands into their pockets to hastily make wagers.

Back on his toes, Tanko released a quick one-two which Bo took on the chin and quickly recovered from to land a punch to the abdomen. Shaking his fist, he stepped nimbly away as Tanko counterattacked.

"What the hell are you feeding him? Iron girders?" Bo yelled at Donka as he narrowly avoided a blow to the head.

"You don't feed a lion, you let him hunt!" she responded.

"Has anyone got a gun?" Bo yelled as he frantically weaved between Tanko's flying fists.

"Do we have a gun?" Mirela shouted at my side, and I laughed in reply.

Assuring my daughter that the men were only playing, the words were quickly stolen by a flash of blue light. Around us, the banter stalled as others took notice, and everyone's attention shifted towards the road. Seconds later, Bo and Tanko staggered to a halt; belatedly realising they were only amusing themselves. Twenty metres away a police car crawled along the edge of the site. From its windows, the faceless forms of three men looked in our direction.

"What do they want?" Mirela whispered.

"Nothing, it's just a patrol," I answered, although there was rarely anything 'just' about a random police patrol of a Romani site.

Disappearing from sight, and into the curve of a lay-by, the car turned, only to creep back along the road it had come down. As it passed, a window lowered and a small flash signalled a photo had been taken. The blue lights were killed. And the vehicle drove off.

"Bastards!" shouted Bo.

"They have no right!" cried his father

"Just leave it be, Rami," the Big Man responded, more quietly yet firmly.

Rami shook his head and raised his hands in bewilderment. He wasn't alone in his outrage. The evening had been spoiled, the laughter had died, and one by one the families around us collected their children to return to their homes. Taking Mirela's hand, Miko signalled that we should also head back to our caravan.

"And so it starts," was his only comment.

Chapter Nine

Many years before we left Romania, when I was still naive and I mingled with the *gadje*, I read a report tucked away in the back of a newspaper. It sat there, sandwiched between the TV section and the sports pages, like an afterthought or a footnote to the important news of the day. And perhaps it was. The article announced a new initiative – A Decade of Roma Inclusion – an unprecedented commitment by European governments to improve our lives.

There was no picture accompanying the report. There wasn't even a quote. The headline simply stated 'Roma Get 10 Years'. The year was 2005 and I remember reading the article whilst sat in the library. Self-consciously, I glanced around to see a handful of white faces sat on spongy chairs, gorging on books that fed an intellect nurtured by the state. Their eyes were hard, their stance unwelcoming and I could smell their disdain festering under supermarket deodorants and cheap perfume. With my dark skin and long skirt, I didn't belong in their hall – touching their books, taking their knowledge – and everyone knew it. If I sat too close, they moved. If I sat at the computer I'd be moved. It was a dance that mirrored our lives.

In those days Romania had yet to enter the European Union so, as interesting as the article was, I assumed it would have little or no impact on our lives. Still, as I left the building, I imagined all those countries beyond our borders, all those places where politicians promised to improve our status. I wanted to believe them. I dared hope that people might care. And this was the great trick that naivety played on my heart.

Today, we are halfway through the Decade of Roma Inclusion and here – parked in the heart of Europe – I see that nothing has changed. Old Europe simply wears a different shade of the same prejudice. Whilst her politicians talk about rights, those with no voice are denied them. The French Roma struggle to find accommodation, and nothing is done to cater to their customs or culture. Inclusion in the *gadje* world means integration. We have to become them, or at least a poorer version of them. For all their fine words and signed documents, Europe's politicians offer only a lifeline to a slow and pitiful extinction. And for those of us in possession of the wrong passports, the only talk is that of exclusion.

"Will they come for us?" Mirela whispered.

"Not like before," I answered honestly, holding her close and feeling her heart pounding against my own.

"France is a good place," Miko assured our daughter. "There are laws. There's no need to be afraid."

"But the police…"

"The police protect people," Miko insisted. He raised his head above the pillow, over the head of our daughter, and I read the doubt in his gaze. "No one will ever hurt you again," he gruffly promised before turning away to extinguish the candle.

Plunged into darkness, Mirela's questions ceased, but only a fool would assume her mind had stopped turning and for an hour or more she lay still and awake. Gradually, as the world grew quiet, she began to twitch as her body surrendered to sleep. Her shallow breaths were soon joined by Miko's soft snore. And I listened with envy, unable to join them.

In the still of the night my mind grew loud; I heard the anguish of a mother mourning her son; the despair of the unwanted, kicked from pillar to post; and the snarls of men who had once marched to end us. Even now, despite everything I knew, I couldn't fathom their hatred. It followed our people as surely as our shadows. But why? We were only people; a collection of families, nothing more than a speck on the landscape, and yet no one wanted us to stop, and there was nowhere to hide. The world that we lived in had no room for our kind.

Burying my head into the pillow, I fought to contain the despair welling in my chest. Then, as I slipped on the verge of sleep my last thought was of my grandmother.

"Get a grip, Mala," she advised. "You're making my bones ache."

After a sluggish start, I managed to coax Mirela from bed shortly after 9am. Once she had washed, I carefully applied the ointment she needed.

"It hurts," she protested, slapping at my hand.

"I know, my love. And I'm sorry for that."

"Then stop it!"

"I can't."

Mirela began to weep, but it was more out of frustration than pain. Nonetheless, her tears served to increase my sense of guilt. Returning from the water pump, Miko took in our upset and kissed both our heads. He reached to wipe away the fatigue clinging to my eyes before instructing me to prepare our things.

"Are we leaving?" I asked.

Miko shrugged, shook his head and then sighed.

"I've no idea," he muttered. "Not today I don't think, but we should be ready."

"I guess you're right."

"I'd prefer not to be," he admitted.

As Miko left the caravan, I followed him, pausing to open the door and let in the day. Outside, I saw that most of the men had remained on site; other husbands and fathers unsure of what the future might bring, burying their concerns in the engines of their vehicles and the arms of their children as their women stood by, boxing their belongings.

"I hate this," Donka shouted over to me, surveying the same scene from the steps of her caravan.

"You hate what?"

"This," she repeated, waving an arm before her. "Scurrying like rats because a cat has walked by."

"People are nervous, Donka."

"People are afraid."

"And you're not?"

"Not of them," she insisted, jerking her head backwards, indicating a place beyond the fields.

"Well, maybe you should be," I warned.

Donka stepped to the ground, her eyes defiant, her lips ready to argue, but then Mirela appeared with a bucket in her hands and the woman's look softened. She walked over and handed me a slip of paper.

"Can you read this?" she asked.

I took the sheet Donka offered. It was a letter, crumpled and worn at the edges, and I was reminded of a similar note I had caught her hiding in her skirts, some time ago, before we grew friendlier.

"I'm sorry. It must be in French," I apologised. "I don't understand it. Is it important?"

"Probably not," she replie"Who's it from?"

Donka sucked at her lips and frowned. Her face looked thinner than it used to.

"Maybe you can ask Drina to translate it," I suggested.

"She can't read."

"I could read the words to her. Maybe she could make sense of them."

"I don't want everyone knowing my business," Donka snapped, and though I was stung, I wasn't offended.

"If it's important, Donka..."

"It's not important," she insisted. And before I could say more, she turned away, digging for a cigarette in the pocket of her skirt as she returned to her home.

Given the turn of events, and everyone's fraught nerves, when Jack arrived shortly before 2pm any interest in his 'gypsy heart' had all but vanished and it was to Francoise that the Romanies came running.

"Did they stop? Did the police say anything?" she asked as she tried to make sense of the previous night's drive-by. The Big Man told her the officers had stayed in their car, but they had taken a photograph.

Francoise looked puzzled. "I can't see how a photo would serve any official purpose unless they were investigating a crime."

To her right, Bo and Tanko shifted on their feet, moving their hands to mask the bruises colouring their faces.

"We've no criminals here," the Big Man stated, stepping in front of the two men.

"Then there's nothing to worry about," Francoise replied. "You've had no official visit?"

The Big Man shook his head.

"Have the Press been?"

Again, he shook his head.

"Well, if the authorities want to move you, they'll have to speak to you first. Really, I'd relax for now. I'll make some inquiries when I get back to the city."

"That would be very civil of you," the Big Man acknowledged. Around us, the other men also did their best to thank Francoise, mainly employing nods because they were unused to being beholden to women. They then scoured the area for something to sit on. I took a deep breath and steeled myself. As gratifying as their interest was, I hadn't expected an audience when I first agreed to speak to the *gadje*, and the presence of our neighbours filled me with nerves. It was another pressure – to get things right, to do right by them all.

As Francoise translated the finer points of the site's concerns to Jack, Miko and I nipped behind the caravan to salvage the visitors' cups from the dust and the wildlife.

"What's the topic this time?" he asked.

"Wallachia."

Miko released a tuneless whistle between his teeth.

"Well, I suppose it's time," he replied.

"Yes, and as you pointed out earlier, we may not have much of it left. Even so, this is nothing I want Mirela to overhear."

"Agreed. I'll take her away for the day."

"Thank you."

"For what?"

"For just, you know... for everything."

Glancing about him, and finding only a stringy dog watching the two of us, Miko placed a hand on the back of my neck and drew me in. His lips tasted of coffee and cigarettes, but they also tasted of love. Beautiful, honest, hard-earned love. As he pulled away, he held my gaze for a second, maybe longer. I could hear his heart beating.

"Okay," he whispered, "Now go and tell those mother fuckers what the world stole from us."

WALLACHIA

1772

Chapter Ten

Born in the dying days of Byzantium, the Roma clung to the shadows of the realm for close to three centuries, remaining aloof and largely tolerated. During that time, some groups filtered west – driven by hardship, warfare and basic curiosity – and many more followed after the pestilence rolled in. However, their sudden influx into Europe, combined with their dark skin, made the Romanies culpable in the eyes of many for the plague's relentless march west. From the outset, the Roma triggered suspicion because – at that point in time, in that part of the world – God favoured only the white.

Though the Roma left Byzantium no richer than when they arrived, the wealth of their language revealed the path they had taken. As India grew distant, they looked to the skies and counted Greek 'magpies'. They worked with 'lead' and 'copper' and built 'chairs' using 'saws', 'nails' and 'planks.' Taking 'roads' into 'towns', they occasionally turned 'left' – whilst dispensing with the right – and they chose to keep 'more', but not less.

The Romanies' moment in the Empire had left another indelible mark.

Through the dense forests and lush valleys of Europe, the Roma travelled as tradesmen, firing copper, carving wood, and proficiently recycling whatever they gathered, long before the process became fashionable. Their skills alone ought to have been enough to sustain them, but the iron grip of the guilds worked to block this route and their craftsmen were slowly forced to seek less legitimate paths – plying their trade in a twilight world made up of backhanders, black markets, and blagging. Only in the last outpost of Christendom, in kingdoms half-drowning in the midst of the Ottoman swirl, were the Romanies ever welcomed for their expertise. The Latin-speaking Vlachs of Moldavia and Wallachia instantly recognised the Roma's worth – so much so that they became too valuable to lose.

The people there called us '*Cigan*'. In time it became synonymous with 'slave'.

Chapter Eleven

Livia was only a child, but she knew there were things in her life that weren't quite right. She lived in a castle yet she was confined to a kitchen. Beds filled the rooms, but she slept on the floor. She had her own language, but she spoke it in secret. And though her mother named her Livia, the Boyar called her Dishrag.

"There was a time when we could speak how we liked and go where we pleased," Basil muttered over a dinner of old potatoes. "But that was an age ago, well before the laws. Now we daren't empty our bowels without first getting permission."

Livia listened to the old man grumble – because that's what he did – and among everything she recognised as not being quite right, she had to include him. Basil's voice was high for a man and his hips were a touch too round. Her mother said it was due to a loss of "essence," but as Livia was only a child, she wouldn't understand that explanation for some time to come.

Unlike Basil, Livia's mother rarely complained. Instead, she spent her days working for people she quietly despised. She once had a husband, but he had been killed. She used to have sons, but they had been sold. And she used to possess beauty until she cut it away. Though her name was Luminitsa, the Boyar called her 'Whore'.

The year was 1772, Livia was ten years old, and her life was one of eternal drudgery and appalling food. It was a time when a man's worth was measured by the colour of his skin, and Livia's mother was as dark as burnt wood. In contrast, Livia was pale to the point of white and possessed startling green eyes. Whenever the girl thought about this, she could only conclude that she wasn't right either.

"You've got your mother's heart. That's all that matters," Basil assured the girl.

"That's what you say."

"That's what I say."

"Whereas the cook says I'm the bastard child of a scar-faced mongrel."

Basil spluttered, emitting pipe smoke and spit from his open mouth.

"You pay no heed to the cook. She's nought but a fat Wallachian peasant."

"But she shouts."

"Then close your ears."

"Like this?"

Livia placed her hands over her ears and grinned. Rather like Basil, she hated the cook only a little less than she hated the Boyar and his wife.

The Boyar was the main source of terror in Livia's not-right world, which might have been the whole world as far as she knew. Built like an ox, he was perpetually unpleasant and rarely seen without a whip tucked into his boots. When his anger was roused, he unleashed it across the backs and faces of those who displeased him. There wasn't a slave on the Dragos Estate that hadn't been stung by the Master's fury, and though Livia was beaten only once, the scar that ran along the back of her leg would remain there a lifetime.

At some point in the past, three daughters played in the castle, but they had long since left – to marry other rich men who carried whips in their boots. They rarely returned home. No one trapped there could blame them.

However, once every summer others came to visit, and they rattled up the driveway in an array of pretty coaches, all driven by slaves in various states of decrepitude. On those occasions, the castle breathed back to life with feasts and banquets and all manner of games. For the slaves, however, the festivities merely signalled a new kind of terror as extra workers were drafted in to make everything just so, and suffer the consequences if it wasn't.

"The *Cioce* severed the hand of one of our grubs last week," a guest once remarked as she glided from gilded carriage to tiled hall.

"Theft?" the Master inquired as he took the lady's arm.

"Isn't it always?"

"And yet they never learn," replied the Boyar. "The trouble is they don't feel pain, not in the way normal people do. Or even the cold for that matter."

"Well, the child will be neither use nor ornament now."

"Then cut him loose. Let him beg on the streets of Vatzi."

"Yes, I know. We probably will, but it's the ingratitude that galls."

"Madam, if the gypsies possessed any redeeming qualities at all then they wouldn't be slaves."

"Well, isn't that the truth," the woman agreed before handing her cape to Luminitsa who stood silently at the door, ready to serve the Master's every whim.

Though schools were unknown to slaves, lessons were not and one of Livia's most memorable came at the age of seven when she was sat in the sunshine on a glorious spring day. A clatter of hooves brought her mother running from the kitchen and Livia got to her feet to be ushered indoors. But then, as the Boyar's horse stamped to a halt, her mother seemed to change her mind. Behind the master's stallion was a teenage boy – on his knees, tied to the end of a rope. The shredded rags he wore matched the colour of his skin, immediately revealing his sex and his status. The Boyar dismounted and took the rope to bind the slave's legs. Snatching the whip from his boot he attacked the boy's feet. He didn't stop until the soles were shredded, no longer feet but bloody flaps of skin.

"Now let's see how far you can run," the Master challenged before walking away, rubbing his hands on his breeches and ordering Basil to pick up the pieces.

Luminitsa looked at her daughter.

"Do you understand?" she asked, and Livia nodded.

When a gypsy was born into a world that wasn't quite right there were only two options; the castle or death.

"Can't we get some dry bread to go with this dry bread?" Basil moaned even as he choked on the crumbs clogging his throat.

"You get what the Master leaves you," the cook replied, ignoring the sarcasm in the old groom's voice. "I'm not paid to cater to slaves."

"You're not paid to kill them either."

Basil got up from his seat and filled a tankard from the drip pan hanging over the fire. The cook watched, but made no attempt to stop him.

"*Mamo* says dry bread makes you clever," Livia remarked.

"Not clever enough that you'll leave your seat and get your own sauce though, eh?"

Basil poured half the tankard onto his plate and the rest onto Livia's. In response, the cook took a shawl from a peg and threw it around her shoulders.

"Make sure your mother has the kitchen ready by the morning and don't use up the candles," she ordered the girl.

As the wooden door clattered shut, Basil raised his eyes to the low ceiling.

"A woman with all the allure of a pickled pig's trotter," he commented, taking advantage of her absence to speak his own language.

"I'd say she was more of a pig's ass," Livia corrected and the old man chuckled. "And really, Basil, you say she's not paid to kill us, but I don't see why she's paid at all when we're not."

"It's because the pig's ass is a peasant," he calmly explained. "Whereas we, my green-eyed beauty, are the cattle of this land, and a farmer doesn't pay his cows to make milk, does he?"

"It's not fair."

"No, it's not, but that's how life is – you live it, you die from it and somewhere in between some bastard cuts off your gonads."

"What are gonads?"

"Never you mind."

Livia rose from the table to set a pan of water over the fire. As it warmed, she took the dirty plates used by the Master and his wife, as well as those of the guards who lived next to the stables, and she washed them.

"Do you think dry bread really does make you clever?" she asked Basil.

"I think your mother's clever if she's able to convince you that eating crap is anything other than eating crap."

"Isn't that the truth." Livia laughed before disappearing outside to tip the grease from the pan. After collecting water from the trough, she returned to the kitchen and set it on the fire. When the water was warm, she scrubbed the floor and wiped the surfaces after which she disappeared again to empty the pan, refill it, and put it on the boil, ready for her mother. These were the last of Livia's chores, although Basil assured her there would be many more to come, the older she got. It wasn't the greatest promise a child of ten wanted to hear.

As Luminitsa was little more than a fleeting presence until the Master and his wife retired to bed, Livia spent all of her evenings with Basil, listening to stories that may, or may not, have been true. He was her best friend, as well as her only friend. And as far as Basil was concerned, Livia was the closest thing he had to family.

Basil was sold to the Dragos Estate at the tender age of nine. Torn from his mother's arms, his new owners strapped him to a table and swiftly castrated him. No longer deemed a threat to decent women, he then became the driver for Dragos' mother. When she died, he was passed on to the Boyar's wife. Though his job was unpaid and largely thankless, it was better than most because inclement weather failed to agree with the Madam which meant he was usually left to his own devices. And because the Boyar's wife was unusually tolerant of Basil, if not fond of him, the cook was careful around him, in a way that she wasn't with Livia or her mother.

"Has she gone?"

Luminitsa entered the kitchen, glancing around the place to see how careful she needed to be.

"Gone," Livia confirmed and her mother relaxed knowing she could speak as she liked without risking a whipping.

"You've been busy," Luminitsa remarked.

"Not as busy as you," Livia replied, and her mother acknowledged that truth with a shrug. Taking the pan from the fire, she tested the water before plunging in both hands. For a moment she enjoyed the comfort of being still, feeling the warmth crawl up her fingers and into her arms. For more than five hours Luminitsa had been bent to the floor, and every bone in her back groaned like the rusty hinges of a door.

"You're looking well," Basil commented dryly, and Luminitsa stared at him blankly. The skirts under her smock were tattered and dirty; her body was a collection of bones; and the scars on her face were livid from exertion and cold.

"Do you think?" she finally asked.

"Never better," he replied.

"Then it must be the sea air," she joked and they both managed to laugh because neither of them had ever seen the sea let alone felt its benefit. Furthermore, Luminitsa looked about as well as a mangy donkey.

When spring arrived to transform the icy draughts that blew through the castle into gentle gusts of tolerable cold, the Madam emerged from hibernation, still wrapped in her furs, to trouble Basil with trips into Vatzi. Naturally, Luminitsa and Livia were also needed; to fetch and carry whilst Basil tended the horse.

As a rule, the trips were short and efficiently to the point because Madam found the town vulgar and malodorous. Her nerves were further antagonised by the sight of slaves on the estate which is why, when they travelled, she always focussed on a point in the distance so she might remain untroubled by the privations of the poor. Though Luminitsa also stared ahead, it was for vastly different reasons. In contrast, Livia loved to get out of the castle, and in the fields that they passed she searched for the eyes of her brothers within the mud and the rags.

"They were taken elsewhere," Luminitsa insisted the first time she noticed her daughter searching.

"Perhaps," Livia had replied, but because she thought that a man who was capable of selling human beings was more than capable of telling lies, she continued to look.

As they bounced from one grassy knoll to another, the heavens opened and the Madam pulled up her hood to protect the tower of her hair. Beside her, Luminitsa barely blinked as raindrops clung to her lashes. Basil pulled up his collar, though it made little difference, and Livia merely wiped her face and carried on searching.

Passing a muddy river, Livia gazed at a line of men, their necks gripped by long wooden yokes as they sifted for gold. Though the rain had washed the filth from their faces, they all looked the same; black-skinned, half-naked, starved and defeated. Even so, Livia inspected each and every one of them, determined to find her brothers who – if her prayers had been answered – would be recognisable from their beautiful green eyes.

Roughly a mile from the town, the rain began to ease as they trotted past a number of moss-domed huts that, from a distance, looked like giant mole hills belching black ants. Livia recognised her people in much the same way that she recognised the shackled 'gypsy' painted on a poster that had been nailed to a tree on the outskirts of Vatzi.

"Please God, not today," she prayed. She then crossed her fingers for added luck.

Arriving in town, Basil steered their cart around pockets of rich, white-faced men. Many were in jocular mood, standing in threes or fours, drinking ale, passing comment and counting their money. In the centre of it all, in a square bordered by factories and shops, a platform had been erected upon which stood a tall man dressed in furs and knee-length leather boots. Beneath a wide-brimmed hat, his hair was thick and curled, and he carried two whips in his hands that he flicked like a dance in front of the crowd. Livia recognised the uniform of the *Cioce* and her childish heart sank.

The *Cioce* were the sticks that the landowners beat their slaves with. They enforced discipline and collected taxes, and once a month one of them appeared at the castle to hand the Boyar his dues from the earnings of the *Laiesi* – the slaves who worked as smiths, basket makers and gold washers. Unlike the house slaves, the *Laiesi* were permitted to roam between the nobles' estates so that they might find the money to pay their monthly tribute. Another group of the superficially-free were the musicians known as *Lautari*. Everyone else was trapped. And if a slave was found wandering the land with no owner to speak of, and no seal to prove it, he automatically became the property of the state. This was how life was, and it wasn't quite right.

Basil reined in their horse outside Vatzi's one and only fabric store just as the *Cioce* began to reel in his audience. The old man stepped from the cart to help the Madam from her seat, and with no order given, Luminitsa followed her inside whilst Livia waited behind. Basil took out his pipe and turned to watch the spectacle on stage. Unable to stop herself, Livia did too.

By now, the *Cioce* was into his stride; tempting the crowd with the quality of his lots, teasing and flattering the market's big spenders. To general disinterest, the first slaves were hauled on stage; three teenage boys, all thin and all tired-looking despite their young age. Ignoring the jeers, the *Cioce* described the youths as hard-working, of good record, and in handsome condition. He then invited bids.

"Come on gentlemen, these are skilled labourers. They are as able with the hoe as they are with the scythe, strong as cart horses and quicker than rabbits. Be reasonable, who will start the bidding?"

With theatrical reluctance, one of the boyars stepped forward. Holding a cane, he prodded a boy before demanding all three of them lift their rags so he might inspect their upper bodies. With dead eyes, the slaves hitched up their sack-cloth smocks. Beneath the dirt, their ribs were pronounced and a number of sores ate into their flesh. The *Cioce's* potential buyer returned to the crowd, shaking his head to show there would be no joy from him. Undeterred, the *Cioce* continued to cajole the crowd, and other men climbed on stage to prod, to poke, and pull back lips to check the boys' teeth. Eventually, as the audience grew restless, someone closed the deal with a bid of 40 horseshoes. The *Cioce* looked to his right where a man in a felt hat nodded his consent.

"Sold!" he declared, and the slaves were herded away into a waiting cart.

"Now, allow me a brief sigh of contentment," the *Cioce* continued, taking the hat from his head in order to wipe the sweat from his heavy brow. "I swear by everything I hold dear that my next lot is a treasure beyond measure brought to you from the reputable confines of the Basarab Estate. Yes, respected gentlemen, we have a young woman looking for a good home; a maiden of 14 gentle years, healthy, able-bodied and, I'm honestly assured, perfectly untouched."

The *Cioce* nodded at one of his helpers and to great applause and general mirth, a child was dragged onto the platform. From her seat, Livia saw the whites of her eyes before noticing her beauty. The girl was tiny with shining black hair, exquisitely fine features and strong, straight teeth. The audience murmured its appreciation and the *Cioce* smiled. Playfully flicking his whip at the girl's ankles, he stepped closer and lifted up her skirt to casually display her legs. With a wink to the crowd, he squeezed one of the girl's thighs and she instinctively lashed out despite the shackles binding her wrists. The *Cioce* laughed, as did the crowd, but he kept his fists still because she was too valuable to mark. Instead, he grabbed her by the hair, pulled back her head, and ripped away her modesty. At the sight of bare breasts, the men hollered their approval and the clamour for bids soon drowned the girl's screams.

Basil spat his disgust onto the floor and turned away, just as the Madam and Luminitsa emerged from the store. In her arms, Livia's mother carried two rolls of silk freshly arrived from Flanders. The Madam carried nothing. As

Basil offered his arm to the Boyar's wife, helping her into the cart, the sun broke through the clouds.

"My, what a perfectly lovely day," Madam observed, apparently oblivious to the half-naked girl standing twenty yards away, crying on stage surrounded by fat, baying men.

It was a sight Livia would never forget. And that night, as she struggled to sleep on the hard floor that was her bed, she whispered to her mother, "Will they do that to me when I'm older?"

Luminitsa bolted upright, pulling her daughter with her. Taking hold of Livia's face, she stared hard into her eyes. "I swear on my life that I will kill the man who tries to touch you."

"But..."

"There will never be a 'but', there will never be a 'what if'. If something happens, I will protect you."

Roughly embracing her child, Luminitsa lay back on the blanket and pretended to sleep. The next morning, while the world was still dark, she dragged herself from the floor, built the fire, collected the water, and prepared the kitchen for the cook's arrival. When the time had come to wake her daughter, she handed her a tiny blue flower.

"There will always be beauty in the world," she said.

Without another word, Luminitsa left the kitchen to set the table for the Master's breakfast and prepare the bath for the Madam's ablutions. Livia rose from the floor, wiped the sleep from her eyes, folded the blanket that was their bed, kissed the flower she had been gifted – and quietly thanked God for not having given her breasts in the night.

Two months after the slavery market, the Boyar's wife had transformed the rolls of silk she had bought into a fine summer dress that she wore for the one event of the year that everyone in the castle looked forward to – the arrival of the *Lautari*.

Every year the musicians played for the Boyar and his friends, and for at least two nights the castle became a place of music and merriment. Extra slaves were plucked from the estate and the stone walls carried the intricate skills of the Romani players to all those who were excluded from the great hall.

Although her face never showed it, Livia knew her mother welcomed the *Lautari's* arrival as much as the next slave, and Basil, well, he was like a man reborn, albeit with none of the regular equipment.

"If I die now, I'll die happy," he declared, tapping his feet to the beats that echoed along the corridors.

"If you died now, I'd be happy too," retorted the cook, her fat face flushed with the exertion of having to cater to more than she was used to.

Basil smiled in spite of the insult because the woman would always be a peasant whereas, tonight, his people played with angels.

The leader of the *Lautari* was a tall, silent man named Jozka. His hair was poker-straight and it ran like a river down his back. His moustache was trimmed and teased into points and his cheekbones were high and sharply defined. He was handsome in a way that was mysterious and unnerving, and his black eyes watched everything while giving away nothing. Though he rarely spoke, Jozka was always quick to his feet should he find Luminitsa struggling in the chaos. There was nothing lascivious about his attentions. Every gesture was careful and courteous. Enslaved as he was, Jozka exuded dignity, and he afforded respect to all those he considered worthy. Naturally, the cook wasn't included in this group.

"Aye, he's a fine Romani," Basil agreed when Livia expressed her admiration for the violinist.

"He steals my breath," the girl replied, and because the old man felt much the same way he urged her to follow him to the back of the castle where he hoisted her onto his shoulders so that she might get to watch Jozka play through the gaps of a broken shutter.

After adjusting her eyes, Livia found her mother and a handful of other slaves standing in the corner of a candlelit room, waiting to serve the needs of the privileged. However, with the *Lautari* playing, the guests had largely forgotten about their stomachs and, either side of the five-piece band, the wives and husbands sat immersed in their respective clouds of perfume and pipe smoke, completely and utterly entranced. In the centre of it all stood Jozka – a violin tucked under his chin, his arm moving to the demands of his bow. He commanded every eye in the room and with the merest flick of his wrist he aroused memories of sunshine and rain, anger and love. In Jozka's midst, there was no world but his, and he played to an audience he hardly seemed to see. When the performance ended, the slave owners applauded with gasps of admiration and grudging praise, but if Jozka appreciated the moment it never showed on his face. His black eyes continued to stare into the distance – hard and detached from the beauty he had created.

In Livia's eleventh year the little freedom she had enjoyed was steadily picked away, not by the Boyar or his wife, but by her own mother. No longer was she permitted to sit in the sunshine or creep along the walls. Her orders were to stay in the kitchen, to work and be quiet, to keep clean and become gradually invisible. Naturally, Basil was sympathetic, but in the end, he had to admit he agreed with the girl's mother.

"You're getting older."

"I'm no different to how I was yesterday."

"Not to us, but these differences are subtle and one day someone will notice and when they do, you'll wish that they hadn't."

Livia dismissed Basil's concerns, largely because she didn't understand them. However, two months later the old man was proved right when a handful of men arrived at the castle to spend the evening with the Boyar. Appearing earlier than was customary, Luminitsa walked into the kitchen.

"You must come with me," she informed her daughter.

"Where?"

"The Master wants to see you."

"What for?"

For the life of her, Luminitsa couldn't bring herself to explain, and as Livia waited for her mother to try, she felt the world grind to a halt. Basil's pipe smoke seemed to hang in the hole of his mouth and the cook's arm stopped stirring as she lowered her head to mutter a prayer.

"You must come," Luminitsa repeated more urgently, and Livia removed her soiled apron to follow her mother up the stone slabs leading to the Master's quarters.

Along the damp corridors Livia was conscious of the cold seeping into her feet. Her heart was beating like a bird in her chest and her mother's silence was scaring her. Stopping in front of a large oak door, Luminitsa squeezed Livia's arm.

"Do what he says," she whispered, hurriedly. "Don't cry, don't be afraid. I will be here."

"But what does he..."

"I will be here, Livia."

Before the child could say more, Luminitsa pushed open the door and ushered Livia into the room. Inside, an open fire met her, bathing the walls in orange and red. The air was thick with pipe smoke and the gruff sounds of middle-aged men. From his seat in the centre of the room, the Boyar turned. Sitting on a long couch, a little to his right, Livia saw two male guests having their hands washed by a couple of young women. Another waited by the Boyar's side, dark-skinned and still as a statue.

"About time," muttered the Master as Luminitsa closed the door. "Come here, Dishrag."

Luminitsa gently pushed her daughter forward. When Livia came into reach, the Boyar grabbed her roughly. His shirt was unbuttoned and she felt the heat rising from his chest. Alcohol flushed his face and infected his breath.

"What did I tell you gentlemen, a beauty wouldn't you say?"

The Boyar forced Livia closer, and though she resisted it seemed only to amuse him. He pinned her to his side as one of the guests glanced up from his hands to inspect the new goods.

"She'll fetch a decent price," the man confirmed.

"Oh, I'll not be selling her."

"Well, she's too young for the other."

"But they grow up so quickly!"

The men in the room laughed at the Boyar's observation, whilst the women stayed silent.

"And what do you say, Dishrag?"

Livia didn't know what to say. Things weren't right and she suddenly needed to pee.

"Another quiet one," the Master noted, apparently pleased with the discovery. He pinched the girl's cheeks, holding her so close she could count the pores on his doughy face and the wine stains on his lip. Livia's knees began to shake. The Boyar's eyes were glassy and uncomfortably familiar, but when he leant in to kiss Livia, they looked not at her, but at her mother.

"Sweet," he declared as he pulled away. "But as you say, John, still some time before it ripens."

Releasing his grip, the Boyar span Livia back to her mother, patting the child's bottom as she went.

"Go now," he ordered, and Luminitsa hurriedly grabbed her daughter's hand, knowing she was running out of time.

Nothing was the same again after the Boyar demanded to see Livia, and in the nights that followed her mother shared every horror she had saved from the child.

With little emotion in her voice, Luminitsa revealed how she had grown up deep in the mud and the weeds of the estate, tilling the land and living in one of the molehill huts that circled the town. Despite their lowly status, the family was well-regarded. Music played and occasionally the Boyar's mother would come to have her hand read by Luminitsa's sister who had been born with the gift.

"The rich have the wealth of the world, but they still need to hear they deserve more," Luminitsa sneered.

On one of these occasions, the Old Madam was accompanied by her son, Dragos. He was then in his early 20s and in the space of an afternoon, Luminitsa's fate was sealed. Ten years later, when he inherited the estate and all the slaves in it, Dragos returned to the village to find what he wanted. By then, Luminitsa was married with five sons of her own. Her husband was a good man, not a musician or a smith, but a barber and labourer. All their boys were healthy and strong, and Luminitsa thought she was as content as she could ever hope to be.

Within days of the Boyar's appearance, the *Cioce* arrived with orders to investigate the theft of a bullock. Despite no evidence, Luminitsa's husband was taken away "for questioning". In the Boyar's courtyard he was hanged by his feet over a burning fire until his face was gone and he eventually stopped screaming. The day after they buried him, Luminitsa's eldest boys were snatched from her arms and loaded onto a cart. They were required for sale, the *Cioce* informed her. He then dragged Luminitsa to the Master's castle with her youngest son still clasped to her breast. In the space of a week, the baby was all she had left of the family she had known and she paid for his life by giving up her own. By the time Livia was born, her brother was four years old. When Livia reached three, the boy was deemed old enough to sell.

Though Luminitsa fought like a tigress, the *Cioce* took the child away and Luminitsa had no option but to carry on because there was another child who needed her. Even so, she saw the pattern that was forming and one night, as the castle slept, she took a knife to her face, releasing her disgust in deep gouges that ran along her cheeks, forehead, and chin.

"You cried when you saw me," Luminitsa told Livia. "It was the only time I ever felt sorry. Eventually, you stopped remembering and you accepted what I had become."

When the Boyar saw Luminitsa's face, he struggled to swallow the revulsion surging from his gut. In contrast, his wife remained calm, appearing almost pleased by the nightmare that greeted her. She forbade her husband from showing Luminitsa the door.

"You took what you wanted, now give me what I'm due," she demanded.

Up unto that point Luminitsa had never known whether the Madam had the measure of the man she had married. When she understood that she did, Luminitsa saw the Boyar's wife was no better than the thug who had held her down and raped her for the past four years.

"Is the Boyar my father?" Livia asked, half-strangled by the pain of her mother's abuse and the realisation that came with it.

"God is your father," her mother replied, and she refused to discuss the matter further.

Once everything was said that needed to be said, Luminitsa stopped talking and started planning. For hours she sat with Basil, working out a way, in the dying embers of the kitchen fire, whilst Livia listened to their conversation, horrified and scared.

"I don't want this," she whimpered.

"It's the only way," her mother replied. "This is my one chance of happiness, Livia. Don't take it from me."

Noting the determination in her mother's eyes and hearing the plea in her voice, Livia never protested again.

Shortly before her twelfth birthday, there came some respite from the gloom as the castle once again prepared for the arrival of its summertime guests and the great *Lautari*. As ever, Jozka reappeared with his sweet violin and Livia saw some of the worry drop from her mother's shoulders. Though it was only a passing moment, too quick to be noticed in the chaos, Livia also saw the whispered exchange as the violinist helped pull a long-handled pan from the fire. The knot in Livia's stomach tightened.

Once the guests had all dined and the guards had retired to their barracks, the musicians carried their instruments into the cavern of the great hall, taking their seats as the sun sank beyond the hills. It was to be the last time the *Lautari* would ever play at the castle. And some time later – when the blood had dried and scores had been settled – everyone present would swear they saw the devil dance among them that night.

As the castle fell under the *Lautari's* spell, Luminitsa slipped from the hall to return to the kitchen. To her frustration the cook was still present, fiddling with cuts of cold meat to feed guests who refused to sleep. Basil was already gone and Livia was sat on a chair, looking wide-eyed and bereft. Both

Luminitsa and her daughter glanced at the vast expanse of the immoveable cook.

"I know what you're up to," the woman muttered, not bothering to look up from her work.

Livia caught her breath and for the first time in her life, she saw tears clouding her mother's resolve. Luminitsa wiped roughly at her eyes as the cook turned to face her.

"I *know*," she repeated emphatically.

Through the crack of the door, Jozka's violin picked up Luminitsa's pain. She took the hand of her daughter. "Please," she urged, unable to find more.

The cook stopped her work and wiped her hands on her apron. Without a word she took a square of muslin and wrapped a slab of meat, a cut of hard cheese, and a dozen loaves within it. She passed the parcel to Luminitsa.

"I'm a mother myself," she admitted quietly. Turning back to the stove she added briskly, "There was more ale than meat in the stew tonight. I doubt the Master or his guards will see much of the morning."

With a nod that the cook didn't see, Luminitsa grabbed Livia's hand and pulled her from the kitchen. Under the half-moon, they scurried to the stables where they found Basil waiting. A horse was harnessed to the Madam's cart, the floor of which was covered in blankets and a number of furs taken from the Master's rooms. Basil heaved himself into his seat and Luminitsa lifted her daughter behind him.

"Be brave. I love you," was all she said. She reached up and took the old man's hands. "Go with God."

"Stay with God," he replied.

Giving Livia a last kiss, Luminitsa hurried back to the kitchen. At the door, she choked back her tears before closing it on everything she loved. Pausing briefly to thank the cook, who gave no reply, she made her way back to the dark corner of the great hall where Jozka slashed his bow across the face of his violin, forcing the other players to match his pace with their lutes, pipes and fiddles.

Under the cover of night, and the protection of the *Lautari's* talent, Basil urged his horse forward and the cart rolled along the rough track leading away from the castle. Once the music died on the wind, the old man gave the horse her head, and he pretended not to notice when Livia's tears began to fall.

True to the cook's promise, the Master didn't stir from his bed until shortly after midday. Neither did his guests. Even so, Luminitsa stood at her station waiting to serve and waiting for trouble. To her relief no one suspected a thing, not until long after three when the Madam and her ladies decided to take air and Basil was nowhere to be found.

At the dining table, the Master wiped the lethargy from his face as he dealt with his wife's questions. In the corner of the room, Luminitsa took a deep breath and steeled herself for the last chance she had to gain her daughter more time.

"The old fool must be somewhere," the Boyar muttered and turning to Luminitsa he ordered her to run to the guardhouse and bring back the captain.

Though habit nagged at her legs and fear gnawed at her courage, Luminitsa stayed where she stood. The Boyar didn't even notice, he was so unused to sedition, and it took a pointed cough from his wife before he looked in Luminitsa's direction.

"Did you not hear what I said?" he shouted, ripping the napkin from his neck as he rose from his seat.

Luminitsa flinched as the Boyar neared. But in her mind, she had lived this moment a million times. She knew she was more than ready. And when the Master lunged to strike, she took the opportunity to jump at him, propelled by a force gained from a lifetime of hurt. To her surprise, she felt the knife slip into his flesh with the ease of warm butter. Embedded deep in his groin, she forced the blade upwards until it mutilated everything he was. As the blood warmed her fingers she lifted her head – convinced she heard Basil's laughter rising above the screams of the Boyar's wife.

"May you rot in Hell!" Luminitsa snarled.

As the Master fell to the floor, she spat into his blanched face feeling the full power of the curse in the beauty of her own language.

For a week, possibly more, Luminitsa sat in a dank cell, under the weight of the castle, watching brown sludge slide down the wall until it soaked into moss. Each day, water arrived to keep her alive, and occasionally a husk of bread was thrown at her feet. She never ate it because she saw no sense in it. The only hunger she had was for news – and it drifted through the bars of the window above her. To her surprise, the Boyar lived. But it mattered little – he had been damaged for eternity – and judging by the quiet and inactivity, her daughter had escaped. This was her one source of pleasure, this was her one pride, and after a while Luminitsa stopped feeling the bugs crawling over her skin or the rats skipping across her toes. She was happy and ready to die.

Finally, when the count of days had been lost and she floated between heaven and earth, the *Cioce* came to rouse her. Luminitsa opened her eyes, seeing only his leather boots.

"Do your worst," she smiled.

And the *Cioce* obliged.

Once his torturer was done, the Boyar ordered Luminitsa's body to be hung at a crossroads at the foot of his estate. Her clothes were gone, her hair was ripped from its roots and everything that marked her as a woman had been carved away. The sight was dreadful. The message was clear. Yet later that evening, under a slither of moonlight, Luminitsa's body danced in the breeze to the strains of the most beautiful violin. As the melody travelled, the world fell silent, the castle shivered, and the Boyar's wife grew afraid. She recalled the *Cioce* and told him to investigate. Slapping the felt hat upon his head, he loaded a musket. It was dark on the road and he had more reason to fear it than most, but when he arrived at the crossroads, he found not a ghost, but the *Lautari* musician they called Jozka. He sat playing his violin beneath the rotting stumps of Luminitsa's legs. His eyes stared into the distance, black and unreadable.

Without a word, the *Cioce* walked away because he'd worked the estate long enough to recognise the dead woman's brother.

Livia wrapped herself in the Boyar's furs and tried to find sleep under the cart which Basil swore would protect her from not only the rain, but also the attentions of wolves. Older, and apparently less bothered by the wet or indeed creatures that might eat them, the old man tended the fire while their horse grazed nearby.

"We should get a dog, for protection and the suchlike," Basil said. "Dogs are useful, not clean like a horse, but useful nonetheless. I've a mind to keep an eye out for one. We can teach it to hunt. Get some meat in our bellies. I tell you, I'm sick of living on grass. Oh, and if you're listening, Livia, I'd be happy if you'd eat more tomorrow."

Livia raised her head to show she had heard, but they both knew she was a long way from listening. For a little over a month, they had been on the run with Basil talking incessantly about fresh starts and lands of opportunity whereas Livia felt done with the world.

"Your mother wouldn't have…"

"I know!" Livia snapped, tired of hearing about a sacrifice she had never requested.

Her mother was dead. She knew it a week after they fled when Livia looked to the sky and saw the moon had turned red. Basil snorted and said the moon had done no such thing, but Livia saw the colour as clear as the fingers on her hands. The moon dripped with her mother's blood, and the realisation left her distraught. She hated herself. She had abandoned the only person who had ever loved her, like a rat fleeing a fire. She was despicable, a weak and loathsome worm crawling upon the shit of the earth, and every day she woke up, it felt nothing short of betrayal. Eating was merely another act of treachery, one more heaped upon the last. And though she slept under the cart, at Basil's insistence, Livia prayed with all her might that a pack of wolves would come and rip her to pieces. In fact, the only reason she didn't kill herself was because of Basil. She recognised the old man was scared, despite the courage of his words – it was clear in the twitch of his eyes and the reins that trembled in his fingers. So, with no one else to live for, she existed solely for him. Livia allowed Basil to save her because she saw that he needed to do it.

Having spoken with Jozka, Basil's original idea had been to join with a band of escaped slaves known as the *Netoci*. It was a sensible enough plan, but it was one he quickly abandoned as the great peaks of the Carpathians loomed into view and he saw the rebel hideout being eaten by flames. At the foot of the forest, Wallachian soldiers shot at anyone caught fleeing the blaze. Up unto that point Basil had half-believed the *Netoci* were a myth.

"Out of the frying pan," he muttered as he steered their horse in a new direction.

"So where next?" Livia asked, though she hardly cared.

"Elsewhere that's where."

"You don't know, do you?"

"Well, I know we won't be going up there," he replied pointing towards the flames licking the skirts of the mountains. "And neither are we going back there," he added, jerking his thumb towards the place they had left behind. "We'll head down the road and camp for the night, so I can think on it. And I warn you now, girl, you best get some sleep; it'll be an early start in the morning."

"It's always an early start."

"Well, that's the problem with mornings; they tend to come early."

True to the old man's word, he never took Livia 'up there' or 'back there' and in the end they simply rolled westwards, stopping in isolated copses, relieving fields of whatever was growing, finding wood to patch up their wagon, and swiping clothes to replace those that had rotted. The going was tough and there were days when the rain fell like a river, soaking them to the bone. When the snow came it was a prettier form of torture, and as night fell Basil would tip the cart onto its side so they might use it as a shield. To beat the freeze, they huddled together under a mountain of damp furs next to the steaming belly of their horse.

As the seasons came and went, and the land they travelled on adopted new colours, the air changed its smell and the language around them began to slip into something unfathomable.

"Taking an educated guess, I'd say we're out of it," Basil commented.

He removed a stick from the belly of a pheasant he had roasted, a bird they had somehow frightened from the jaws of a fox earlier in the day.

"Do you know where we are?" Livia asked.

"I've no idea, but I know it's not where we were. Now hurry up and eat, I'm a minute from death."

Livia sighed, wearily expressing the full inconvenience of the demand. Putting a morsel into her mouth she pointedly swallowed. Basil waited patiently – quietly salivating – until he was satisfied the girl had eaten enough to keep her from fainting. He then took his turn, humming as he chewed because the pheasant was delicious and the sound of his pleasure blocked the worry messing with his head.

To Basil's relief, and also his surprise, there had been few challenges on the path out of Wallachia. Because of the *Lautari* he had been half-prepared, thanks to the names they had supplied him of all the landowners en route to the *Netoci*. However, once they changed course, he had been forced to change tack, and that's when Basil ordered Livia to shake the grief from her limbs and take the seat next to him. Coating his words with uncommon authority, he instructed the girl to cover her rags with the Boyar's furs, to claw the hair from her eyes, and affect the air of a lady being driven by her sexless *skopica*. Although Livia resented the charade, she saw the sense in Basil's plan. Even so, it made her feel dirty, from her skin to her guts.

"I hate it because I hate them," she later complained.

"Grow up, Livia! There's good and evil in all people," Basil declared, more out of necessity than belief.

"I will never forgive them."

"You don't need to forgive them. You just need to stay away from them."

"Always," Livia promised, and she meant it.

Although the girl would never know what happened to her mother, she wasn't so naive as to think her death would have come easy. Cruelty lay at the heart of Wallachian power and it seeped into every layer of the social structure, from the princes to the boyars to the peasants.

"Vlad Tepes, now there was a devil," Basil informed her on the evening they acquired a dog from an inattentive farmer and named him after the Wallachian Prince. "The people also had another name for him, they called him The Impaler, and the evil that he wrought brought blood falling from the skies."

"Blood from the skies, Basil?"

"True as I'm sat here," the old man insisted. He poked the small fire keeping them warm. Above their heads, the moon shone bright and the light breaking through the trees brought shadows creeping upon them from every direction. Livia shivered.

"Why do you always tell these tales at night?" she asked.

"They're not tales; it's history," Basil corrected. "And it comes out at night because that's when I think of it."

"That's when you're scared, you mean."

"That too."

Livia stretched out her legs, watching the fire's light play across her toes. At her side slept the scrawny form of Tepes, a dog that had yet to inherit any of the attributes of his namesake.

"I can't see as The Impaler was all bad," Livia stated, suddenly awake and hungry for sport.

"Not so bad?" spluttered Basil. "Have you lost your mind?"

"He killed the boyars, didn't he?"

"He didn't just kill the boyars, he killed everyone! I tell you girl, there's evil that exists in the hearts of men and then there's evil that walks in the form of them."

"And he was the latter?"

"Yes, he was the latter!"

Livia giggled as the old man wiped the exasperation from his chin. She then fell silent as a familiar guilt coursed through her veins. Oblivious to the girl's change of mood, Basil threw more twigs onto the fire and continued.

"You may think you're braver than a bull by making fun of what you don't know, but you're tempting the devil with such talk. Words are carried on the breeze and they get heard in the trees and they pass into the realm between waking and sleeping. This is how evil works. This is how it gathers its knowledge. We know Vlad existed, but where's the proof that he died? I'm not so sure that he did. And the boyars weren't the only ones he killed. Our people suffered too."

"As slaves?"

"As slaves, as prisoners, as entertainment. The story goes..."

"Don't you mean the history?"

Basil cast Livia a withering look before correcting himself.

"The historical story goes, that on one occasion Vlad Tepes returned from battle dragging 12,000 *Cigan* behind him. After plying them with drink he threw a few thousand on the fire, others he boiled alive or impaled – nailing their limbs to posts in order to stop them from squirming as he skewered them. A few he kept alive just so he could force them to eat the burnt flesh of their brothers – our brothers, Livia. God rest their tortured souls."

Basil crossed himself and because he was watching her, Livia followed suit. Beside them, Tepes stirred, idly stretching his legs before yawning. Much to Basil's chagrin, the dog had proved disappointing as an agent of terror. However, Livia found his lethargy helped make the darkness seem that little less threatening. Granted, he wasn't much to look at, but Livia was fond of

Tepes. His coat was rancid and his breath could have felled a horse, but he had slotted into their family as easy as a key in the right door. And they were a family; Livia, Basil and Tepes.

"You know, the devil is a clever creature," Livia admitted softly. "He dresses himself in the skin of white men and then convinces the world that evil is black. I swear when I'm older I'll marry with the darkest man I can find."

"If we find any," Basil muttered.

"We will," Livia insisted. "I can feel it."

And almost two years after they fled Wallachia, in a city topped by a white castle, they did.

By her fourteenth year, Livia stood as tall as Basil. It was a vantage point that allowed her to see that all was not well. While the old groom had always been ancient, he had suddenly become frail. The meat had dropped from his cheeks, leaving him with overly large ears attached to a wizened head. Brittle as a fallen tree, he was prone to exhaustion and infuriatingly preoccupied with visions of his death.

"Never bury me," he muttered, not for the first time that day. "Release me in fire. I don't want to be planted in a place that's been nought but a prison and a shithole."

"I'll burn you," Livia confirmed wearily.

"Make sure you do."

"I will."

"That's fine then."

"Glad you think so. Can I go now?"

Basil shrugged, grimaced, and nodded.

"Bring me an apple. I'd die for an apple."

"I'll bring you an apple."

Livia pulled their cart to a stop. With Basil's fingers freezing with arthritis, she had taken charge of the driving, as well as the foraging, the thieving and repairs to their wagon.

"Don't lose Tepes," she ordered as she jumped to the ground. Basil glanced to where the dog lay sleeping.

"I've more chance of losing my virginity. Don't forget the apple."

"I won't, Basil!"

Livia grabbed the woollen cloak she had acquired earlier that year. Though it was the height of summer, she used it to hide the sorry state of her clothes because shopping was less troublesome with the illusion of money. Suitably attired, she walked towards the shadow of the castle under which she found a bustling market.

Feigning a casual interest in the goods on display, Livia stopped to lift a tomato – sniffing its skin, checking its ripeness – whilst her free hand slipped whatever was nearest into the folds of her skirt. Occasionally a stallholder attempted to engage her in conversation, but as she hadn't the words to reply she largely ignored them.

Within half an hour Livia's hidden pockets were sufficiently laden and she strolled towards Basil, breathing easier the more distance she put between herself and her crimes. She rarely enjoyed their trips into town, the people were unfriendly – if not to her then certainly to Basil – but a busy market was too good an opportunity to pass by. The fact was they needed to eat, and the season's crops were yielding increasingly sparse pickings. Of course, with greater opportunity came greater risk and when someone pulled roughly at Livia's cloak there was a moment of panic as her heart stilled and her legs tensed to run.

Setting her face into one of haughty indignation, Livia turned to confront her accuser. To her utter confusion, she found a small woman pawing at her palm. A cloying smile distorted the shape of her lips and her dark eyes hooked onto her own. With no invitation, the woman grabbed Livia's hand as she chattered incessantly, her gaze obsequious and overbearing. Though she was small and curiously round, a red turban added substantially to her height. Gold shone in her ears. Her skin was on the cusp of black, and Livia felt goose bumps tickling her arms. Releasing Livia's hand, the woman stroked her palm again, looking increasingly dejected. When Livia remained silent, the stranger finally lost patience. She shuffled away, throwing an insult over her shoulder.

"What did you say?" Livia demanded, suddenly finding her voice.

The woman stopped walking and slowly span around.

"What did *you* say, more like?"

Livia paused. Though the accent was odd, less guttural than she was used to, the words were too familiar to belong to anyone else.

"Sister, I am you," Livia gasped, feeling relief catch her by the throat.

"And yet you're not," the woman challenged, clearly unmoved.

"But I am!"

"You don't look it."

"Yes, I know! Christ, don't you think I know that?"

And because Livia had spent two years dreaming of such a moment, and this was not how it had played out in the theatre of her mind, she started to unravel.

"Oh mercy, don't cry," the woman scowled. "You'll get me stoned."

"But I am you," Livia sobbed. "And we've come so far, and you're the first person who speaks like us, and to hear it, here, in this place, so far away, and then the way you are, with your black eyes, and your lovely skin, it's just, it's because, well, you see, I'm, oh God help me, my mother is dead!"

Livia slumped to the ground, her body shaking. As she gulped for air, a number of people stopped to watch the spectacle. "My mother, oh God, my mother!"

"Shush now, child," the woman whispered harshly, quickly stooping to pick up the apples rolling from the girl's skirts.

"I want my mother!"

"Yes, I know, I know. We all do sometimes,"

Feeling increasingly conspicuous, the woman whose name was Kizzy, pulled Livia to her feet – not without care, but certainly with a degree of urgency.

Kizzy lived a mile from the city in a painted wagon that was more like a house fixed onto wheels. She wasn't alone; there was her husband Harman and their six boisterous children. Her neighbours were a collection of sisters, brothers, cousins and strays. All in all, there were perhaps 60 people, all of them camped in a field that they claimed was common land. Not that Livia saw any sign of the area's commoners.

"They'll return when we're moved on," Harman stated.

"Moved on?" Basil repeated, his shoulders drooping under the weight of his disappointment.

"It happens eventually, when the town folk get fidgety or we've exhausted the Church's charity. Sometimes, if we're lucky, they'll pay us to leave. Mostly, they just turn up with their dogs."

"Will they come soon?"

"It's hard to tell. Maybe not, we've given them no trouble. But don't worry, Uncle. When we go, we'd be honoured to have you travel with us."

Basil smiled broadly and crashed tankards with Kizzy's husband, a man who also happened to be the elected leader of the group. Also known as 'The Big Man', Harman was taller, but far leaner than his wife. His lips were quick to smile, his eyes were round and generous and he exuded confidence and charm. In his company, Basil lit up and Livia was struck by the sudden change in her friend. She also saw he was drunk.

"I don't think Basil's ever tasted ale," Livia remarked to Kizzy.

"Little wonder you skipped your country then," the woman teased, before clasping a hand to her mouth. "I'm sorry, it was a joke."

"It's fine, Kizzy. Everyone likes a joke, even ex-slaves."

Livia gazed around the field, abruptly and acutely aware of being different. Everywhere she looked there were children running, in packs of three or four, scattering chickens in their wake while dogs barked in excitement. Livia had never watched children play before. She'd never enjoyed such freedom of movement. Thanks to the Boyar and his wife, she and Basil had been cruelly and coldly disconnected from their own people – from life itself.

Even Tepes was different to the other camp dogs; shadowing his keepers rather than running with his breed. All three of them were timid in a way that the others were not. Every family among them shone bright and vivacious; their tempers were quick and their clothes were as colourful as their language, with golden buttons glinting from the tunics of men whilst the women glittered with coins they had weaved into their hair.

"We call ourselves Romani," Kizzy explained, as they swapped memories and stories. "Everyone else we call *gadje*."

"And if you're half of one and half of the other?"

Kizzy paused and pulled the girl into her hard, round stomach, roughly embracing her.

"You are Romani, Livia. No different than the rest of us."

Raised poorly but with good manners, Livia thanked the woman for her kind words. She even promised herself she would try to believe them.

According to Kizzy, there were thousands of Romanies in the land they now travelled.

"And do they all speak like you?"

The woman both nodded and shook her head. "Every nation has its peculiarities, but the root is the same. I imagine you'll catch our dialect, in time."

Kizzy heaved herself from the steps of her wagon only to return a few minutes later carrying a rabbit stew, still hot in the pot.

"You need to eat more," she chided, and Livia smiled because she sounded like Basil. Out of habit, she glanced at the old man who was sat at the far end of a large fire, surrounded by men, feeding his belly and laughing with the best of them, even though he couldn't have hoped to catch every word they said.

"Is Basil your grandfather?" Kizzy asked, following Livia's gaze.

"No, my friend."

"Then he's taken you?"

Livia's face revealed her confusion, so Kizzy explained, without a hint of embarrassment.

"Oh, good Lord, no!" Livia replied, genuinely shocked.

"Well, men are men. It wouldn't be so strange."

"It would be for Basil; he's a *skopica*."

This time it was Kizzy's turn to be baffled. Though it felt disloyal, Livia whispered the explanation.

"May the devil damn them," the older woman muttered before shaking her head. "This isn't unknown to us. Many of us bear the scars of what the *gadje* have taken."

Lifting up her long hair, Kizzy revealed a ragged hole behind her left cheekbone, in the place where her ear ought to have sat.

"This was a gift from the French after we overstayed our welcome," she stated. "If I go back, and they find the proof of this warning, they're at liberty to kill me. It's written into their laws – evidence that they are a civilised people not simply murdering barbarians."

"They sound like murdering barbarians."

"They are. I was being sarcastic."

Despite her appetite being further diminished by the sight of the hole in Kizzy's head, Livia attempted to eat the stew the older woman had prepared.

After a brave effort, she put the pan aside and considered the revelation of the *gadje's* murderous legislation. "I thought our people were free here; that they could come and go as they pleased."

"We're free to move, as long as we don't go anywhere that they don't want us to go. Unfortunately, that's pretty much everywhere these days."

"And this place?"

"Here, we are so far tolerated, but feelings change faster than the wind. It's important to know what's going on."

Kizzy paused to scour the camp. Her eyes settled on a wagon on the far side of the field. In the dusk, Livia saw a silhouetted man, black against the horizon, perched on steps, eating alone.

"That's Walther," Kizzy revealed, "one of my cousins, naturally. He's the eyes and ears of our family. He's got the knowledge, you see; the writing and stuff. He goes into towns to discover what's going on in the *gadje's* newspapers and the posters they sometimes pin onto boards. It's useful to have someone like Walther in the company. He's helped us escape a few scrapes in our time because the *gadje* tend to moan before they strike."

As if sensing their interest, Kizzy's cousin stood up. He ambled towards the fire where the other men greeted him warmly. With less distance between them, Livia could see Walther was slim and perhaps a decade older than herself. It didn't escape her notice that his skin was as dark as the night drawing in. Straining for a better view through the haze of the flames, she couldn't be certain, but she thought she saw him watching her.

Despite the universal acceptance of Livia and Basil into the company, concerns were raised over Livia's pale face and green eyes. In short, the older women wanted her kept out of sight.

"The *gadje* already think we steal their babies," one complained as they gathered to air their reservations.

"She's not a baby, she's a woman," Kizzy replied tersely. It was a fact that not only finished the debate, but stirred the strangest sensation within Livia's stomach. She hadn't yet considered herself to be a woman and the public recognition of her status sent her eyes searching for Walther. As ever, she found him perched at the edge of the gathering, seemingly disinterested in the conversation taking place.

Livia was not a little disappointed.

"You don't catch a hawk by staring at it," Basil whispered as he came to sit by her side.

"I've no idea what you're talking about."

"Of course you don't," the old man chuckled. "No idea at all."

In front of them, Kizzy rose to her feet, a vision in red and gold.

"Are you ready?" she asked, and Livia replied that she was.

The previous night the two of them had hatched up a plan to lure the reticent *gadje* into parting with their money. They would make their way into the busiest area of the city where Livia would pretend to be a fine lady having her palm read. She would subsequently feign astonishment, delight and, if she could manage them, tears of gratitude.

"The *gadje* are gullible," Kizzy had informed her as they practiced their roles, and Livia had quipped that they needed to be. The foreign words she'd been taught bounced hard and round in her mouth, as though knowing they didn't belong there.

"*Jo! Na! Gut! Unglaublich!*"

Though Livia kept forgetting the meaning, there was a definite order to the words if she was to reel in the *gadje*. Once they were hooked, she was free to shut her mouth and wander the city to filch a few apples. The charade didn't seem so taxing, and in practice it wasn't. When the two women returned later that afternoon – their hands spilling with silver and fruit – even the old women seemed impressed. After that, nobody mentioned Livia's differences again and slowly, but surely, and with Kizzy's gentle guidance, she became the Romani she was.

Whilst Livia normally spent her days in the city, Basil stayed behind to assist where he could. A few of the men still toiled with metal, but the hold of the guilds found them few orders and even fewer openings so most earned their keep by weaving reeds into baskets or by poaching and fruit picking. Women not tied to the field by old age or new babies usually worked the town; selling their husband's wares or promises of good fortune while their young hovered close by, begging for pennies. Though Basil's arthritic hands limited his involvement, he gladly fetched water and attended the fires, while regaling gathered grandmothers with tales of Wallachian evil.

In the space of only weeks, there wasn't a man, woman or child who didn't adore Basil, and when Livia noticed the lightness return to her old friend's step she almost welled up as she reflected on his life and how lonely it must have been knowing he would never be reunited with his own family, or ever have the capability to start a new one. The more she contemplated this tragedy, the more determined she became to build a family of her own. Once again, her eyes drifted towards a man who parked his wagon on the furthest edge of the camp.

In comparison with the other Rom, Walther was a strange fellow; plainly dressed, quiet, and reserved. His face was angular and his hair was hacked shorter than the preferred fashion, which was mainly long with a complement of curls. He clearly lived alone because Livia had watched for other women and found none, but though he sometimes glanced in her direction that was attentive as he got. If anything, his interest appeared to lie more with Basil.

Late in the evenings, once the children were packed off to bed, Walther would leave his wagon to join the other men. Around the fire, he would encourage Basil to speak about his experiences, not that the old man needed any encouragement; Basil could talk a deaf man into submission. As he spoke, Walther sometimes interjected, asking for further details or the definition of a word, which he would then scratch onto a pile of yellow paper.

"The man's a genius," Basil informed Livia as he settled down for the night under a blanket on the grass below her. "I believe he's also looking for a wife."

Livia sat up from her bed in the open-top cart.

"I thought that would grab your attention," the old man chuckled.

"I *was* listening."

"Maybe so, but you're listening extra hard now, aren't you?"

"I'm doing no such thing."

"As you like."

Livia waited a moment before realising the old man wasn't about to make things easy. "So, is he then?"

"Is he what?"

"Is he looking for a wife?"

"Well, he hasn't actually said so, no, but as he's not got one, I'd assume that he is."

Livia rolled her eyes and lay back down. Basil's answer wasn't as reassuring as it might have been. "So, what's he been telling you?"

"Who?"

Walther!"

"Oh, Walther," Basil repeated, and Livia could have crowned him. "Usually, it's stuff about the old days, back there and here, in this place. We're in the Holy Roman Empire, you know. And that river we passed – the one with all the barges on it – it carries salt. The *gadje* call it White Gold."

"The river?"

"No, the salt. And that castle sitting on top of the city, it's known as the Salt Castle."

"That's kind of pretty."

"I guess. If you like salt. Anyhow, Walther says the Romanies arrived here after some religion called Protestantism drove them from wherever they were."

"Maybe France," Livia interjected. Basil turned his head. "Kizzy told me that's where they cut off her ear."

"They cut off her ear?"

"With a knife."

"That's a damn disgrace," Basil grumbled. "They've no right cutting a woman's ear off."

"But they did."

"I tell you, these *gadje* are devils, the lot of them." Basil paused to spit his disgust into the night. "So, where was I?"

"A religion called Protestantism…"

"Oh yes," he interrupted, picking up the line Livia hadn't finished throwing. "So, the Romanies came here from somewhere that might have been Frank…"

"France."

"There too, and they came hoping to fare better among the Catholics. You see, the Salt City doesn't like non-Catholics and not so long ago they kicked out a load of Protestants and took over their land. It was a mirror image of the Romanies plight, if you like, without the land part. The Protestants were forced to seek shelter in cities belonging to Protestant princes. On the road they were set upon by highwaymen and they had to pay all manner of taxes and tolls."

"Sounds like Wallachia."

"That's what I thought, but it's not really, and the truth is those refugees weren't like us at all; they were given shelter for a start, by countries practicing the same religion, whereas we – who will gladly take up anyone's god for the sake of a good night's sleep – are given refuge by no man."

"I wouldn't live among them even if they paid me," Livia insisted.

Instead of the approval she expected to hear, Basil emitted a loud sigh. "I hear what you say, child, but sometimes I find myself wondering what it must be like to sleep on a mattress in front of a fire with meat in the kitchen and water in a bath."

"Basil, the ground is your mattress. The fire you have, here. There's meat in the forest and water in the river."

"And all of that's very fine when you have youth on your side, but I don't. I swear the next winter that comes will kill me."

"It will do no such thing, Basil. See how far we've come. We actually have a home now, with people who respect us. And we are free."

"Maybe so, but it's not the same as peace, child. That's all I'm saying."

Livia paused to think of a way to shake the optimism back into her friend.

"I tell you what, I'll build us a proper wagon for the winter," she finally said, "with a roof and a tiny stove, like the one Kizzy and Harman have. Then you can sleep the whole day if you want to, just like Tepes."

"I'd rather sleep like the dead," he grumbled. "And when I go, Livia…"

"I know, Basil."

"Just see that you do."

On a morning much like any other, Livia dressed for her role as a Salt City madam and went to pick up Kizzy, only to find her friend had disappeared in the night. Naturally, Livia was anxious. More than that, she was astounded that no one appeared to share her concern. Not even Harman. When Livia pushed for answers, her questions were met with smiles, nothing more. Even Basil was baffled.

"Maybe they've killed her."

"Basil!" Livia protested.

"I'm just saying, that's all."

A week later, Kizzy reappeared, holding a baby in her arms. Livia was astonished, not only by the arrival of a baby, but by the reaction of the Romanies, which appeared to be no reaction at all.

"This is how things are done," Kizzy explained, which was hardly sufficient to answer all the questions swimming in Livia's head. She scoured her friend's face. Kizzy looked exhausted, virtually depleted, unlike her belly which appeared to be as full as the night she had left.

"But where did you go? Why didn't you stay?"

"Birth is a gift, but it also brings pollution. No one wants that in the community."

Kizzy covered her breast and lifted her baby over her shoulder, gently soothing the child's back until it vomited. Livia watched, unable to grasp the reasoning behind feeding a baby if a second later it was encouraged to throw up. As the question formed in her mouth, it was abruptly stolen by the determined approach of Walther. He was heading straight for them, carrying ink and a sheet of paper.

"Kizzy," he greeted.

"Walther."

"Got a name yet?"

"Naturally."

Walther sat on the grass, resting the paper on his knee. He looked up expectantly and Kizzy coughed. She paused a few seconds to rack up the tension.

"My daughter shall be named Luminitsa."

Livia gasped. "It's..."

"Yes," Kizzy admitted, knowing the girl's history from their nights by the fire. "And it's a fine name, an honourable name."

"Luminitsa it is," Walther confirmed. He wrote on the sheet of paper, adding the name to a long list of others.

"Can I see?" Livia asked. He pointed a finger at the latest entry. The ink was wet, glisteningly fresh, and it made the words look beautifully, wonderfully alive.

"Lum-in-it-sa," Walther said softly, in rhythm with the movement of his finger that glided beneath the shapes he had made.

"Lum-in-it-sa," Livia repeated. Her mother's name, recorded for eternity.

"Do you read at all?" Walther asked.

Livia tore her eyes from the page only to be startled by his proximity. They were sat so close their noses almost touched.

"No, I don't," Livia admitted, suddenly conscious they were sharing their first conversation.

"So, you don't write?"

"No."

"And do you want to?"

"I can't see as I'd have any use for it."

Livia smiled in a way that she hoped looked feminine and inviting.

"Fair enough," Walther replied, and he got to his feet and walked away.

Livia was mortified. Kizzy looked up from Baby Luminitsa, and chuckled. "You really do have a lot to learn."

Basil pulled Tepes roughly from the back of their wagon. The dog's brown eyes looked wounded and his tail hung between his legs.

"It's not natural," the old man grumbled, glancing at the other dogs with something close to envy, "sleeping all day, only waking to eat."

"He's a man after all," Livia teased.

She took hold of a plank and hammered it onto one of the posts she had fixed to the wagon's edges. Basil's face was unconvinced.

"It looks like a scabby hedgehog."

Though Livia ignored him, she inwardly conceded he had a point. She'd never built a home before but though it was unlikely to be a palace, she was quietly pleased with her efforts. Livia had promised Basil a shelter for the winter, and with the summer growing old she was running out of time to fulfil it. The nights were already chilly, and when the morning arrived it brought drizzle dampening their faces. Naturally, Harman offered his help, when he saw what the two of them were up to, but Basil wouldn't hear of it. Apparently, they needed to prove they could fend for themselves.

"We're not invalids."

"One of us isn't far off it," Livia retorted, and Basil slumped to the ground.

Rubbing a gnarled hand over his face, Basil apologised for his decrepitude. His regret hit like a dagger in Livia's heart.

"No, I'm sorry. It was a joke. I shouldn't have said it."

"Why not? It's the truth, isn't it? I know I'm no use to you."

"Of course you are, Basil!"

"No, I'm not. Look at me; sat here, giving a girl orders, to do a man's job. It's shameful, that's what it is."

"It's no such thing."

"Yes, it is."

Livia continued hammering. She told herself there was no reaching Basil when he was in one of his moods, but the truth was the noise dulled her guilt. It had been a really bad joke.

Over the years Livia had come to love the old man. Her attachment wasn't solely due to their shared past; she genuinely valued the former groom. Basil had been her teacher and guide, but above all her saviour. She would have eaten broken glass to protect him and though he never said it, the feeling was mutual, which is why – with winter approaching, along with his imminent death – Basil had been drawing up plans for Livia's safe future. As far as he was concerned, he'd given the child her life and now the time had come for her to share it with another. It hadn't taken Basil long to whittle down the contenders; most of the men in the vicinity were married. There could be only one and Walther would be a good match – despite the disgrace that had left him bookish and withdrawn.

"He had a wife once," Basil stated out of nowhere.

"Who did?"

"Walther."

Livia's heart stopped, unlike the hammer she wielded which caught her squarely on the thumb. With a tight-lipped curse, she sucked at her nail and took a break.

"Did she die? Walther's wife?"

"No, she got banished."

"Banished?"

"It's another of those things that they do here, though I've heard similar. Romani communities have a court system and when a crime gets committed, they settle it amongst themselves. Five men sit on a committee, no women of course, and the accused gets to speak, as well as the accuser, and in between everyone else can throw in their views, as long as they're men. Eventually, once all's been said that needs to be said, the five men lock heads and one of them decides on guilt, and then punishment. It's a good system."

Livia reached behind her back to stroke the tension stiffening her neck. She tried to remain patient, but as interesting as the Romanies' sense of justice was, their court system wasn't the most salient part of this discussion.

"And Walther's wife?" she reminded.

"Ah yes, the wife – or the sister-in-law – hard to figure out which really."

"Basil!"

The old man frowned. He wasn't fond of being rushed. "Walther's wife was caught with Walther's younger brother."

"You're kidding?"

"Am I laughing? As you can imagine, their position was untenable. The traitors had to go."

"Go where?"

"Away."

"And will they come back?"

"Unlikely," the old man declared. "A few months after they were banished, the two of them were found dumped in a river. Their necks had been slit. The woman's skirts were missing. They think it was brigands."

Livia crossed herself. Basil followed suit.

"It's dangerous when you go it alone, Livia. When I think back to our journey from Wallachia, knowing all that I know now, I have to say we were damn lucky. But luck runs out and when it does, I don't want you on your own. I want you with people who will protect you."

Livia smiled at her old friend's concern. "I'll always have you."

"No, you won't. I'll be dead by the winter."

"No, you won't Basil!"

"Yes, I will! And I'm not arguing about it because the main point of this discussion is to inform you that I've sorted your wedding."

"You've what?"

"I've sorted your wedding. Come the morning, you'll be marrying Walther."

Livia's feet slid from under her. Picking herself from the ground, she rubbed her rump, shook her head, and released an exasperated scream at Basil before running for Kizzy. It was a short distance, and Livia quickly found her waiting on the steps of her home, a wide smile painting her face.

"He's told you then."

"So, it's true?"

"It's a good match."

"Am I the last to know of it?" Livia asked despairingly, before contemplating something far worse. "Does Walther even know?"

"Of course he does."

Kizzy laughed and ushered the girl inside. As they moved into the wagon, their steps made music of the glass balls that hung in lines along the walls of her home. In a corner, baby Luminitsa slept on a pillow.

"Harman and the boys will stay with Walther tonight," Kizzy informed Livia. "There's much to be done if you're to be a fitting bride for my cousin."

Livia plunged her head into her hands. "I don't believe this is happening."

"Believe it."

Forcing Livia to look up, Kizzy ran a critical eye over the girl's face and got to work. The first transformation involved a needle, which she promptly stabbed through Livia's ears.

"Don't worry, the blood will stop by tomorrow," she promised.

Given her shock, as well as her panic and the hellish throbbing of her ears, Livia barely slept a wink on the eve of her wedding, so when it took place, it felt nothing short of a dream. There was no ceremony to speak of, simply a bizarre ritual involving bread and salt, and the rest of the day passed in a blur of dancing, feasting and worrying advice from the company's grandmothers, all of whom were hell-bent on preparing Livia for the coming horror that the night would bring.

As the women fussed, the men took breaks from their tin plates to salvage Livia's ramshackle attempt at building a roof-topped wagon. Their assistance was the dowry Basil had earned, if not through blood than through care.

"We'll give it a dash of colour in the morning," Harman promised, and the old man thanked him for his help, smiling broadly and feeling richer than a king.

Once the sun had set, the men carried Livia on a wooden litter decorated with flowers to the door of her new home. The short journey was accompanied by the women who either sang or winked at her knowingly. Stepping into Walther's wagon, Livia looked at the blanket on the floor that was destined to be their bed and she waited for her husband, feeling both terrified and elated. When he joined her moments later Walther sighed. He made an awkward joke about the long ears of his brothers before smiling. He pulled Livia towards him. The top buttons of his shirt were undone and she smelt the day's exertions in the heat of his body. Sweeping back her long hair, Walther kissed his new wife for the first time. He then did his tender best to ensure her next experience would be a good one.

Before Livia was aware of the night being over, the sun warmed her face through the slats of the wagon. Her pillow was a warm chest and she blinked in surprise before remembering where she was.

"Are you happy?" he asked.

Startled a second time because she hadn't realised Walther was awake, Livia nodded shyly.

"Truly happy?" he pressed, and realising he expected more she took a moment to think about it.

"Well, my ears hurt."

"I'm sorry?"

"It's the rings. They're burning the crap out of me, like hot pokers."

Walther paused, somewhat unprepared for the conversation they were having. "Well, I'm sure they'll feel better soon, once they've healed."

"Yes, Kizzy said much the same thing."

"But other than that, other than your ears, I mean... everything's alright?"

"Oh yes," Livia beamed turning to look at her husband. "Everything's more than alright. I've just about had the happiest night of my life!"

An hour later, and with her skin prickling with the excitement of being loved, Livia ran to find Basil, keen to invite him for breakfast in her new home. Reaching the old cart, which had also undergone something of a transformation in the night, she greeted Tepes. He was tied to the wheel and seemed pretty upset by it. As she freed him, Livia noticed Basil's tethered horse watching her, bored and expectant. Something wasn't quite right. And even before she looked inside the wagon, she knew Basil had gone.

In the early hours of the morning, the old man had passed away, in his own bed, in his own home, with a contented smile on his sweet, shrunken face. Many times over, Livia had imagined Basil's death – thanks mainly to his fascination with it – but the sense of loss was different to what she had expected. This wasn't the pit of grief that had accompanied her mother's passing, but rather a sense of peace. Basil had worked hard for this moment, and for the next two hours, Livia stayed by her friend's side, stroking his soft white hair, as she told him everything that he had ever meant to her. Once she was finished, she picked herself up and shared her sadness with the rest of the company.

"He said the winter would kill him, not my marriage," Livia told Walther as they stood, hand in hand, watching the flames swallow Basil and the home he still laid in.

"It was his time," Walther replied softly. "He swore to protect you, which he did. Now you have me to protect you. His duty was done. He's at rest, Livia. It's a blessing."

Because she agreed, Livia shed only a few tears for the man she owed her life to. When the black smoke carried Basil away, she whispered, "Tell my mother I love her." As if in answer, Tepes stretched his neck to the moon and howled. His lament was quickly taken up by the other dogs in the camp, and somewhere in the distance – within stone houses standing in the shadow of a great castle – the *gadje* looked out of their shuttered windows and shivered. Unnerved by the flames and the ghostly howls in the night, fathers bolted their doors, mothers pushed crucifixes into their children's hands, and fires were kept burning well into morning. When it came, they gathered.

Before dawn had barely begun, the city folk congregated in the market square. Their mumbling fear soon gained strength in numbers. It was said that a child had fallen ill in the night. A calf was born with three legs. A red mist appeared in the baker's parlour. A woman had lost much of her hair. 'Witches!' someone shouted. The city had been cursed! Snatching torches from their brackets, they marched from the square, galvanising the panic in their chests into hate and mob fury. Armed with pitchforks, knives and pistols, they swarmed out of the city, gathering more on their way as a man of God ran between them, feeding their anger with righteous fury and prophecies of doom. With snarling threats, they broke into the clearing that used to be their land, brandishing fire, screaming hate and demanding blood. But their fever died on the wind. The field was empty. The Romanies had gone.

Because sound travels swifter than feet in the valleys, Harman ordered everyone into their wagons at the first rumble of trouble. Livia was stunned by the speed of the evacuation.

"Fear is an uncontrollable pest," Walther told his wife as they followed the trail leading away from Salt City. "Once it takes, it quickly spreads. Your only hope is to outrun it."

Livia stared at the wagon in front of her. She saw little urgency in its speed. In fact, she could have passed it at a brisk walk. Beside her, Walther rested his arms on his knees as he played with the leather reins that were looped casually between his fingers. Along the grassy verge, a number of children had already vacated their seats to run with their dogs. Even the beady eyes of the chickens stared at her, unperturbed. Livia could only assume that in the space of a morning they had outrun the uncontrollable pest. Behind their wagon, she heard the steady beat of soft hooves as Basil's horse followed them.

"Do you think it was the funeral fire that scared the *gadje*?"

Walther tipped his head towards her, in possible confirmation. Livia sighed in response and pulled Tepes onto her lap. Despite her husband's protests, the dog sat on the seat next to them.

"It's funny how someone's death could bring the *gadje* screaming for more."

"It wasn't Basil's death that scared them, but the night and fears of their own making," Walther replied. "The *gadje* are so disconnected from the earth that they forget all she is. They hear threats in the howls of dogs; they see blood-suckers in the flight of bats; and flesh-eaters in the blizzards that cut them off in the mountains. There is evil abroad, that's for certain, and there are creatures walking among us that are caught between sleep and waking. But there is also nature, the very clothes worn by Mother Earth. She is our protector, and she works for the good of all of her children, even the greedy ones. Though the *gadje* might try to cut and divide her skin, there's no place on earth that a person doesn't belong. But these fools suffer from a form of gluttony, one that has brought them nothing but misery and war. This is not our way. Romanies respect the land that feeds us. We know her sights and sounds. And this is what the *gadje* have lost. Today, they believe only in their own purses."

Walther turned his head towards Livia. He was clearly expecting some kind of response, but she had lost the thread of his argument at the hairy flesh-eaters.

"Do you eat a lot of dry bread?" she suddenly asked, recalling something her mother once said.

Not for the first time, Walther was speechless.

Crawling along the shadows of mountains, skirting lakes that shone like mirrors, the Romani caravan moved eastwards, occasionally stopping at towns that would either tolerate them, pay them to leave, or threaten to destroy them. With the arrival of winter, life became harder, and for some of them it was a suffering too many. One morning Livia woke up to discover Tepes sleeping the long sleep under the wheels of their wagon.

"He was lazy but loyal," she said, after they cracked the frozen earth to bury him. Walther didn't reply immediately because he was too embarrassed. No one buried dogs.

"Really Livia, they're filthy creatures, no better than cats," he later chided. "They carry diseases that can blind a man. In future I'd have you save your attachment for your husband and children."

Livia shrugged at what she guessed was a reprimand. She then patted her stomach and gifted her husband a smile, promising she would endeavour to do as she was told.

"Don't try, do!" Walther instructed.

"I do! I do! I do!" Livia yelled. "Honestly, you're worse than Basil sometimes."

Flicking the reins of his horse, Walther ignored his wife's teasing, largely because he didn't want to encourage her. If he was brutally honest, he had hoped she would be quieter than she was. But she was young and he was partly to blame, having done little to knock the sense into her. Violence simply wasn't his way.

Blissfully unaware of her husband's discontent, Livia considered herself to be nothing short of blessed. Walther was calm, strong and reassuringly black – a gift from God, come to dilute the shame of her heritage. In fact, her only quibble had nothing to do with the man but rather his home. Livia had been enchanted by the glittering grotto of Kizzy's wagon and she yearned to decorate her own with a few trinkets. Sadly, Walther favoured study over style and he refused to make space among the piles of yellowing paper stacked against the walls.

"Words are more valuable than trinkets or gold," Walther insisted. "They are the wealth of our past and the signposts to our future. For hundreds of years, our grandmothers have passed on their wisdom in the form of stories and fables, and as our collective memory fades and we lose sight of our cousins, it is more important than ever to keep a written account of our experiences. In those papers behind us you will find the roots of our birth. It is a work of respect, in honour of our ancestors and as necessary to our harmony as any of the herbs Kizzy burns around her family or the rituals we follow at every birth or death. In those papers, there are lives written many times over. Some are only a few lines, others have pages, but all of them tell of who we are and of the events that shaped us. It is a work with no end, and when we have gone, our children will carry it on, doing our memories and our people proud."

Livia scowled in irritation. "I don't mean any disrespect," she said, "but I really think you need to get out more."

Walther looked up from the reins in his hands. "I'm serious," he said.

"So am I," Livia laughed, and Walther shook his head.

Refusing to speak another word, Walther got his revenge later that evening, when the Romani caravan groaned to a halt and he banned his wife from the daily gossip she appeared to enjoy with the other women.

"We are writers," he stated with a broad smile. He handed Livia a chalk and slate. "And a writer must learn to write."

"Lord, have mercy, Walther."

"God can't help you now, my love."

And closing his ears to Livia's protests, Walther picked up his own work, sorting through his papers as his wife struggled to copy the letters he had chalked on the slate.

Despite his wife's disinterest, and the cynicism of their community, Walther steadfastly believed that in the years to come there wouldn't be a man on earth who wouldn't know how to read or write. When that time came the *gadje* would come to realise their mistakes from the written memories of those they had denied, and armed with this knowledge the world would find a new way of living, free of prejudice, free of war and free of ignorance. This would be how the Romanies would find their place. But until that time came, Walther would continue to safeguard the key and travel with his company – following Harman and Kizzy's trinket-laden wagon as it jangled ever eastwards.

At first Livia said nothing about the direction they were taking, but after she disappeared for a week to return with her first child, her sense of unease could no longer be ignored and she voiced her fears.

"I've travelled this path before, Walther, and I don't wish to retread it."

"It is not the same path," he assured her.

"Yes, it is! I see where the sun rises and see where it sets and I see where it leads us. I will not go back there. I tell you, I won't."

Walther pulled his wife towards him as gently as his patience would allow. "I understand why you're scared, and I tell you we are not going there."

Releasing her, he picked up their son. The child was fat, healthy, and dark – everything Livia had prayed for. And because her husband felt equally blessed, he raised no objection when she called him Basil. In truth he thought it a good omen given they were following a route the old man had unwittingly suggested during his soliloquies by the fire. Royal Hungary was to be their next destination.

Having spent enough time in the west to accept they were running out of luck, the Romanies had listened to Basil as he talked of a place that neighboured the one he had fled. Despite popular opinion, the men in their caravan weren't habitual thieves or hopeless vagabonds; they were skilled artisans deprived of an income by the greed of Europe's guilds. Basil had sworn this wouldn't be the case in Royal Hungary. It was a land, he said, where men were neither slaves nor outcasts, but workers appreciated for the skills they brought.

"I don't know…" Livia replied warily, once Walther revealed the course they were taking.

"But you should know," he responded tartly, and he meant it quite literally.

The next time they rested, he pulled out a bundle of papers. He untied the twine and began to read to his wife. He told of a mighty empire that had been ruled by Greeks and ravaged by plague. He said the tragedy had driven the Romanies westwards, some blindly walking into slavery, others finding a fate that was different, but no less appalling.

"Arriving in Europe, our ancestors were greeted as curiosities from Egypt or as pilgrims fleeing the scourge of Islam. They arrived on horses and mules and they scattered to the four corners of the Holy Roman Empire, like autumn leaves blown by the wind. Remembering the Latin hordes and their doomed Crusades, the Romanies shrouded themselves in the fascination of the time. They appointed 'Counts' or 'Dukes' to follow and they spoke of great suffering at the hands of child-eating Turks. Some of the 'Counts' claimed to have been driven from their homes. Others said they had left willingly; as punishment for converting to Islam. They were penitent Christians, they said, required by God to roam the earth for seven long years and, as such, the subjects of the Holy Roman Empire behaved charitably, if not always kindly. However, even at the start, there were grumbles of suspicion.

"In the German-speaking territories, the Romanies' dark skin saw them despised as Turks or as criminals. The people there didn't recognise our language as a foreign tongue, but rather a cant of the underworld, designed to hide criminal activity and accommodate spying. It became increasingly clear that a pilgrim's safe passage could not rely on the name of God alone. Thankfully, there were those blessed with the skills to deal with the problem; not the famous musicians or the coppersmiths or bear trainers, but the writers.

"When the going had been good, the Romanies had acquired letters from various nobles who sought salvation in acts of charity, and there was no greater act of benevolence than aiding a pilgrim on his travels. These letters were addressed to the officials within their kingdoms and they demanded the Romanies be treated kindly and given roof, hearth and fire. The order wasn't always heeded, but a number of towns donated cows, herrings, and casks of ale, as well as straw for the pilgrims' animals. Given the irregular nature of such generosity, the Romanies also indulged in petty theft, fortune-telling, and the occasional counterfeiting of coins. By and large, however, the Romanies took only what they needed.

"One of the most valuable letters they possessed came from the Holy Roman Emperor himself. He wrote that the Romanies were to be greeted with love wherever they travelled. They were to be given no hindrance or trouble and they were to be preserved from all impediments and vexations. Truly, it was a very fine letter, the best among the crop, and with the skills of the Romani writers, it was faithfully copied and passed on, time and again.

"For a while the subterfuge worked; the appointed 'Counts' rode on horseback whilst their faithful subjects followed on foot. They covered vast distances and came to be known all over Europe; from Bologna to Paris; Amiens to Rotterdam; Utrecht to Fermo. However, as the decades rolled by the charm of the seven-year pilgrimage began to lose its lustre. Furthermore, the Church had grown irritable and it accused the Romani fortune-tellers of sowing discord within decent, Christian households. Slowly, but surely, Europe began to batten down her hatches.

"A hundred years after their arrival, the Romanies were no longer seen as honest pilgrims fleeing the Islamic devil, but as traitors, spies and thieves. The writers of the day castigated the scurrilous 'gypcians' as "the dregs and bilge water of various peoples". Eventually their word spread and it is what the Romanies became in the eyes of other men.

"Seemingly from nowhere, laws sprang up to deal with those now demoted from pilgrims to pests. Cities refused them entry; they were forcibly ejected; paid to leave; and jailed at random. Anti-gypsy legislation was adopted in

Lucerne, Brandenburg, Spain, Germany, Holland, Portugal, England, Denmark, France, Flanders, Scotland, Bohemia, Poland, Lithuania and Sweden. Romanies were no longer worthy of house or shelter, orders were given for their expulsion, and once they were officially cast as outlaws it was only a matter of time before permission was granted to kill them. In order to survive, the larger companies fractured into ever-smaller groups, making them more mobile and less conspicuous. Even then, the persecution continued.

"During those dreadful years the countryside was plagued with beggars: maimed soldiers from the Hundred Year War; Catholic priests evicted from their monasteries; and displaced peasants, pirates, and brigands. And yet, there was only one group that was consistently hunted and that was the Romani people. Europe meant to finish them.

"As the laws increased throughout the continent, the Romanies were chased, banned and punished. Their cheeks were branded; ears were severed; women and children had their heads shaved; they were flogged; arrested; and sent to work on the galleys. The Church disowned her dark-skinned children, and the Romanies were rejected, country by country, with no thought to where they might go or to what might welcome them. They were hanged without trial, put in hospices and workhouses, and when they hid themselves in the cloak of the forests, the *gadje* hunted them like foxes, winning rewards for their severed heads.

"And there you have it, Livia. This is how Europe was and this is how Europe is. This is the Europe we are leaving. I know you're scared about heading east, but I promise you truly, we will only travel on part of the path that brought you to me."

For months after Walther's revelations, Livia was plagued by nightmares, most of them involving the death of her husband and the slaughter of her child. Every evening, when she joined her friends around the fire, her enjoyment was ruined by the constant anxiety of sufferings yet to happen. A boy's playful shouts became the screams of the mutilated; a missing face was the victim of a 'gypsy hunt'. By the end of another summer, Livia couldn't have left Europe fast enough and her distress only increased when she gave birth to another boy – another potential victim of the merciless *gadje*.

Basil was in his second year when Emilian arrived. And thanks be to God, the baby was perfect in every way. Blessed with the handsome, stern face of his father, he was quiet and easily satisfied. Walther was overjoyed to have a second son. In turn, Basil was curious and he proceeded to acquaint himself with his new brother by putting his feet into his mouth at every given opportunity.

"Life continues, no matter what," Walther mused as they packed up their wagon to continue their seemingly endless journey.

"How far is it now?" Livia moaned.

"Not far!" shouted Kizzy. She threw Livia a wink from the front seat of her wagon. Livia felt no need to reply because it was a claim Kizzy made every morning.

Walther snapped his reins and their wagon lurched forward to take up the rear of the caravan. As the train of twenty or so wagons pulled away, rolling up a small incline, Livia was reminded of one of her husband's stories, and she imagined the wagons in front of her were the lumbering backsides of leathery elephants, swinging their way to war, seven hundred years earlier. She had to admit that compared to their ancestors, their own journey was but a moment, nothing more, and by the time Livia felt a third child stirring in her belly, her caravan of friends and family penetrated the invisible borders of Royal Hungary. Livia was 20 years old.

Far from the new start that Walther had envisaged, Royal Hungary proved to be depressingly familiar. Everywhere the Romanies stopped, they were watched by eyes guarded by suspicion and bubbling resentment. The only positive was that the locals were few and far between. With great swathes of land owned by lords ensconced within castles, the country was sparsely populated and easy to hide in, if you had the mind for it.

"It feels like Wallachia; cold and unfriendly," Livia grumbled as she skinned a rabbit Walther had caught.

"It's not Wallachia," her husband insisted.

"But it is cold and unfriendly?"

"Well, yes. It is."

Despite the chilly reception, the Romanies found they could enter towns and practise their trades with little or no hindrance. It was a novelty that gave birth to thoughts of settling. After conferring with the other men, Harman chose to establish a more permanent base outside a city called Kassa.

Initially, everything appeared to go well; the men dusted off their anvils, hooked up supplies, and the women took their finished plates into the city to sell. But then, in the second week of their arrival, Harman received a number of visitors.

Without warning, a group of twenty or more men descended on their site. They were hard-faced with iron bars swinging casually in their hands. Taking the lead was a man who introduced himself as Ferka. Harman greeted the men cordially, because he saw they were different, yet also the same. The strangers wore their hair short, their legs were hidden by billowing cloth, yet Ferka's speech was familiar, and when he spoke there was no malice in his demands. Kassa was the birthright of his company, he explained. If times were easier, it wouldn't be a problem, but times weren't easy and there was no room for more. He was truly sorry, he said, but he had come to ask Harman to move on.

Being a man of honour – and genuinely respecting the prior claim of a Romani brother armed with an iron bar – Harman said his people had meant no disrespect and that they would be gone by the morning. The two men shook hands, the tension dropped from the air, and everyone breathed again. Ferka then waved an arm and a cart drawn by men rolled into the clearing. It carried barrels of ale and a band of musicians.

"I guess I can kiss goodbye to my husband for the night," Kizzy said wearily, and for the first time in a long while, Livia laughed.

As Kizzy predicted, the arrival of the Hungarian Roma and their brotherly generosity, brought a celebration that lasted well into the morning. The musicians were astounding, their music sublime, and it charmed the hearts and ears of every one of them in the field. Even Walther got to his feet to dance with his boys. As he caroused with his sons, he flashed Livia a broad smile, and one of the old women hobbled over to point at Livia's stomach.

"You best get that one out quick. I've a feeling your husband will be bringing you another tonight."

Around them, the women all cackled in agreement and Livia blushed furiously. Away from the men, the chatter of their women could curl even the straightest hair.

As the moon began her descent, the players began to grow weary and their melodies less cohesive the drunker they got. Finally, the chief violinist ended the performance. He finished with a sweet lament that brought chills to the back of Livia's neck, reminding her of another violinist from another time. As she looked around the fire, she saw sadness reflected in each and every eye.

"Were times not what they are," Ferka apologised to Harman, his voice sad and slurred.

"If only," the Big Man agreed. "But what went wrong here?"

Ferka snorted loudly. Accepting another measure of ale, he stroked the sorrow from his cheeks before answering.

"It never used to be bad," he admitted. "But that was long ago, in the time of our grandfathers' grandfathers, possibly longer. For a while everyone lived side by side, and our lives were relatively peaceful. Then, in some corner of the empire, the peasants revolted. It signalled the end for all of us. After they were beaten into submission, the royal prince instructed the smiths in Temesvar to fashion a throne out of iron as well as a crown and a sceptre. The Romanies did as they were ordered because it was a job like any other.

Had they known what the prince was up to, they might have refused. You see, the prince took the crown and the sceptre and he placed them into a great fire. When they were red hot, he forced the peasants' leader onto a burning throne. He then stamped the glowing crown over the man's head and thrust the flaming sceptre into his hands. After his death, his followers were forced to eat his charred flesh. From that day on, the peasants never forgave the Romanies."

Around the fire, everyone listening made the mark of the cross on their chests. Ferka paused for a slug of ale. "After we provided the tools that tortured their hero, things went from bad to worse. Where once we used to roam freely, now a fool would wander alone. Not that we're actually allowed to. Twenty odd years ago, the Empress banned travelling. She forced us to settle and, the next thing we knew, the treasury was at our door demanding taxes."

"You became slaves?" Livia interrupted, unable to stop herself as her eyes darted to the faces of her children.

"Not slaves as such, serfs I suppose," corrected Ferka. "We were banned from owning horses and we were told to stay in our villages. Before we knew what was happening, we couldn't even call ourselves Romani. We were 'New Hungarians'. From now on, we weren't to set ourselves apart from the Old Hungarians in any way – from our language to our dress. I mean, look at these clothes; I look like a goddamn peasant. Pretty soon, new laws were passed banning us from marrying our own kind and bringing up our kids. Children under five were to be taken away and brought up in non-gypsy families. Well, you can imagine how that news was taken. Law or no law we won't have a white man carry off our children. Luckily, the Empress appeared to be alone in many of her ideas and most of her subjects found it easier to turn a blind eye. But it's the threat of what they could do that makes our lives uncomfortable. And that's how we live today, walking like ghosts among people, hoping they won't change their minds and steal our children."

After Ferka and his men returned to their settled lives, Livia put her sleeping boys to bed and confided in her husband. She was scared, she said. Walther squeezed her hand and turned away before she could read his eyes.

"Try to get some sleep. Everything will be fine," he whispered.

"Are you not going to sleep?"

"Later, once I've written up Ferka's stories."

Walther forced a smile to his lips and because Livia trusted him, she tried to return it. The next morning, he left at dawn and went to sit with other bleary-eyed men who had gathered around the still-smoking embers of the previous night's fire. Once Harman joined them it was unanimously decided that they would take the road west.

"A life's a life, but it's worth nothing without your children," Walther told Livia as he explained why they would be chancing their luck again in Europe.

"I'm so relieved," Livia admitted as she pulled herself onto the seat of their wagon.

"Me too," shouted Basil, placing himself between his parents.

"Me! Me! Me!" chorused Emilian.

"Well, nothing new there then," Walther teased, and Livia laughed as he passed their son over.

After so long travelling – and despite every pain, grumble and worry that came with it – Livia relaxed as she felt the wheels turning beneath her. On the road, with the wind catching her hair and the breath of the horses misting their path, she felt safe in a way she couldn't explain. Livia placed a hand on her growing bump, feeling the warmth of new life waking inside her. She looked at her sons, drinking in their wide-eyed innocence, and at the man who had made their lives possible. As long as they had each other, as long as the wheels kept turning, they could be happy. Livia was sure of it. Just as long as the wheels kept turning.

Two days into their journey, Harman brought the caravan to halt in a place called Hont County and Livia felt her nerves return, itching like bugs under her skin, longing to be gone. Although he may have shared her disquiet, Walther began to lose patience; telling his wife that men had to sleep. But as she watched him snore, Livia could find no rest, no matter what he said. She tossed and turned, unable to relax no matter which way she lay. She could find no tangible reason for her worry. All she knew was that she was incapable of shaking it. Adding to her distress was a baby kicking fiercely against her bladder. Eventually, after a fruitless hour spent trying to ignore the need, Livia left her bed to find some relief. As soon as she opened the door, her mouth fell open.

"We've got to go!" she shouted as she hurried back inside.

Walther jumped from sleep, automatically reaching for an iron bar. "What's happened? Is someone here?"

"Not yet," Livia replied. She grabbed the boys from their beds. "But Walther, please trust me. God help us, we have to go! We really have to go!"

"I trust you," Walther assured her, trying to sound calm as he pulled on his breeches in order to wake the rest of the company. By the time he jumped from the wagon, he found Livia's shouts had beaten him to it.

"What is it?" Kizzy demanded rushing to speak with him, closely followed by her husband.

"It's Livia, she's seen something or feels something, I don't know what, but she's determined we leave."

"Then we'll leave," Harman agreed, "But in the morning. It's not safe for the horses to be travelling at night."

Livia yelled from the wagon, insisting tomorrow would be too late.

"Wait, Harman," Kizzy instructed her husband. She reached for his arm as he turned to go. "Let me speak with her."

Harman threw his hands into the air, but his silence revealed his consent. Wrapping her shawl about her, Kizzy climbed into Walther's wagon. Livia hardly noticed she was so busy anchoring her belongings. On the floor, Basil watched his mother, half-dazed. Emilian was crying. Kizzy picked up the baby.

"Livia, not so fast, love. What have you seen?"

Livia looked up and the woman paled at the fear she found in the girl's eyes.

"It's something I've seen only once before, Kizzy, on the night I knew my mother had died. It's the moon; it's blood red. I swear to you, this isn't a joke or an act of lunacy, we've really got to go."

Kizzy crossed her chest. She had also seen the moon that night, and it was round and perfectly white.

"So be it," she agreed, handing Emilian back to his mother. Kizzy then stepped from the wagon and told her husband they must leave, "Right now."

Because Harman trusted his wife's instinct, even above his own eyes, he hollered her instructions to the rest of the camp. The response was immediate. The women dressed their children, locked up their wagons and the men harnessed their horses. Within twenty minutes, the company was ready to go. Their horses pawed at the ground sensing the urgency. Their dogs stood ready to run with the wheels. And everyone kept their eyes on Harman, waiting for his signal. Only it was too late.

Before his arm went up, a river of fire flickered in the dark, heading straight for them. Seeing the danger, the women yelled in panic as the men urged on their horses, but their exit was quickly blocked. Livia held onto her children as Walther turned their wagon searching for an opening. But there was nowhere to run and within minutes they were encircled by a sea of white faces brandishing torches and guns.

Livia held on to her sons, sat on the dirt that their fears had turned into mud. On a stool in front of her, a guard kept watch while his superiors tried to make sense of her appearance. His eyes were cold and the set jaw revealed his irritation at the task. Emilian whimpered in her arms. Basil was mute with fear. And somewhere, out of sight, Livia heard the wails of women she knew. She almost wished she were with them.

Like cattle, the Romanies had been herded into the centre of a town. Not only Livia's company, but dozens more, plucked from their beds to answer allegations of theft. When the man in charge saw Livia's green eyes, he came over to speak with her. One of the Hungarian Romni managed to shout a translation before being silenced by a fist.

"He thinks you're a white woman! Save yourself, tell them you are!"

Of course, Livia could do no such thing. She hadn't the words. And confused by her silence, the armed men pulled her from her family to deal with her later. As they grabbed her, Livia slipped from their hands to run back for her children. With a nod, the man who seemed to be in charge permitted her to take her boys. They were led to a wooden pen, away from the square, but in hearing distance of those left behind. The screams that followed would stay with her until the day that she died.

Four days after her arrest, Livia was told she was free. She then she learned the full cruelty of what had occurred. More than 150 Romanies had been rounded-up, investigated and judged. An initial charge of theft had been swiftly forgotten during the course of the interrogation as news arrived of another more serious crime; apparently, a number of men had disappeared from a village. Their bodies were missing and it was presumed they had been eaten. The torture that followed brought confessions of cannibalism.

In front of a cheering crowd, six Romanies were broken on the wheel, fifteen were hanged, two were quartered and eighteen were beheaded. Their screams scared the birds from the trees. Their blood flowed faster than a river. And then two days later, the human wreckage of what was left of their people was suddenly unshackled. Somehow, the ruling family had come to hear of the case. Following another investigation, it was ascertained that the missing men were not only alive, but sitting in their homes. The *gadje's* 'error' had cost the Roma 41 lives, including that of Livia's husband and the woman who had first given her a home. Kizzy was gone. Walther was gone. Livia was grief-stricken.

For weeks after their release, the Romanies travelled in a daze with no sense of direction, no fear of the unknown, unable to shake a vision of hell. Though Harman survived, he was a shell without his wife. Even so, the company followed him because they knew no other way.

Although their wagons were returned, every home had been ransacked, every memory stolen. Livia had never possessed much, but her clothes and even the tiny stove were gone. All that remained were Walther's papers, ripped from their binding to be scattered like rubbish. With tears blinding her eyes, Livia collected every sheet, feeling her husband's touch on each and every page. His life's work was intact. It had survived his death, just as he predicted.

As the days melted into weeks, perhaps into months, the company rode through sunlight and rain until they felt the breath of winter burrow into their bones. Livia could hold on no longer, and seeing her dilemma the company halted. A week later they resumed their journey, and the new mothers around her lined up to feed the baby in her arms because Livia's own breasts were unfit for the job. It hardly needed saying, but Livia named her son Walther.

As Harman continued to push the caravan on, nobody dared ask where they were heading, and in truth it scarcely mattered. The Romanies kept moving because stopping meant dying. At Livia's side, Basil stared into the distance. The chattering boy gone, never to return. Though Emilian was too young to understand, the grief around him weighed heavy on his shoulders and he spoke only in order to answer. Only baby Walther behaved according to his nature, incessantly crying for the milk his mother hadn't the strength to supply. Livia snapped at the reins of their horse, forcing them forward, trying not to see her husband's fingers in the leather thongs she now held.

Finally, as the snow began to fall and the earth began her sleep, the Romanies found their path blocked by a tall man dressed in furs. A felt hat covered his long hair and tucked inside his leather boots was a whip. Livia's heart chilled.

"Who do you belong to?" the stranger demanded.

Of course, no one could answer him because they hadn't the means. No one apart from Livia. And with no name to offer the *Cioce* she knew they were destined to become the property of the state. She stepped down from her wagon to translate.

"Will they kill us?" asked Kizzy's eldest boy.

"I don't think so. Not if we work for nothing and don't try to escape."

"Then that's good enough for me," interrupted Harman. The matter was closed. Livia nodded, accepting the decision.

"We have no master," she informed the *Cioce*.

Livia was 75 years old when she died and for 67 of those years she lived as a slave. However, when the time came for her to breathe her last, she left her body as a freewoman.

Having been seized by the state, she worked for many years as a domestic in the royal household. The conditions were tolerable and she was permitted to stay with her family. Each of her three boys worked on the land and they all grew up to be men. They were never shackled, and Livia was thankful for that, but the days were long and always exhausting and, in the end, Livia outlived them all. Naturally, each death took its toll and there were occasions when she could barely drag her body from the floor, her mind was so crowded with the faces she had lost. But for every end there was also a beginning, and Livia was blessed with nineteen grandchildren. It was these sparks of happiness that kept her heart beating, that kept her writing, and that kept her teaching. And it was her grandchildren that she called for when the young Prince startled the world with a longed-for announcement.

Keen to emulate their European cousins, slavery had grown unfashionable among Wallachia's nobles. Coupled with the advent of machinery, it had also become uneconomical. Therefore, in 1837, the Prince freed all the slaves on his estate.

As soon as she heard the news, Livia rose from her bed, where she had been confined for the past three years. For an hour or more, she gathered and ordered a lifetime of work, stroking each page in farewell. Though she was no longer able to see the words, she felt the power of them within her hands. She knew they would live on. Then, walking unaided from the hut her family had been permitted to build, Livia gathered her grandchildren before her, as well as their wives, husbands and children. After kissing them all, she wished them a safe journey.

"You can burn me now," she told them quietly. "I think it's time I went to thank my mother."

Chapter Twelve

Although there was a moment of guilty pleasure as I watched the colour drain from Jack's face as he comprehended the scale of calamity that had visited a people he may, or may not, have been related to, this paled into insignificance the following morning when I finished my chores to find Florian loitering beside our caravan, his meaty arms penning three sullen-eyed children into compliance. He pushed the youngsters towards me. His eyes were bloodshot and a number of dark holes gaped where his teeth had once stood.

"Tell them things," was the brief instruction, and with a cursory nod at his flesh and blood he turned away leaving his children staring at me, somewhat resentful and clearly suspicious. I was insanely delighted by the development.

"Well, isn't this is a nice surprise?"

"It's a surprise all right," muttered the oldest boy.

"And you are?"

"Telus."

"That's a fine name."

"If you say so. I had no hand in it."

A miniature version of his father, Telus was round and churlish. The black t-shirt he wore clung to his body like the casing of a sausage, and though his arms were folded, I saw his hands were clenched into fists. The effect was rather fierce on a twelve-year-old boy. Nonetheless, I smiled in encouragement. It was a gesture the child felt no need to reciprocate.

Ushering the youngsters inside – sensing that any dithering would only allow the moment to grow mutinous – I opened the windows and ordered Mirela to gather more pens. I sat everyone around a small table that collapsed into the wall when we needed the space to sleep.

"Pens or pencils?" Mirela inquired.

Telus opted for a pen. It was a choice echoed by his younger siblings.

"A pencil might be better, just in case you make a mistake," my daughter advised.

"Are you saying we're stupid?" Telus challenged.

"No."

"Well, it sounds like you are."

"Then I'd say you were deaf."

"Mirela..." I warned.

My daughter pursed her lips and rolled her eyes. Although he smirked, Telus discarded the pen and, after some theatrical deliberation, he took a blue pencil from my daughter's hands. She nodded sternly to show her approval. Though it was only a small triumph in the sea of crap that we sailed on, I couldn't have felt prouder of my daughter if she'd wrestled the little sod to the ground and blackened his eye.

Florian's children spoke with the Vlach dialect that revealed our shared birthplace, and once they began to relax, the caravan slowly hummed into life. Of course, the lazy profanities that littered their speech were less than pleasing, but in a way, I saw they also told their own story.

Telus's younger brother was named Ion, their sister Claudia. And though Mirela's new classmates were some years older than her, it became quickly apparent that they were some years behind her. Unlike the French on site, they were unused to the discipline of learning, having rarely attended school. As a consequence, they brandished their pencils as though they were weapons and it took the regular invocation of their father's name before they took a stab at the exercises I laid in front of them. The effort required to deal with this inconvenience revealed itself in further scowling, protruding tongues, and bitten lips. Twenty minutes later, I was little surprised when their concentration faltered and they fell back on the tactics employed by most capable children when they don't want to do something. One by one, they began to ask questions.

"Why are we doing this?"

"Why am I here?"

"What's the point?"

"Who made you the boss?"

"Can I water the horses?"

While ignoring all questions not starting with a "How do I?" or a "Can you show me?" I did allow Telus to relieve himself. After his siblings had exhausted the same option, we took a much-needed break from the grievous issue of letters to concentrate instead on the real reason they had been brought to me. Naturally, I began with a story.

"One late autumn evening, a fine-looking fox was prowling the boundary of a farm…"

"What farm?" Telus interrupted.

"What do you mean what farm?"

"Well, where was it?"

"Does it matter?"

"It might."

"Then let's say it was a farm in France."

"So, this is a story about a French fox?"

"That would be correct."

"Was it called Carla Bruni?"

As the other children sniggered, I raised a bewildered eyebrow. "How do you even know that name?"

"Bo told me," the boy admitted. "He said the President's wife is a supermodel and he'd like to do to her exactly what her husband is doing to us."

"And what's that?" asked Mirela.

"Fu..."

I clamped my hand over the child's mouth whilst informing the rest of the class that the French fox was actually a male fox and, if nobody minded, we'd get back to his wanderings around the farm.

"As it was getting late, and the fox was feeling hungry, he circled the farm hoping to sniff out a hen before finding a place to sleep for the night. As the fox searched for his dinner he passed a wooden kennel. At first, he thought nothing of it, not until a deep growl echoed from the doorway and a huge dog burst into the open. The fox almost died from fright. Running as fast as his little legs could carry him, he sprinted for the woods. Within seconds he heard the dog gaining on him and felt its hot breath heating the back of his neck."

"Do foxes have necks?"

"Yes, Telus, they do," I replied. And God forgive me, but I pinched the little bugger on the back of his arm.

"That hurt!"

"Don't be such a baby."

Beside him, Claudia giggled. "She called you a baby."

"I'll pinch you too if you don't behave," I warned, and like cogs turning a wheel, the two of them quietened to re-evaluate our teacher-pupil relationship.

"As the dog's shadow loomed over the fox, the poor creature held his breath, said his prayers, and prepared to die. But then, the fox heard a terrible yelp pierce the evening air. Curious, he looked behind him to find the dog lying on its back, poleaxed by a chain that stretched from collar to kennel. The fox stopped running and turned to check on the animal. 'Well, you can relax now,' the dog grumbled. 'Can't you see I can't reach you?' The fox looked around him and saw the truth of the dog's words. So, he sat in the grass to catch his breath whilst the hound flopped onto his belly. After a while the dog spoke again. 'Tell me something,' he said. "As you can see, I have a fine house. I have food brought to me every day. I am watered and I am looked after. In return all I have to do is guard the hens. I have an easy life, a good life. So why do you insist on living like you do?' The fox thought about the question. As he did so, he looked at the dog's fat belly, his shining coat and healthy wet nose and he saw that it was true; the dog did have an easy life. In contrast, the fox could hear his tummy rumbling and his feet ached from walking. He looked at the house that gave the dog shelter and he wondered where he might sleep that night. Yes, the dog had a comfortable life. Even so, the fox didn't believe it was a good life. 'I see you are fed,' the fox informed the dog. 'I see that you have water and a beautiful house, but I also see the chain around your neck. Me? I have little or nothing, I often go hungry, I am chased and despised, and yet I have something you will never know. I have my freedom.' And with that the fox walked away smiling; knowing some things in life were more valuable than a full belly and a warm bed."

Finished, I sat back and scrutinised the class. I read a level of understanding in the eyes of only one of my pupils; my daughter. The other three looked baffled.

"It's an analogy," I prompted.

"A what?" asked Ion.

Mirela sighed and shook her head with all the gravitas and despair of the seasoned academic.

"We are the fox," she explained. "The *gadje* are the dog."

"That is so lame," stated Claudia. "If I'm anything, I'm a wolf,"

"Bugger that, I'm a man."

"Yes," I interjected patiently. "You are a man, Ion – or at least you will be when you grow up – but what I'm trying to show you is that the Roma are like the foxes of the world; poor but free. Don't you think it's better to be free than to be chained like a dog?"

The three children paused to consider the idea. After swapping glances, two of them acknowledged 'perhaps.' However, Telus wasn't so easily convinced.

"We don't live in a house," he said slowly, his chubby face creasing with concentration. "But I don't see how that makes us free. We are pushed here and there and everywhere. Not even the French Roma are free. Bo has to have his papers stamped every three months. Yet the *gadje*, they don't have to report themselves, do they? They can go where they like for as long as they like. So no, I don't see how we're like a fox. We're more like the dog – but on a longer chain with no one bothering to feed us."

"The fat kid has a point," Miko stated, after I regaled him with the failure of that day's lesson over a dinner of buttered potatoes and peppered cabbage.

"Perhaps, but I was hoping to give the children something to believe in; something that made them special and better than the *gadje*."

"And that would be freedom? Do you honestly believe we have any?"

"Oh, I don't know," I admitted, suddenly defeated by the day and the un-sugared facts of Miko's conversation. Unable to face the challenge, my eyes drifted from his face to land on a crow pecking at a mouse by the hedge. The mouse was dead. I also noticed that the rubber seal was coming away at one of our windows. "I'm sorry, but I have to believe in something, Miko."

Mirela dropped her spoon into the bowl. Winning our attention, she declared her absolute belief in the fox even if no one else did, and I smiled at my daughter, despite her face looking more kind than convinced.

"Thank you, *shukariyo*."

"You're welcome, *Mamo*."

After finishing the rest of our meal in silence, I took away the bowls to wash them at the pump. By the time I returned, Mirela had gone to find Bo. It was silly, but I felt bereft at her absence. I sank onto the lino, dipping my head into my skirts. On the back of my head, Miko's hand came to console me. God help me, I couldn't stop the tears.

No matter what the papers said, or what the politicians claimed, I knew we were good people; people with families that we loved and who loved us back. We possessed a long and proud history. We were once warriors. We were among the privileged. So how had it come to this? We had worked hard and honestly all of our lives. We had paid our bills, when it was demanded, and we had planned for our future. Now, there was nothing; no house, no future, not even any bills. With no cause, we had found ourselves vilified for the crime of trying to find a place less lethal to raise our kids. So yes, perhaps Telus was right. The Roma weren't foxes after all, but neither were we dogs. We were people, trapped and moulded into something to be feared and despised, simply for having the audacity to breathe the same patch of air.

"It's not fair," I spluttered.

"Yet it's better than it was," Miko replied calmly.

And though he was right, it brought me little comfort.

Once Donka had finished washing, she wiped the hair from her face, lit up a cigarette and came to sit next to me as I patched a hole in one of Mirela's skirts. She said nothing, and I told her not to worry. Being her default reaction in most things, Donka snorted. Before stubbing out what was left of her cigarette, she used it to light another. By the third, Drina arrived and I was struck, not for the first time, by the softness of her skin as it brushed against my cheek in welcome.

"What do you need?" asked the Big Man's wife.

I glanced at Donka, but her eyes had turned towards her home and I saw she was a moment from bolting for it.

"Donka?" I encouraged.

"Yes, I know," she hissed, before repeating more softly. "I know."

Stamping the stub of her cigarette into the dirt, she rummaged in her skirt and handed me the piece of paper she had been nursing for who knew how long.

"Drina we'd like you to try and translate this," I said.

The older woman read the concern on our faces. "Off you go then."

I opened the letter. At the top was a date under a collection of larger letters, which I ignored. Instead, I moved straight to the body of text that might hold the clue to Donka's bout of ill humour. As I sounded the words, Drina interrupted at intervals asking me to repeat and enunciate more clearly until eventually she held up her hand.

"This is a doctor's letter?"

Donka nodded.

"Where did you get it?"

"From the doctor, where do you think?"

"Why did you go to a doctor, Donka?"

"Why does anyone go to a doctor?"

"Donka…"

The younger woman clamped shut her jaw. A vein pulsed at the base of her neck and reaching for the hem of her skirt, she wiped roughly at her face.

"I have some pain," she finally admitted, stabbing a thumb into her abdomen. "I don't know what it is, why it came, but there are times when I can hardly speak with it. On top of that there's no sign …"

Donka tailed away. Drina and I shared a look and waited. Another cigarette was lit and after inhaling deeply, the words rushed from Donka's lips with the speed and fury of a long-dammed river.

"For two years I've been married and still nothing; still no children. And with this pain in my stomach and the bloating – not like the monthly bloating, something different – well I thought it might be, that perhaps it was a baby; a baby that was trapped and couldn't find its way out. And so, I went to the doctor. And, oh God forgive me, it was shameful. But after I dressed the doctor took me to a calendar that showed I should come back the next day. I did and that's when a woman gave me this letter. She spoke to me and I nodded, but I didn't understand and I didn't know how to tell her I didn't understand. Since then, I've been staring at these words, praying they'd start to make some kind of sense. But they haven't, and I've been trying to be a better Roma – you've seen me, you've seen that I try – I've been praying to our ancestors, but I still hurt and I still know nothing. I'm in the dark with my eyes sewn shut. I don't know what to do. I only know that Tanko mustn't know. Please, don't tell my husband I did this."

As Donka burst into tears, I placed a hand on her arm only to pull it away again as Drina hit the younger woman over the head. Not violently, but not so softly either.

"Donka you're a stubborn mule. I can hardly believe it. You should have come to me sooner than this, much, much sooner. This doctor is saying you need to go to a hospital. It's an appointment. And you've missed it."

Pausing to rub at the silver cross lying over her blouse, Drina pulled Donka towards her. She placed a rough kiss upon her thick, black hair.

"No matter, we will return to this doctor tomorrow and we will demand a new appointment. I'll go with you. We'll get a new time and when we have it, I'll go to the hospital with you. Don't worry, child. We'll fix your problem. It's what we women do."

Donka pulled herself from Drina's arms, rubbing roughly at her eyes. Her fingers were shaking and she admitted she was scared.

"Everything will be fine," Drina assured her.

"But the *gadje*," Donka insisted. "They hate us. I've listened to your stories, Mala. I've seen what happened to your family. And listen, I'm not as stupid as I look. I know a little myself and I've heard the *gadje* poison our wombs. I know all of this. And I tell you I am scared."

As the tears returned, I kissed the back of Donka's hand, feeling the wall of rings burn hot against my lips. Even so, I couldn't find the words to comfort her. Over the years, unspeakable crimes had been committed against our people. I thought she had every right to feel afraid.

Although I considered telling Miko of Donka's predicament – given our own past disappointments – in the end I decided against it, mainly because Donka had begged me not to and partly because I had developed a migraine from thinking about it. The ability to bear children was perhaps the greatest gift bestowed on a woman. The act of bearing them was the greatest duty of a Romani wife. For years I had struggled to conceive, often blaming myself for the inadequacies of my body, and finding punishment in the mistakes of a past that I raked over time and again to find answers. I knew the agony of wanting and the embarrassment of failure, and I felt Donka's pain in the memory of my own. We were not destined to be great friends, but we had grown used to each other. We were both from Romania and as such we shared an affinity no matter how tenuous. Of course, it went without saying that her husband terrified me. Tanko was brash and intimidating, and I was a stranger to the level of poverty that had spawned him. However, I understood what had shaped him and therefore a little about him. I also understood that though he might love his wife he would expect her to supply children. Any failure to do so would be Donka's fault, justified or not. More than that, a childless marriage might be viewed as the penalty for the scandal they had caused. Donka had eloped with Tanko, which was not a wholly unforgiveable sin, but Tanko had been betrothed to Donka's sister at the time. It was a terrible slight and a stain on both their families. There would be no easy way back for either of them. Donka had dishonoured her parents and visited shame on her older sister who was now in very real danger of being viewed as 'defective'. Though Donka and Tanko never acted out of malice, love wasn't reason enough for what they did, which is how they ended up in France – two more strays taken in by Drina and Marko. Unfortunately, if no children came to bless the marriage it could mean only one thing; that the ancestors, the saints, and all the gods of the past and present had turned their back on the couple. It would be the final rejection.

I was on my hands and knees, scrubbing the floor of the caravan and worrying about Donka, when Miko loomed above me to reveal the Big Man had called a meeting.

"What about?" I asked.

"I don't know. He didn't get a programme printed."

I threw the wet cloth at Miko's head before grabbing a shawl and following my husband to Marko and Drina's campervan. Swapping curious glances, we joined the small crowd gathered outside. Everyone appeared to be present, but this was little surprise; the families were spooked and the sporadic work the men relied on had withered in the heat of the current political climate. Somewhere ahead of us a clap of hands signalled the start of the meeting. As most of us stood, the Big Man clambered onto a table so that he might be seen. Holding a rolled-up newspaper in his hand, Marko began by thanking us for our time before quickly getting down to business. As he spoke, the table wobbled beneath his feet, but his voice remained steady. Below him, Drina's eyes carried the concern he hid.

"There has been a lot of talk lately and a lot of dangerous talk at that," he stated. "The politicians have accused us of trafficking, among other crimes, and the *gadje* appear to believe them. Despite the criminals making up less than one percent of who we are, the Roma once again find ourselves judged as a nation. Now, many of you here have listened to Mala's history lessons. They have brought us not only pride, but also sorrow and disbelief. Believe me, she spins no fairytales. This is how it happened."

The Big Man paused to applaud me. His eyes were followed by eight score more and I began to melt under the heat of them.

"So, you see," continued Marko, "we are a people with history, and one that's mostly involved some form of persecution. How little times change, eh? For this reason, we are bound by blood and compassion to shelter our Romanian cousins. Now, I know some of you think we create only trouble for ourselves in doing this, especially the young ones among you, but I say, speak to your grandparents. Ask what they know of the past, not from another's stories, but from their own memories. This talk of antisocial elements, the insult of state-run sites; it's a path we've walked down before. And I'm telling you, it didn't end well. But, I'm not here to lead you. You are your own men. It's my role to advise you, and to let you know what's been brought to the table. Apart from me, that is."

After pointing to his feet, and allowing time for the joke to filter through the audience, Marko unfolded the newspaper he held.

"There'll be no surprise in hearing that our time here is coming to an end," he continued. "For the Romanians, this is most definitely true. It says here, in this newspaper, that for every foreign Roma agreeing to go back to wherever they came from, they'll get three hundred Euros. A child will receive one hundred."

"So, we take it and return!" shouted Tanko over the murmurs the revelation brought.

"Son, do you think they'd make it that easy?" Marko asked Tanko. "If you take the money, you give your details and Old Europe will close its doors to you. You may find another road in, but it'll get harder and harder to find. So, my advice is this; be ready to move if you don't wish to go. However, if you want the cash then rest easy and wait for the authorities to find you. In the meantime, the wife and I will wait as well. When the police come, I expect they'll move us on and ship you out. And that's where we're at. Does anyone have any questions?"

For a second there was nothing but silence as everyone weighed up the options. It was one of the French Roma, stood at the front, who was the first to voice his concerns.

"I don't want my kids around when the police come," he stated calmly, but firmly. It was a concern quickly echoed by other parents.

"I don't blame you, Loiza," the Big Man replied. "Many of us have seen what happens. Please, take some time and think on it. My door is open to anyone who needs me."

As the Big Man was helped from the table, the crowd slowly dispersed, largely mute, largely uncomplaining. A little to my left, I heard Tanko ask his wife whether they should take the money on offer. When I turned to look, I saw the struggle in Donka's eyes.

"Let's see what tomorrow brings," she replied. Her gaze briefly caught mine before she dropped her head and hurried home.

As it transpired, tomorrow did nothing more than bring Donka a new complication – she was given a hospital appointment set for ten days' time. Of course, nobody knew whether we had a week left in the area, let alone ten days, but before we had time to discuss her options, the increasingly familiar figures of Jack and Francoise arrived.

The Frenchman brought with him a fistful of Euros which I duly shared between the Big Man and my purse. Francoise brought with her a copy of the local paper. The front page declared 'Travellers Give Cause for Concern.'

As Francoise read the article – first in French, then in Romanian – the accusations of spiralling crime and potential health hazards brought murmurs of protests from the gathering Roma. As everyone sat down to debate the issue, I disappeared behind the caravan to recover the *gadje's* mugs. By the time I returned with hot tea, the crowd had largely quietened because the newspaper hadn't actually revealed anything they hadn't heard before. Therefore, the scene was relatively calm – until Jack started talking.

"I think you all know me well enough by now to see that I come as a friend," the Frenchman announced, pausing briefly to accept an affirmation that didn't come. "Yes, well, I do come as a friend. I can assure you of that," he muttered. "However, and though I know you in a way that many do not and never will, I remain confused. It is clear that this place, where you live, is not ideal; there is limited water, one generator and all this… well, rubbish everywhere. It seems, how should I put it? Unusual perhaps, maybe even a little stubborn, that you don't park your homes within designated sites with all the amenities the authorities have to offer. So why is that?"

Before I was given chance to understand the words, I saw the Big Man bristle. As Francoise finished translating, Tanko offered his own somewhat forceful opinion.

"There's no one offering me and my wife a place to stay!"

Tanko slapped aggressively at the top of his arm and a wasp fell to the ground. He didn't even flinch and I was mildly impressed.

"Yes, quite…" came Jack's meek response after Francoise had repeated and explained that the wasp-killing guy with the bare chest came from Romania. "But many of you here are French-born, no?"

The Big Man nodded his confirmation.

"So, given the facilities on these sites why do you reject them? Surely life would be easier."

"And there speaks a man who's never lived on one," scoffed Bo.

The young man was sat on the grass, whittling a piece of wood in order to keep his hands busy in the presence of his father who disapproved of him smoking. Around us, a few voices rose up in support of Rami's boy until, eventually, The Big Man raised his hand to restore order.

"Monsieur Caron…"

"Jack, please."

"Monsieur Caron," the Big Man repeated. "These sites aren't built for our comfort. They're built to contain us. Yes, there's running water, electricity, and whatever else it is that you think makes for a better standard of living. But there is a price. There are rules that don't lend themselves to our way of life. We have animals. We eat and talk around open fires. We pay rent only when we have to, but more than that, these sites are camps, and as a human being, I find that notion offensive."

As Francoise translated, it was evident from Jack's hesitation that the Big Man had lost him. Seeing I could rectify the confusion, I seized the chance to move on, and get the day over with.

"Monsieur Caron, do you remember the first time you visited us; the day you made a joke about Darwin?"

Jack turned to me, admitting to "vaguely" remembering the conversation. "About creation or something, wasn't it?"

"Yes, and it was a throwaway line," I conceded. "But for us, Darwin's theories are no laughing matter. Many years ago, he concluded that natural selection and the fight for survival were the very things that shaped nature. Applied to society, this meant that western civilisation, with all of its comforts and healthcare, had disturbed the possible higher development of humans and that a form of degeneration, both physical and moral, had set in as a consequence. It was a finding that was echoed some 80 years later by a physician named Robert Ritter. For many years this man studied our people. He visited our homes and wagons bringing with him pen and paper, callipers and syringes, tape measures, colour charts and pots of wax. He took masks of our people's faces. He copied records that were held in public offices, from the Church to the Police, and in the end, he concluded that we were, in essence, a primitive people belonging to an alien race. We were a population of parasites. We lacked ambition. We were inherently workshy. This is what Robert Ritter said, and he said this in a place called Germany. At that time, the leader of the country was Adolf Hitler – a man who you may recall also had a fondness for camps.

"What I tell you now comes from my own grandmother's memories. This is the story of Florica and Marcia."

ROMANIA
1954

Chapter Thirteen

Florica's eyes snapped open. Her sheet was sodden, her mouth was dry, and screams tore through her head.

"Get them off! God have mercy, get them off me!"

Alone in the dark, the girl drew a cross over her heart and reached for a glass of water that stood by the mattress she slept on. Downstairs in the kitchen she heard her mother running. A second later the screams grew louder as a door opened, and Florica imagined her mother rushing to help; bringing a wet cloth to wipe Marcia's neck and wash away the bugs that only one of them could see.

"I can feel them! You don't find them all!"

"I will find them."

"You won't! God help me, I know you won't!"

Florica covered her ears. It had been the same routine every night, ever since the old woman appeared, and everyone listening to Marcia's torment knew she was correct because the lice that prevented her from sleeping lived only in her head.

"They were everywhere," Florica's mother explained, the first morning after the first night that the old woman's screams had woken them. "The straw was crawling with lice and when the dead were pulled from their bunks their necks would be covered in them, like a black scarf come to strangle them in their sleep."

"It sounds disgusting," Florica mumbled.

"It was."

Downstairs, Marcia's sobs quietened. For tonight, the nightmare was over. Florica curled into a ball and tried to find sleep. As the sweat cooled on her skin, she shivered.

Marcia's arrival in Florica's life was strange for two reasons. Firstly, she didn't belong there and secondly, she brought with her a pair of knitting needles and a ball of red wool that never reached its end. Florica's mother Esma said the old woman had been sent by God. Her father Grigor said she had been chased there by the devil. And Marcia said that once her knitting was done, she would die. Knowing this, it was Esma who gave the wool its magical lifespan by replacing the ball every few nights, quite often in differing shades of red which the old woman never seemed to notice. Florica wasn't overly surprised; Marcia appeared to be oblivious to most things around her, not least the fact that she was living in somebody else's house.

"Now, Berlin – there was a city," Marcia croaked over the constant clickety clack of her needles.

Florica sighed and raised herself from her bed, coming to rest on her elbows.

"Are you here again?" she whined.

As was customary, the old woman ignored her. As was her habit, she was dressed in black, from her head to her stockinged toes.

"Buildings higher than mountains, roads bigger than rivers, and churches, well God himself couldn't have built a finer cathedral than the Dom. Berlin was paradise, a heaven upon earth, a hotbed of culture and learning."

"Bucharest is pretty good."

Marcia sucked air in between her broken, blackened teeth.

"Bucharest is a crap hole, like the rest of Romania."

"You've never been to Bucharest!"

"I don't need to go down a sewer to know it's full of shit."

Florica fell back on her bed, stunned once again by Marcia's foul tongue. The sick needed rest – and grapes, if the ration allowed it – not a mad witch from another country who dreamt about lice and talked about crap holes.

"She's killing me!" Florica informed her mother as she implored her, not for the first time, to keep the old woman away from her room.

"She's looking after you," Esma insisted.

"She swears!"

"So does your father."

"She calls our capital a crap hole."

"Beauty's subjective."

"I don't even know what that means, but she also passes wind. All of the time!"

"Well, she's an old lady and that sometimes happens."

"*Mamo!*"

"No, Flo'. Still your tongue and learn some respect. I want you to listen to Marcia. One day you'll see why."

"If I don't die first."

"If you don't die first."

"I'm halfway there as it is."

"You're no such thing."

"Am so."

For as long as she could remember Florica had been ill. Her legs appeared ambivalent to the task of supporting her body, her head was often woozy, and she was cursed by a sporadic fever that heated her blood to boiling. Her mother blamed Antonescu, but she held him responsible for most of the country's ills. When their leader sided with the Germans – throwing the Roma to the wolves of Transnistria – Esma said there had been nothing to live on but fear, and she believed its insidious impact had seeped into the very soul of her unborn child.

"It's a miracle you were born at all," she informed her daughter.

Although Florica was largely ignorant of who Antonescu was, or why he had persecuted the Roma, she grew up mad as hell at him nonetheless.

"Such nonsense," Marcia declared, not bothering to look up from her knitting. "Not enough meat, that's your downfall. In Berlin we ate sausages every day. Grand things they were, not like the apologies I've seen here. The butchers would hang them in their windows like huge coral necklaces. Even after the Great War, none of my children went without meat, or dumplings for that matter. Oh, you should have seen the dumplings; plump as yellow balls of wool. And the bacon, well you've not known happiness until you've tasted our bacon."

Not content with enthusing about Berlin being better than, well, anywhere, Marcia also spoke at length about food. Florica had yet to discover the word 'ironic', but she saw it characterised in the chattering bag of bones before her.

"You're very thin seeing as you ate all that food."

Marcia lowered her knitting. "Well, that's the thing about food; you have to keep eating it if you're going to be fat." She blew her nose into a handkerchief and resumed work. "Now, my Joe, there was a boy who liked his food. Handsome he was and healthy as a thoroughbred. He loved sausages and he grew into a hero. Decorated in the war he was, for bravery. Not that it counted for much in the end, not once the storm blew in. But by then none of us counted for anything. Not even my Joe; a war hero."

On the occasions that Florica fell ill she was moved downstairs because her father couldn't cope with his wife walking above his head whenever she needed to tend to their daughter. As Marcia was old – and beyond the age of womanly pollution – she was permitted to roam all over the house, which is how she came to take over the burden of Florica's care. The girl was less than pleased with this arrangement.

"What on earth are you making?" she asked, pushing aside the pickles and bread her mother had sent up. She stared disdainfully at the hill of wool piling upon the old woman's knees.

"It's a scarf. Even a blind man can see that."

"Who for?"

"For them."

Marcia jerked her head upwards and Florica looked to the ceiling, thinking of the rats that sometimes played above it.

"It gets cold you see. Colder than you'd ever believe," the old woman continued.

"Where?"

"There."

Florica rolled her eyes and turned to face the wall. It was an act of disinterest designed to discourage further conversation, but it failed.

"Joe was tormented by the winter." Marcia spoke in the hard accent of her homeland. "I remember one year his toes turned blue. He was only a lad. Stefan was a minute from hacking at his feet. Can you imagine it? And my husband, an educated man! Needless to say, I picked up a knife bigger than the one he held and he soon changed his mind. We even laughed about it later. We were a happy family, see? At least for a while…"

Florica heard the regret in the old woman's voice and turned around to check she wasn't crying.

"It was spring when Joe left us," Marcia continued, keeping her eyes firmly on her knitting. "He was a volunteer, well a volunteer of sorts. Of course, it never occurred to me that he might need a scarf and by the time he got back from The Front, the snow was upon us and there was no wool to be found."

"I guess you miss Joe?"

Marcia's nostrils twitched in reply. Shockingly, she lifted one of the needles she held and pushed it deep into the palm of her hand, until it reached blood.

"Marcia!"

"Berlin was a beautiful city," she said. "We were really happy there."

Some hours later, and with the grip of fever somewhat nullified by Marcia's self-mutilation, Florica headed downstairs to support her mother as she closed the door on another of the old woman's nightmares. In the glow of candlelight, Esma broke the wool attached to Marcia's knitting before knotting a new ball onto the frayed thread. Even in the gloom, Florica saw the effect was hardly subtle.

"It's more pink than red," she remarked.

"It's close enough."

"Doesn't she ever notice?"

"She hasn't yet."

"I think she's crazy."

"You may be right."

"Then why is she here, *Mamo*?"

Esma replaced the knitting on the table in roughly the same position she had found it. She pulled her daughter onto her lap.

"Marcia is here because she needs to be," she whispered. "Now go back to bed. The sun is only an hour or two away."

Sent away with a kiss, Florica returned to her room. Scarcely had she closed her eyes when the day seeped through the sheet nailed to the window. To the girl's frustration, she woke to find Marcia already sat there, cross-legged on the floor, knitting with the pink wool, believing it was red.

"What's the point in having your own room if people come in whenever they feel like it?" Florica demanded, pulling the sheet over her face to display the full depth of her discontent.

"How old are you now?" Marcia asked.

It was a question that surprised Florica, not because it showed a typical lack of concern for her right to privacy, but because the old woman rarely addressed her. It seemed an unnecessary part of their relationship.

"I'm nearly nine," Florica mumbled.

"You're what?"

"I'm nearly nine!" Florica shouted, kicking the covers from her face as she did so.

"My, you're small for your age."

"In case you haven't noticed, I'm pretty sick."

"I've noticed a lot of things," Marcia replied calmly.

"Well, you could have fooled me!"

Florica got up and stomped to the bowl waiting for her in the corner of the room. Turning her back on Marcia, she undressed before taking the flannel to wash herself. The water was lukewarm and Florica had to wonder how long the old woman had been sat there.

Barking an instruction for the girl to wash behind her ears, Marcia resumed her knitting.

"My Ava was your age when the Games came to the city."

Florica stared hard at the wall. In the end, her curiosity got the better of her.

"What games?"

"What games?" Marcia mimicked, and the girl rolled her eyes. "I'm talking about the only games there are, child. The Olympic ones, the greatest games on earth brought to the greatest city on earth."

"That would be Berlin, I take it?"

To Florica's astonishment Marcia laughed. Unable to help herself, she smiled back.

"Yes, that would be Berlin, the greatest city on earth. Of course, with the world suddenly looking there had to be changes. For a start, we were overrun with your kind of people; cluttering the streets, thieving and begging. You know, looking back, I sometimes wonder if that's what started it all. But perhaps not. The devil always finds his way. And no one deserved Marzahn."

"What's Marzahn?"

"A camp, the first of many to come. It was a place where your lot could stay out of sight."

Florica slapped her flannel into the bowl. "Why do you keep saying 'your lot'? You're Roma, too."

"I am no such thing!" Marcia retorted, swiftly laying aside her knitting in protest. "Who told you such filthy lies?"

Florica was speechless. She was also naked. Grabbing her dress, she decided the old woman wasn't only a nuisance, but also a lunatic. "You speak the same as us, so you must be one of us."

"I speak like you because it's the only way I can be heard," Marcia spat back. She rubbed angrily at her left arm. "But I am not you, absolutely not. I am Sinti and proud of it."

"God save us all, that's like saying you're a terrier and not a dog!"

"It is no such thing! And how dare you compare me to a dog? I'm a human being, nothing less than that. And I deserve respect! I am Sinti, do you hear me? How dare you!"

Before Florica could apologise, the old woman gathered her scarf and left the room in tears. The girl was stunned. It was a shock that quickly dissolved into shame. Marcia may have been tiny, but her absence left a hole in the room as vast as a canyon. Reeling from the mess she had created, Florica finished dressing and went in search of her mother. She found her at the bottom of the stairs, already waiting.

"Don't worry. She doesn't mean anything by it. It's just a little complicated," Esma told her.

"But you said the Sinti were Roma."

"And they are, more or less. Unfortunately, the ties that bind us aren't as strong as they once were. Marcia was born in Germany. Her mother was born in Germany. Her grandmother was born in Germany. And so on and so on, as far back as any of them can remember. German-born Romanies call themselves Sinti. They see themselves as a very different and distinct group."

"What's distinct?"

"Something like 'special'. However, when the Nazis came to power…"

"The Hitler people?"

"Yes, the Hitler people. Well, the Nazis were blind to everything that makes people special. Because of that, they started to get rid of anyone they didn't like such as the activists, the homosexuals, the ones touched by God, and the Jews. When that was done, the Nazis turned their attention on the Sinti and Roma. As far as they were concerned there was no distinction – both groups were '*Zigeuner*', the German word for gypsy, and they were classed as 'asocial' like the homeless and the criminals. I think that's why Marcia insists on being called Sinti, not because she doesn't like us, but because it's the very thing that makes her special. And if that's what she want, well, it's a small thing to give her."

"I didn't mean to make Marcia cry," Florica confessed.

"I know you didn't, and she knows that too."

"Shall I speak to her?"

"Later. She's gone for a walk, but when she returns, you can talk to her. I'm sure she'll be glad of it."

Florica nodded, grateful for her mother's good sense, and slightly surprised she hadn't mentioned Antonescu. After filling a glass with water, she went to sit on the front step to wait for Marcia. With nothing else to do, she contemplated the error of her ways in a line of washing swinging in the breeze. As boredom began to tug at her, Florica's eyes fell on the cracked bowl of a toilet at the far end of the garden. It had sat there ever since her parents escaped from Transnistria. On their return, her father had ejected the *gadje* he discovered squatting in his house, as well as the toilet they must have used during their stay. As far as Florica's father was concerned, one couldn't be too careful in matters of pollution.

For more than three hours Florica waited on the step, watching ants run into the soles of her shoes and birds pecking for bugs, until eventually Marcia appeared, walking purposefully down the street, her small frame harried by two mangy-looking dogs. With a final 'shoo!' she entered the yard. Ignoring the girl's practised apology, she disappeared into the kitchen and demanded a frying pan. Florica followed and stood by her mother as they watched Marcia pull a sausage from her skirts. Esma couldn't have been more surprised if the old woman had dumped a sack of gold on the kitchen table. Covered in greasy white fat, the sausage was dropped into the hot pan where it sizzled and spat. With great care, she turned the meat with a fork just as Florica's father walked in.

"That smells good," he declared, bending over the pan as he did so to waft the smoke into his face.

"Never mind what it smells like," Marcia ordered, pushing him away. "It's not for you."

Taking the sausage from the pan she placed it onto a plate. Pulling a knife from her skirt, an act which also caused some astonishment, she cut it into six bite-size pieces, all of which she placed in front of Florica.

"Eat," she ordered. "It will make you strong."

Later that evening, as Grigor visited his friends and Esma attempted to claw back the sleep that eluded her most nights, Marcia and Florica sought to undo the damage they had caused each other during the day. In the girl's bedroom, with dusk casting shadows upon the ceiling, they sat together on one of the cushions lining the wall. As Marcia knitted, Florica collected the ever-growing scarf in her lap.

"We were all guilty at the start," Marcia admitted quietly, her tone softer than it had previously been. "When the Nazis rounded up the criminals everyone agreed it was a good thing. Then, when the beggars, vagabonds, prostitutes and the plain bone idle were taken away, it seemed a natural progression of a general desire to restore order. We were still recovering from the First War, you see. Times were hard. We were in a depression, with the victors of France and Britain robbing us blind, and there simply wasn't enough money – or indeed compassion – to go around. But then the decrees started to change. Suddenly, crime was not down to bad individuals but bad racial stock. The Jews were targeted first, may God now keep them safe. After them it was us; the so-called 'Gypsy Menace'. And do you know what hurts most? No one said a word. Not even the Church."

Instinctively, Florica fingered the cross that hung about her neck. The symbol of Christ that her mother swore would protect her.

"What's racial stock?" she asked.

Marcia frowned as she searched for an explanation.

"It's kinds of people. Like the whites, or the blacks, or the Jews or even us, the Romanies."

Marcia laid special emphasis on the word 'Romanies'. Florica tried to smile at the gesture, but it couldn't fight its way through the remorse she felt.

"I'm sorry, Marcia. I didn't mean what I said. It's fine if you want to be Sinti."

"I am Sinti, child. But you are right, I am also Romani. We need to be proud of the names we give ourselves. The Germans had their own word for us. They called us Zigeuner. It was a word that made thieves and criminals of us all. Here..."

Laying down her knitting, Marcia pulled back the sleeve of her cotton top. Etched into the skin on her left forearm were a series of numbers marked in black ink. In front of the digits was the letter Z.

"Z for Zigeuner," Marcia explained.

Florica ran her fingers over the tattoo.

"Where did you get it?"

"At a camp called Auschwitz. The Germans did it."

"Why?"

"Because they could," Marcia replied with a shrug. "They stole everything they could possibly steal from us, and then they took our identity."

Florica had never had cause to assess the issue of her identity. She was what she was. Even though the communists insisted on making Romanians of everyone, she remained Roma. Her family continued to practise the traditions they knew, and her father only toiled in the collective farms of the state because he had to. No matter what life threw at them, they never forgot who they were, and they largely ignored the *gadje's* determination to integrate them into a society they didn't trust. Everyone she knew was Roma, and proud of it. Therefore, it came as something of a shock later that week, when Florica heard her parents arguing about putting her into school, something that was a distinctly *gadje* institution.

"With Romanians?" she asked, visibly appalled.

"With Romanians," her father confirmed, "but there might be other kids that you know."

Esma stirred furiously at the soup she was making, clearly unconvinced that this was the correct course of action for their one and only child. She turned to face her husband, pointing the ladle close to his face. As Grigor rose from his chair, Marcia all but jumped to her feet. She quickly ushered Florica out of the house, and away from the argument about to take place. As they left, the old woman grabbed a bowl from the sink.

"Let's hunt for blackberries," she suggested, and because Florica was still somewhat dazed by the recent development in her life, and she rather liked picking fruit, she nodded in mute agreement.

"You know, school isn't so bad," Marcia assured her as they scoured a bramble hedge on the roadside. "Of course, it does depend on which one you go to because school can also be a place where you'll get your head kicked in."

Florica stopped in her tracks. Of all the objections she had to going to school, of which there were many, physical violence hadn't yet factored.

"Did that happen to you?"

"Sometimes it did, but not all of the time. Things were different when I was young. We travelled a lot, whenever the seasonal work was good, and our schooling was often fleeting and, it has to be said, occasionally hostile. But then my father got a job sorting mail and, what with the restrictions, one year we simply stopped moving. For a while, we kept our horses, in a field nearby, and all of us kids were put into a permanent school."

"And did they kick your head in then?"

"No, not then..."

Marcia's eyes darted downwards. She breathed heavily through her nose as if to dislodge a smell that had become trapped in her nostrils. After wiping herself clean, she shuffled further down the road. Florica picked a couple of fat berries they had missed before running to catch up.

"It must have been a grand life when you were travelling," she declared, throwing the fruit into Marcia's bowl. "I'd love to see the world one day, all the cities and mountains and seas. You must have had the best adventures, you know, until they took away your freedom and made you go to school."

"Well, yes and no," Marcia confirmed and denied. "Our life was hard and every one of us had to work, but there were many fun days too; playing with other children, eating out, building dens, riding the ponies. But even when we stopped – when the wagon was gone – we still had our freedom. We kids didn't think so at the time, but freedom is one of those things you only truly understand when it's gone."

"Are you talking about when you went to the camp?"

"Camps, plural," Marcia corrected. "But yes, that's when I started to value what we had lost. It was the same for us all, I imagine. Everyone ended up in the camps, one way or another. Initially, it was only the travellers who didn't have regular work and who relied on handouts. They were rounded up and dumped in what they called 'residential camps.' The name sounds laughable now, but that's the power of the right word – it can turn a prison into a welfare project, and a people into Zigeuner. The fact was that these so-called residential camps were guarded by the police for the security of the locals, or so they said. The residents had to abide by a curfew, they had to attend roll calls, and they had to give the Nazi salute. As you can imagine, once everyone got to know what they were really about, every traveller scrambled to find a place to settle themselves. But the Nazis had thought about that. They pressured landlords not to rent to Romanies and the travellers had no choice but to park their wagons and build their huts on land off-limits to them. Of course, this gave the Nazis a new reason to round them up and shift them into camps. And the more camps that they built, the worse they became. Within a matter of years, the residential camps were not only guarded, but also surrounded by barbed wire with sleeping areas fitted with barred windows and steel doors that locked from the outside. Then in 1939 the new war began and a new law was passed to deal with the antisocial and workshy. The residential camps became concentration camps, with inmates working for the pleasure of staying there. And do you know the worst of it?"

"No," Florica answered honestly.

"I still didn't appreciate the danger. Not even then. I thought only of myself and of my own family. That was my big mistake." Marcia paused to shake the bowl she carried. "Alright, I think we've picked enough berries. We ought to get back."

Florica dropped the last of the fruit she held into the bowl and licked her fingers clean. As she did so, she noticed the state of the yellow dress she wore; clean on that morning and now striped with purple stains.

"Oh, great. *Mamo's* going to kill me," she moaned.

Of course, Esma did no such thing. However, the next morning she handed a task to her daughter that was part punishment, part education. Florica found herself in the front yard hunched over a bowl of warm soapy water. As she scrubbed the berry juice from her dress, Esma hauled bed linen over a washboard whilst Marcia washed her skirts in an old tin bath. Because chores remained a relatively novel pastime, Florica declared she was quite enjoying the experience.

"That'll change," her mother grumbled, and the old woman at her side chuckled. Both Esma and Florica were briefly stilled by the sound.

"I wasn't always a grouch!" Marcia felt forced to explain.

"I've never said you were," Esma responded.

"I might have done," Florica admitted, and Marcia laughed again. In fact, she laughed so hard that tears shone in her eyes

Two hours later, with their washing drying in the breeze, the three of them rested for lunch. As the sun was warm, they ate in the yard. The two women sat on chairs they had taken from the kitchen whilst Florica made do with the stone step at the door to their home.

"We used to love eating in the sunshine," Marcia revealed as she sucked on a wedge of ham that her teeth were no longer able to cut through.

"Who did?" Florica asked.

"Me and my family"

"What happened to them?"

Esma turned her head abruptly, to silence her daughter.

"It's alright." Marcia waved her arm calmly. "The child can ask."

She moved her chair to face Florica.

"They were taken from me; that's what happened – one lost to life, the rest to the Nazis. When I was younger, but some years older than your mother here, there were six of us in total. Not a large family by Sinti standards, but large enough for us. Freddie, he was my eldest. Then there was Joe, then Ava and finally Bea. Freddie was the first to go. He was hit by a bus as he walked to work on the Bundesstrasse. If he'd had the money, he might have been on it, but he didn't and he ended up under it. When the police arrived, it damn near broke my heart. Freddie was 15 years old, a mere boy, even if he thought himself a man. He would have been married the following year. With Freddie being the eldest of our children, and the first of his sons, Stefan was inconsolable. In truth, I don't think he ever recovered. But men are different to women; they lose themselves quickly whereas women have to carry on. The next of my children to die were Joe and Ava. Joe went to the army. Ava went to her husband's family. I didn't hear of their deaths until long after they happened. Then there was Bea..." Marcia's face crumbled as she fought to blink back tears. "Bea died in my arms. I swear I'll never forgive them for that. Even today, even now, I can feel her blood soaking through my skirts."

As the tears poured from Marcia's eyes, she spluttered an apology as Esma moved to console her. Though she tried not to, Florica wept too. And in the nights that followed, sleep eluded them all.

Lying in her bed, listening to her mother running to still the screams of a woman strangled by imaginary lice, Florica clenched her fists and thumped the side of her head, in punishment for the guilt she felt. Her mother had tried to warn her. She'd tried to silence her questions, but Florica hadn't listened, and she'd broken Marcia's heart all over again. If she didn't learn to be careful, they'd all drown in the old woman's tears.

Pulling back the bedsheet, Florica knelt on the floor and prayed with all her might. In urgent whispers, she begged God to help Marcia; to be kind to the family she had lost; and to protect her own from the evils of other men. She didn't pray for herself because she felt unworthy of God's grace. And when Florica woke the next morning, still on her knees with her head balanced on the end of the mattress, she embraced the stiffness in her neck with the zeal of the penitent.

"Pain doesn't disappear because no one speaks of it," Marcia informed Florica when she later apologised for the tears she had caused.

"But if I hadn't made you remember..."

"I'll always remember, child, and I'll always have dreams. They are a part of me now. What's done cannot be undone."

Florica turned from Marcia, not knowing what else to say without making matters worse. In the far corner of the room, her mother was busy wafting a tin of smoking herbs, and Florica offered a prayer to St Basil. Though she wasn't sure who Basil was, her mother claimed he was on the side of the Roma, and Florica reckoned they needed all the help they could get right now. An hour or so later, with her own prayers still ringing in her ears, she was given cause to doubt Saint Basil's allegiance to her people when her father returned from the collective to tell her she would start school in three weeks.

"Grigor, no..." his wife protested.

"It's that or the workhouse," he insisted.

"But they'll kick my head in!" Florica shouted, genuinely alarmed by the announcement. "Tell them, Marcia! Tell them what school's like!"

The old woman glanced up from her knitting. Despite the drama that was making her head spin, Florica noticed that the ball of wool she worked with was more maroon than red.

"School's a necessary evil," Marcia stated.

Satisfied he had the backing of at least one woman in the house, Grigor nodded.

"I need to lie down," Florica moaned, and she walked to her room employing the heavy footsteps of the walking dead.

A little while later, Marcia appeared carrying a tray holding cups of sweet tea and a couple of plums.

"Get up and stop being so dramatic," she muttered.

"I'm sick!"

"You're no such thing. You're spoilt, that's all."

"Look at my fingers! See how they shiver."

Florica raised her hands which were in fact trembling. Unluckily for her, Marcia had witnessed too much to be swayed by childish hysterics. Taking the knife from her pocket, she cut the plums into pieces and dropped them into the hot tea. After stirring a while, she tipped part of the liquid into two bowls and offered one to Florica. The girl accepted it with a forlorn look.

"I'll try," she said, "but it might not stay down, what with me being so sick and all."

"You can only do your best," Marcia agreed.

The old woman slurped at the contents of her bowl and for a moment neither of them spoke. It was an easy silence, and Florica was surprised by how far they had come, though it wasn't far enough to convince her of the merits of school.

"Reading and writing is a good thing," Marcia insisted.

"I can do that already. Dad taught me. It's not so hard."

"No, it's not so hard, but it's not enough either. To get on in this world you need education. That's what school gives you. With an education you can beat the *gadje* at their own game, in the parliaments and the courts and the suchlike."

Marcia lowered her bowl and filled it with the rest of the plum tea waiting in her cup.

"All of my children could read and write, but at that time I didn't understand how the world worked. I thought reading and writing was enough to get by, only it wasn't. Nowhere near it, in fact. That's why, when the Nazis made their decrees and unveiled their laws we didn't see the full danger. By the time we caught up, the rock had fallen on our heads, and stone by stone the Nazis broke us. First, they made us carry identity papers. The full-blooded Sinti carried brown and the mixed-bloods had brown striped with blue. My family was mixed blood, like many others. Not too much, but enough. Likewise, there were *gadje* with Romani blood, not that you could tell by looking at them, all blond hair and blue eyes, but the authorities soon sniffed it out. It only took two members in a family, going back to the great-great-grandparents, to have these blond-haired Germans declared *Zigeuner*."

"Is that when they took you to the camps, when you got your papers?"

"No, not straightaway. As I explained before, the troublemakers were picked up first, but gradually new crimes were dreamt up for us, some of them so ludicrous it beggared belief. When the Nazis heard that fortune-tellers were predicting an end to the war, they issued a decree against them. Those convicted, or even under suspicion, of fortune-telling were taken into custody."

"Didn't they see it coming?" Florica asked, repeating a line she had heard from her father.

"You think this is funny?"

Under the heat of Marcia's sharp eyes, Florica wilted.

"I'm sorry. That was stupid."

"And that's why you need school."

Florica and Marcia locked stares; knowing that one of them had been out manoeuvred. Acknowledging the defeat, the child tipped more tea into her bowl.

"What happened after the fortune tellers?" she asked.

"Terrible things," Marcia admitted. "It started with a whisper in the neighbourhood, of plans to dump all the *Zigeuner* in Poland – tens of thousands of us. Another rumour quickly followed saying that families with sons serving in the army would be spared and, God bless him, Joe walked out from the house when he heard this, and immediately signed up. My daughter Ava's husband did likewise. That poor boy died in a matter of months, during the Battle of Brody. They never found enough of him to bring a body home."

"That's awful."

"Yes, it was tragic. My daughter went into labour when she heard the news. Two days after giving birth, I went to visit her, but she was gone. The house was empty. Everyone had vanished. I went to the town hall, even to the Gestapo, looking for answers. Eventually I was told my daughter had been taken to Ravensbrück, with her new baby and her in-laws."

"Ravensbrück?"

"It was another camp, filled with women, although some men were held there too."

Marcia rolled onto her knees so she might get to her feet more easily.

"Well, I think that's me done for the day," she confessed and Florica helped her place the empty cups onto the tray. Before the old woman disappeared, she took her knitting from the pocket of her apron and showed it to the girl.

"Does this look wet to you?" she asked.

"No, why?"

"I don't know it just seems darker than usual."

Florica turned away to stop her eyes from betraying her.

"It must be the light. It looks the same as always to me."

"Right you are," the old woman said.

As the door closed behind her, Florica collapsed onto the mattress, her heart thumping in her chest. She really was the most dreadful liar.

Florica's world centred on her house in a rundown suburb the *gadje* called 'Gypsy Town'. Even so, she was aware that another world lay beyond the perimeters of safety her parents had set. The nearest big city was Sibiu and though it was part of Romania, it hadn't always been. In fact, it used to be full of Germans until the end of the war when it was advised they better pack up and leave. Perhaps for that reason, Marcia attracted the attention of some of the older women in their community who occasionally visited to drink sweet tea and punctuate their chatter with words they had learned, but which were no longer deemed to be acceptable for civilised company. Mostly, however, they simply swapped stories of shared miseries. The madness that took hold of Germany ran unchecked under the shadow of the swastika, and none of them were spared its cruelty.

"When I sit with them, I feel partly to blame," Marcia told Esma after the women had left. "Perhaps, if we had protested at the start, if we'd had the courage to stand up and say 'no', things might have been different and those women wouldn't have suffered like they did. You wouldn't have suffered."

Esma shook her head, dismissing the suggestion. She raised a floury hand to scratch at the tip of her nose and then carried on kneading a lump of dough on the table. "The people responsible are them that gave the orders."

"What about those that carried them out?"

"Well, yes, them as well," Esma admitted, "but lines get blurred in wartime. Everyone gets scared. Even so, good people remain. I don't think I've told you this, but one of the women here escaped from Transnistria by train. Obviously, she had no ticket and when the conductor appeared she didn't have time to hide. By rights that man should have handed her over, only he didn't. He simply ignored her and stamped the tickets of the other passengers. When the train came to a halt, she passed the conductor and though she wanted to thank him she was too scared. But as she descended the steps this man handed her a coin. He told her, 'Go with God, little gypsy girl.' So, you see, there's good and bad in all walks of life, and in all regimes."

"Who was the girl?" Florica shouted from her place on the doorstep.

"Afina," Esma replied.

"Gabi's *Mamo*?"

"Yes."

"Well, you'd think she'd be nicer to Gabi then. She works her like a slave."

"We don't use that word in this house, Flo'."

"Like a donkey then! Gabi's *Mamo* works her like a donkey."

"In comparison to you, maybe," Esma retorted. "You've had it too easy, girl."

"Hardly my fault when I've been weakened by Antonescu!"

Esma rolled her eyes at Marcia, indicating that she blamed herself for the ready excuse she had supplied her daughter. Marcia chuckled.

"You've an exceptionally bright girl, there," she stated. "I'm glad I got to know her."

Collecting her knitting, Marcia left the kitchen to sit in the sunshine where she found Florica picking at a scab on her elbow.

"You'll make it bleed."

"Too late," Florica replied, pulling the crust away.

Marcia handed her a tissue. As she bent towards her, Florica lifted her head, her nose twitching at something on the breeze.

"Can you smell jasmine?" she asked.

Marcia sniffed, and said she couldn't. For the briefest of moments, Florica held on to the old woman's gaze. The child couldn't explain it, but she felt time slipping away from them.

"I think you should finish your story," she whispered.

"Do you?" Marcia whispered in reply.

When Florica nodded, Marcia read the sincerity in her face.

"Perhaps you are right," she said.

Taking hold of the grey knitting needles that had become so much a part of her she seemed naked without them, she hooked one under each arm and announced the year – 1942.

"It was the year that defeated hope," Marcia explained. "A new law was passed and we saw there was no way back. From that point on, any Romanies not in camps had to work in special groups, well away from the Germans. Our boys could no longer be apprentices, welfare benefits were stopped, and we lost any right to sick pay. We were also required to pay a 15 percent tax on top of the tax we already paid. Stefan lost his job in the post room, the same place my own father had worked, and he was employed instead in a munitions factory. It was also the year that Joe came back from the frontline. It was winter when he arrived, his least favourite season, and it was clear from the start that he was no longer the boy who had left us. All day, Joe's big, black eyes would gaze at a place none of us had seen, and he barely glanced at the food that I made him. Then, barely a week into his leave, he was told to report to his commanding officer. My boy never came back. Joe was a decorated soldier, he had fought for his country, yet he was taken to a concentration camp. For weeks afterwards, I searched for answers taking with me a photograph of my son, looking handsome and proud in his uniform. Eventually in a room at the end of a cold corridor I was told he was in Buchenwald. I remember falling to my knees, telling them they had made the most terrible mistake, but I was brushed out of the office, like rubbish. "*Zigeuner*," the official spat after me, as if that was reason enough. I tell you Flo', I ran from that place as though the devil himself was licking my heels. That evening, as Stefan cried into his hands and Bea rocked on the floor at his feet, I closed every shutter of our home and never opened them again. For months we lived in the dark, we kept ourselves quiet, and we prayed to God Almighty to save us.

"The next spring, before dawn had even woken the birds, we heard a knock at the door. Stefan answered and I heard boots violating the sanctuary of our home. Bea ran to me and we both ran to Stefan. In the parlour, we saw one of the Gestapo. He was looking at our papers, and he checked our names on a list he carried. When he was done, we were ordered out of the house. Outside, a truck waited for us, filling up fast with our neighbours."

Marcia stopped speaking and rubbed at her arm. Through the open door of the kitchen, Florica saw her mother take a break from the bread she was kneading. Placing a damp cloth over the dough, she pulled a chair towards the door. As she sat down, Esma placed her hands upon her daughter's shoulders.

"The trucks took us to a train," Marcia continued. "I don't remember much of the journey, only the noise; the wailing of people no longer in control of their lives. Forced at gunpoint into a wagon, the space kept filling up around us until there was hardly room to breathe. I clung to my husband and daughter. Bea was barely twelve years old. I couldn't bear to look at her, to see the fear in her eyes, so I crushed her into the heart of me and wept into her hair. As the door slid shut, it felt as final as a coffin lid closing.

"In the dark, the panic seemed to subside and as our eyes adjusted to the light coming from the slits above our heads, I remember seeing a young woman fighting for room in the crush of the wagon. She wore her hair like you; long, with thick plaits running in front of her ears. She was also pregnant and it was clear from the strain on her face that she was about to give birth. Stefan moved quickly. God rest his soul. He told everyone to make space and though it seemed an impossible request, children climbed onto the shoulders of their fathers, and brothers stepped on each other's toes, until eventually the young girl was able to hunch down, holding onto the arms of her mother. As the train pulled out of the station, her effort was echoed in the piercing screech of iron wheels. Seven hours later, with people fainting from heat and dehydration, the baby arrived. The girl's mother bent down to break the cord with her teeth and the realities of childbirth merged into the mess of those who'd had no choice, but to relieve themselves where they stood."

Florica gasped, Marcia paused to cross herself, and Esma quickly followed suit. Because Florica was both horrified and impressionable, she copied them both.

"We suffered similar, on the trains to Transnistria," Esma admitted quietly, her voice barely more than a whisper. "Many of the old died before they even reached the Bug River. As long as I draw breath, the stench of those wagons will stay with me. It was the smell of Hell."

At her feet, Florica stiffened. Her mother was fanatically clean, as were most of the Roma. In their culture the hem of a woman's skirt was enough to defile a man, and yet here they were; two women from different countries talking of the same horror, both of them victims of an unspeakable hatred.

"How can people do that to each other?" Florica asked, shaking her head in dismay.

"People are capable of anything," her mother replied. "And those who aren't usually stop looking."

Florica's eyes snapped open. Her lungs were on fire and she found herself struggling with a sheet that threatened to strangle her. Tearing herself free, she bolted upright, blinking rapidly and breathing heavily. There then followed a moment of confusion as she realised the nightmare hadn't come from the room below, but from scenes still lingering in her head.

She had dreamt of school. It was her first day and kids had circled her, every one of them bigger than adults. They each held a white card in their hands, which they flapped in her face. Then she looked down to see she also held something; a sheet of brown paper striped with blue lines. In panic, she turned to run only to trip and land in a pit. At her feet, hundreds of snakes wriggled and hissed at her ankles. She lost control and wet herself. Now, wide awake while the rest of the house slept, Florica could still hear the children's laughter.

Wiping the sweat from her face, Florica walked to the window to lift up the sheet. The sun was a long way from rising, but she decided to wait for it. Some hours later she finally heard her mother getting up. She gave her time to wash and prepare before going downstairs. To Florica's surprise, she was singing.

"What happened to you?" the girl asked.

"A good night's sleep, that's what happened. Although I still had to change the 'you know what'."

Esma's fingers fiddled with a pair of imaginary needles and wool. Instinctively, Florica's eyes searched for Marcia who was already up and sitting outside. In the still-cold day, her hands were busy with her knitting whilst her feet soaked in a bowl of warm water. Florica rubbed at her face. The world had gone mad.

"What are you doing, Marcia?"

"And good morning to you, too. What does it look like I'm doing?"

"But when did you get up?"

"About the same time as you."

Marcia looked knowingly at the girl, but Florica didn't believe her because she knew she had been awake since forever.

"In answer to your question, I am enjoying one of life's luxuries," Marcia proclaimed as she lifted her feet from the bowl. The blue veins protruding from her skin reminded Florica of frozen worms. "Back in the days of you know when, we stood for hours in the open, usually as some kind of punishment. Through heat wave or blizzard, we had to keep to our lines, sometimes all through the night. Standing might not sound like too big a deal, but it is, and today, nearly ten years later, I still suffer the effects."

Marcia gestured for Florica to pass her a towel that was hanging on the front door handle.

"I think I would have died at Auschwitz," the young girl declared, immediately regretting it as Marcia raised her eyebrows.

"That was stupid," she quickly confessed, and the old woman did nothing to dissuade her of that fact. "Can I ask you something, Marcia? When you talk about the bad times, doesn't it make it worse? You know; the nightmares and stuff?"

"Sometimes it does, sometimes it doesn't," the old woman admitted. "The thing is I want to be rid of it. I don't want to join my family hanging onto the weight of the past. Besides, too much is lost with the dead. If nothing remains, nothing can be learned. People will eventually forget and once they do that, the same mistakes will be made, time and again."

Florica poked her head into the kitchen. Satisfied her mother was busy, she came to whisper in Marcia's ear.

"I dreamt that I shamed myself last night," she confessed. "It was my first day at school."

Florica moved her head backwards as Marcia shook her own in violent denial.

"If there's one thing you'll never do, it is shame yourself at school," she replied firmly. "You'll be a credit to your family, and also to your people. I know this because I've seen it in your palm."

"When did you see my palm?"

"When you were asleep. No matter what comes, Florica, I will always watch over you."

"Well, thank goodness someone feels the need to," the child retorted loudly, still stinging from her dreams and her parents' attempts to make them come true. Behind the door, Esma's heart sank as she listened to her daughter's tantrum.

As soon as her husband awoke, after allowing him time to wash the sleep from his mouth, she repeated all she had overheard.

"I'll speak to her later," Grigor promised, and because he was unused to having to reason with eight year olds, he spent much of the working day worrying over what he might say.

Unlike his wife, Grigor wasn't comfortable with small talk or feelings. He recognised he was a fleeting presence in his daughter's life, but he loved her to distraction. He also hoped his actions spoke for him, such as the time worms were thrown in his daughter's face. He had tracked down the boys responsible, kicked their asses and administered the same punishment. When their fathers took umbrage, he attempted to reason with them before giving up and boxing their ears too. There wasn't a man alive who didn't know how much Grigor prized his daughter. Of course, sometimes little girls needed to know that too.

Unsurprisingly, Florica's eyes narrowed with suspicion when Grigor came to sit beside her. He had to admit he was quietly impressed; there were enough fools in the world without having added to the quota. Taking his penknife to a piece of wood, he punctured the wary silence between them by asking if she was alright. Florica answered with a shrug.

"Your mother is under the impression that you think we don't care about you," he persisted.

"Really?" replied Florica, innocence dripping from her huge eyes. "I don't know why she'd think that."

"Perhaps because she heard you say so this morning."

"Oh."

"Yes, oh."

Florica breathed in, embarrassed. Biting her bottom lip, she turned to look at her father. Though his knife continued to carve away slithers of wood, his eyes were on her.

"I was just mad that's all," Florica confessed. "I had a bad dream, about school."

Grigor nodded. Reaching into his trouser pocket he pulled out a chunk of toffee wrapped in paper. He cracked it with the blunt end of his knife and shared it.

"Don't tell your mother," he warned, "she'll say it's a bribe."

"Is it?"

"Of course, it is."

Grigor laughed gently and pulled his daughter closer. Florica leaned into his side, enjoying the toffee and the rare attention.

"I know school is a big deal, Flo'. But I want you to go because I know you'll benefit from the experience. It makes no difference to me or your mother if you stay at home. But there are rules to follow, which I know most of our people ignore, and one of them is sending your child to school."

"But if others ignore the rule…"

"It doesn't make them right. Look, I'm sure there'll be other children you know. School is part of what life is. More than that, it's a good thing. Your *Mamo* is suspicious because she's never been to school and she can't forget what the authorities did to us. But that time has gone and I tell you this, girl: I would fight the devil to keep you safe."

That said, and with his daughter's teeth glued by toffee thereby preventing any further challenge, Grigor rose to his feet and entered the house. As he passed his wife on the way from the kitchen to the bedroom, she squeezed his arm softly.

"Is that an invitation?" he joked, and Esma blushed furiously because Marcia was sat by the stove watching them. As Grigor left the room, the old woman sighed in a way that wasn't for once weary or depressed. 'Men,' she added with a chuckle and Esma smiled, admitting her parents had matched her with one of the good ones.

"My Stefan was a fine man," Marcia replied. "I tell you Esma, a good man is a blessing. A bad man is plain hard work."

Esma laughed. She took a frying pan from the shelf and reached for the eggs the good man in her life had brought from the farm.

"You've never told me what happened to Stefan," she ventured, leaving Marcia room to take up the conversation or not.

Marcia tilted her head slightly. "He was murdered," she replied, the shock of the statement at odds with its matter-of-fact delivery.

"I'm sorry, Marcia."

"Yes, me too, but then, in a funny way, I wasn't," the old woman confessed. "Stefan's death spared him from a lot that was to come. I've since taken comfort in that fact. The truth was he died as soon as he set foot in Auschwitz. As we left the train that had taken us there, he demanded water for that young girl and her new baby. The guard that Stefan asked tried to move him along, but he persisted. From nowhere it seemed, an officer stepped forward. He grabbed the soldier's gun and smashed the butt of it into my husband's head, cracking it like one of those eggs you're holding."

Esma glanced at her hands. When Marcia continued talking, she quietly returned the eggs to the sideboard.

"I tried to get to Stefan, but the guards forced us back. Bea was distraught, of course, and fighting to get to her father, but from where we stood, I could see the light had gone from his eyes. I pulled Bea away because there was nothing I could do. Nothing, I swear on my life. The Nazis murdered my husband, and for what? For having the gall to ask for a cup of water to give to a young mother and her baby."

As the horror of school drew ever nearer, Marcia did her best to distract Florica with tales of horrors far worse during walks they took away from the concrete jungle of 'Gypsy Town'.

"Nature is the most wonderful thing," Marcia declared as they disappeared into the countryside. "When I was a girl, about your age, I was obsessed with cornfields."

"Why?"

"I don't know, probably because they seemed so unusual. All those huge fields filled with giant stalks, their roots poking out like pink and purple spider's legs, and their leaves filled with tiny corn dollies sprouting red and yellow hair. I just loved them."

"I love flowers in trees," Florica revealed. "And fruit, I also love fruit. Cherries are my favourite."

"Oh, cherries are marvellous, growing in pairs, like two parts of the same soul. Apples are my favourite."

"They're not bad," Florica agreed. "Did you get any apples in the Auschwitz camp?"

"Only once," Marcia replied. She stopped to rest under the shade of an old tree. After scouting for a rock to sit on, Florica joined her.

"In fact, I received my one and only apple from a Roma girl called Violca. She was one of your people. In fact, she came from this place. A tiny little thing she was, and timid, like a pretty mouse dropped in a world of hungry cats. We met on my second night in Auschwitz, after we'd spent the first in some kind of storage shed. I can't remember much of that night, only my grief and Bea's tears. Did your mother tell you?"

"Yes," Florica confessed, her mind filling with the image of Marcia's dead husband, lying on the ground with his skull cracked like an egg.

"Good," Marcia stated, firmly nodding her head. "The next day in Auschwitz, when the sun came up, we were moved and herded into lines. Any possessions we had, which were few, were abandoned on the floor to be picked over by the Nazi crows. After that, we were shaved, branded and given a black patch."

"They shaved off your hair?"

Florica glanced at the grey plait peeking from under Marcia's black scarf.

"Yes," she confirmed. "They only did it the once. We were able to grow our hair again unlike others in the camp, but the damage had been done, the dishonour had been felt. We were also permitted to keep the clothes we wore, which was some comfort, until the lice got in them. Once the tattoos were done, we were taken from that part of the camp and marched to another. Oh Florica, Auschwitz was a vast and ugly place; a huge prison patrolled by soldiers and dogs and surrounded by barbed wire fences. As far as the eye could see there were rows upon rows of wooden barracks, each of them crammed to the hilt, like giant bee hives. I imagine I would have been terrified if I wasn't so beaten.

"The *Zigeuner* compound had 32 barracks, each holding more than 500 people. We were taken to a hut and ordered to find a place. I didn't know where to start. There were two rows of bunk beds, three tiers high, all of them displaying faces that just stared at us. I remember seeing nothing behind those eyes. After I'd been there a while, I obviously knew why.

"Inside the barrack, a Sinti man took charge. He was a prisoner, like us, but we were told to call him 'Kapo'. There were many Kapos in Auschwitz, some of them as brutal as the guards who beat us. At first, such thuggery felt like an unforgiveable betrayal, but again, after I'd been there a while, I understood more.

"As whole families ran for a bunk, I was left standing, holding on to Bea, lost and bewildered. From somewhere a young man appeared. 'Mother, come this way,' he said. He led me to a place on the bottom row. Inviting us to sit, he revealed his name was Tobar. In the corner of the straw mattress, with her knees tucked under her chin, was Tobar's wife; Violca.

"My God, that girl was beautiful, Flo', even in rags. She was also incomprehensible. Married for only six months, Tobar was her second cousin and a second-generation Roma in Germany. He explained that Violca had begun to learn our speech, but once they were arrested, she refused to utter another word tainted by German influence. As a result, Tobar endeavoured to pick through the maze of his wife's dialect. During the hours sat in their bunk, Bea and I learned to do the same."

"That's how you can speak like us?"

"That's how I can speak like you," Marcia confirmed. "And do you know, after everything they had done to us, all those faceless bureaucrats, politicians and dead-eyed soldiers, I found myself agreeing with Violca. The Germans had unleashed a plague on us all and I wanted nothing more to do with them either, not their country, not their speech, not their anything. May God curse their shit-smeared souls to Hell."

Florica raised her eyebrows, but she let the language pass. After everything Marcia had been through, she had earned the right to swear like a sailor. At least that's what her father said.

For a while the old woman sat motionless, unspeaking, unblinking. Florica busied herself by watching the birds in the trees. When a wasp landed on her arm, she sprinted from her seat to lose it. She then rejoined the old woman, wondering aloud how awful it must have been to live on a straw mattress that wriggled with lice with four of her family dead or missing.

"It was awful," Marcia agreed. "We had nothing in Auschwitz; no food, no privacy, no nothing. The hunger was absolutely fierce on us. Once a day, we were given a loaf of rye bread that had to be shared between five. It was usually old or wet, but after a while you stopped caring. You were so hungry you'd eat anything, even the mould that grew on the sides. There was also soup, usually made of turnips, so thin you couldn't tell it from tap water. And the latrines, my God, it was a block overflowing with all of life's indignities. As you can imagine, diseases ran wild and because one of them, something called typhus, also threatened the guards, we had to be deloused once a month. After undressing in our barracks, we were made to walk naked to the delousing area where they spread ointment on our bones using a brush. It was shameful, it really was. Grandmothers and great-grandmothers, paraded in front of other prisoners as naked as the day they came into the world. Though the men had to watch, they did their best to stare through us. It was the only dignity they could give us. Of course, not everyone blinded their eyes and I'm almost certain that it was on one of these days that the Nazis set their sights on Violca.

"She and her husband had arrived the month before us in February, part of the first transport of the *Zigeuner* to Auschwitz. In that short time they had witnessed everything we would come to know; the fresh tallies of death each morning; the bodies thrown onto carts with less care than a slaughtered pig; the fights that broke out as the Nazis played with our minds; the beatings; the punishments; the days stood standing in the rain; the soldiers laying bets as they forced the elderly to race along broken rocks on their hands and knees; and of course, all the diseases that dirt and poverty bring; typhus, diarrhoea, diphtheria, tuberculosis, scarlet fever and scabies. But do you know what was worse than all of that?"

Florica shook her head, unable to comprehend anything worse than what she had so far heard.

"We were the lucky ones," Marcia revealed "We lived in a 'family block' and we weren't Jews. Those people Flo', they were treated like nothing at all. Their heads were kept shaved, they were clothed in striped uniforms, and it seemed there wasn't a day that went past when they weren't shipped in and lined up for inspection. Those unfit for work didn't even make it to a bunk. They were taken to buildings that they called 'showers', only to reappear later as smoke. The Jews were gassed and burned in their thousands. Auschwitz was a factory, a conveyor belt of death, and the chimneys melted in the heat of their murders. We saw it all because one of the crematoriums was next to us. This is why I considered us lucky because degraded, beaten, abused, starved and killed as we were, we weren't sent to the shower. Not at first anyway. Only at the end, in the dying days of the Nazi terror, did our luck run out, but before it deserted us, we did what we needed to in order to survive. Just as Violca did what she had to do.

"After roll call one evening, Violca was called forward. The guards ordered her and a handful of other women to join them in their private quarters. As expected, Tobar ran after his wife, but he was stopped before he got anywhere. Two soldiers grabbed him by the arms and an officer stepped forward. I remember he smiled at Tobar. It was the coldest smile I'd ever seen on a man's face. The officer then shouted for the musicians. Yes, as crazy as it sounds, the Romanies had a band, one that played only for the amusement of the guards. On the officer's orders, the musicians struck up a lively reel, even as they blinked back tears. As the Romanies played, the Nazi guards took it in turns to beat Tobar, each blow delivered to the rhythm of the musicians' tune and the claps of the other soldiers. Only when Tobar's eyes closed and his legs gave way, did the guards eventually drop him.

"Throughout Tobar's punishment, Violca was forced to watch. She was then taken away to entertain the very men who had beaten her husband. During the long night that followed, I did everything possible to nurse the boy's wounds, but there was nothing I could give him. Three teeth had been knocked from his mouth. One eye had closed. Every inch of him was cut and bruised. There was no medicine. There was nothing to dull his pain.

"The next morning when Violca returned, she brought with her an apple. We all saw the insult and Violca shoved the apple into my hands, telling me to share it with Bea. I tried to urge her to eat some, it was food after all and God knew we needed it, but she shook her head. 'It would choke me,' she replied. And that was the first and the last time that I ate fruit in Auschwitz."

A week before Florica was due to start school, her health took a turn for the worse. With no warning she vomited her dinner onto the floor and Esma asked Marcia to take the child to bed while she cleaned up. Esma next suggested her husband might like to join his male friends a little earlier than usual so she could go upstairs to attend to their daughter without causing any issues of defilement.

"It's only nerves," he insisted, but he agreed to vacate the premises because the stern set of his wife's jaw indicated this would be the wisest option.

A minute after her husband left, Esma went to check on their daughter. She found Marcia wiping Florica's forehead with a damp cloth.

"It's only nerves," the old woman reassured her.

"I know what it is!" Esma snapped. "Don't you think I know my own daughter?"

Esma slapped a hand over her mouth in horror. Tears welled in her eyes and she slumped to her knees as Marcia muttered an apology. Esma shook her head and offered one of her own.

"No, I'm sorry. That was uncalled for. It's just this blessed school business. I'm jittery as a wasp in a jar these days. It seems Flo' isn't the only one suffering from nerves."

"It's not nerves!" Florica loudly asserted, impatiently wiping the hair from her face. She kicked away the sheet as though the weight of it was crushing her. "I'm truly sick. I swear I am. Look at me! I think I've got scabies!"

Both Esma and Marcia stared at the child.

"You think you've got what?" Esma asked.

Beside her, Marcia sucked on her lips and shrugged, apologetically. Esma shook her head.

"You haven't got scabies," she informed Florica. "And if you value your life, you won't repeat that again, especially not in school; they'll have you home before your feet can touch the ground."

Florica raised her head at the revelation.

"Don't even think about it," her mother warned. "Trust me you'll never get a husband if you tell everyone you've got scabies."

As this was just about the worst threat a Roma mother could give to her daughter, Florica reassessed her illness.

"Perhaps it's diphtheria then," she offered, and Marcia started chuckling.

"You do remind me of Bea, sometimes," she said by way of explanation. "Now you pay heed to your mother, she knows what she's saying."

Marcia squeezed the wet cloth into a bowl, and kissed the girl lightly on the forehead before leaving the room. As the door closed, Esma came to sit on the mattress and Florica moved up, lodging herself under her mother's arm. For a while neither of them spoke. But then Florica got bored.

"Marcia misses Bea, doesn't she?"

"She misses all of her children," Esma replied. "But I guess, with Bea being the youngest, she plays most on her mind."

"What happened to her?"

"She died."

"I guessed that."

Esma gazed at her daughter, hardly able to believe where the years had gone. The child was the most precious thing in her life and yet every day that passed Esma felt closer to losing her. Not in the terrible way Marcia had lost Bea, but rather through the passage of time. In a matter of years, Florica would be a woman and she would go to live in another house, with another family. The very idea of it sent shivers running along Esma's shoulders.

"I love you, Flo'."

"That's all very well, *Mamo*, but what happened to Bea?"

Esma sighed. Sometimes her daughter was very much the product of her father.

"As you know, Bea was in Auschwitz with Marcia. About six months into her imprisonment, she was taken to the infirmary on the orders of a man called Dr Carl."

"Was she sick?"

"Not in a way that needed this doctor."

"Why? Who was he?"

"He was an evil man – an evil, evil man – and knowing this Marcia fought like a tigress to keep her child with her. Unfortunately, this brought the Kapo running. He took a stick to Marcia and knocked her feet from the floor. When she came round, Bea was back, but the girl was bleeding between her legs."

Florica's eyes grew wide and Esma hesitated, uncertain how far she should go. Her next thought was of Bea and of everything the girl had endured, and she decided there was no justice to be had in denial.

"The evil doctor had injected liquid acid into Bea's uterus – the place where babies grow," Esma explained. "They called it sterilisation, but it was murder. They did it to as many women as they could. Some of the older ones survived the ordeal – which was no great blessing – but Bea was only twelve years old. Her body was too young and too traumatised by fear and starvation to survive the procedure. She died in her mother's arms."

"Poor Bea," Florica whispered.

"Yes."

"But why did they stera women?"

"They *sterilised* women – and also men – so that there would be no more babies, and one day there would be no more Roma."

"But why? What had we done?"

"Nothing, we had done nothing, Flo'. And this was the great crime of the Nazis."

Esma tucked her daughter's head under her chin. For an hour, maybe more, they lay on the bed together, lost in their own thoughts. More than ever before, Esma felt the great gift God had given her and though her daughter stayed silent, she felt this gratitude reciprocated.

The following morning, Florica woke early for breakfast. Her mother was already cracking eggs into a pan while her father was doing what he had to in the washroom. Marcia was sat outside, her old feet standing in a bowl of warm water.

"Feeling any better?" her father asked as he entered the kitchen.

"A lot better," Florica answered. "I don't think it was anything serious, just nerves."

Grigor nodded, throwing a quick glance at his wife. "Well, it's a worrying time, going to your first school."

"Not really. There are bigger things to worry about than school."

Florica grabbed a cut of bread and disappeared out to the yard to sit with Marcia. As she approached the old woman, she gave her a kiss on the cheek. Marcia bit her lip and carried on knitting.

"I was like a ghost when they took Bea from me," Marcia confessed, once she had ascertained that Esma had taken on the hardest part of her story. "There's no pain that compares with losing a child, Flo'. I pray to God that you will never know it, I really do."

"I can't even think how you got over it."

"I've never got over it. But Violca was the one who kept me going. She reminded me over and again of the children I still had, both waiting for me somewhere, in different camps. If it wasn't for her, well, who knows? That girl may have been tiny, but she was tough. She simply refused to give in. Whenever the Nazis took her for sport, she accepted it as the only way to survive. And when Tobar was beaten for the third time, a savage attack that cost him the sight in his eye, she put down her foot. She told him that if he couldn't support her, she would run into the fence and have the Nazis shoot her. You see, she suffered her indignity because she had something to live for; she had Tobar, her husband. And she insisted it had to be the same with me.

"Of course, even amidst the pain, I saw Violca was right and so I tried to concentrate less on what had been taken and more on what remained; on Ava and Joe. And I looked at those chimneys that continued to smoke, and the gas chambers where scratch marks on the walls were all that remained to show lives had been taken, and I grew angry.

"Violca often said it was oblivion that scared her most; the possibility that she may die and no one would know it. She was so far from home, you see. 'How would anyone even hear of my passing?' she asked. Though I didn't want to comment, she was plagued by this fear and so in the end I promised that I'd do everything humanly possible to get the truth to her family, if it ever came to it. I remember she hugged me for that, for the promise of explaining her death. That's how low we had fallen; we no longer believed we had a place in the future."

"Is that why you came to Romania?" Florica interrupted.

"God sent me."

"And I suppose you also believe He's the one sending me to school tomorrow."

"Probably. Are you scared?"

"Not anymore."

"Good girl."

Marcia placed her knitting on the table. She rubbed at her eyes before pinching the bridge of her nose. Florica thought about leaving her to rest, but seeming to sense the girl's pity, Marcia sniffed and picked up her needles.

"Where was I?" she asked.

"Violca wanted you to let people know if she died."

Marcia nodded. "Actually, I guess it wasn't so strange a request. In those days, death preyed on everyone's minds. Hidden away as we were, none of us had a clue what was happening outside. We didn't know if the Germans were winning or losing. We only knew hunger and suffering. Every day the war went on, more of us died. I felt my bones pressing against my skin and I watched my teeth slip from my gums. All of us were skeletons, skeletons dressed in rags, and the lice that crawled on us brought infections and disease. Our bodies were plagued with open sores, and in the autumn something new swept through our barracks. The medics called it 'water cancer'. It affected children the most, the poor mites. Their faces were left scarred by ulcers that had chewed their flesh down to the bone. As the disease spread, the head doctor, a man called Josef Mengele, took the afflicted into his hospital. Only a few came back to reveal what happened. Initially treated well, they were given clean bedding, better food and good water, the patients even started to recover. Then, each of these luxuries was taken away, and those who had been improving rapidly deteriorated. For Mengele and his doctors, the disease was just another experiment, and as people died, they simply stood by and took notes."

"That's disgusting," Florica declared, genuinely outraged. "Doctors are supposed to help people."

"But these weren't proper doctors and, to my mind, Mengele was the worst of them all because he pretended to be something he wasn't. Many a day I saw that man giving sweets to the children. He even had a play area built for them, with a sand box. Because the little ones didn't know any better, they called him 'Uncle', and do you know how he repaid their affection? He picked them off, one by one, to perform experiments on their tiny, emaciated bodies. Even now, I can't bear to think about the rumours that followed a missing child. Really, I can't. I won't speak of them either. Not ever."

Marcia laid down her knitting, and Florica saw they were done.

Despite her fears, Florica's first day at school was nothing like she had envisaged. She didn't wet herself for a start. Furthermore, there were no gangs of giant-sized kids and she learned nothing she didn't already know.

"I had to write my name on a board," she told her mother.

"Is that all?"

"Yes."

"Then I hope you spelt it correctly," her father interrupted.

"I did, if you spelt it right in the first place."

Grigor looked up from his stew, raising an eyebrow to indicate he accepted his daughter's fun, but it wasn't to go any further.

"Where's Marcia?" Florica asked.

"Lying in her room. She said she was tired."

Being a professional in suffering herself, Florica inquired whether she was eating.

"She ate some bread today, but not much. She's also stopped knitting." Esma dropped her voice. "I didn't change the wool last night because she'd hardly touched it."

"I'll go and see if she's alright."

"You'll eat your dinner first," her father ordered, and because he was the head of the house she did as she was told.

After escaping the table, Florica knocked on Marcia's door. When there was no answer, she pushed it open. Inside the room, she found the old woman lying on a mattress, facing the wall. The only decoration was a picture of Jesus and a rosary hanging from a nail. Her black scarf was draped over a small chair.

"Are you awake?" Florica whispered.

When no reply came, she tried again.

"Marcia... Marcia... Are you awake? Speak if you're awake."

"Well, I am now," the old woman grumbled, rolling over to face the child.

Florica flinched at what she saw. Marcia's hair, that was so thick down her back, was a long way from her forehead, like a wig that had slipped. Her skin was paler than milk, and dark circles dragged at her eyes.

"I'm sorry. I've disturbed you."

"And what? You think I can sleep now you've woken me? Come, sit yourself here."

Marcia raised herself to pat the chair by her mattress. She reached for the scarf as Florica moved reluctantly closer. As she took her seat, she smelt jasmine.

"How was school?"

"Not so bad. The teachers don't pay me much attention, but I'm practically a genius compared to the rest of the kids. Most of them don't know anything, not even their ABCs."

"Well, that's nothing to gloat about."

"Don't you think?" Florica laughed, and despite herself Marcia smiled too.

"Alright, perhaps it merits a small gloat. A very small one, mind."

Florica brought her knees up to her chest and squatted on the chair. She smiled at Marcia, relieved to see the scarf back on her head, and found it hard to believe the old woman hadn't always been in their lives she now seemed such a part of it.

"I'm glad God sent you," Florica informed her.

"Me too," Marcia confessed. "It's been an interesting lesson."

"Lesson?"

Marcia reached for the glass of water beside her bed. Taking a sip, she washed her mouth and swallowed.

"Everything that comes in life is a kind of lesson, sort of like the ones you're now learning in school, but different. For example, and I know it sounds terrible, but for many years when I saw a Roma woman in the streets of Berlin, with her skirts and plaited hair, I saw only our differences. On the evidence of others, I didn't see a person but a crime waiting to happen. More than that, I despised these women for pushing their poverty in our faces. I didn't give a second thought to their other lives, as mothers, daughters, sisters or wives. I felt only my own discomfort. Isn't that awful?"

"Yes, it's pretty bad," Florica agreed.

"Of course, I think differently now, thanks largely to Violca," Marcia admitted. "I've seen prejudice taken to the extreme and the effects of ignorance in the wounded flesh and broken bones of human beings. Auschwitz taught me to fear those I don't know. Your family taught me to appreciate those I did. The fact is Flo' that Violca was your mother's cousin. It is because of her that I found you."

Florica's legs slipped from under her chin. She slid herself back onto the chair, stunned.

"Does my mother know?"

Marcia stared at the girl.

"Yes, of course she does," Florica added hastily. "No one tells me anything."

"Really?"

"Well, you know what I mean. So, what happened to her – to Violca?"

"Sadly, after opening my mind, I had no way to thank her. One evening Violca was taken away and she never came back. She died in the Nazis' rooms. Tobar went mad when he found out. He ran screaming for the first guard he saw. He smashed that man's head into the ground until his tin helmet came away. Tobar then grabbed a rock. As he lifted it, a dog was released and it leapt at the boy's throat. Within seconds, he was dead."

Marcia paused to draw the mark of the cross on her chest, and for a second or two her eyes focussed on a place hidden from Florica's view. From the kitchen, Esma shouted for her daughter to come.

"You best go," Marcia advised.

"I'm not sure I want to."

"You should."

Florica rose from the chair. "Shall I pass you your knitting?"

"Not just yet," Marcia replied. "I think I'll rest a little more. I'm very tired these days. Really, more than you could know."

Florica nodded and wished Marcia 'sleep tight'. It was the last she would see of the old woman for the next two days.

In Marcia's absence, Florica pestered her mother for details of the woman who had brought them together. Despite the sadness that crept into her eyes, Esma spoke fondly of Violca who she described as a small girl with a quick tongue and uncommon beauty. She recalled days in the rain picking fruit from the trees and vegetables from the earth, of weddings and dances, of shared punishments and jokes, and she remembered a young woman leaving for a new country who was excited to be getting married. Esma then apologised for keeping her daughter in the dark.

"Marcia came to us because she had a life to remember and a story to tell. I didn't want to take that from her. She had travelled so far, and she had searched for so long, that I saw this was her purpose."

"Do you think we'll ever see her again," Florica asked, once the day had gone and they both sat staring at Marcia's closed door.

"Yes, when she's ready," Esma replied, sounding more confident than she felt. Though Esma hadn't voiced her concerns, and she continued with her daily chores as though nothing had changed, the truth was she was worried. The food she prepared went untouched and every offer she made to wash Marcia's clothes, or to brush her thinning hair was met with a smiling rejection.

"I don't know what's worse; the screams or this quiet," Esma finally confessed as she and Florica sat alone in the dark, almost willing the nightmares to begin.

The girl sighed and rested a hand on her mother's arm. She didn't know how she knew, she just did, and she told her mother, "Marcia will be leaving us soon."

As she spoke, Florica felt no sense of regret, but rather a shy happiness that seemed to circle the house, dancing around them, a little out of reach. Beside her, Esma crossed herself and later that night, whilst everyone slept, she got up twice to check the old woman was breathing.

On the third day of her retreat, Marcia emerged from her room looking much younger than when she went in. There was colour in her cheeks and her skin appeared softer, as though she were wearing powder.

"What are you all looking at?" she demanded.

Marcia surveyed the family that had adopted her, watching them staring at her with open mouths, like baby birds waiting to be fed. Jolted from their rudeness, the kitchen turned busy as everyone pretended that they weren't looking at anything at all; especially not an old woman who had hidden in her room for two days, apparently rejuvenating.

"I'll walk you to school today," Marcia informed Florica.

The child agreed, though it appeared she really had no option. As Marcia shuffled out of the house, Florica waved her parents goodbye and ran to catch up. On the road, they joined the trail of recalcitrant children dawdling to the gate of a large rundown building.

"Doesn't look much," Marcia observed, and Florica revealed it was little better inside. She then had an urge to reveal something more urgent.

"Marcia, I'll miss you when you go."

"Is that so?"

"Yes, it is. Honestly, it is."

Marcia stopped walking. She kept her eyes on the school yard ahead. "How does the gift come to you?"

"Do you mean how do I know?"

"Yes."

"It's a smell," Florica explained. "I smell jasmine around you."

Marcia raised her eyebrows a fraction. "That's nice. I've always liked jasmine. Perhaps, when you return from school, you ought to come to my room. There's still more to be said."

Florica agreed before running to join other children lining up in front of the main building, waiting to be led them into class. Marcia watched for a second before turning away. The sight of anyone standing in line made her uncomfortable. Rubbing at her left arm, she hurried back the way she had come.

That afternoon, as promised, Florica appeared in Marcia's room. The old woman prepared two bowls of plum tea before getting quickly down to business.

"So much occurred it's hard to recount it all," she confessed. "No words can do justice to the suffering in Auschwitz. There was simply too much of it. Even the small things, which might sound silly to you – like an old man crying for the loss of the moustache it took him a lifetime to grow – they all make me shudder now. The fact was, Auschwitz was an ugly place, the likes of which I pray will never be seen again. It was a place where pliers pulled gold teeth from the dead; where black bins overflowed with bodies; where blue flames threw souls to the sky long before their time. It was enough to break any man's spirit – and I thought that it had, until the Germans tried to make Jews of us.

"Roughly a year after we arrived, changes occurred. One of the rows in our block was emptied and thousands of Sinti and Roma were transported to other camps. Their places were filled with Jews. It seemed the Nazis couldn't kill them fast enough and they were running out of space. And it was during this period that a rumour reached us revealing our time had also come for the 'showers'.

"Of course, some said the warning was nonsense, but they soon changed their minds when the SS surrounded our block. We were informed there would be a 7pm curfew. When we filed into our barracks nobody said a word, but we were prepared. Some 6,000 of us were still in Auschwitz and we wouldn't go to the gas chambers with the dignified defeat preferred by the Jews. If we were going to die, we would fight to the death and the bastards would have to drag our bodies to the chimneys themselves.

"I can't pretend we weren't scared, Flo'. We were terrified, of course we were. But that night, when the Nazis tried to move us, we launched ourselves at the guards, wielding crowbars, planks, stones, and even hard bread. Every man, woman and child of us. And we screamed as if our toes were already dipping in the eternal fire of Hell.

"When the Nazis fell back, hurriedly locking us into our barracks, we were elated and then suspicious. People began to mutter that we would be burned alive in the wooden huts where we stood and I swear at one point I even smelled gasoline. But the guards didn't come. Instead, over the coming weeks – with all of us still living on our nerves – they started to wean the healthy from the weak. Those fit to work were suddenly transported in groups. At the end of May I was moved too. I was put on a train out of Auschwitz. I had survived.

"Sadly, I heard later, much, much later, that the ones left behind, some 3,000 elderly, the sick and the orphans, were sent to the gas chambers. No longer a force to be reckoned with, they left Auschwitz the same way as the Jews, as smoke pouring into the sky.

"From Auschwitz I was sent to Ravensbrück, and for the first time in a very long time, I found some kind of purpose. It was the camp Ava had been sent to and as soon as I arrived, I began searching for her. I inspected every pair of eyes. I asked every prisoner I passed. But the answer always came back the same. No one knew of Ava. Some of them were sorry for that, but most were too traumatised to feel anything at all. Even so, I kept looking because I had no other option; it was the only way to continue.

"Ravensbrück was mainly for women, and all of us worked. I was sent to the munitions factory and I have to say, the irony of keeping the Nazi war machine alive wasn't lost on me. In Ravensbrück we worked or we were beaten to death. Other than that, little had changed; the food was unfit for the troughs of pigs; we were regularly deloused; female guards were free to shoot us or set their dogs on us; and chimneys released people into the sky. Then, to my horror, I recognised a familiar face.

"One day, walking to the infirmary, I saw the doctor who had butchered Bea. The thought of him there consumed me, and in the nights that followed, I plotted that bastard's death a million times over. If God heard me, maybe Dr Carl got what he deserved, I don't know. I never found out because the Nazis suddenly stopped working us in order to kill us. Week after week, barracks were emptied. The gas chambers were filled. The chimneys smoked. Women, who had long ago lost sense of the differences that had sent them to that place, were marched to their deaths, in thousands upon thousands. The intent was clear; we were all to be exterminated and every day I saw my moment creep nearer.

"One day, when I was ordered to stay in our barracks, I thought my time had come, and I almost welcomed it. Outside, I could hear a tremendous commotion, as though Hell itself had come to our door. There were gun shots, screams, cries for help, barked orders, revving engines and the march of tens of thousands of feet. Then, as quickly as it started, it fell quiet. The next time our doors were pulled open we were faced with soldiers we no longer recognised. They were white, but their uniforms were different and their language was nothing I knew. Around me, women dropped to their knees, weeping and praying. It was like a dream no one dared believe."

"You were free?"

"Yes, I guess we were. The Russians had come and the Nazis had fled, taking 20,000 prisoners on a death march north. I have no idea why I was spared; it might have been a mistake. All I know is that I found no joy in it. In less than six years, millions upon millions had died. Many more were scarred for life, both physically and mentally. And though I couldn't wait to get out of there, I stayed. I needed to find answers.

"It took a week to hear the truth, and I learned it from the records left by the Nazis. Ava had died in the gas chambers along with her child. The man who told me came from Moscow. A huge man he was, with arms as big as boulders. I thanked him for his time, and left his office. The next day I saw this man again because he had information about Joe. He told me my son had died in Buchenwald. The paperwork in front of him blamed 'natural causes' and I remember looking at this Russian and seeing the lie written in his eyes. Young men don't die of natural causes. They die because someone killed them.

"In that room, in front of that man with arms as big as boulders, I fell to my knees and wept like I'd never wept before. Everything poured out of me; every humiliation; every suffering; every hurt; every death. I cried because there was nothing else that I could do. There was no one left to look for, there was no one left to look after. I was alone.

"I don't know how long I lay there, slumped on the floor, but eventually the man from Moscow pulled me to my feet. I guess he had delivered a lot of bad news that week because when I looked up, I saw his eyes were also wet with tears. I'll never forget that. It seems such a small thing, I know, but his sadness was a reminder of a humanity I had long ago forgotten.

"And there you have it, Flo'; that is my story, which I hand to you so that you might make it your own. Whatever you do in life, make sure you honour it. Whether Sinti or Roma we are one people and this is as much your history as mine. And now that I'm done, I guess I better prepare my clothes."

It was still night when Esma's sobs echoed through the house. Florica was awake when she heard them, having been prevented from sleep by the clicking of Marcia's needles, but once her father's voice travelled up the stairs, she left her bed to support her parents.

At Marcia's door, she found her mother holding a scarf. It was incredibly long, in differing shades of red, and perfectly complete. Without a word, Florica entered the old woman's room. In the candlelight, she saw Marcia lying on her bed, dressed in the clothes she had washed that afternoon. One of the sleeves had been picked away and as Florica moved closer she noticed a fresh burn lying on Marcia's left forearm. It was clearly in the shape of her mother's iron, erasing all that had marked her before. Marcia was no longer a *Zigeuner* with a number. She was a Romani Sinti – and Florica felt honoured to have met her.

Offering a sad smile to her parents, Florica returned to her room. As she pulled the sheet to her chin, she smelt the deep scent of Jasmine that had woken her many hours earlier. When she closed her eyes, her mind danced with a million tiny stars.

"Goodnight, Marcia," she whispered.

Chapter Fourteen

"Only in recent years has the suffering of the Roma during World War II been acknowledged. There are some who still deny that our people were victims of the Holocaust. Even in death it seems we are denied the right to equal status. But what would you call it when a race of people is gassed, executed, beaten and worked to death? When half a million or more are systematically and brutally robbed of their lives? When our men and women are butchered to stop us breeding? Is this not slaughter on a mass scale? Is this not a holocaust?"

Jack leaned forward as he listened to Francoise's translation. When she finished, I continued before he could answer. "I'll tell you what we call it, Monsieur Caron; we call it *O Baro Porrajmos* – The Great Devouring."

Jack scribbled in his notebook. He tilted the page towards Francoise who indicated the accuracy with a nod. He then tucked the pen behind his ear.

"I had no idea," he admitted, carefully. "The Jews, well yes, everybody knows what happened to the Jews. But the *Gitans*..."

"Romanies, Monsieur Caron!" the Big Man barked from his seat. "We are Romanies!"

"Yes, of course. Excuse me, I meant no disrespect."

"No one ever does," Rami muttered from his seat next to Marko.

As Francoise repeated the exchange, I spied Miko and Mirela returning from their walk. They both held flowers in their hands, plucked from the roadside during their wanderings. Although Mirela knew part of our history, I hadn't burdened her with all the details. She knew only a little of our time in slavery and she knew nothing of *O Baro Porrajmos*. One day, she would be old enough to hear it all, but not now. She was still a child, no more than a little girl, and she had already seen too much. Fear had come to take my daughter early and she was already aware that she was hated. This child, no more than a little girl, my beautiful Mirela.

Feeling a familiar knot rising to my throat, I lifted a hand; begging five more minutes from my husband. Miko nodded. He turned away from the crowd gathered before our caravan, taking our daughter with him. I turned my attention back to Jack who was looking increasingly uncomfortable under the glare of the silent Roma. His top lip glistened under their scrutiny. It was clear the time had come for answers.

"Jack," I said, tugging his attention towards me as softly as I was able. "How could it be that you know none of our history? Not even of The Great Devouring? Your grandmother was a Romani, was she not?"

My question hit the Frenchman with the force of a bullet. His breath caught in his chest. His eyes widened. He then coughed so hard that he choked, bringing spidery red veins to his startled gaze. "My grandmother?"

"Yes," I confirmed patiently. "She was Hungarian Roma. We read it on the back of your record, *My Gypsy Heart Beats On*."

"Oh God," he groaned. He looked at the sea of faces before him and ran his fingers through his thick hair. "This is really quite embarrassing."

As Francoise repeated, her pale eyes revealed her confusion. She glanced at me, raising an eyebrow, apparently seeking an explanation that wasn't mine to give. I tipped my head towards Jack – her possible boyfriend, a possible gypsy – and her shoulders tensed. Beside her, Jack shrugged apologetically, pulling the corners of his lips down, towards his chin. It was pathetic really, and the colour crawled up Francoise's neck. As the shocked silence dripped into awkwardness, Jack finally confessed, with more sheepish shrugs, that both of his grandmothers came from Toulouse.

"The Roma persona was created by my record company. Terrible, isn't it?"

"Why?" I asked.

"Because it was a lie."

"Yes, I gathered that, but why did your record company do this?"

"Who knows, maybe because the *Gitans*, sorry, the Romanies," Jack hurriedly corrected, "were in vogue at the time. It was the seventies; hippy flower power, easy love, unprecedented freedom. When I was discovered, my hair was long and I had a nice tan. I was also busking in Saintes Marie de la Mer, long before it became fashionable. Out of nowhere, this scout approached me. He told me his idea, and I thought 'why not? It'll be a gas.' Soon after, Jack Caron the Gypsy Lover, was born. This was just before punk rock arrived and the fizz soon went out of the market. After some initial success – two singles in the Top Ten and a Number One album – I couldn't sell a record for love nor money. The record guys dropped me like a brick. To be honest, it was pretty disheartening, but that's the way the industry is. It's fickle and phoney. In fact, my name isn't even Jack or Jacques. It's Alain."

"Hellfire, he's got more names than I have!" Bo interrupted.

The joke caused a ripple of laughter among the men around him, many of whom often used multiple names in their dealings with the *gadje*. It also helped lighten the mood with some declaring they had known all along that Jack was no Roma.

"No Rom has his luck with women!" Tanko stated, and even Bo laughed at that. In fact, it was only Francoise who seemed to be remotely upset by the deception and the more those around her relaxed, the straighter her back became until I could see the sharpness of her anger in the shoulder blades spearing the cotton blouse she wore.

"But why?" she asked in a harsh whisper. Once again, Jack who was really Alain, shrugged.

"Actually, there's something I'd like to know," I said, and the crowd stilled. I found their respect uncommon and gratifying. "Monsieur Caron, I've told you our history, or at least parts of it, and yet I still don't understand your interest in us, even less now we know you share no blood. So, tell me, why do you come here?"

Jack nodded as Francoise translated, but his eyes never left mine and for the first time I saw the subterfuge that shrouded him lifting. Beneath the arrogance he was simply a man trying to find his seat in a world, a world that had turned its back and forgotten him. Pulling at the tip of his nose, he recalled a day, long after he had been famous, when a stranger remembered who he was.

"I had never met the guy before. I had never seen him before. And yet he assumed he knew me. He called me 'gypsy' and he swung a fist at me that knocked me off my feet. He then spat in my face as he walked over me on the street. Nobody stopped to help. In fact, I saw another man, possibly a friend of this thug, approach to high-five him. I was shocked. Sometime later, I was furious. But in the seconds after he hit me, I was too much of a coward to confront him."

Jack raised his hands in apology, acknowledging his weakness before the other men.

"You could have told him the truth," Rami mumbled, sad and embarrassed for their guest.

Jack nodded. "I could have told him, yes, but it would have been no less upsetting. The fact was, my time as a Roma, or rather my time pretending to be one, had been good to me. It was too late to declare the truth. More than that, when I replayed the incident in my mind and though about what other, better, reactions I might have given, I realised a denial would have felt like a betrayal. Odd you may think, but that's how I felt. Besides, I doubt this stranger would have believed me even if I had told him the truth."

"That'd be right," agreed Rami.

"Of course, after a while I simply forgot about the attack. It grated from time to time, but nothing had been broken and I was working as a salesman in an electrical shop. It hardly seemed to matter; one man's memory of a character I'd once played. But then, this year, when all of this anti-Roma resentment started to build, I got to thinking about that man again. And I got to wondering about why the world was so openly hostile to your people, beyond all others it seems. It became an itch within me. One I couldn't scratch. In the end, I contacted an organisation in Paris with an idea. They passed me on to Francoise, who was not only Romanian but also an advocate specialising in Roma discrimination. And we came here, to speak to you."

"But what for?" I persisted. "To what end?"

"At this stage, I don't exactly know," Jack confessed. "I was hoping a plan might come to me the more we talked. Ideally, I'd like to use the impact of my misspent youth to do something worthy. Perhaps, being who I am, and being remembered for whom I am not, I might offer some kind of platform to counter the discrimination that you guys face. At least that's the hope. Truly, I only want to help."

As Jack finished, his palms held out to us, his eyes large and wary, I had to admit I thought he was sincere. I saw my belief mirrored in most of the faces around me.

"Well, I'm not sure there's anything you can do," Rami said quietly.

"There must be something," Jack replied.

To my right, Bo got to his feet. "At least you can try," he told Jack. "Let's face it, there's nobody out there who feels the need to listen to *us*."

When I later informed Miko that Jack's heart wasn't quite as gypsy as he would have once had everyone believe, my husband was as unbothered by the deceit as most of our neighbours.

"It seems a strange sort of prison to build yourself," he commented, raising his head to rest it on his hand. Between us, Mirela slept soundly. Her left cheek faced the pillow and she looked something like the girl we used to know.

"I don't think I've ever heard of one of the *gadje* pretending to be Roma before," I said. "Even during the communist times when they mimed to our songs on TV, it wasn't because they were pretending to be us; they solely wanted to keep our faces off the screen."

"It is unusual," Miko agreed. "Let's face it, there are Roma out there who don't want to be known as Roma."

I frowned a little, knowing he was alluding to my sister, Afina. She was six years older than me, bright, beautiful and somehow lost to us. Against our parents' wishes, she had married out of the community. As a result, she lived in a nice house, in a nice area. She drove a decent car. Her kids were in a good school. She worked at a bank and she had prospects. But though Afina had carved herself a future, she had given up her past. The price of progress had been her Romani roots. Our parents were mortified, and ashamed, both for her and for them. By denying who she was she had sullied us all. Even so, I didn't blame her. She simply wanted more than our community could offer. And she was safe now, in a way that those she left behind were not.

"I sometimes wonder whether it's pride that brought us to this," I whispered.

"Brought us to what, this patch of scrubland in France?"

I dipped my eyes towards our daughter and the laughter died on Miko's lips.

"We are who we are," he replied, twelve years of marriage enabling him to read my thoughts as easy as the most gifted among us. "To deny it would be an insult to all those who walked before us. You know it, Mala, you taught me the history as well, remember. And I never tire of hearing it. Honest, I don't. Our people have suffered, we continue to suffer, but walking away is no solution. If we cannot take pride in who we are, in who we were, and in who we will one day be, then the *gadje* wins. Hate will have conquered humanity. Our people will become extinct, not through climate change or evolution, but because we lost the will to believe in ourselves. Pride is our strength, not our weakness."

Miko moved his arm towards me, gently wiping away the tear that had slipped from eye to cheek. I held his hand to my face, pressing his conviction into my bones, feeling my heart expand with the great love I possessed for him.

"Twelve years and still you cry," he muttered sourly, but the smile had returned to his face. I laughed at the complaint, recalling our wedding night, another lifetime ago, and the tears that had drenched our pillow as the fear of wifely duty didn't so much override decorum as grab it by the throat and wipe the floor with it. In that simple room, at the back of his parents' home, Miko had looked on astonished. He then reminded me that sheets had to be seen, and he was too drunk to slice a vein and spare me the torment. Of course, the mention of blood only made my tears tumble faster, but eventually nature took its course thanks to the tender coaxing of my new husband. Miko had helped me then, he had helped me ever since.

"We'll be going soon, won't we?" I asked.

Miko's chocolate eyes softened. Before he could answer, Mirela's legs kicked out to steal the moment. As her tiny hands clawed at the sheet lying over us, I took them in my own and drew her to me. Miko turned away to nip the light flickering at our heads.

"Two eyes, two hands, two legs, pain in the eyes go away into the legs. Go away from the legs into the earth. Go away from the earth into death."

I heard the voices first – angry shouts that I couldn't make sense of. Seconds later, a pulsing blue light lit up the dark giving partial explanation to the growing clamour beyond our windows. Dazed and hijacked by old fears, my body refused to move. Beside me, Miko jumped to his feet, dragging his jeans on, over his pyjama bottoms. He reached for an iron bar, its serrated edges revealing it had once belonged to something larger. Experience had taught us much, but the most valuable lesson had been to keep something heavy at hand.

"Stay here," he instructed.

Next to me, Mirela reacted to the commotion outside. "Oh God, not again, not again..."

I pulled her into my stomach, unable to meet the terror stretching her eyes. I needed to say something, but I couldn't find my voice. I wanted to comfort her, to assure her everything would be alright, but my mouth was dry with the ashes of past lies. Nothing would ever be alright. There would never be an escape. Not until we were dead in the ground and the bastards danced on our graves.

The door clattered behind Miko as he ran from the caravan. Outside, more angry voices joined the fray. I heard Marko. He was speaking in French, but his alarm was apparent. Somewhere, glass smashed. Doors banged. A dog barked. It didn't sound like one of our own. Then the sound of feet came, running nearby. More barks, clearly more than one dog. The blue lights continued to flash. And before I could gather my wits to stop her, Mirela wrenched herself from my arms. She flung herself at the window behind us, the one that looked onto the dry fields beyond the hedge of our boundary.

"Run, Bo! Run!" she screamed.

Finally galvanised into action, I jumped to my feet to pull Mirela away. Halfway across the field, in the dirty grey of the coming dawn, I saw Bo scramble to his feet. He must have twisted his leg as he fell, because he limped as he ran, now employing great lolloping strides like a wounded animal fleeing the hunt. A blur of black streaked after him. Reaching the horizon, the silhouette of a German Shepherd pounced and dragged Bo to the ground. I gasped for air and pulled Mirela to the floor, hiding her head in my lap as Bo's screams tore through our heads.

After the police bundled Bo into a wagon, the Big Man phoned Francoise. She arrived with Jack, who must have been with her when the call came – perhaps having shared her bed, somewhere in a quiet flat, in a quiet street where the police didn't come to wake them with batons and dogs. There was an allegation of theft, she had managed to ascertain, now coupled with a charge of resisting arrest.

"A computer shop was burgled," Francoise revealed. "A witness saw Bo with an item from the store."

"But he fixes old computers!" Rami protested.

Francoise sighed in sympathy. "I'm sure the police will realise their mistake."

"You think?" Rami demanded, unconvinced.

"We should go down there," Stevo remarked.

"I wouldn't," Francoise advised. "I think you should wait. He'll be released soon enough, even if they charge him, which I doubt they will," she added hurriedly. "When Bo returns, I'll speak to him and if he needs my assistance, I'll do everything I can. I promise."

"Will they release him?" I asked Miko when he returned to our caravan to reveal the conversation that had taken place.

"Who knows? Every country has its own laws and I don't know what they are here."

I glanced at Mirela. She was sleeping on the blanket. Her face was moist, with sweat from the August heat and the tears she had shed since morning. My palms itched. The time had come.

"I'm going to speak with the *gadje*," I informed my husband. "I need to finish what I started. After that we go. Stay here, listen at the window. When the time comes – you'll know when – I want you to bring Mirela outside to meet them."

Miko nodded. "You're right. Let's finish this."

Chapter Fifteen

"I'll keep this short because I'm going to talk about my life. It's not yet over, it's not yet history, it's not yet another's story to tell. It is my life. It is the one that God gave me, the one that I endeavoured to do the best with, and the one they tried to end. When I say 'they', you know I mean the *'gadje'*. And when I say the *'gadje'* I mean you – every man among you who never raised a voice to protect us. Savage acts against the Roma have been instigated and sanctioned by your people, time and again. They continue today. Silence is not an option. Mumbled condemnations are no longer sufficient. If you sit back and allow prejudice to fester – to gain sustenance from the stew of ill-informed belief, ignorance and fear – you are not only part of the system, but an arm of the disease. Strip us to the skin and the only difference between us is colour. Traditions, culture, history, customs these are merely the clothes we wear. They are also the shields that protect your eyes from the truth. Because when the punch is thrown, when the knife goes in, when the bullets fly, the flames are fanned and the gas is released, the victim is no longer a gypsy or a gitano, ijito, gjupci, sipsiwn, or yiftos. The victim is a man, a woman, a child. The victim is a husband, brother, father and son. The victim is a wife, sister, mother and daughter. The victim is a person who harboured hopes, battled fears, dared to dream and struggled to get by. A person not unlike you, only different in colour. Trust me I have to try to remember this myself when I'm consumed with rage and, yes, also with hatred over what you have done. But that reminds me of one other fundamental difference between us; we have never set out to destroy you."

ROMANIA
1993 – 2009

Chapter Sixteen

I was ten years old when my grandmother opened up her books to me. There were five in total, all of them huge. Standing on the floor, they came up to my thighs. I have no idea how she came by them. She claimed they had always been there. Cased in black board, grown soft as old leather, they were the books that salvaged our history in words that never lay still. The yellowing pages were filled with corrections, new admissions and fanciful details imagined by different hands at different times. When I was older, I read them all. When I was educated, I breathed new life into them, just as *Mami* had once done, and others before her. They became a part of me, just as she said they would.

I cannot say with any certainty, because the reasons behind decisions are quickly lost in the execution of them, but I believe the books and *Mami's* belief in them are what stirred my desire to learn. When I was teased at school, when my hair was pulled, when the teachers turned their backs pretending not to see my raised hand, I ignored it all. And when friends urged me to play truant or misbehave, I ignored them too. I had a purpose, you see, and the purpose lay in the completion of my grandmother's books.

No doubt due to the passage of time, and periods of disinterest, many details were lacking within those yellowing pages. There were names and allusions to dates. There were tender memories that were sometimes accompanied by doodles and drawings, such as a face, a flower or a butterfly. There were accounts of wars, and tales of hardship, sometimes documented with a heavy hand, displaying words that appeared to have been seared into the paper. And there were pages upon pages of unimaginable grief where the ink would suddenly fade away, as though losing heart with the telling. What they lacked, however, was any evidence to separate fact from fable, and I understood from the start that this was to be my role. I felt the weight of this responsibility from the moment the books were revealed to me. With the right tools, I knew I could add substance to my grandmother's stories, and reveal the history that they fought to preserve.

Of course, enthusiasm wasn't enough to do justice to the catalogue of injustices laid before me. I needed knowledge. But Romani history was never part of the school curriculum and the glory of Ceausescu, followed by the glory of those who deposed him, could only ever have a minor bearing on the Five Books of Truth, as I had so whimsically named them. It was clear I would have to be patient. And really, that wasn't so difficult. I was the youngest of eight children. I was used to waiting in line.

I won't bore you with the names of my siblings; they would only confuse you to the point where you'd choose to forget them. Suffice to say, we were a large family and largely happy. We lived near Sibiu, at the foot of the Cindrel Mountains, close to the olive green waters of the Olt River. Our home had been provided by the communists after they bulldozed the old one, along with 7,000 other communities, in their rush towards modernization. I guess, in their way, the communists had sought to improve our lives. Some Romanians even called Ceausescu the Father of the Gypsies, citing the preferential treatment he apparently showed our people. But Ceausescu wasn't a Roma, he was a *gadje* and in the end he sought to improve our lives in the only way the *gadje* know how, by forcing us to settle and forget who we were. Travelling was outlawed. Dealing was no longer tolerated. Traditional trades were stymied by state monopolies on industries and resources. We were forced into soulless factories and agricultural cooperatives. For all their words, the Communists only succeeded in binding us to the chain of relentless misery that the *gadje* seem to favour. It never occurred to them that we might be a people who worked to live, not the other way round, and the daily slog of employment was like a torture to us. However, having been fed into the labour machine there was little to differentiate us from the Romanians. Our shared suffering allowed us to be tolerated. But Ceausescu's programme of systemisation didn't stop the rot – it merely sowed the seeds of a later discontent.

The Roma who had lost their homes or had been forced to stop travelling were given empty houses within *gadje* communities or offered new ones in blocks built on the fringes of towns. Grumbles soon followed, with many claiming the Roma didn't know how to respect property, that they broke windows and built fires in rooms. And maybe some of it was true. But it's not so hard to imagine an old man who had lived his whole life on the road suddenly finding himself trapped in a concrete square. It's not so hard to imagine the winter rolling in and him building a fire, like he had always done. It's not so hard to imagine how the transition could have been perplexing, in much the same way that a *gadje* might struggle to survive in the open. The fact is you only know what you know until someone teaches you different. But the nomadic Roma weren't taught a thing. They simply had their horses taken away and their wagons confiscated before being entombed in a world they had no knowledge of. Even so, my grandmother insisted, shortly before she died, that these were the good times. And in many ways, they were. Although we were treated with contempt, joked about and prohibited from performing or singing in our own language, we were never attacked. Violence, or the fear of it, only entered our lives following the revolution, when Ceausescu and his wife left the world with bullets in their heads.

The year was 1989 and I was six years old when the National Salvation Front came into power. I remember there were flowers thrown onto roads, people were crying, laughing, and giving each other gifts. A collective madness took hold of the country with everyone apparently very pleased with the change. But then the attacks started: Turu Lung; Lunga; Cilnic; Huedin; Mihail Kogalniceanu; Bolintin Deal; Ogrezini; Bolintin Vale; Plaiesii De Sus. Suddenly the Roma were no longer to be tolerated. Houses were razed to the ground. Our people were beaten. Whole families were chased from their villages. And the innocent died, one of them a three-year-old boy who burned to death in a haystack.

In some cases, there was a reason, of sorts, for the violence, like Bolintin Deal. A student died in a fight and though a Rom was arrested, thousands later gathered in front of the victim's home. From there they marched to the Roma quarter. They torched 27 homes and three cars. All the families had to flee. Families who had done nothing to anyone. For a while, they slept on construction sites and camped in the open. When some tried to return home, the mob chased them away again before torching the last remaining houses. And what did the government do during this period of mob rule? Did they try to reason with the masses? Did they punish those who took the law into their own hands and made a mockery of it? No. At the height of the attacks they chose to honour Marshal Antonescu with a minute's silence in parliament. Yes, the great dictator who'd sent our people in their thousands to die on the plains of Transnistria. It was hardly the support, or the leadership, we'd been hoping for.

This was the new revolutionary Romania and, to be fair, it wasn't only the Roma who suffered. When President Ion Iliescu brought a train-load of miners to Bucharest we found ourselves in illustrious company as they got to work on not only us, but the capital's students and intellectuals. However, in the frenzy of hate that ran unchecked through our villages between 1990 and 1991 we were the sole targets, and yet we were the only ones arrested. Is it any wonder our people lost faith in *gadje* justice?

Of course, at the time of the troubles I was too young to appreciate the full horror of these attacks. I only knew that my mother stopped taking the bus into town because she was afraid.

Seven years later, when I was 15, the country was quieter, our people were guarded rather than fearful, and I found myself married. My parents had chosen well and though custom required that I live with my in-laws, I retained much of the freedom I had enjoyed in my youth. Miko, my husband, allowed me to continue my schooling. It was a kindness, and one that wasn't common in our communities where study is a luxury few can afford. More surprising, however, was the support of my mother-in-law. When I showed her the Five Books of Truth that *Mami* had gifted me, she grudgingly agreed to this abnormality in her life, as long as I was first from sleep, the last to retire, and I fulfilled the duties of a good Romani wife. This I did, and much more besides, but when my last day at school arrived, I walked away no wiser than when I had started. In the candlelight of my bedroom, I sensed the disappointment fluttering within the pages of the Five Books of Truth.

By then it was 1998 and, thankfully, Romania was not the place it once used to be. Nine years after the revolution, the Roma had their own newspapers as well as political parties and, as narrow as my education had been, it pointed me towards doors waiting to be opened. The first one led me to the library.

Given the enormous role it played in my life, it's disappointing to recall the dank, cold chamber that was the nearest town library. On the tired walls, paint flaked away like the petals of a dying flower. The air was musty and eyes followed me as I walked through the narrow wooden passageways. And yet, the moment I stepped into that hall it felt like every window of the world flew open, bathing me in sunshine. Rows of books lined multi-tiered shelves, some of them tattered, some stained, some squeakily clean and wrapped in polythene. They all screamed for my attention, but I chose to start with an atlas. I heaved the great volume from its dusty resting place, searching for the paths that our people had taken. My fingers trembled as they followed the line: from Kanauj to Ghazna; from Ghazna to Khorasan; from Khorasan to Constantinople; from Constantinople to, well, everywhere. Encyclopaedias and geography manuals further revealed the sights and tastes of each part of our journey. History books threw fresh meaning on foreign names. And late in the evening back in my room, once the meals had been cooked and the chores had been completed, I felt the Five Books of Truth come alive with my discoveries. Though I knew it was the blood pounding from my heart to my fingers I felt the pages pulse beneath my fingers.

Occasionally, during the hours spent scrubbing or the endless pursuit of relieving potatoes of their skins, my husband's mother would grumble a complaint, claiming I was bordering on obsession, but these were relatively rare gripes triggered by her own daily frustrations. In contrast, Miko was constant in his support and his obvious pride validated my endeavours.

Unfortunately, in those days there was only so much a Romanian library could supply the Roma researcher, but as I came close to exhausting the state-sanctioned resources, another door opened. In 2001 a computer was installed and it introduced me to the internet. Well, if the library had opened the windows of the world, this new technology kicked out the doors and blasted holes in the wings. With each click of the mouse my heart began to race with the seemingly endless wealth of information now at my fingertips; academic papers, magazines, organisations, novels, discussions, and, some years later, even videos on You Tube. I blinked rapidly to still my blurring vision. After years in the wilderness, with our nation scattered to the winds, we were finding each other; the Kalderash, the Lovara, the Machraya, the Churara, the many branches of our ancient tree, reaching out and uniting in a world in which there were finally no borders. I could have wept, which in fact I did, and another door opened.

I had been reading about Famous Romanies – Matéo Maximoff, Michael Caine, Charlie Chaplin, Bill Clinton, Rita Hayworth, Jean-Baptiste Reinhardt, Papusza, La Liance – when a man approached me.

"Are you OK?" he asked.

I was startled, and somewhat embarrassed by the tears glistening in my eyes, so I ignored the man's concern. Without a word, I relinquished my seat. He seemed surprised. He even tried to convince me to stay, but as I walked away, he thanked me before mumbling something about an urgent email. I didn't let it show on my face, but I too was surprised; I was normally unseated with far fewer manners. When the man finished, and he was actually very fast, he held the chair back for me and invited me to retake it. I thanked him, thinking it polite, and was trying to remember the name of the site I had been looking at when he interrupted me again.

"Are you researching your people?" he asked, quickly explaining he had noted the page I was reading before closing it.

It was such an innocent observation, but it was one that left me feeling as naked as a plucked chicken, as though I'd been caught doing something I shouldn't. I mumbled an affirmation that sounded more like an apology. Instinctively, I looked around, noticing a handful of eyes following our exchange. The man noticed too.

"Well, I've taken up too much of your time. Please, go ahead," he said. Then he was gone.

Four days later, I saw him again. We were back in the library. On this occasion I wasn't at the computer because I'd been obliged to make way for a young woman, a student, judging by her clothes. I was sitting instead at one of the large writing desks. In front of me lay an open medical book and I was jotting down symptoms of the Black Death. A smile stretched my face, which may have appeared odd given the subject matter, but I couldn't help it, the grim reality of the plague tallied with the stories I had inherited.

To my astonishment and, yes, embarrassment, the Romanian joined me at the table. Without a word, he pulled the medical book towards him with the casual ease of the more powerful. I didn't say anything, not until he spoke, and when he did, well, it was like the pieces of a jigsaw slotting together.

The man's name was Radu and he said he came from Constanta. I asked if he was lost, given he was a long way from the Black Sea, and he seemed oddly pleased by the joke.

"No, I'm not lost," he replied. "Although I think I may have found something I've been searching for."

It was a remark that might have sounded creepy coming from another mouth, but Radu possessed a wide, clean face. He didn't look like a playboy, or a pimp. His eyes were hazel, his nose a touch dumpy, and his smile was easy and genuine. He worked in education, he said. His group was funded by the European Union and he dealt predominantly with the schooling of Romani children.

"It is clear you read and write Romanian," he said, waving a hand at the book before me, "But what about Romani?"

Though I could have felt justifiably insulted at the inference that I might not know my own language, strangely I wasn't. Radu's questions, as clumsy as they were, were luring me to a place that felt suspiciously like destiny. According to him, one of the greatest obstacles facing the Roma was a lack of education. It was hardly a Eureka moment, but I was less cynical at that time and I let the comment pass.

"Many children are disadvantaged from the outset," he said. "Locked inside their own communities, many of them speak little or no Romanian by the time they reach school age. To our shame, the state solves this by placing them in special schools more suited to the mentally and physically handicapped. Either that or we ignore them. However, there are organisations working to correct this. My own group creates programmes to enable Romani children to be taught in mainstream schools. We place Romani educators in classrooms with staff teachers. They are the bridge between our two worlds. They translate where needed and advise on matters of cultural sensitivity. It is a new initiative, still early days, but it is one that has proved successful in a number of pilot projects."

As Radu spoke, I found myself excitedly telling him how much I agreed with his initiative and what a wonderful idea it was, getting Roma into mainstream schools, as though he had stumbled upon a breakthrough of apple-Newton proportions. In my defence, I was still young and easily impressed by good intentions, which is why I revealed how lucky I had been in terms of my own education. And that's when the next door opened. Radu offered me a job.

Naturally, the money was nothing. It was a volunteer position with paid expenses. Naturally, Miko had to approve, which he did after meeting Radu at one of the many pretty cafes lining Sibiu's cobbled streets. I remember sitting by my husband as he discussed my potential employment. It was a blistering hot day, and though my ears were listening my eyes were drawn to an old Roma woman crouched by a wall, out of the sun, her hand lifted in timid supplication as people walked by, stoically ignoring her. At another table, at another cafe, I watched a tourist break off a part of his sandwich and throw it at a waiting stray dog.

After Radu had explained his plans, Miko laid out his terms. He said I could join Radu's programme for a trial period. During that time, I had to be treated fairly and equally. Any concerns I had were to be properly addressed. And if any harm came to me, my husband would find Radu and rip his head from his shoulders. The Romanian smiled in agreement.

"But please, should it ever come to it try not to mark my face," he begged. "My mother loves it if no one else does."

And that's how I became a teacher, of sorts.

I was ridiculously nervous, that first day of my first job. The classroom was small, tucked away at the back of a shabby school, with three rows of tired desks facing a worn-out blackboard, scratched and faded by use and misuse. To my relief, the Roma children, all five of them, weren't seated at the back of the class as I'd half-expected, but as a group huddled near the front. They were aged six to nine – three girls, two boys – and their poverty was displayed in the ill-fitting clothes they wore, the rough haircuts and the physical defects that may have been genetic or social. Though the other children were by no means rich, my pupils looked achingly out of place and I was struck, possibly for the first time, by the realisation that I had been so consumed by the past I had grown blind to the present. Modern times had rendered a section of our people invisible. The children in front of me were like wraiths, clinging to the underskirts of life. They were beyond poor, and as a consequence I saw how a large section of society assumed they were beyond help.

To put the tragedy of their lives into some kind of context, the house where I lived was in a quiet neighbourhood. There were cars, in various states of disorder, parked on grass verges in front of homes hidden by drooping grape vines. Dogs wandered listlessly looking for shade under benches and chairs where old women gathered to swap miseries as they watched the traffic pass by. The aroma of roasting meat mingled with the breeze. Chubby toddlers and round-bellied men pointed to a level of prosperity. I guess you could say we were the middle ground, the land between rich and poor, and rather like any other society we aspired to become like those above us whilst ignoring the ones below, such as the children I had been tasked with teaching. Truly, I felt ashamed – not of the children in my care, not even of the *gadje*, but of me and everyone like me who had allowed our brothers and sisters to fall so low they were in danger of being lost forever. On that first morning, in that tired old classroom, I saw how close we had come to that day.

From a discussion during the break, I learned that one of the boy's fathers was a street cleaner. The rest were unemployed. One girl revealed her mother searched waste bins for discarded cans she could sell for scrap. Communism had robbed these children and their parents of trades that would have sustained them. When the regime collapsed, discrimination denied them jobs in the factories and cooperatives that had fallen into private hands. Forced integration had failed in its objective. Instead of assimilating the Roma, it merely created a new class of dependents on the state. *Gadje* prejudice had turned the Roma into the very thing it set out to destroy.

The day this realisation hit me, I turned to the internet to read documents I had previously discounted as being nothing more than the ignorant, racist bile of madmen. I had previously skipped over them because they threw no light on my grandmother's stories, and they were dripping with the rants of the deranged. But this was a mistake. Many of the authors were not in fact unhinged; they were respected scholars, authors and journalists. People listened to them. People read their words. And in doing so, they used them to form an opinion of us that was grossly at odds with the reality.

Historical diaries dating back to the 18th Century accused us of eating dogs, cats, mice and sick animals. Our children were described as 'black worms'. We stole babies. We were dirty. We were parasites. We didn't know the difference between right or wrong. We were dishonest. A more recent newspaper report about an eviction in England told of the applause that greeted the revelation that a Roma mother was suffering from cancer. Hundreds more articles told of 'Roma criminals' peddling drugs and prostitutes, and ringing cars. I had to admit, that if the media was my only source of information, it would be hard to find any redeeming factors in the Romani people at all. Even the well-intentioned had unwittingly added fuel to the fire, declaring with all the certainty and gravitas of their scholarly credentials, that there were no Romani words for 'duty', 'possession', 'truth', 'beautiful', 'read', 'write', 'time', 'danger', 'warmth' or 'quiet'. It's preposterous, of course, and one might consider it a trifling matter, but the natural assumption is that a people who have no word for 'truth' live in a world of lies. If you are not 'beautiful' you can only be ugly. If you have no sense of 'duty' you can only know treachery. It was an understanding that hit like a hammer to my heart. I felt winded and broken.

"The Roma are not the only ones in need of educating," Radu sympathised when I repeated what I had read. "It is not an impossible task. There are organisations and political parties working to address these misconceptions. You should look into them. They might be of interest to you."

And they were of interest to me, initially. But like most political initiatives, they ultimately proved disappointing. Dipping into the myriad of websites and forums, I learned there were a number of parties representing our people's interests. However, instead of forming into one cohesive platform, they had dived into the pool of politics from so many differing springboards they ended up banging heads in the water. There were splits between the nomads and sedentary Roma, splits based on professions, there were even splits within splits. However, there was one article that did give me cause for hope; it spoke about the Comité International Tsigane. Established in Paris in 1965, the aim was not to adapt the Roma to the modern world, but to end the injustice meted out to them. To this end, a number of demonstrations took place; there was fierce lobbying; and publicity campaigns. Then, in 1971, they held the first World Romani Congress in London where delegates from 14 countries formally adopted the term 'Rom' to describe our people. Furthermore, they agreed upon a flag and a slogan; Opré Roma! – Roma Arise!

I have to admit, I was inspired. Change felt long overdue. It was surely time for our people to help ourselves, not wait for the rest of the world to accept us. We had to stand on our feet and demand to be counted, not hide in the shadows, hoping to be overlooked. The internet, with its far-reaching arms could be the very tool to rally our people. We could regroup. We could find strength in one another. We were once warriors. And it was time to take up the sword again. Opré Roma!

And yes, it was a glorious dream while it lasted.

I had been teaching at the school for two years, enjoying progress and suffering disappointment in equal measure, when my mother-in-law sat me down at the kitchen table one evening. Her face was hard and her hands were clasped like locks guarding the gate of her stomach. Miko was out, building the fledgling car dealership he had started, and I was confronted by a growing wall of female determination as his aunts filed into the kitchen followed by his sisters and cousins. It was apparent they needed to get something off their bountiful chests. My mother-in-law coughed before voicing her concerns. History books were fine, she said, even charming, but this new militancy...

I swallowed my surprise.

Yes, she said, it was true Miko had supported my wish to teach at the school. But what of this man Radu? Who was he really? What was his interest? Why was it that he happened to pick you, a slip of a girl, reading in a library on her own?

Heat flushed my cheeks.

"And five years married now," she muttered. "Five long years, teaching, reading, visiting the library, sitting until all hours, scribbling in books, scrawling on paper, mixing with the *gadje*, and yet no children? No children at all. Not even a lost one."

My public shaming was complete.

The inference was clear; Miko's mother blamed me for not bearing her son a child. More than that, our ancestors couldn't be happy either. It's not easy for the outsider to understand, but our culture demands balance in all things. Time spent in the non-Romani world drained energy. When spiritual balance or harmony wasn't maintained, the spirits of our ancestors felt little inclination to lend a helping hand. Once displeased, they meted out punishments or warnings, depending on the nature of the transgression. It could be a stubbed toe. It could be sickness or death. It could be infertility.

Though small families were not unheard of in the community, my own great-grandmother Esma had only ever had one child, it was unusual. And the fact remains that a Roma woman's first duty is to her husband. As much as I resented the women's intrusion, I understood it. The following morning, I resigned from my job. I was a teacher no more. The decision was painful, my sense of loss palpable, but two months later my sacrifice was rewarded with the first sign that I was to be a mother.

I won't bore you with the details of how wonderful it was to feel my baby grow inside me, or the beauty of holding my own child in my arms or the catalogue of miracles that charted her progress from cot to floor, from crawling to walking. Suffice to say, I was as happy as a mother who feared she would never be one. This rare light in my soul has never dimmed. I carry it still. I'll carry it always. Whatever may come.

As well as incalculable pleasure, my daughter's arrival also brought me freedom. With a family to call my own, at last, we were given leave to vacate the home of my in-laws and move into our own. After so many years waiting, Miko was more than prepared. He had bought land and a house quickly followed. It was small, nothing ostentatious, built on two levels with a terracotta tiled roof. It was protected by a shoulder-high mortared stone wall. The wheel of a wagon was carved into the wooden gate. Inside was a kitchen, a sitting room, two bathrooms – his and hers, naturally – and a couple of bedrooms. To the side of the house was a patio with a bread oven and grill. At the back of the house, a small plot of land was to yield vegetables until the time came when we needed to expand. Our home was small, but it was lovely and though the details might seem unnecessary to you, I'd ask you to humour me. This was my first house. And yes, it was also to be my last.

Beyond my daughter's arrival, one of my greatest joys was that my grandmother Florica had lived to see the day I became a mother.

"I told you she would come," *Mami* whispered as she bent to kiss my baby.

As she neared, she suddenly blew through her nose as if expelling a bad smell. I thought little of it at the time, the air was heavy with pollen, my grandmother was old, but now the memory of it haunts me. I should have asked, but I didn't, perhaps because I was frightened of what I might hear.

Unlike Miko's female relatives, *Mami* had been a vocal follower of my journey from student to teacher, from historian to militant.

"Opré Roma!" she had spat when she discovered I'd been shamed into giving up my job. "Hard to 'arise' when the women around you conspire to keep you on your back."

My grandmother was nothing if not opinionated. Naturally, Miko was terrified of her even though I knew she respected him, in her own way. He wasn't the academic she had hoped I would marry, but she saw he supported me, and in a marriage that's no small blessing. *Mami* was less than charitable about our new neighbours, however. Some of whom attracted the regular attention of the police.

"Your husband has moved you into a den of thieves," she muttered as we walked past a Mercedes being quickly stripped of its plates by a group of men without the means to buy one. She was partly correct. The men were thieves, that was blatantly apparent, but they were one family among thirty or more in our quarter. Of course, the *gadje* might say that it takes only one drop of poison to pollute a well.

My daughter was two years old when *Mami* died and she was too young to register her absence in the pool of our many relatives. But I felt it. *Mami's* loss was my first experience of grief and for a while I thought I'd never clear the taste of it from my mouth. Perhaps that's why I returned to the Five Books of Truth; the memories she had safeguarded and which I had allowed to lie dormant since retiring from teaching. Miko, being the man he is, encouraged my recovered interest, so much so that one day he appeared in our sitting room brandishing five new books. He dropped them at my feet. They were as large as gravestones, which seemed apt, and he told me he'd had them specially made.

"Most shops only stock A4," he explained.

I was ridiculously delighted by Miko's efforts and after rewarding him with a handsome dinner, I resumed the responsibility my grandmother had spent her life preparing me for. Slowly and carefully, I began to fill the pages with my own take on old memories, fattening the bones of the past with the details I had scavenged from today. I also returned to the library.

Unwilling to test the patience of our ancestors with a repeat of past obsessions, I kept my visits to once a week. Sometimes I'd merely check a minor detail destined to go into the Five Books of Truth (Part II). Sometimes, I simply sat and read the newspapers. Sometimes I'd pick a topic to study, simply for the hell of learning it. One year I even attempted

English. I have to say, it wasn't as easy as the blurb on the textbook promised. The letters were different to what I knew and it took the best part of six months simply to understand them. By the time I gave up, I could write any name phonetically, but I was no nearer to understanding the language. Perhaps if I'd had more time, things might have been different, but in the autumn of 2009 a terrible accident occurred, and time ran out.

It was late afternoon. The sun had already lost its strength but the wind remained warm. It was the kind of weather that comes to throw a magic gauze over the world, making its edges indistinct, its possibilities infinite, its people reckless. Perhaps that's why the little boy ran into the road without looking. Perhaps that's why the driver failed to see him. And perhaps that's why the men dragged the driver from his car and left him bleeding by the tyres that had run over the boy.

As the news circulated to find us, Miko and I saw the sadness in it all: the injured child; the angry relatives; the driver who may or may not have been speeding, but who certainly didn't leave his home that day to intentionally harm someone's son. These are the circumstances that came to change everything; the facts of an accident that mutated with every retelling until they evolved into an irresistible force that could only find satisfaction in further tragedy.

Six hours after the driver was beaten, a mob descended on our homes. It was dark and I had no sense of the danger until the first window shattered. By the second smash of glass, I smelt burning. In the street outside, men were gathered. Their faces were covered and their hands hurled bottles spewing burning rags. One of them went sailing through the upper window of our house – instantly lighting the room where our daughter slept.

Chapter Seventeen

Miko emerged from the caravan. I opened my arms and Mirela walked into them. With a reassuring smile I turned her towards our guests. Their eyes widened, but only for a second, nothing more. After the initial shock, their gaze ran through the gamut of expected emotions, ranging from pity to disbelief. Even so, the response felt inadequate. It always did. Empathy was not an understanding of pain. To understand it, you had to live it.

I stroked my daughter's black hair and pulled it away from her face, the left side of which was scarred beyond recognition. The melted skin that disfigured her features dripped down her neck. The lashes were gone, an eyebrow was missing and the flesh was a swirl of vivid red welts. With the right of Mirela's face being perfectly untouched, the effect was that of an exquisite oil painting vandalised by fate before it had had the chance to dry.

"This is Mirela," I said. I kissed her gently and pulled her onto my lap. "I don't need to tell you how my daughter has suffered. You can see it. She suffers today and she will suffer in future because more operations will be needed as her body grows and her damaged skin struggles to meet the change."

"My God, Mala. I'm so sorry," Francoise gasped.

I accepted her sympathy and acknowledged the regret clouding Jack's eyes.

"Now do you understand why we chose to leave Romania?" I asked him. "After everything that happened, how could we stay? How could we ever sleep in our beds at night thinking we would be safe?" Mirela shifted uncomfortably on my knees and I slipped her backwards, onto the fleshy seat of my thighs. "You know Jack, there are many reasons the Roma choose to travel. Sometimes it's a calling, an affliction of the blood. Sometimes they have no other choice; in Romania many families live on less than two dollars a day. Occasionally though we leave for the simple reason that we are afraid."

Behind me, Miko's hand landed on my shoulder, timely coming to calm the tears that were threatening to fall. He took the chair Marko graciously gave up, and he introduced himself.

"As you have heard, we were not poor," he continued. Mirela leaned towards him and he pulled her onto his lap. "But trust me, when your family is in danger there's no money in the world that can buy you back peace. As you have heard, I am not educated, not like my wife, but I'm not ignorant either, and when I hear people shouting at us to go home, I wonder where that place might be exactly. To Romania, where they burned my child? Or India, a land so far behind us it might as well be the moon? Or perhaps they mean any number of other countries we once travelled through, the ones in which we were enslaved, hunted, and murdered."

Miko paused as Francoise translated. When I saw he had nothing further to say I continued.

"We are not all criminals, Monsieur Caron, no matter what the newspapers imply. And none of us are animals. We came to your country, not for its benefits or easy living. We came for our daughter. It was my wish, not Miko's. I wanted to take her to Saintes Marie de la Mer, to the church housing Saint Sarah, to the sea where they bathe her, like our people once honoured the Goddess Kali. In doing this pilgrimage, I hoped Saint Sarah might agree to look kindly upon us, that she might bless Mirela and keep her safe. This was my prayer, this was my hope, but now, as I sit here worrying what will become of us, I have to wonder whether our trip was in vain. It's a doubt that weighs heavily on my mind because of its blasphemous implications, and so I have to dig deep into my faith to find the trust I once possessed. The fact is our Saints move in mysterious ways. Who knows what Sarah's plan might be? She might even have sent you."

No sooner had the words left my mouth then I regretted them. I rarely spoke without thinking and the realisation that I had said too much, that I had *gifted* him too much, now jarred in my throat. It was a disquiet exacerbated by the sudden shine in Jack's eyes; the glassy glow of the perpetual dreamer. Of course, when he said he would do everything in his power to help us, I nearly laughed. Some nations get Ban Ki-Moon, the Roma get a busker from Toulouse.

Behind me, I heard Marko clap his hands together. The meeting was adjourned and I was grateful for the intervention. Even so, as everyone moved from their chairs, or their upturned buckets and patches of grass, I felt a sense of lightness sweep over me. A second later, I recognised the sensation for what it was – relief.

Having said all that needed to be said I realised the exercise had been close to cathartic, an exorcism, of sorts. I was acutely aware of the many stories I had omitted – other times, other places and other names – but I had narrated the few I knew best, the ones that I'd worked on until they were engraved on my mind, as sure as an epitaph on stone. I had fulfilled the Big Man's request. My duty was done.

"You did us proud," Miko told me, as ever reading my thoughts.

I reached for his hand and matched my daughter's smile with one of my own.

Although no one encouraged them to stay, Jack and Francoise seemed reluctant to leave once I stopped talking. Eventually, Marko and Drina ushered the pair towards their campervan and I picked up the mugs they had used, discarding them in their usual place behind our caravan, in the dirt. I didn't see either of the *gadje* again, not until the sun began to set and Bo made a triumphant return to the site.

Naturally, Mirela sprinted to greet the object of her affections, but as the boy was quickly swamped by the attentions of his brothers, she had to wait patiently on the edges of the huddle until Bo noticed her. Emerging from the throng, beaming and breathless, he swooped to pick her up. Bo then came to speak with us, still holding our daughter in his arms.

"No charge," he revealed, and Miko and I expressed our relief even though the swollen cheek and a fresh cut on Bo's upper lip revealed a fine had been paid nonetheless.

To the detectives' surprise, and irritation, I imagine, Bo's contact had come forward to vouch for him. He informed the police that they were indeed in business together, selling reconditioned computers to the Africans. Bo's speedy release was further aided by the arrest of a French teenager, after the burglary victim found his stolen goods being peddled on eBay.

"Amateurs," Bo said with an exasperated sigh.

He set Mirela on the ground just as a shrill whistle called for his attention. We all swung our heads to find his brother Stevo gesturing.

"I think they're planning a little party in my honour." Bo grinned. "You're all invited, of course. The old man has even invited the *gadje*. He must be losing his marbles."

"We'll bring what we've got," Miko replied, just as Tanko appeared by our side. He gathered Bo in his arms and kissed him hard on both cheeks before punching him energetically in the stomach. Bo doubled over in pain.

"You've got to stop doing that," he whined.

Mirela, who had grown accustomed to the men's games, laughed in Bo's face. Miko joined her and I even managed a giggle of my own. The evening was taking on a giddy air and it felt good, almost liberating.

As was customary, it took a little over two hours to prepare the food for Bo's party and a little under twenty minutes to consume it. As I helped the other women clear away, a cool breeze played around our ankles. Darting in between the adults, the children continued to eat on the run, throwing finished bones to the dogs as they played. As ever, Mirela loitered around the guest of honour. As Bo humoured her, I noticed Jack's eyes occasionally fall on her face.

Having washed and put away, I joined the women who had gathered around Drina. The men were close by, sat in their own masculine huddles, passing beer bottles and bad jokes – blissfully unaware that one of their women was busy regaling the others with a story I found unexpectedly ripe. I accepted a glass of sweet wine poured by the Big Man's wife. Before I got the chance to taste it, I noticed Jack beckoning Francoise to his side. From their glances it was clear that I played a part in their discussion. A minute or two later, they approached.

Jack sat himself on the grass by my feet. Francoise knelt by his side. Both of them appeared uncharacteristically relaxed and I found their faces all the fresher for it. I also had to wonder whether they were drunk. Inching his knees to his chest, Jack asked me what had become of the Five Books of Truth. The question was offered so casually it must have been rehearsed. I told him, somewhat flatly, the truth; that they had gone up in smoke, along with the rest of our belongings. It was a fact that seemed to energise the Frenchman and he almost fell over his words in his haste to release them. Though Francoise was calmer, I could see the excitement reciprocated in her eyes.

"An idea has come to me, Mala. I think, and I'm sure we could make it work, I think we should rewrite the Five Books together, for the French market." Jack paused waiting for a reply that I couldn't yet give. "I know it might seem like I'm taking a liberty," he admitted, "they are, after all, your stories, but perhaps, with my past being what it is, it might generate some interest, a bit more than such a book might do otherwise. Unfortunately, these days everything needs a gimmick. And I could be that gimmick! Of course, I'd make it abundantly clear that you're the primary author. As I said, these are your stories after all. What do you say? Do you think it's an idea?"

Well, it was certainly an idea, and I can't say the initial sound of it didn't thrill me. During the lifetime I'd spent writing, I'd always wondered 'what if?' On one occasion, during my descent into militancy, I'd even considered writing a blog. I'd watched the internet grow in sophistication and I saw the possibilities it had to offer. Of course, it was a thought that quickly crumbled under further consideration because managing a blog would have been all but impossible on a shared computer in a public library that made me feel as welcome as smallpox. But a book, a published book, well, that was the stuff of dreams. Of course, the problem with dreams is that reality rarely has the scope to realise them, which is why, whenever I used to sit in front of *Mami's Five Books of Truth*, imagining them typed, and smaller than they wanted to be, I always sensed their disappointment. Hidden in those pages were centuries of stories – precious memories and untold agonies. Now they were gone there would always be gaps, yet I was sure I could retrieve the heart of them, that I could bring them back to something close to what they once were, and for that reason I knew I could never agree to Jack's plans, no matter how tempting the prospect. *Mami's* books were never a collection of words; they were a living, breathing part of me. To confine them now would be like closing a door on them, and our time was not yet over. I couldn't do it. Physically, I couldn't do it, and when I told Jack as much, I noticed Miko listening. My husband nodded his head and smiled.

"Well, perhaps we can discuss it again tomorrow," Jack mumbled, deflated but not yet ready to be beaten.

"Perhaps," I replied.

A sudden flurry of applause erupted around us, which confused me for a moment until I saw Stevo approaching, holding a guitar in his hands. With a glint in his eye, he asked Jack if he'd do the honours. To his credit, Jack replied that he'd be honoured to. He took hold of the instrument, resting the curve of its body on his half-raised knee and strummed a lazy chord. The guitar revealed it needed no tuning and Jack nodded his head towards Stevo in a gesture of respect. After a cough, and a quick 'one-two', Jack launched into an easy tune that wasn't wholly unknown to us, detailing as it did his conquests "from Savannah to Havana, Santa Fe to Mandalay and Arizona to Daytona". This time, however, there was none of the hilarity that had accompanied the lyrics the first time we heard them. Instead, Bo and his brothers sang along as the other men clapped. When Jack finished, his face flushed with pride and exertion, he apologised for his voice not being as supple as it used to be.

Taking back the guitar, Stevo struck the chords to a song that was as familiar to us as those of the birds in the trees. When he sang, the other men tapped out the rhythm on buckets and tins, and I looked over at Rami who had tears in his eyes. Noticing me watching, Drina leaned over to reveal that it was once Rami's wife who was the singer of the family.

"She had a voice like honey," Drina remembered.

"I went, I went on long roads,
"I met happy Roma.
"O' Roma where do you come from
"With tents on happy roads?
"O' Roma, O' brothers.

"I once had a great family,
"The Black Legions murdered them.
"Come with me Roma from all the world
"For the Roma roads have opened.

"Now is the time, rise up Roma now,
"We will rise high if we act.
"O' Roma, O' brothers."

Stevo finished to thunderous applause. Even Jack and Francoise were moved, if not by the words than by the music and the obvious emotions it stirred. It was a beautiful song, one that was known by many names, but I knew it only as *Djelem Djelem* – the National Anthem of our people. It was a fine way to end the evening.

The sun had barely had time to make an impact, when Miko woke me. He held a finger to his lips and pointed to the window. Outside, I heard vehicles arriving. There were no flashing lights, there was no sense of panic, but it was enough to make us move.

Miko got to his feet, pulled on his jeans and scooped Mirela into his arms. As she protested, he told her to hush. I checked the windows. A number of our neighbours were running towards the barricaded gate at the entrance to the site. Without a word, Miko pulled open the door of our caravan and we crept around the back of it. Ignoring the barbs of the prickly hedge, we forced our way through a gap and into the open field. As I stumbled, Miko used his free hand to drag me to my feet. It was so early, the earth was still grey and we fled to the brow of the hill where we could watch what was happening, protected by a sparse copse of trees.

As one, Miko, Mirela and I slumped to the ground, facing the site, like a family of snipers. The world was silent, even the birds had yet to wake, and the sound of our breathing was all that filled our ears. Gradually, as the sun began to find her way, she threw light on the action downhill. By now, there were a number of men milling about the gate; *gadje* men holding clipboards. Standing behind them was a contingent of police. Their bodies were padded, their heads were bare. Ten yards away, the Roma faced them like a wall. From where we lay, I saw hands raised in gestures of outrage, followed by shouts, fierce but largely inaudible. I strained to listen, but the sudden rustling of leaves behind us grabbed my attention. I span my head around to meet the threat, and found Tanko crawling towards us, closely followed by Donka.

"Morning," he greeted.

"Morning," Miko replied.

The two men shared a grim smile before returning their attention to the action below where the men with clipboards had now entered the site. The police followed them before branching away to investigate the caravans. Rami's sons moved quickly. Stevo ran to the steps of Tanko's home. Bo walked at a more leisurely pace to our own. From the gesticulations that followed they appeared to be claiming the properties. Bo reached into his back pocket and an officer checked the papers he handed him. The policeman then pretended to return the documents. His reach was contemptuous and the papers fell to the ground between them. I could almost see the smile of easy acceptance playing on Bo's bruised face. With our home protected, I turned back to the throng at the centre of the site. The men with clipboards were attempting to speak with Florian and his family. Telus stood by his father, his tiny fists clenched and resting on his hips.

From a bag, passports materialised. The officials took them, copied the details and handed them back. A clipboard was pushed towards Florian who appeared to sign it. As the exchange took place, the rest of the Roma, who were mostly French, shouted indignantly, but it was mainly theatrics. After the officials spoke to the police officers, they turned away, only to be followed by Florian. From the way his hands pulled at his empty pockets it appeared he was asking for his Euros. Less than 45 minutes later, the vehicles drove off. The *gadje* had gone.

"Stay here," Miko ordered. He rose to his feet, pausing only to slap the dirt from his knees, before accompanying Tanko back to the site. Meanwhile, I held Mirela's hand and waited.

Donka got up from her stomach to sit facing me with her knees pulled towards her chest.

"I need a cigarette," she moaned.

"It should be alright," I replied. "No one will see the smoke."

Donka raised a tired eyebrow.

"Oh, I see," I smiled, realising my mistake. "You've left them in the caravan."

Donka nodded and when Mirela told her she really shouldn't be smoking because it was bad for her health, she nodded again.

"I guess that was the eviction squad," Donka finally said.

I told her I thought she had guessed correctly.

"What will you do?" she asked.

I looked towards Mirela, silently indicating that this was not a discussion for my daughter's ears. Donka accepted my wish with a jerk of her head. She turned back to the scene below us and sighed. It wasn't a gentle sound. It was a heavy breath loaded with fear and regret.

"I suspect we shall leave," she confided.

"But what about your appointment..."

The young woman shrugged. "I know. But what can I do? If there was time to find out, I might have done. Drina discovered from the doctor that I have some kind of lump."

"What kind of lump?" Mirela asked, turning her attention from her father and, no doubt, Bo.

"None of your business," I chided, closing her ears with my hands.

Donka lifted herself higher, to whisper above Mirela's head. "Apparently, the doctors at the hospital need to cut some of it away so they can carry out tests."

"A biopsy," I stated.

"A whatever," Donka replied. "But I'm damned if I'll let the *gadje* cut me up. No, maybe this thing..." she paused to wave a hand towards our homes, "the timing of it and all, well maybe it's a sign from God, you know, to walk away."

I closed my eyes, feeling my heart sink. I had no love for the *gadje*, but sometimes they were our only hope. Without them, Mirela might not be with me today. It was a painful truth, but one that couldn't be denied. They were the cause and the solution to my daughter's pain.

"You must go to the hospital," I urged.

"I must do no such thing," Donka snapped. "I have my husband. I have breath in my lungs and I put myself in God's hands. He will provide."

"And if He can't?"

Donka puffed out her cheeks in exasperation. "Well, if He can't, I'll throw a feast for St Basil and see what he can do!"

Donka laughed, but though her eyes asked me to join her, I couldn't. I could only reach for her hand and hold it for as long as she would allow me.

Miko backed our battered Dacia Sedan towards the caravan. As Marko helped him secure the hitch on the towball, I hugged Drina tightly and thanked her for the thousand kindnesses she had showered on our family. The old woman sniffed and claimed it was nothing.

"Go with God, Mala."

"Stay with God," I replied.

I gazed around the site, now busy with families packing away their belongings, ready to vacate the patch of wasteland that had given them the chance to rest for a while. I wandered over to Florian and his family to wish them good luck on their journey home. They had opted to pocket the Euros on offer, and the authorities would come for them the next morning.

"Nine hundred Euros," he said with a shrug. "It's a lot of money for people like me."

"For anyone," I agreed.

At his side, Telus had his small meaty fists clenched around a notebook and a handful of pencils that I had gifted him and his siblings.

"Remember, you're a fox," I ordered with a smile.

"I'll remember you pinched me," he retorted.

Florian looked at us quizzically and I quickly ruffled the boy's hair muttering something banal about the blessings of kids. Before the moment had time to grow awkward, Donka stepped forward, to take my arm and pull me away.

"Tanko's going to take the money too," she said. She looked up and blew the smoke she had inhaled over my head. "When they come for Florian and his family, we'll go with them."

"Oh Donka..."

"Oh Mala..." she mimicked. "Look, don't worry, everything will be fine. It's for the best. I'm sure of it. Anyway, that's not why I wanted to speak to you. I just wanted to say thank you, that's all. I know we haven't been close, but everything you told the *gadje*, all those stories about where we came from, well it was good, you know. I'm glad I was here to hear it. Really, you should think about putting them in a book."

I gazed at the woman, knowing that though we hadn't been friends we had been neighbours. More than that, we would always be sisters.

"Go with God, Donka."

"Stay with God, Mala."

Behind me, I heard the rattling chokes of the Dacia stirring into life. With a last nod I took Mirela from Bo's arms. She was crying, but it was a different pain to the one she was used to and I knew that it would quickly melt into fond memory. I strapped her into the back seat of the car before taking my place next to Miko. His hair was wet and he had swept it back and away from his handsome face.

"OK, where to?" I asked, reaching to buckle my belt.

"Well, funny you should ask, it's something I've been giving some thought to lately," he confessed. His smile was bright in his tanned face. His eyes were warm. I didn't think I had ever loved him more. "How do you feel about America?"

"America," I hummed. "Well, they do say it's the land of opportunity."

"Exactly, Mala, which means we only have to decide on the route – via Ireland or Japan?"

"I hear Japan is lovely at this time of year."

"True enough, but I hear Ireland is closer and we have to think about the petrol."

"For environmental reasons?"

"But of course." Miko's face creased with mock sincerity. After turning to wink at our daughter, he released the handbrake and we pulled away from the place that had been our home for the past two months.

Behind us, Mirela moaned in the back of the car, claiming she couldn't breathe in the heat and the agony of her broken heart. I shook my head at her histrionics and Miko laughed. I then thought briefly of Jack and Francoise and how they would arrive later that day, hoping to convince me of their plans for a book and finding only the empty space where my family had been; a tired patch of grass and two forgotten mugs on the ground, one of them painted with a tractor on the front.

"Get ready to wave," Miko ordered as we neared the gate. At the entrance, everyone had gathered and I felt a lump rise in my throat as I watched Drina drag a hankie across her eyes.

With a shudder, the Dacia groaned its relief as the caravan connected with tarmac. So, this was it, I thought. We were on our way again. Driving to somewhere, hoping it would be home. Not that I was upset. It was the journey rather than the destination that brought me the most comfort these days. So perhaps home wasn't a place, after all. Perhaps it was the car that you travelled in or the wagon you owned; the space that housed the people you loved, the space that kept you safe and secure. Place or space, they seemed one and the same, yet they weren't. They were wholly different. Space couldn't be boxed. It couldn't be penned in, bordered and possessed. Space was infinite. I knew this because an encyclopaedia once told me it was so. It was a fact that I was about to share with Miko, because he appeared to enjoy the meanderings of my mind, when a loud whistle demanded our attention. Miko immediately stepped on the brake and we all peered out of our open windows – me, Miko and Mirela – craning our necks to see what it was we had forgotten. Behind us we saw Bo, stood on his own in the middle of the road. His face was serious and after a second's pause, he bid us goodbye in the best way he knew how. With one arm raised, he clenched his fist in defiance before shouting two words.

"Opré Roma!"

"...But the time has come
to honour my people,
and free them from
the evil spell that I will

break with the spell I make.
They won't be dogs any more,
they will be what they were
they will return to being the Roma –
Gypsies as you would say."

The Gypsy from India by Nicolas Jimenes Gonzalez

"The persistent, relentless portrayal of Roma as rootless, lawless, immoral, childlike thieves, as a people for whom the basic human concepts of truth and beauty, obligation and ownership do not exist and who are ignorant of danger and never seek warmth or peace or quiet... will ensure that anti-gypsy prejudice will remain firmly a part of Euro-American racist attitudes."

Professor Ian Hancock.

ACKNOWLEDGEMENTS

In The Words That Made Us I have endeavoured to be true to Romani history and culture, although there remains debate surrounding the Indian exodus. Therefore I am deeply indebted to the following publications: *We are the Romani People* by Ian Hancock; *Shared Sorrow: A Gypsy Family Remembers the Holocaust* by Toby Sonneman; *Winter Time: Memoirs of a German Sinto who Survived Auschwitz* by Walter Winter; *The Nazi Persecution of the Gypsies* by Guenter Lewy; *Our Forgotten Years* by Maggie Smith-Bendell; *The Pariah Syndrome* by Ian Hancock; *The Roads of the Roma* edited by Ian Hancock, Siobhan Dowd and Rajko Djurić; *Destroying Ethnic Identity: The Persecution of Gypsies in Romania* by Helsinki Watch; *E Zhivindi Yag – The Living Fire* by Ronald Lee; *The Gypsies of Eastern Europe* edited by David Crowe and John Kolsti; *Rromane Paramichi: Stories and Legends of the Gurbeti Roma* by Hedina Tahirović Sijerčić; *In the Shadow of the Swastika: The Gypsies During the Second World War* by Centre de Reserches Tsiganes; *The Final Chapter: The Gypsies During the Second World War* edited by Donald Kenrick; *Constantinople: Capital of Byzantium* by Jonathan Harris; *Romani Culture and Gypsy Identity* edited by Thomas Acton and Gary Mundy; *The Gypsies* by Angus Fraser; *Danger! Educated Gypsy* by Ian Hancock; *Gypsies: From the Ganges to the Thames* by Donald Kenrick; *Gypsies in the Ottoman Empire* by Elena Marushiakova and Vesselin Popov; *India* by John Keay; *The Black Death* by Robert S. Gottfried; *The Romani World* by Donald Kenrick; *Storm on Horseback: The Seljuk Warriors of Turkey* by John Freely; *History of Kanauj* by Rama Shankar Tripathi; *Gypsy*

Law: Romani Legal Traditions and Culture edited by Walter O. Weyrauch; and *Romani Dictionary Kalderash – English* by Ronald Lee.

My special thanks go to the author Ronald Lee and Prof. Ian Hancock for their patience and advice regarding this novel and all things Roma.

On a more personal note, I'd like to thank my family and friends for their unwavering support, help and guidance. As ever my mum was a constant presence throughout the writing and editing process. My dad and my sister, Louise, also gave much appreciated encouragement, chapter by chapter. And to the friends who took the time to read and advise – Hélène Collon, James McLeod Hatch, Janey Harvey and Christa Tragatschnig – I thank you from the bottom of my heart. A xx